GLENMILL

Author's Note

Ten years ago I visited Israel with my family. We spent much of our time in East Jerusalem and the West Bank. It was a tense time and the people were held in a vice-like grip by the Israeli army. Despite their desperate situation, we found the Palestinians to be the most hospitable and friendly people we have ever had the privilege to meet. On numerous occasions we asked what we could do in return for the spectacular hospitality we were shown. The answer never varied. "Please tell or story. Please tell the truth." We duly promised to do our best. Well, it has taken ten years, but I hope that 'Red Zone' does them justice.

I must point out that this is a work of fiction. For those of you who know Sighthill well, please don't agonise over the exact geography. The place is real. The tower blocks and places described in the book are not. There will be many who will feel that I have exaggerated the experiences of the asylum seekers both in their home countries and in Sighthill. Sadly I have not.

I couldn't possibly have done this story justice without the help of Ghazi and his family. What Ghazi and his children have endured warrants a book on its own. But that is their story, not mine. Ghazi lived through nightmares that most of us cannot even begin to imagine in the torture rooms of the Syrian Police. Despite all his suffering he is still one of the most friendly and charming people I have ever met. I feel honoured to call him my friend.

D0529847

A Glenmill Publication

First published in 2003

Glenmill
Dumfries
Scotland
DG2 8PX

tel: 0776 149 3542

http://www.thecull.com

British Library Cataloguing in Publication Data.

A catalogue record of this book
is available from the British Library.

ISBN 0 9535944 8 3

Origination & Typesetting: Ψasmin
email: nomad@blueyonder.co.uk

Printed and bound in Great Britain

RED ZONE

MARK FRANKLAND

In the spring of 2003 the lightning advance of the 3rd Infantry
Division of the American Army reached Iraq's holy city of
Kerbala. Ahead of them lay Saddam Hussein's much vaunted
Republican Guard who were dug in at the gates of Baghdad.

The American officers who briefed the world's press in
their Hollywood style Media Centre in Qatar found a typically
colourful description for the stretch of land that their
forces were about to cross. They called it the 'Red Zone'.

Acknowledgements

It is all too easy for a 'thriller' writer to go over the top
and wander into the realms of Hollywood. I am lucky
because my partner Carol reads everything that I write and lets
me know in no uncertain terms when I have crossed the line.

I must also thank Sheila, Alison, Ghana, Abraham
and all the others who have helped me with the story.

Finally I must mention a charming young man in a baseball bat
who threatened my children and many others with his equally
charming dog. He took great exception to the fact that they were
all enjoying a game of football. He gave us a fond send-off from
Sighthill that night with a torrent of foul-mouthed abuse. He also
let us know exactly what would happen if we ever dared to return.
Sadly he never gave us his name so I cannot thank him in person.

Why thank him at all? Simple. Motivation.
All writers need motivation and when he threatened my
children he gave me all the motivation I could ever need.

C o n t e n t s

PART ONE   Page   1

Killings in the night

PART TWO   Page   63

A journey to the West

PART THREE   Page 243

Red Zone

EPILOGUE   Page 373

Contents

PART ONE   Page   1
Railways in the early
...

PART TWO   Page   61
A Journey to D... West

PART THREE   Page 261
The T... ...

EPILOGUE   ... 373

PART ONE

Killings in the night

The man from Afghanistan stood by the window.

It was how he spent most of his time. Had anyone been there to watch him they would have been struck by how little he moved. Stillness came easily to him. For most of his life he had lived among the empty dry mountains above Khandahar. There had been times when stillness had been a necessity to him. A talent. A tool. Like the times when he had waited for hours to shoot a rabbit or small deer to take home for the family pot. Or other times he had waited for days to send a rocket-propelled grenade towards a Russian personnel carrier.

Sometimes his stillness had been merely a habit. Times spent high on rocky hillsides tending his small flock of sheep. These were times when each hour melted into the next without relevance. And then of course there were the years he had spent in the prison cell of the Taliban. Times when he had come to know every small crack in the stone floor. Every tiny notch in the tired concrete of the walls. Every knot and gnarl in the rough wood of the door. Once again the hours had melted into days and the days had melted into years. He was a man who had learnt to pass the time quietly.

But now he was angry.

For days the damp walls of the flat had been slowly closing in on him. Out of his window on the fourteenth floor there was endless space. Below him the greyness of Glasgow in wintertime rolled out to the dreary hills on the horizon. For days he had simply stood and watched as the days had unfolded, flickered and died. The strange city gave off no sound.

3

The greasy windows were double-glazed and would only open a crack. Suicide from inside a flat was a tough option for the residents of the fourteenth floor of the Fountainwell flats in Sighthill. Maybe a lumphammer would have done the job. It was something that he had often thought of. At times he yearned to smash away the filthy glass to let in some air, some sound, some kind of life.

Each day saw orange turn to grey and then the grey would fade back to orange. The city at night was a carpet of thousands and thousands of orange street lights. They let off a dull glow that leaked up into the night to stain the clouds that blanketed the city. Even on the occasions when the night sky was clear, the all-contaminating orange would hide the stars. The stars here were a sad spectacle. He yearned for the sparkling canopy that shone out every night in the clear mountain air of his homeland.

Everything here was dirty. Filthy. The corridor outside his flat. The litter-strewn areas of grass where no children dared to play. The miserable offices where irritable officials lost their patience at his lack of English. The miserable little shops where food came in frozen packets and the vegetables were never fresh. Even the night sky was soiled by the endless filth of the city.

He was always there at his window for the break of the dawn. Every now and then it was a thing of beauty. A sight to lift his tired soul as a big red sun climbed up over the edge of the world and started to pick out the crazy latticework of streets and buildings. He would watch as a seemingly endless number of tiny cars of all shapes and colours would fill the roads. These were the mornings when there was a small flicker of life in his dark expressionless eyes. Most mornings there was no more than a dreary lifting of the gloom as the darkness of the night slowly lightened into grey whilst the rain lashed at his window.

The city below was still a thing of fascination to him. Even after two years of taking a bird's-eye view from his high window he was still in awe of its sheer size. He would never have imagined that any city could be so big. The villages at home were tiny places. Collections of clay-built houses hanging onto the steep sides of valleys. Khandahar was the centre of the world, but compared to the city below him it was a mere village.

It was place where he would never be at home. Everything was alien to him. When he had first arrived he had spent many days walking. He had tried to get some kind of a feel for his new environment. Hour after hour he would walk the streets flanked by the great grey buildings as he slowly tried to find his bearings, his landmarks, all the time trying to believe that this place could one day be home. There was so much that was beyond his understanding. The wealth of the place was beyond him. How could people have so much? So many cars. So many shops filled to overflowing with goods. Where could such wealth come from? The land around the city seemed poor. The grass in the fields was tired. Where were all the farm animals? Nothing made sense.

It was a place of a million faces and hardly any sound. The roads were packed with cars but their horns never blared. Every other door was some kind of a shop but nobody plied his or her trade on the pavements. The people seemed to want for nothing and yet they never smiled.

It had been the people who had slowly driven him back behind his door on the fourteenth floor. It had not been fear. He would never have let that happen. His was a people who despised fear. It was why the foreigners had never managed to stay for long in the hills where his people lived. For hundreds of years they had tried. They had tried to frighten his people with all the weapons that they could bring. From swords to rifles to helicopter gunships to the stooping MiG fighter planes with their napalm canisters. There had never been a terror great enough. His people had never been broken. They would never accept fear. He would never accept fear. It was his creed. A possession that could never be stolen. Something he had taken from his father. Something that his father had taken from his grandfather. Something that was as old as the great ragged peaks that reached for the clear cold blue of the empty Afghan skies.

In the days when he had walked the grey streets of the city there had been plenty of people who had tried to frighten him. Shouts of abuse. Pointing fingers. Deliberate shoulder-barges. Pale, thin-faced kids throwing stones. Loud, angry women with cigarettes and prams. Faces filled with hostility. Words he could not understand. And it had all washed over him. Sometimes he met the abuse with a small private smile. Who did these people think he was? Did they really believe that their shouts and stares could frighten him? These were people who had no concept of fear. They lived out their angry little lives in the cold safety of their grey city. They had no idea of how it was to feel the air thump with the sound of an approaching helicopter. They had no idea of how it was when the lines of tracers arced through the cold of the night smelling out the hole where you hid. They had no concept of the sound of the keys in the lock of the prison door as the men came to collect you for torture. And these people thought they could frighten him with their tame hostility.

It was the contempt that slowly ate away at him. His was a proud people. There were those who had come to his land to try to break them, to defeat them. And the men who had come had brought with them all the hate in the world. There had been no limit to the evil that they had brought to the quiet mountains. The British. The Russians. The Taliban. They had brought their hate. An endless hate. But never contempt. Never the utter contempt that he saw every day on the faces of the people of Glasgow. To them he was something to despise. Something dirty. Something worthless. Dog shit on their shoes. Bird shit on the windscreens of their cars. Unflushed shit in the pan of their toilets.

The hate he could deal with. The hate he was used to. The hate merely made him stiffen his back and walk through it. Hate would never break him. Not in the high hills. Not in the heat of a fire fight. Not in the prison of the Taliban. It was the contempt that had forced him back behind his door. Contempt was something that he had never known. Before there had always been respect. Nobody would look on his people with contempt. His were the people of the mountains. People to be wary of. People to step away from on the dusty pavements. People to meet with a small deferential nod. People to inspire fear. Never contempt. The contempt showed him just how far he was from his home. How hopelessly far.

In the end it had broken him. The days of walking passed. He retreated back behind the door of flat 14b. Nobody came. There was just him. Sometimes he would stare for hours at the screen of his TV. The endless stream of gaudy adverts and idiotic grinning faces were beyond him. He watched with dumb fascination. Other times he just slept. Sometimes he would sleep for days at a time just as he had done in the prison of the Taliban. And other times he would stand at his window and stare away the empty hours. And all the while the same nagging question ate away at him like a fat hungry maggot.

Why had he come? Why had he run away? Why had he not stayed to accept his fate?

It had been the Russians who had taken his wife and his two sons. The air strike had come in seconds out of the blue of the sky. Just a brief moment to watch the two jets flashing up the valley in silence. Like toys. Like two shiny birds. Far too fast for there to be any sound. Graceful. Beautiful. Awesome. Far too fast for the brain to register the danger. And then the bombs gliding through the air and down toward the village. Nothing to be frightened of. Not like a storm or a blizzard. Just shapes twisting and turning like carelessly thrown stones. And then a feeling as if a giant had come to suck the air from the valley. At last the sound of the planes caught up and his ears had nearly burst as the jets looped up and away from him. The explosions consumed everything. His senses disintegrated. Somehow blind instinct must have taken a hold of him. Somehow his body had reacted and he had thrown himself down into the dust covering his two-year-old daughter. The shrapnel had lanced across his back. A chip of rock had slashed into the back of his thigh. And then the roar and heat of the explosion had faded to silence. His house was just a pile of bricks. His wife and sons were just blackened charred things. In seconds his life had been shredded.

His little girl had been twelve the day that the Taliban had come for her. There had been three of them, drawn by her beauty, her dark eyes and her creamy limbs. He had been too late when he had run down from his flock on the hillside. All three had raped her. One after another. Leaving their stink. Their filth. He had been a year out of their prison. A year away from the leering face of his torturer. A year from the stick with the rusty nails which they hammered into the flesh of his back. A year when the hate in his stomach had hardened. He could hear the screams of his little girl as he had run down the track to his home. He recognised the old jeep parked outside. The jeep of the bastard officer who loved to take the young girls of the villages. The leering bastard with the big black beard. He was beyond all thought when he crashed down the door of his house. The old pistol was ready in his hand. He shot the first one in the face from a foot away. He shot the second in the chest as he tried for his gun. He waited a small moment as the big officer hauled his body off the broken mess of his little girl's limbs. He waited to see the gleam of fear in the dark piggy eyes as the man wrenched at his trousers. He shot him from inches away. In the face. Obliterating it.

They had run. High into the sanctuary of the hills and all the hours his little girl had wept silent tears. She had never slackened the pace. She had never complained even through the blood seeped from her vagina. And something inside him had died. He had done what he could to treat the wound but it had been hopeless. Her soul was dead. They had taken away her will. Death came on a cold night high up above the snow line. Death had been mercy. Death had been the only freedom that was available to her.

He had buried her as best he could under a pile of rocks. And he had walked. He had walked like a robot. There was no going back. Not after he had shot down three of the men of the Taliban. All he could do was to walk east. In the end he had arrived in the refugee camps of Peshawar. Once he had embarked on his journey there was no reason to stop. He had cut a man's throat for his money. He had paid his way to the west. And he had come to Glasgow, to Sighthill, to flat 14b, to the contempt of these people he would never understand.

He hated himself for not going back when he had buried the broken body of his little girl. It would have been better to go back to face the guns of the Taliban. Better to have sought a death. Better to have gone to his wife and his sons and his little girl. Better than the pointless journey to this place. This hopelessness. This dull and empty despair.

A small light came to his eyes. No more. He would go out. He would walk until he stopped. What did he care if there was contempt? What did it matter? Nothing mattered. It was over. There was no point in hiding any more.

There were three of them. There had always been the three of them. Kev, Spik and Migs. They had been with each other in the playground at their primary school. They had roamed together through the bored days of the summer holidays. They had sniffed at solvents in the hidden concrete corners of the sprawling estate. They had shoplifted together. They had scrapped together. They were mates. They were a part of each other's furniture. They could not have imagined life without each other any more than they could have imagined a life away from the blank staring blocks of Sighthill. Sighthill was their world. Their turf. The place that made them. And life was moving. They were leaving behind the time of catapults and mud ramps for their BMX bikes. They were at the dawn of becoming men. Fifteen years old and already they had come up with a tenner each to lose their virginity to Doreen Hughes, the smackhead tart from Block 7 who had chewed her gum with glazed eyes as they had cheered each other on. Manhood had come on a rainy night for the price of three tenner-bags of Glasgow brown.

For a long time it had looked like being a bad day. A blank day. A day spent in and around the side streets off Sauchihall Street waiting for an opportunity. Another day soaked to the skin waiting on a chance. The chance had not come until just after seven. The woman had been in a hurry. Late out of the office. Late for a hurried rush round Tesco to get some tea for the man waiting at home. Late and talking breathlessly on her mobile phone and not looking, not thinking, not taking a couple of extra minutes to stay in the light. Kev had reached out and dragged her by the hair into the small yard where the skips were kept. He had slapped her hard across the face and shown her the knife. She had been too frightened to scream. They had been quick. The phone and her bag and away, their wet trainers pounding the pavement whilst the woman sat in a puddle and cried.

The purse had yielded 30 quid and a credit card. They shared the cash and split a bottle of vodka as they walked back through the rain to Sighthill. Donny Henderson gave them a twenty for the card and three wraps of whizz for the phone. They snorted down the speed in the lift in Donny's block and burst out into the rain of the dark night. They were kings in their castle, lords of their manor. Their voices were up a notch. The vodka and the speed took away the cold and the damp that had seeped through the thin fabric of their shoes. They talked hard and fast and loud. They were in charge of the empty streets of the night. They were Glasgow's newest and finest. They had the world laid out in front of them. They had twenty each in their pockets and Doreen Hughes would do it without a johnny for twenty quid.

They saw the man from 100 yards. They saw him coming towards them on the other side of the street. A huddled figure in the rain. It was past ten now. Sighthill was quiet as a graveyard in the dark of a cold night. It wasn't something that they needed to discuss. It was a decision made telepathically. It was too good to be true. The Pakis never came out at night. They hid away and cooked their stinking shit food. They only dared to come out of their holes in daylight when there were people around. This was unknown. This was a bonus. They drifted across the street like ghosts in baseball caps. They allowed the distance to close in silence. They filled the pavement and waited as the small man approached.

He only noticed them when one of them shouted. The one in the middle. The man from Afghanistan had been staring down as he walked. His thoughts had been a thousand miles away until he heard the shout. He looked up to find three of them blocking his way. Kids acting like men. Pale thin faces like the plastic cartons they sold their butter in. Bad skin. Bad yellow teeth. Gleaming eyes. Crazy eyes. High on something. Wound up tight. Full of themselves. Convinced of themselves. Pathetic boys. Skinny. Weak. No respect. No clue of what life meant. Like the idiotic faces on the TV. Like the stupid women in the shops. Dressed in their stupid clothes and whoring their fat pale flesh. Smoking in the street. Like whores. A whore of a people who did not know about respect. About dignity. Like these three. Arrogant in their stupid track suits and American caps. Stupid in their belief that they knew anything. Stupid in their miserable grey home.

It wasn't how they had anticipated. The man just stopped and stared. He straightened himself and became very still. There was something about the eyes. Black eyes. Bottomless eyes. No fear there. Something else. Something out of the half-forgotten nightmares of their childhood. Something from a place they didn't know. It was Kev who broke the spell.

"What the fuck do you think you're staring at you Paki bastard . . .?"

And on cue the others joined in. They twisted their thin faces and spat out their abuse. Contempt. They leaned in at him and shouted to make him cower. But he didn't cower. He started to shout back. Strange words. Angry. Spoken in a deep cracked voice. Words that met theirs and refused to back off. It went on for 30 seconds. Abuse in two languages. Abuse thrown by voices that became louder. The boys edged forward. They closed the space. They demanded that the small man should back off. They needed him to cower. To cringe. Instead he stayed as still as a tree. Instead a small mocking smile came to his face as he shouted at them in a language they could not understand. And in less that a minute they came to a place from which they could not retreat. He had come thousands of miles from the broken body of his little girl. They had come from a tenner's worth of manhood with Doreen Hughes. They couldn't back away. It was unthinkable. Not here. Not on their own turf. Not to some little Paki asylum seeker. No way.

Kev pulled his knife. It was his prize possession. A flick of the thumb brought out the blade to glint in the light of the street. "There you go Paki. What do you think of that then? Still going to mouth it off are you? Are you? Piece of fucking shite. Come on. Let's hear you shout now you smelly bastard. COME ON . . .!"

The knife stopped the shouting. The man fell quiet. His dark eyes locked onto the blade as the boy edged forward into his space. And all the while the smile stayed on his lips. Mocking. Taunting. Goading. No words required. The smile an open invitation. A dare. A taunt.

And Kev felt the onset of fear. Alarm bells were sounding somewhere in the corners of his mind. But the vodka and the speed were too much in control of him. He had carried his knife for three years. Waiting. Waiting for the moment when he would take his chance and prove himself. Waiting for now. Waiting to show them all that he wasn't a boy any more. Waiting to become one of the ones that people talked about in quiet voices. Like his Dad. Like Tac Brennan. And now was the moment. The moment when the vodka and the speed and the adrenalin all surged together in his mind. A moment to deliver the cut.

He was so much slower than the instructor had been. The man from America who had taught unarmed combat to the fighters of the mujahidin had been ten times quicker. The boy was slow. Predictable. An easy mark. The man from Afghanistan stepped out of the way of the knife thrust like a dancer. He closed a hard hand over the boy's wrist and snapped down. There was the sound of a crack and a piercing scream. The knife clattered to the pavement and things all went much too fast. Kev tripped and fell forward with his face twisted in pain from the broken wrist. The man stooped quickly to pick up the knife. His body turned with a kind of grace as he buried the knife deep into the boy's back. The others hadn't started to register what had happened when the man turned on them. Fast. Light on his feet. Almost dancing. The smile even bigger now. His arm flashed out and the blade cut through Spik's windpipe and jugular vein. Migs was just starting to try to turn and run when the knife shot between his ribs and into his heart. The man stepped back. Kev was breathing in huge ragged gasps. The man took a handful of his hair and tugged back his head. He sliced the boy's throat with no more emotion than he had shown a hundred times before when he had slaughtered one of his goats.

He tossed the knife to the floor. He sat down on the small wall by the pavement and searched his pocket for his cigarettes. He lit one and drew deeply. He looked down on the corpses at his feet quite impassively. There would be no more contempt now. Hatred yes. All the hate in the world. But not contempt. Not now. Not again.

Constables Campbell Swann and Bob Teague were killing time. They were seven hours into their shift and an hour remained. It had been quiet. It had been as quiet as a wet Wednesday night in April warranted. They had dealt with a domestic violence call-out. A neighbour had said that it sounded like someone was being killed. The couple swore blind that the neighbour was a nosy old bitch who should mind her own business. The woman looked as if she had done five rounds with Lennox Lewis. It was the way it was. Just paperwork and a feeling of time wasted.

Later they had helped to pick-up a pensioner who had fallen flat on his face outside a bar. He had rearranged his nose but he was drunk enough to barely notice. They sat him down and waited for the ambulance whilst he told them all about the Anzio beachhead as if it had only been the week before.

A window had been put through in a primary school and a nicked car had been set alight. Seven hours of Glasgow police work. They had picked up coffees at the McDonalds on the Kirkintilloch road and now they talked football without much enthusiasm as the rain blurred the windscreen. Campbell was idly considering whether to take a curry or a Chinese back to his bedsit when the squawk of the radio snatched at his attention. The controller's voice seemed unusually agitated. As the guts of the message came out, Campbell tossed his coffee cup out of the window and hit the gas. The details nailed into him one by on. Fountainwell Avenue. Multiple homicide. Reported three. Knife attack. All units . . . He radioed in confirmation of their ETA. Five minutes. The siren wailed into the night as they crashed red lights at 75.

Sighthill was coming alive as they pulled into Fountainwell Avenue. There was a growing cluster of people halfway down the avenue. He took in the first impressions. Already there was the beginning of chaos. Nothing good. A man shouting into a mobile phone. A youth vomiting over the wall. A woman with an arm around another youth with his head in his hands as he sat on the wall. People's faces betrayed extremes of emotion. Some displayed a raw killing anger. Others were blank and numbed by the horror of what lay before them. The residents of Sighthill were no strangers to violence. It wasn't unusual for a bit of blood to be spilled on the pavements of the estate. But now there was something different in the air.

Swann parted the small group. The horror hit him hard. Blood everywhere. A lake of it dripping into the gutter. Three bodies, already soaked by the rain. Staring eyes. Young. Terribly young. Jesus, throats cut like slaughtered pigs. He took a long breath and fought for control. He looked for Teague. Nowhere to be found. Stupid twat. Then he saw him doubled-up and vomiting. Fiasco. Faces were being pushed into him. There was shouting. Anger. Blazing anger. He forced himself to become organised.

"OK. Shut up. All of you. NOW!" He threw his arms out to back up the crowd that was growing by the minute. It was then that he noticed the man. How the hell had he not seen him before? Just sitting there like something straight out of hell. Still as a statue covered in blood and his eyes staring out of Sighthill to some place far away. Not British. Asian. Indian. Pakistani. Oh Christ. An asylum seeker.

The sheer magnitude of the situation hit Campbell. An asylum seeker coated in blood. A crowd about to become a mob. Teague with the plot lost chucking his guts onto the road. Three dead kids, two of them with their throats cut to the neck bone. And voices all around him that were starting to bay for revenge. Decision Campbell. A decision to make and seconds to make it.

He made it. He decided to forget the integrity of the crime scene. The forensic lads could bitch about it later. He took a few quick steps to where a chalk-white Teague was bent over with his hands on his knees. He roughly pulled him upright and slapped him hard across the face.

"Get a fucking grip Teague. Get it now." He stared hard into the bewildered face for a moment. The light was back on. His junior colleague was coming round to being angry about the slap. "OK. In the car now. Get the engine running. We're out of here. Got that?"

Teague nodded and jumped into the car. Campbell moved through the crowd to where the man sat. They were closing in on him. And he just sat there and smiled as the rain swept down his face.

"OK sunshine, on your feet." Campbell took a handful of the man's jacket and yanked him to his feet. A look of vague bewilderment came onto the man's face. Campbell was a big man, a little over six three. He spun the smaller man around and pulled his arms together. He snapped on the handcuffs and frog-marched him to the car. Teague had at last come to his senses and had got the back door open. Campbell almost threw the man onto the back seat. The crowd had been caught unawares by the speed of Campbell's action. But only for a moment. The realisation was dawning fast now. He was about to take the man away and it wasn't going to sit well. Hands were reaching for the door as Campbell dragged it closed behind him.

"GO! NOW!"

Teague didn't need asking twice. The wheels of the squad car spun and then bit into the soaked tarmac. The car bounced with a couple of kicks and a fist on the roof and then it was clear with the siren wailing. Teague's knuckles were white on the steering wheel and there was a frantic gleam in his eyes.

"Where to Campbell?"

Campbell took a couple of breaths and considered. The local station would only be asking for trouble, it would become a magnet for the mob once it gathered properly.

"Get us over to Central. Fast as you can."

He pulled out the radio and demanded to be patched through to the controller on the desk of Strathclyde Central police station. He pre-warned that they were coming in with a triple murder suspect and that their ETA was five minutes. No point in trying to explain any more. As Teague threw the car through the quiet streets of the city centre Campbell tried to get his thoughts into some kind of order.

He had been a policeman for two years. He was one of the new order, having joined up as a graduate of St Andrew's University. Training school had been good. His first 24 months had been good. All the boxes were getting ticked. They had put him into the tough areas and he had come through fine. The file was filling up in all the right places and CID was no more than a couple of years away. But he was painfully aware that the decisions that he had just made in Fountainwell Avenue in a matter of seconds could have changed everything on a permanent basis.

He deliberately slowed his mind down and started to put the facts together. The triple killing would become the most notorious murder that the city had seen in years. In all probability he had the perpetrator in the back seat of the car. And what had they done? Teague had chucked his guts up whilst Campbell had thrown the suspect into the back of the car like a bag of shopping without reading him his rights. They had departed the crime scene leaving all the evidence to be trampled by a growing mob and washed away by the rain. He was going to have to convince his superiors that if he hadn't acted in this way his suspect in all likelihood would have been lynched. Lynched! For fuck's sake Campbell. When was the last time that somebody got lynched in Scotland? Christ, it was beginning to sound thin. It was beginning to sound as if they had bottled it and legged it.

He shuddered as the pieces started to assemble themselves. What the hell had he done and why in the name of Christ had he done it? But when he really posed the question to himself he knew the answer only too well. He hadn't had long to look at the corpses on the Sighthill pavement but there had been long enough. He knew the lads and he knew one of them in particular. He had recognised Kevin Brennan. Kev was Tac Brennan's lad and everyone on Sighthill knew all about Tac Brennan. The consequences of what had happened were beyond belief. In the tinderbox of the tower blocks it was only ever going to take the smallest spark to set the whole place alight. For an asylum seeker to slice up three local kids was always going to be rather more than a small spark. For an asylum seeker to slit Tac Brennan's son's throat from ear to ear was more like a ten-pound lump of Semtex.

The sergeant was primed and ready for them as they shoved their prisoner through the front door of the central police station. He was in the process of opening his mouth to deliver his tirade when Campbell held up his hands to stop him. What the hell. He was already up to his chest in it, might as well get right in up to his neck.

"Sorry Sarge, but there isn't time. Believe me. This is the perp. Read him his rights. Book him. Bang him up. Before that, speak to anyone who will listen. There is a shit storm about to break up there and we need as many men as possible. We have three dead bodies on the pavement. Two have had their throats cut. They're local lads and one of them is Kevin Brennan. His dad is Tac Brennan and believe me he is hell on wheels. Once he gets to the scene the whole place is going to blow. Got that? As many men as possible. Immediately. We need to get back. Sorry Sarge. Come on Teague. Let's move."

He pushed his bewildered colleague to the door and they were out before the sergeant had a chance to speak. It was all going way too fast for Teague. He was just twelve months into the job and going back to Fountainwell Avenue wasn't even nearly what he had signed up for. He stopped and brushed away Campbell's hand.

"No. For fuck's sake Campbell. Slow down. There is no way we're going back up there. They'll bloody murder us. It's madness. We should stay here and book the bastard that did it. Come on, he's our collar."

Campbell looked at the younger man's chubby face and saw fear among the bad skin and the acne. He didn't blame him. Anyone in their right mind would be bricking it. He tried to moderate his tone.

"Look, Bob. I don't think that you get this. We took the call. We didn't secure the crime scene. In fact we buggered-off from the crime scene. We cuffed the suspect and chucked him into the car without reading him his rights in front of twenty witnesses. We've ignored just about every rule in the book. Now I know, and you know, that if we hadn't removed the perp from the situation they would have lynched him, especially when Tac Brennan showed up. But that's just you and me Bob. Every other bastard will say that we shat it and scarpered. Now that isn't what is going to happen. So we go back and we try and do our fucking job. Yeah? Get the picture?"

Campbell Swann had always intimidated Teague. He had everything the younger man wanted. The university degree. The lean six-foot-three frame. The thick blond hair and the film star good looks. A girlfriend that half the Strathclyde police force dreamed of shagging. And tonight it had just got a whole lot worse. He had chucked up all over his uniform and Campbell had slapped him like a ten-year-old. And now he was going to force him back up to Sighthill and a complete bloody nightmare. And he was going to go. Of course he was because he was always going to be bullied by Campbell bastard Swann. He shrugged his shoulders petulantly and threw himself into the driver's seat. They didn't talk as they made their way back up the hill from the city centre to the coffin-shaped tower blocks that loomed up into the orange of the sky.

Desk sergeant Higgins called up help. Two policemen took the man from Afghanistan through a door and processed him. 10.45 p.m. The waiting area was as quiet as the grave. Not for bloody long he thought. He could feel it in his bones. This was going to be a big one. Probably the biggest since the Ibrox Stadium disaster. He checked behind him. Nobody. Just him. That would all change soon enough once the shit started flying. He pulled out his mobile phone and scrolled through the memory. Hendon. He hit "dial". It rang out for longer than he would have hoped. He was on the verge of giving up when it was answered by a groggy voice.

"Yeah."

"Johnny?"

"Yeah. Who's that?"

Another look around. "It's Higgins. Listen up Johnny. I'm going to make this quick. I've got the biggest story you've ever seen and it can be yours before any bastard in town. It'll cost you five grand. No ifs. No buts. No nothing. You take it or I ring the next number on the list. You've got twenty seconds."

"Fucking hell Walter, give a man a break, five grand and you won't even . . ."

"The clock's ticking Johnny. You've got ten seconds left."

A pause. An endless chasm of a pause. Bite, you bastard.

"OK. Done."

Higgins allowed a slow breath out. Unbelievable. He's bitten. One phone call and he could come up with the new conservatory that Vera had been nagging him to death over. He speeded up. Time to get it over and done with.

"OK. Only once. Fountainwell Avenue. Sighthill. About 10.30 tonight. An asylum seeker went berserk with a knife. He's killed three local lads. Just kids. Fifteen. Sixteen. I'm not sure. He carved them. Two of them got their throats slashed."

"Jesus."

"It gets better Johnny. One of them is Tac Brennan's lad. There is a mob building and things are about to blow. Over to you Johnny boy. Happy hunting. I don't need to remind you just how poor your life will be if you don't pay me."

He touched the end button almost gently. As he started to raise the brass from their beds he had a smile on his face not dissimilar to that worn by the man from Afghanistan an hour earlier.

Johnny Hendon stared dumbly at the mobile phone in his hand. Five grand. What the hell had he just done? Five grand! He was three thousand over his overdraft limit, two months behind on the rent and he didn't have a credit card that worked any more and he had just agreed to five grand. Madness. Utter bloody madness. And yet despite the madness of what he had just done he felt the excitement all through him. This could just be the best five grand he had ever spent. It could be corner-turning time. Play this one right Johnny boy and the good times can start to roll again.

He hauled himself up from the battered old couch where he had been sprawled and started to pull clothes off the floor. His flat told the story of his life much more eloquently than any biography could have done. Just three years before he had taken the keys to a new apartment on the gentrified banks of the Clyde within spitting distance of the city centre. It had been the peak of the good times. Ten thousand quids' worth of designer furniture, the wide-screen TV before anyone else had one, the surroundsound music system, the fully-stocked drinks cabinet in the bedroom. It was when he had hit his peak. The boy from Parkhead made good. He had felt indestructible. Unassailable. Halfway up a ladder that led straight up into the clouds. And all of it before he was 23.

Now it was all gone. Gone without a trace. Sold on. Repossessed. Pawned. Now it was this one-roomer on the fourth floor about a million light years from the gentrified banks of the Clyde. There was just the one relic left. It was only left because it had no value to anyone but him. No value to the pawnbrokers. He remembered proudly hanging the picture on the wall in his sparkling new apartment. It had been the proof that he had arrived. The reason for his arrival. "Scottish Reporter of the Year 1999 – John Hendon. *The Scottish Recorder.*" And now? Now he was just another two-bit freelancer that didn't get his calls answered. He carried the smell of catastrophe. He was living evidence of just how far and how fast a man could fall. Johnny Hendon, loser in residence.

He had blagged his way into a junior reporter's job on the *Kirkintilloch Herald* when he had left school at eighteen. His exams would have walked him into any university he might have chosen. It had been a disappointment to his school. They wanted to see one of theirs make it to a hallowed place. A rare result for a school drawing on the youth from the schemes of Glasgow's south side. It hadn't appealed to Johnny Hendon. He was ready for the real world, not ivory towers. His decision was soon vindicated. The *Kirky Herald* turned out to be a six-month stepping stone. By the time he was twenty he was on the crime team of *The Recorder* and bringing home the bacon every week. The heartbeat of Glasgow's world of crime was to be found deep in the high-rise schemes of the city. Not places for policemen. Not places for social workers. Certainly not places for reporters from a Scottish broadsheet. But it was where Johnny had come from. These were places that he knew. He had blended in for twenty years for no other reason than he was a born and bred part of the furniture. It was no big thing to simply carry on.

He was a natural. His editor always said that he had a nose for it. Nobody could make a hundred quid go further. No matter how deep it was buried, Johnny Hendon would dig it out. Several of his stories made the big time. *The Recorder* started to gain a hard-hitting reputation that it had not enjoyed for 50 years. Readers all over Scotland started to automatically turn to the Johnny Hendon column.

The pay cheques got fatter. The big nights got bigger. A season ticket at Celtic Park. Complimentary tickets to all the right gigs. Holidays in sunny places that were never to be found in the Thomson brochure. And girls. An endless stream of girls. Girls on tap.

Then one night he had picked up a whisper. Just the smallest breath of a whisper. A whisper about a brothel with a difference. It had taken him four months but he had found it. A nice big Victorian house in amongst the solicitors' offices and exclusive apartments for young professionals. They were flying in girls from Kosovo. Pretty young ones who would command the highest prices. Girls who were in no position to moan. It was a joint venture between some Glasgow gangsters and some murderous maniacs in Albania. He had hidden for days patiently clicking away with his camera and night vision equipment. And the gallery started to grow. A judge. Two senior Council men. A Soap star. Two footballers. Day by day his rogues gallery steadily grew. And then the story took a lurch in a whole new direction when he saw Timothy Small enter a side door. Small's family owned a chain of hardware stores across West Scotland. Small wasn't a particularly important face. Nothing compared to what had gone before. What made Small special was that there had been rumours floating around for years about him. Small liked boys. Young boys. The younger the better. Which made Johnny wonder what else might have been going on behind the respectable façade of 57 Orchard Avenue.

It took a while, but he got there. One night he recognised a face and followed it. He painstakingly maintained his watch for a month. Then it all paid off. He was led to an industrial estate on the outskirts of Motherwell. The face supervised whilst other men lifted big wooden crates from the back of a lorry with Polish markings. When the cases stopped being handled, the real cargo was unloaded. Fifteen boys, and not one older than nine years old. They looked half-starved and the sight of their terrified pale faces in the headlights was enough to send tears running down Johnny's cheeks. He was ready to blow the whole thing sky high right there and then but some instinct told him to wait. As ever, his instincts were proved right. Two nights later his camera whirred and he captured a perfect collection of photos showing Chipper Finnighan entering the side door.

Chipper Finnighan had been the uncrowned king of Glasgow's underworld for over a decade. His reputation had become legend. The hardest of the hard men. The biggest of the big men. And here he was going in to get his rocks off buggering a nine-year-old boy from the Balkans.

The paper and the police hatched a deal. The police took over the stakeout from Johnny. A week later twenty armed officers crashed every door of the house half an hour after Finnighan had gone in.

KILLINGS IN THE NIGHT

They cuffed him without his trousers in the company of a weeping young Montenegrin called Pavel. Anything else and Chipper Finnighan's time in Barlinnie would have been fine. But not that. Not with an nine-year-old. Chipper Finnighan was finished beyond repair. And Johnny Hendon became Scottish Reporter of the Year and everyone's hero because he was the man who had caught the beast.

The summer that followed had been the time to end all times. He was on everyone's A-list. Awards. Parties. Weekends in the country. Champagne by the gallon. And Lena.

Lena.

Lena was the far end of the dream. Lena walked straight out of *Vogue* and into his life one afternoon at Ayr races. Lena would have turned heads at a Miss World contest. Lena had it all. Looks. Charm. Brains. Class. Lena was the real deal and they were the number one couple in town. She took him to places he had never dreamed of. And she had introduced him to her best friend Charlie. Snow. Cocaine.

Johnny had been waiting all his life to meet Charlie. It finished him off. It made him perfect. Charlie and Lena. Lena and Charlie. At night. In the afternoon. And then in the morning before getting out of bed. A line a day. Then three. Then 23. And then no remote clue of the count. But it was never a problem. Lena always had Charlie with her. At the start he sometimes asked her about the money. Surely he should contribute. But she would only laugh. Don't be so boring about things Johnny. It's fine. Just enjoy it. Live it Johnny. And so he had. Why look gift-horses in the mouth?

Soon his work started to fall apart. The nose that had always sniffed out stories was now a full-time vacuum cleaner. He got a couple of warnings. They just washed right over him. Who needed a stupid job anyway? Not when he had Lena. Not when he had Charlie. They fired him in the end. It broke the editor's heart. He had felt like a father figure. In the end he was nothing. His star boy from the South Side just sneered when he received his cards. There had been a couple of papers that had been more than happy to take on the boy who had knocked over Chipper Finnighan. But they had soon realised that they had hired a basket case.

Then one morning it all came to an end. He woke to find himself alone in the bed. Lena was gone. The flat held no memory of her. No clothes. No cosmetics in the bathroom. Nothing. She had just evaporated from his life. For a while he had waited but never with a great deal of hope. Lena had merely hitched herself to a shooting star. He had been her ticket to the parties and the weekends. All the right places. Once his star was all burned out Lena had moved on. The next fortnight was a bad wake-up. He tried to get a handle on all the bills that he had stuffed into the drawer. And then things took a big turn for the worse. Two men he didn't know and didn't want to know arrived at the door. They brought along the biggest bill of them all. For months Lena had been buying their cocaine on account. His account. It was the way they had always worked before with Lena. And her gentlemen had always paid up, just like he would pay up, assuming that he had a fondness for his legs.

In a way he was lucky. The apartment complex on the gentrified banks of the Clyde had rocketed in value. He sold it on for enough profit to pay the men off. The other debts took on a life of their own, generating a constant stream of summons letters. In the end there was no point in fighting them and he went bankrupt.

There was only one legacy from his golden year. Lena had gone. The high-flying job had gone. The luxury apartment had gone. Everything had gone, leaving only the cocaine, which hung onto him with the devoted loyalty of an unwanted mongrel. And so Johnny entered the twilight world. A story sold meant a few more lines. No story meant the sweats. His addiction pushed his career into desperate places. Somehow he just about managed to come up with the goods. Editors learned the habit of throwing him the impossible leads, the ones that no reporter in their right mind would follow. Give it to Crazy Johnny. He's mad enough. Maybe he'll get something. Crazy Johnny who never bothers about the risks. It had earned him a few good kickings along the way.

And now a half-forgotten contact had tossed him a lifeline. The biggest, juiciest murder the city had seen in years. His dulled instincts thrilled to the few facts that he had already learned. There was no way around it. The story seemed to have everything. And there was the promise of more to come. He grinned as he pulled on a sweater and checked over his digital camera. It was extraordinary. Of all the two bit yobs in the city the asylum seeker had chosen to cut the throat of Tac Brennan's lad. What were the odds on that? Millions. Zillions. Tac wasn't the biggest hoodlum in the city. Not big at all. He was no kind of legend outside of Sighthill. Small time really. But Johnny knew him. He had met him a couple of times whilst chasing up stories that no other journalist in town would touch with a barge pole. He wasn't the biggest or the richest and he didn't have the most men on the books. He worked a small patch of a few tower blocks in Sighthill. Money lending. Drugs. All the usual stuff. No bigger than 50 other small-time godfathers across the city. And yet there was something about him. Something that Johnny had never quite been able to put a finger on. Certainly nothing he had ever been able to tie down into a sellable story. Something that ate away in the pit of his belly. Something darker than dark. And now an asylum seeker had cut up Brennan's son. Whatever was about to happen up in Sighthill was not going to be small.

Tac Brennan was sliding into a bad mood. It was close on eleven and the bar had filled up with punters who could only afford to be there for the last hour. He was sitting in his usual high seat at the bar. Rogan's Bar wasn't a passing trade sort of a place. It catered for a set clientele drawn from the tower blocks. Weekday trade was slow until ten and then there would be a desultory rush. Weekends brought a modest frenzy as Giro cheques were drunk leaving empty cupboards and screaming rows. Rogan's was Tac Brennan's office. It was where he conducted his business. Everyone knew where to find him. It was where he bought and sold and issued instructions. In return for the use of the facilities, Terry the landlord enjoyed an exemption for paying out protection. It was an adequate arrangement. Tac and his boys more or less kept the place going. They were the only punters with any money in their pockets.

The other customers had no great problem with Tac Brennan. If it wasn't him who ran the show it would have been someone else. He was reasonable enough. He only handed out the stick if he was crossed. If debts weren't paid. If respect wasn't shown. He was never one of those who got violent just for the sake of it. His money-lending rates were reasonable. His drugs were of decent quality. He kept his boys on a fairly short leash. In many ways he enjoyed a general popularity that was unusual for a local enforcer. He had become something of a judge and jury in various local issues. If a local heroin addict ripped of a handbag from a pensioner the incident would be reported to Tac Brennan at his seat at the bar. Such behaviour was deemed to be out of order. If the lad was local he would be brought into the back room and given a good slapping. If the goods could be recovered they would be and duly returned. If not, then Tac would arrange a sum of compensation which the lad would repay to him with interest. It was how he worked. And by and large his community liked him for it. They lived in a place where the police were never welcome. Someone had to keep some kind of a lid on things. Tac Brennan wasn't perfect. But he could have been a whole lot worse.

He was by no means the archetypal hard man to look at. He wasn't particularly tall, five eleven. He was by no means all that broad, in fact he was almost wiry. He never dressed flash, but he was never scruffy. He was strictly Marks and Spencer. Slacks. Plain shirts. Golfing jackets. Shoes that were always highly polished. His hair was black and straight, strictly controlled with Brylcream, and swept into a sharp side parting. Most people considered that it was too black. It had to be dyed. But that wasn't something you would think of asking about. A neatly-trimmed black moustache was the central feature of a face that showed more lines than the 47 years on the clock probably warranted. It was a mean face. Often malevolent. Seldom smiling. Not remotely handsome.

Tac Brennan was a man who felt no need to act and dress the part of the hard man. He relied solely on his reputation, which in and among the tower blocks of Sighthill was nothing less than awesome. When a situation needed to be dealt with, he dealt with it. If it required little or no violence, then he used little or no violence. If it needed maximum force, then he used it. It wasn't something he dithered about. On two occasions men who had crossed him had disappeared. Maybe they had just emigrated for their health. Or maybe it was something more permanent. It wasn't something that anyone wanted to discuss much. What mattered was that they had just gone away. It was how Tac Brennan did things. Quiet. Efficient. No fuss.

Right now he was getting annoyed. He was trying to concentrate on the television that was mounted over the bar and he was finding it difficult. Behind him two lads were being louder than they should have been. Too many pints in too much of a hurry. Fair enough except when he was trying to watch the TV. The picture on the screen was strange, distorted, a weird muzzy-green. You needed the commentary to get a proper feel of what was happening. And he couldn't hear what the commentator was saying because there were a pair of wankers behind him acting like ten-year-olds. His patience snapped and he spun round.

"Hey." His voice wasn't dramatically loud. It took a moment for the lads to realise that it was them that he was addressing. They sobered up in an instant, their eyes darting about the room looking for a clue. Tac continued patiently. "Some of us are trying to watch this. Some of us are trying to listen to this. And it is hard when dickheads like you are rabbiting on like a pair of fucking washerwomen. Yeah?"

This brought apologetic nods. They allowed their eyes to wander up to the fuzzy, jumpy pictures on the screen and puzzlement appeared on their faces.

"How you any idea what this is?"

Heads were shaken.

"What you are watching here is the real thing boys. This isn't some tin pot little scrap on the street corner. This isn't a few wannabe hard boys scratching at each other outside a nightclub on a Saturday night. This is ultimate force. The ultimate fighting machine in the history of the world. Yeah?"

They were looking really nervous now. This was the patient, philosophical Tac Brennan that often appeared seconds before the violent, stick fingers in you eyes Tac Brennan. All they could do was nod eagerly. Tac continued, warming to his theme. The whole bar had become his audience.

"Gentlemen, what you are privileged to be watching is the British Army in action. So. What is happening here? We are watching a company of Royal Marines. About 100 guys. How many are they up against? 300? 500? Who knows? The bad guys are dug in. The bad guys have all kinds of modern weapons. Sounds bad, eh? That's because it is bad. Badder than wankers like you would ever believe. See that? RPG. Rocket Propelled Grenade. Boom. Bye bye bad guy. Fire and move. Cover, fire and move. That's what you're watching. It doesn't matter that the boys are out-numbered and out-gunned. They don't give a shite. They'll just go straight at it. And they'll go straight through like a dose of fucking salts. So that, ladies, is what I am trying to watch. The British Army kicking arses. And what I do not need is to listen to a pair of tossers like you pratting around. So put your drinks down and fuck off out of my sight before I get really annoyed."

The two lads didn't need to be asked twice. Tac Brennan turned back to the bar and watched the Royal Marines getting their first taste of life in Saddam's Iraq. He nodded to Terry who duly brought him another half of McEwans and a double Jamesons. The pictures were opening old wounds inside him. Memories of the many times when he had been there in the thick of it. Part of it. Part of something that was unique. It had been twenty years of his life. The best twenty years. He was under no illusions about that. He would only ever have one true home. The sergeant's mess of the First Battalion of the Parachute Regiment. Sighthill was where he was born and bred. Sighthill was where he had cut his teeth. But 1 Para was where he had really belonged. It was killing him inside to watch the green pictures from the Gulf. And here he was sitting in this shit-hole killing the days one by one whilst the boys out there went in and did the business. He slowly lit a cigarette and took a careful draw.

There was a commotion at the door. Two men shoved their way through the thin crowd of drinkers. Locals with frantic faces, both breathless from running on top of 40-a-day.

"Tac. Tac . . . fuck's sake . . ." Bob Hughes gave in to a prolonged burst of coughing that shook his body like a cattle prod. Brennan dragged a barstool to him and grinned.

"Here. Sit yourself down. You're too old for this running shite Bob. What's the fuss?"

The hawking was easing. Hughes sucked in the stale air of the bar and clenched his eyes shut for a moment. At last he felt ready to speak to the expectant bar. His whole demeanour was provoking interest. Something must have gone off to get Bobby Hughes sprinting through the night.

"Christ Tac. There's a fucking nightmare out there. Some bastard has flipped. Killed three lads. Slashed them up. They're just there on the pavement. Bleeding all over the shop. You've never seen anything like it."

Brennan's smile was long gone. He was Sergeant Brennan now. Assess the situation. React. Don't dither about.

"Where?"

"Just down the way. Fountainwell Avenue. Halfway along . . ."

"Who did it?"

"I think it was one of the Pakis. He was just sitting there, blood all over him. You should have seen the bastard Tac. Just sitting there and smoking and grinning . . ."

"What about the Police?"

"Been and gone. Swann and that fat cunt. They just grabbed the Paki and fucked off. Just left the bodies out there. No-one else has come yet."

Tac was on his feet now. He pulled on his jacket, which had been hanging over the back of the chair. He pocketed his cigarettes and knocked back his scotch. It all seemed to be done casually. Never let on that you're in a flap. Leave that to the officers. Just look cool. Look as if you couldn't give a shite. It was how they had always done it. He started for the door but Bob Hughes grabbed at his sleeve. It was only then that Tac noticed the look in his eyes. The look that told him that there was something else. Something that was tearing Hughes inside. Something that he couldn't stand to say. His mouth was flapping around like a goldfish.

"Take a breath Bob. Spit it out."

Hughes looked as if he wanted to burst into tears. "One of them is your Kev, Tac. One of the lads. One of the ones he slashed up."

For a moment Tac Brennan stood very still. It took every minute of his twenty years to make him stay still and show nothing. Remember Tac. You don't give a shite. It's just a job. You get it done. Simple as that. He clamped his teeth down together and held on. He reached out and gently patted Hughes on the top of his arm.

"Thanks Bob. Thanks for telling me."

They were to talk for years about how he had walked out of the bar. Not hurried. His back straight. Just out and into the rain. There was a small pause and then drinks were emptied and everyone followed him as if he were the Pied Piper.

Nicky Jennings had decided on an early night. It was a decision that she had weighed carefully whilst taking a long slow bath. She was tired to the bone. The kids at the High School where she taught English were always a handful. This week they had gone way beyond the handful stage. This week they had been an utter nightmare. It was only Wednesday and already it seemed as if the week had lasted about ten years. And tomorrow it would all start again. Her heart told her to throw on her clothes and head over to Campbell's flat and wait for him with the chilled bottle of wine that was sitting patiently in the fridge. Her head told her to make a hot chocolate and get herself into bed. It wasn't often that Nicky ever listened to what her head told her. Her mum had never shut up about it. You're going too fast Nicky. You'll burn yourself out Nicky. The way she felt tonight she couldn't help but admit that her mum probably had a point. The tiredness seemed to have got deep into her bones. Was it just staying up too late all the time and drinking a little more than she really should have done? Or was it more than that? Was it too much time spent on lost causes? Too much time spent swimming against the tide.

She had never truly realised just how hard the teaching would be. She could handle the lack of interest. Most of the time she could break through that. Nicky Jennings had the knack of kicking down the doors of teenage indifference. She was young enough and she cared enough. Even the most determined found it hard to resist her passion. It was the endless torrents of testosterone that she found hardest to deal with. Nicky was cursed with being a particularly good-looking English teacher. She was young, she dressed well, she was considered to be cool and she had a body that every one of the 643 male teenagers in the school yearned for. She could never walk down a corridor or across the playground without the endless comments. She felt churlish to be so permanently pissed-off about it. They didn't mean any harm. They probably thought she would be flattered. God forbid. She knew that she had to find a way to stop it getting her so down.

Campbell just laughed and moaned that he never had any young girls leching after him, uniform or no uniform. All he got was two fingers and the occasional stone thrown from behind a wall.

Most of the time she felt thoroughly annoyed at herself for being so bothered by the silly comments. After all that was all they were, just silly comments from lads who had reached that dreaded age. It was never going to change. Well, that was wrong. It would change once she got old and raddled. It was only when she got tired that the whole thing got to her. And tonight she was tired. Dog tired.

If keeping up with school and her relationship with Campbell took away just about every ounce of energy she possessed, her work up at

Sighthill took away every last drop. She had started going up there a year before. It had been a colleague in the staff room who had got her into it. Jean was 50 and divorced and had watched both her sons safely flee the nest to university. For Jean, the work up in Sighthill helped to fill the suddenly empty hours. It hadn't seemed too daunting at first. They were just looking for volunteers to help the newly arrived families to settle down. Basic stuff. Help them with their forms. Tell them where the shops could be found. Let them know about how the basics worked. School. Doctors. Electric cards. Just a couple of hours a week. Honestly Nicky, it would be brilliant if you could find a bit of time. You see, we're snowed under. They're coming in every day and we're terribly short of volunteers. It wouldn't be much. A couple of hours a week. You could fit it in with Campbell's night shifts.

Saying no had always been a problem for Nicky. Her dad had said it was because she was sucker. He had probably been right. There had always been something about lost causes that she found to be more or less irresistible. And like a mug she had said yes. Why not? A couple of hours a week wouldn't be a problem. What kind of dreamland did she live in? Two hours a week was fine in theory. After all, how long could it take to show someone how to use an electric card? And then she met her first family. The Khan family had come from a small town in Iraq 50 miles north of Tikrit. For many years their life had never been anything other than ordinary. Mr Khan was a mechanic in a local garage. He had never earned a great deal. But there had always been more or less enough. Life was neither easier nor harder for the Khan family than for most other families in the Iraq of the sanction years.

Then one day they had come. In the true tradition of all twentieth-century secret policemen they had come at three in the morning with dazzling torches and snarling dogs. They had taken Mr Khan away and the family had never seen him again. And everything had changed. Now there was never enough to eat. The children were constantly bullied at school. The neighbours snubbed Mrs Khan at the market as if she had leprosy. And then they had come for her as well. They had no intention of asking her any questions. Once they dragged her down the stone stairs to the basement they only had one goal in mind. There were ten of them and they took their turns with her whilst the others passed the bottle and almost laughed themselves sick. Once they had done, they gave her an hour with the electricity just for kicks. And then they pushed her out onto the dusty street and she had crawled the quarter mile back to the house.

It had been her uncle who had arranged their escape. He had always been the family's black sheep. Nobody really knew exactly what he did. He was a man whom people asked to get things for them. Things that were hard to find in the shops. Things that you would always have to pay a bit extra for. Her dad had disowned his brother and told the family that no good would ever come of him. How wrong he had been. Secret policemen have just as great a need for things as anyone else. Her uncle was useful. There was little point in stealing money if you couldn't spend it on all the latest hi-fi equipment or a dishwasher for the kitchen. The uncle was the man would make it happen and the sanctions had made him a wealthy man. He had the money and he knew the people. He arranged everything. Mrs Khan and her two daughters were taken by a series of lorries across the mountains of Kurdistan. From there it was the Balkans, Austria and a flight to Glasgow.

Jean had asked Nicky to try and get in to see them as soon as she could. As she rode the elevator to the tenth floor Nicky could barely believe what she was doing. There had been no training. Just advice. Just help as best as you can Nicky. You'll be fine. Really.

They hadn't even unpacked. They sat together on the threadbare settee that seemed lost in the room with the peeling walls and filthy window. Nicky tried to be bright and breezy and what was left of the Khan family just sat and stared with eyes that seemed almost dead. She made tea and chatted until she felt frantic. It was her first lesson in the hardest truth that she was to learn. Broken people often turn to stone. The Khans had been emotionally destroyed. Strangely enough it was the electric card that saved the day. The sheer mundane practicality of showing Mrs Khan how it worked forced the first small crack in the ice.

Two hours a week became four hours a night. The oldest girl was six. Her sister was four. It took Nicky weeks and every drop of patience that she possessed, but in the end she broke through. Slowly she taught the family the rudiments of English. Slowly Mrs Khan emerged back into the world and started to come out of hibernation. She was a quick and intelligent lady, and once she grasped the basics, her English progressed quickly. After five months both girls were ready for school. It was the night of their first day that Mrs Khan told her story. The girls were asleep and Nicky was about to leave. A small voice held her back.

"I can talk please Nicky? You can hear me?"

She made tea and sat. It took an hour and at the end Nicky felt as if her emotions had been flushed with bleach. All she could do was to hold the sobbing, destroyed woman until deep into the night. She had no comprehension of the horror that had been unfolded in words of quiet broken English. When she had at last got home she had not slept for a minute. She had cried until her eyes were raw. They all asked about it in the classroom the next morning. She had merely responded with a polite shake of her head. Jean had taken her to one side and held her hand and the tears had started all over again. Even the kids sensed her desperation and managed a day of quiet.

It had been a turning point. The poison was out. From that day Mrs Khan had been able to move on. At last there was some laughter in the flat. There was enthusiasm for weekend trips out to the countryside. And then one day as Nicky was approaching the main entrance to the block she found the oldest sister Aya pinned to the wall by a group of six boys of sixteen and seventeen. Her temper took her over and he dragged the nearest lad away so hard that he caught his heel in a crack in the concrete and fell. His head cracked on the paving and he sprang back to his feet and hit her hard. She flailed out at him but the others were soon at her as well. She went down and tried to make herself into a ball. She screamed to Aya to go. To get inside. To run. But the girl had never moved, her big dark eyes were filled with horror as the kicks came in one after the other.

Then it stopped as suddenly as it had started. She was barely conscious as she heard the sound of training shoes pounding away.

She felt herself being gently eased-up into a sitting position. A pair of thin arms were wrapped around her neck as Aya clamped herself to her. Slowly as she opened her eyes her blurred vision cleared and the sound of a voice clawed its way through the buzzing in her ears.

"It's OK love. Just stay calm. You're fine. Just bashed up a bit, that's all. The ambulance is on its way."

Slowly the face of a blond-haired policeman came into focus. It was crazy, but she started to laugh. The laughing soon turned to coughing and that made her ribs feel as if they were in a million pieces. Her voice sounded completely bizarre.

"Just a bit bashed up. Did you really say that? Just a bit bashed up. I dread to think what it would be like to be a lot bashed up."

The concern on the policeman's face faded into a small smile.

"Aye. You'll be fine. Just keep still. It won't be long."

All of a sudden the smile vanished to be replaced by a look of hostility. Nicky followed the direction of his gaze. A man had come through the small crowd that had gathered and was taking in the scene. She immediately took against him. He had a mean, hard face. There was something malevolent about him.

"How is she constable?"

"She'll be fine Mr Brennan. Nothing for you to be concerned about thank you."

A small smile showed yellow teeth.

"Oh, but I am concerned Constable Swann. We can't be having this kind of thing in the neighbourhood. Out of order. That's how I see it. Even though the young lady would do better to stay clear of this filth and stay where she belongs."

Swann's face was reddening with anger. "That's enough Tac. Why don't you move along? I'm in control here. Your opinions are noted thank you very much." He stood up slowly from his crouching position and stared down into Tac Brennan's face. The older man allowed his smile to widen.

"Now, now big man. No need to get all het up now. We wouldn't want any more unfortunate incidents would we? I must say though, I can't for the life of me understand what gives you the impression that you could be in control of anything in Sighthill."

He held Swann's eyes for a few more seconds and then slowly turned his head to look down at Nicky.

"Sorry this has happened Miss. I can promise you that the boys will be dealt with. In our own way. No need for these gentlemen to be involved. I think I can promise that they won't do it again. Maybe it would be a good idea if you stayed away in future. That face is far too pretty to be kicked . . ."

Campbell pushed him in the chest, much harder than he intended. Tac shot back but found his feet like a cat. The smile vanished in a flash. His voice dropped a notch.

"Careful Swann. You be very, very careful."

Campbell watched him stroll nonchalantly away and felt an icy finger of fear in his stomach. The rest of the small crowd that had gathered drifted away. He crouched back down to where Nicky was gently unpeeling the shivering little girl from her neck. Campbell helped to finish the job. Nicky stared down the front of the block to where Brennan was standing lighting a cigarette with two other men.

"Who is he?"

"Tac Brennan. Our friendly neighbourhood bastard. Thinks he owns the place. Anyway, don't worry about him. He won't do you any harm."

"And the boys, the ones who attacked me?"

"They're in for a kicking. A real kicking. Tac Brennan has certain rules. Mugging women is against the rules. He's right enough. They won't do it again."

"Is there nothing you can do? They were just boys. I suppose it was me that started it in a way."

There was a resigned look about him as he shook his head. "Not a thing. Not a chance. People don't talk to us here. Any problem, they go to Brennan. He's the local judge and jury. The lads will take their beating and they won't say a bloody word. I'm afraid this is the Wild, Wild West Miss."

"Nicky."

"Sorry?"

"Nicky. My name is Nicky."

"Oh. Right. Sure. Nicky."

The ambulance came and Campbell promised to take Aya back to her mum and to assure Mrs Khan that Nicky was fine and would be round as soon as she could. In the end she didn't have to wait. Campbell turned up with Mrs Khan and the girls at the infirmary two nights later. He was out of uniform and explained that the lady from Northern Iraq really hadn't given him any choice in the matter. He brought them again two nights later. The other three times he came on his own, laden with flowers and fruit. They went on their first date a week after she was discharged and had been together ever since.

Nicky made it perfectly clear to Campbell that she had absolutely no intention of heeding Brennan's advice and one look at the angry spark in her eyes was enough to persuade him that it would not be a good idea to argue.

He paid a visit on Tac Brennan the following week. There was a look of grudging respect on Brannan's face as Campbell was shown into his flat.

"I want things made clear Tac. The lady is with me now. She will be coming back to see the Khans once she is better. You don't touch her. Got that? And you put the word out. Nobody touches her. Nobody. Clear?"

Tac Brennan burst into laughter. There were looks of mild surprise from the other men in the room. Tac wasn't much of a one for laughter.

"I'll say one thing Swann. Nobody can ever say you lack bottle. In fact I'd have had you in my platoon any time. OK. Deal. A man deserves respect for showing some bollocks. The lady can come and go as she likes to see her Pakis. Consider it done. Now fuck off before my good mood goes away."

Brennan had been true to his word. Sighthill's young thugs dutifully stepped aside on the pavement when Nicky came to call. After three months Nicky felt sufficiently recovered to adopt her second family. This time it was a mother and son who had fled Robert Mugabe's murder squads in Zimbabwe. Rosemary Mdanga was a tall, formidable woman who was determined to take everything that Sighthill could throw at her in her not inconsiderable stride. At home she had been a school teacher in Bulawayo. Her husband was a solicitor who took on the cases of families who had seen their relatives disappear without trace. They were both from the Matebele tribe who had borne the brunt of Mugabe's oppression from the onset of independence in 1977. The tribal creed had always been a straightforward one: never back-off no matter how great the odds. It was a creed that had led to the annihilation of the great Matebele army at the battle of Blood River in 1895. The warriors of Lobengula's impis had believed that raw courage and spears would be a match for carefully positioned Gattling guns. It had been a terminal error. However the warlike streak still ran through Rosemary's husband, Joshua. He took the fight to the government every day in the old colonial setting of the courthouse in Bulawayo. In the end he took himself to the end of a branch. His high profile with some of the world's press made Mugabe's boys more patient than they would normally have been. They tried beating him. Then they moved on to torture. None of it worked. The blood of the warrior ran too strongly through the tubes of Joshua Mdanga.

Many wives may have urged caution. Not Rosemary. She urged him on in much the same way as her ancestors had sung their men to their many wars.

In the end it was inevitable. They came in the night and Joshua Mdanga joined the list of the disappeared. He fulfilled his own chosen destiny and became yet another martyr to the tribe. At first Rosemary refused to move an inch, but in the end the elders persuaded her otherwise, and reminded her that she had her son Moses to consider. They had money enough to make good their escape. Three months later they arrived in Sighthill and Nicky came to call.

She hit it off with Rosemary from day one. The lady from Matabeleland was in the mood for action. Soon she was taking English classes and numbers of students did not take long to grow. The Muslim women never ceased to be fascinated by the tall lady who wore all the colours of the rainbow. The more they worked together, the more Nicky tended to daydream about giving up her job as a teacher and going to work full time up in Sighthill. If only there was a way of finding the money from somewhere to earn a living.

It was in fact these thoughts that were foremost in her mind as she at last made the decision to do the sensible thing and get an early night. She chose a book and made her way through to the bedroom. Eleven-twenty. Campbell would probably ring just after twelve to see what she was doing. She reckoned she would manage to stay awake until then. She sat up and started to read and hadn't made it halfway down the page before her eyes started to close. She tossed the book aside and reached for the remote control for the TV. A glance along the channels revealed the usual junk. Eventually she decided on *BBC News 24* to kill the next half-hour. Seconds after she switched the channels she was very wide-awake.

" . . . We are receiving reports of a major incident on the Sighthill Estate in Glasgow. Three boys are believed to have been murdered in a knife attack. Reports at this stage are sketchy but we will bring you up to date just as soon as we receive confirmation. The Sighthill Estate houses the majority of Scotland's asylum seekers. At any given time there are upwards of six thousand asylum seekers

35

accommodated in the tower blocks that were built in the 1960s. Tensions have run high in Sighthill over recent years. There have been two murders and numerous assaults over the last two years . . ."

Nicky wasn't listening. She was throwing on clothes and scratching round for her car keys. Her mind was racing. What had happened? Who were the victims? The idea of not going up there never even crossed her mind.

Campbell Swann cursed at the ringing sound at the end of his mobile phone. Damn. He had hoped to catch Nicky before she heard about it on the news. He knew exactly what she would do. She would be her normal bull-at-a-gate self. No answer meant that she had probably heard already. Damn the bloody girl to hell. As if he hadn't got enough problems already. The muscles in his stomach were tightening with tension as the squad car wailed its way over the quiet M8 motorway. He shuddered to imagine how things would have moved on since he and Teague had left the estate 40 minutes before. More than anything else he wondered about Tac Brennan. Had he heard? Probably. Would he be there already? Almost certainly. And then what? Well, there was no point dwelling on it. The job was there to be done and that was all that there was to it.

He glanced across at Teague. Poor bastard. His fat face was chalk white and covered in a thin film of sweat. There wasn't much point in hoping for much back-up from that direction.

Fountainwell Avenue had come awake in a big way. Christ. There must have been hundreds on the street. They left the siren on as the car ploughed slowly through the sea of people. The anger was there. The anger filled the wet night air. All along, the car roof was thumped. Campbell felt the adrenalin begin to surge through him. This wasn't just bad. This was a bloody nightmare, a bloody nightmare that had lurked at the back of his mind ever since he had been given the job of patrolling Sighthill. He grimly wished that the politician who had been responsible for packing so many asylum seekers into the towers had been in the car with them.

He forced these thoughts from his mind. Somehow he needed to be clear. There had to be a way to avoid what was coming next. At last Teague stopped the car a few yards from the bodies on the pavement. Coats had been spread across the faces blocking-off the dead eyes that stared up into the night. The mob had left a respectable space around the bodies. One man stood apart from the crowd and gazed down at the horror.

Tac Brennan looked like an emissary from hell as he slowly looked up to watch Campbell emerge from the car. The rain was streaming down now and his hair was plastered down across his face. All colour seemed to have been bleached from the hard features. His eyes gleamed. He was like a human grenade. Campbell pulled on his hat and went over to him. He felt fear the like of which he had never known. The air felt thick with electricity. His legs felt as if they were made of suet and his heart was thundering the blood through his veins. He glanced over his shoulder to confirm that Teague was with him. The lad looked even worse than he felt. Nightmare. Utter nightmare.

He stopped a couple of feet short of Tac. What to say? That wasn't part of the training was it? What the hell were you supposed to say to Tac Brennan with his only son lain out in the rain with his throat cut from ear to ear.

"I'm sorry Tac. Truly."

For a moment it seemed as if Tac would not say anything. His eyes chewed into Campbell. It took everything he had and more to force his back straight and meet the gaze. Somehow the tension of the moment spread through the crowd and the shouting died down. The silence slowly spread back through the ranks until the only sound was the distance hum of traffic and the raindrops splashing into the puddles on the ground.

Campbell felt his vision starting to swim as the malevolent eyes tunnelled into him. And then at last Brennan spoke. Slowly. Softly. Carefully. Weighing each word as if he were loading into a gun.

"So you're sorry Swann. Isn't that nice? My boy cut up like a pig and you're sorry. You leave him in the gutter. In the rain. Not even the decency to cover him. Oh no. Not even that. Leave him like he is a piece of shite. Here. On the pavement. And you tell me that you're sorry. That right is it Swann? Well fuck it I'm touched Swann. Where is he?"

"Who?"

The voice rising now. Veins on the neck. "Who the fuck do you think? The bastard that did this?"

"Central Police Station."

"Oh yeah. That figures. Get him somewhere safe did you Swann? Wouldn't want anything to happen to him would you Swann? Oh no. That comes first. Get the murdering bastard somewhere nice and safe and sound. So what's happening now Swann? Having a nice cup of tea is he? Warm blanket round the shoulders and a social worker bastard coo cooing in his ear? Why not. Got to look after the asylum seekers haven't we Swann. Must make the bastards welcome." Almost shouting now. Fanning the flames. Fuelling the rage. "And what next then? Pat him on the back? Move him somewhere else? Maybe fly him home? What next Swann? More than my Kev gets, that's what. Because who gives a shite about my Kev? Who gives a shite about any of us? We're just the poor cunts that live here . . ."

Campbell knew he had to stop him. Stop him before his words sent the mob over the edge. The hair on the back of his neck told him just how close that moment was. Somehow he had to bring things back down.

"Tac. TAC! Look give me minute here. Let's try and calm things down a bit. Let's try and get a bit of order."

"And what exactly do you suggest Constable Swann?"

What DID he suggest? What the hell could he suggest? "Tac, we need to calm things down here. A riot won't bring the lads back. We both know that. Nothing good can come if things get out of hand. I need you to go home Tac. If you go, the rest will go. I need you to help here."

The silence once again took a grip. For a moment Campbell felt he saw a slight movement in Brennan's eyes. But the light switched off no sooner than it had been turned on. When he spoke there was real violence in his voice.

"My boy here on the floor. Like a piece of meat. A butchered piece of meat. And you tell me to go home. YOU DARE TO . . ."

Suddenly the crowd found its voice and seemed to roar. Campbell half-turned to see arms closing all around Teague. He struck out wildly and felt the crunch of a nose at the end of a fist. Then they were on him and he was falling . . .

Nicky heard the animal scream, as she was a few yards from the back of the crowd. Somewhere in the middle there was the fluorescent blue flash of a police light. Oh Jesus, not Campbell, please not Campbell.

KILLINGS IN THE NIGHT

Somehow she forced herself forward until she got a glimpse of Campbell at the bottom of a pile of thrashing bodies. Subconsciously she registered the statue-like figure of Tac Brennan watching. Then she lost it. Lost it completely. She waded in screaming like a mad woman. She took a handful of hair and yanked back with strength that she had never imagined. A whole tuft came away in her fist and the man screamed. Somehow the ferocity of her rage cut through the rest of the sound. One by one the men who were assaulting Campbell stepped back. They seemed confused, unsure at quite what to do as she screamed abuse with saliva spilling down her chin. Campbell's face was a mask of red and he seemed unable to move.

And then the sound of sirens filled the air.

Johnny Hendon had arrived seconds after Nicky. The scene before him was spectacular. There must have been 200. Maybe 300. Somewhere in the middle of it all was a police car. The sound of the crowd was unlike anything he had heard before. It chilled him. There was murder in the sound. He climbed up onto the roof of the car and could just about make out the scene in the midst of the crowd. There was a woman there. Screaming. Almost as if she was holding back the crowd. And there was Brennan. In his own space. Just watching. He focused the zoom on the camera and started reeling off shots. Suddenly there was another sound. He took his eye clear of the viewfinder and saw two police vans hurtling toward him from the other end of Fountainwell Avenue. The crowd was slowly becoming aware of them. Those at the back were starting to peel off and run as the vans closed the distance. As the mob thinned he saw that there was another knot of men beating somebody up. The zoom took him to the wrecked, terrified face of Constable Bob Teague. They had been too close in on him for him to fall. He was being held upright as the boots and fists rained in. Johnny winced as his finger automatically worked the shutter. At the last minute they became aware of the police vans that were just yards away and coming on fast.

Later he was to wonder if he had actually been aware of the photographs that he took over the next two seconds. One minute they were holding Teague. Beating him. Pummelling him. Then they broke. Threw him out of the way to get clear of the van. For a

39

moment it was as if the film stopped. It was a moment of terrible inevitability. Teague's falling body seemed to almost hang in the air for a minute as if some giant puppeteer held it. Then it fell hard into the road. Click. The bloodied head of the policeman smacked into the tarmac. Click. The offside wheel of the van went over the head. Click. The van was on three wheels for a brief second. Click. The van screeched to a halt. Click. The back doors flew open and officers in full riot gear sprang out. Click. The crowd spilled away in all directions. Click. The body of Constable Bob Teague motionless on the floor. Click. The woman cradling the smashed head of another officer. Click. Three more bodies, alone again in the rain.

Once again he pulled his eye clear and scanned the scene for Tac Brennan. But Tac Brennan was gone. Long gone. He whistled softly to himself.

"Got your money's worth for your five grand Johnny boy."

He jumped down and got back into the car. Time for a quick exit. His night's work was well and truly done.

Tac Brennan had slipped out of the picture. He was a man who was well enough accustomed to riots. He had seen plenty during his time in Ireland. For a moment he had hesitated. For a moment he had considered staying by the side of his son's dead body. But the anger that had been building through him got its way. Kev was down. Burned. A casualty. He had been there before. No time to be sentimental. That came later. The job came first. He ducked around a corner. Ten of the lads had stuck close by. He checked them over. They were the ones that he would have chosen. Not the kids. These men had all been round the block a time or two. None of them wanted to speak. He nodded to them. Enough to say that things hadn't even started.

Out on the street the scene was beginning to settle. The crowd had flowed away from the police vans and stopped about 50 yards back. About half had gone home. There were still about 150 out in the streets, mainly the young ones. The police were creating a perimeter. There was a blazing argument going on. A big officer was screaming at a younger man who was sat on the floor with his head in his hands. Tac noticed a couple of them over the body of Teague. He put it together quickly. It was the driver who was blubbing it. Not surprising. The feel of running over Teague's head would be with the bastard for years. An ambulance appeared and carved its way through the mob. A couple of coppers waved it over to where they had been doing their best to patch up Campbell Swann. He had managed to sit up and lean back into the chest of his girl who was cradling him. Christ, but wasn't she some girl. But for her he would have been as dead as Teague.

There was no great sign of organisation. They were concentrating on the bodies. Bickering. Looking bemused. Wankers. If this had been Belfast there would have been two or three down already. Then the first stones started to land. It didn't take long for the craze to catch on. The police were electrified into action. Better lads. Better. Several raised their shields to protect Swann and the girl. Others quickly grouped and charged the nearest bunch of kids. Brennan had seen enough.

"OK lads. I'm not leaving this. No way. Who's with me?"

They all nodded.

"Good. We're going to make them pay a price for this. All of them. Pigs. Pakis. The lot. It's time." He touched four of the men on the shoulder. "You. Blow the cars. Every car on the street. That will cause some mayhem. Once you've got the cars going, get in amongst the kids. Try to organise them. Keep them going. We need them out there for another couple of hours if you can manage it. As soon as there are too many pigs on the ground, get them away. Get some kind of masks on before you do anything. They will be taking pictures pretty soon. OK. Five past twelve. Blow the first car at half past."

The four men moved off. Tac turned to the remaining six. "Right. We're going to burn some of these fuckers out. Tonight we send a message. No more. This is our place. Not theirs. Tonight is enough. If any of you don't have the stomach for it say now. It's going to be dirty business. So you in or out?"

They were in. All of them. The deeds of the night would be remembered for many a year. The night that Tac Brennan went ballistic. No ways were any of them about to go home and be remembered as the ones who shat out of it.

The Deputy Superintendent arrived seconds before the first car blew. He had been just about to demand that the TV truck was moved back straight away. He had been ready to blow his top. Who the bloody hell had allowed the sodding media to get this close? Then the night rocked as 43 litres of unleaded went up about 70 yards away. Before anyone could react another one went. Then another.

The air was filled with flying debris. The exploding cars sent the crowd demented and a new volley of stones rained down on the police lines. The problem was that they were basically as good as surrounded. Somehow they had to clear one end of Fountainwell Avenue before there was a chance of establishing any kind of order. He strode over to the nearest car and grabbed a radio. Impatiently he barked out his orders. It took 40 minutes for serious reinforcement to start to arrive. They all collected at the northern end. After a further half-hour they were ready to advance. The crowd soon realised that they were about to be squeezed and melted away down the alleys between the blocks.

Now it was a battle on one front. Finally the police line developed some cohesion. Now the charges started to have more of an impact. Slowly the mob was pushed back a little more each time. It had taken till nearly 1.30 a.m. but finally the police were gaining the upper hand. Then it happened. High above the street on the fifteenth floor there was a crump sound. All heads turned and looked up as a window erupted outwards in a ball of fire. The shards of glass sprinkled down onto the tarmac. It took them a little while. It was a long way down.

The Deputy Superintendent felt a sense of horror spread through him.

"Sweet Jesus no. They're going to start burning them out. Holy Christ."

Seconds later another window exploded three blocks down.

The Khan family were all wide-awake, just like every other family in Sighthill. They had watched the events of the night unfold far below them. Of course it was too far down for them to get any real understanding. The crowd milled to and fro like agitated ants. Police vans were like toys. Cars exploded with a distant thump. However the evil in the air seeped into the sanctuary of the flat. The girls were terrified. Madiya Khan did what she could to calm them. She fussed in the kitchen. She encouraged them to play with their meagre collection of toys. She checked and double-checked the locks on the door. She quietly prayed for the dawn.

The noise in the corridor outside started just after one. Muffled voices. The elevator door opening and closing. Clanking. And then the hammering started. A suddenly huge sound. Splinters started to appear in the centre of the door. Then holes. She got glimpses of men in ski masks with sledgehammers. The door came in after a couple of minutes. Madiya retreated into the lounge and gathered the girls to her. They huddled together in the corner when the figures of men appeared in the door. Figures from a nightmare. The first petrol bomb took her completely by surprise. All her brain registered was confusion as the bottle with the burning rag flew toward them.

Then all was mayhem. The flames erupted across the room. Another bottle. Then another. Then a fourth. Then a big plastic container. The last turned the flat into an inferno. It only took seconds for what was left of the Khan family to die.

They were to bring the death toll for the night in Sighthill to seven. Only Tac Brennan had not driven the family in the flat outside before torching it. Only Tac Brennan had tossed the petrol into a room that contained people.

He rode the elevator to the ground floor. His colleague was shaking and tearing at his balaclava. Tac took hold of his wrist and shook his head.

"Leave it on. Remember the cameras."

They vanished quietly into the wet night. Ten minutes later Tac Brennan was back in his flat. He stood and scrubbed himself for fifteen minutes in a shower that was as hot as he could stand it. He bagged all the clothes that he had worn and ordered one of the younger lads to take them away and burn them. There was quite a crowd in the front room. He got the crates of beer brought in and the party started. Others drank in a frenzy. Voices got louder. Stories of the night got more exaggerated. Tac Brennan sat quietly in his favoured chair and drank steadily. One by one they came to him. It was if they all needed his blessing. No matter how hard and how fast they drank they knew that they had crossed the line. What they had done wouldn't go away. This wasn't just the usual day-to-day violence of Sighthill. This was a war and people were dead. Only Tac Brennan was comfortable with the death they had all seen.

Later those who were in the room were to talk about his eyes. None of them could find the words to explain what they wanted to say. They just said there was something about Tac Brennan that night. The way he was. How calm. How quiet. And those eyes. Christ you should have seen them.

Tac Brennan was mourning his son in his own way. The mourning was carried deep inside and hidden from the view of the world outside. The mourning was a secret thing that belonged to nobody else. Tac Brennan was clearing the emotional decks. He was getting ready for war. Just like he had so many times before.

As Tac Brennan and his comrades swigged away at their cans Noah Cohen was making his slow journey through the deserted streets of Gaza City. It was three hours since he had slipped quietly through the hole that they had cut through the fence. Nobody had paid him any attention. He was only a small man even when he stood up to his full height of five-foot-nine. Even fully clothed he had never pushed the scales beyond ten stones. Noah Cohen stripped to the waist in his shorts at his home Kibbutz was a man who looked remarkably fit for a 40-year-old. However it was a very different Noah Cohen who made his slow way through the dark streets. His back was bowed and he dragged his right leg painfully. He was clothed in a selection of rags, which were badly soiled. He leant heavily on an old stick and the tatty nylon bag on his back looked for all the world as if it would collapse him.

And he stank. Really stank. He had worn the clothes day and night in the week leading up to the mission. He had wet himself several times and had soiled himself once. The shit and urine had seeped deep into the miserable cloth of his clothes and the heat had made the stench almost overwhelming. His long black hair was lank and greasy. People moved away from him on the dirt pavements and muttered comments. Not that there were many about. He had started his journey a little after one. By three the streets were all but empty. Had there been anyone to notice the broken tramp they would have seen that he needed to rest every 50 yards or so.

His journey was only a matter of two miles. After three hours his destination was at last in sight. They had spotted the pile of rubbish from photos taken from helicopters. It was a common enough sight in Gaza City. As the power of the new Palestinian Authority had collapsed, refuse collection had gone much the same way as most of the other civic services. All across the overcrowded and beleaguered strip of land mountains of refuse grew and festered. This one must have been growing for months. It filled the piece of waste ground and had risen to a height of more than twenty feet. A casual glance would have been enough to confirm that the heap was made up of just about everything – old food, cans, plastic containers, rags, newspapers, all the flotsam and jetsam of any poor neighbourhood.

The tramp took another break. He slumped down in front of the heap and seemed to find it hard to breathe properly. The street was utterly quiet. Somewhere around the corner a dog was barking for the sake of it. Traffic was moving a few blocks away. Otherwise the city was asleep. If anyone been awake to watch they would have seen the tramp slowly stand up. It was a painful exercise that suggested something badly wrong with the joints. Then he started to root through the pile of rubbish. Items were picked up, examined and discarded. One or two were thrust into the old bag. As he dug and rooted, the tramp started to climb up the heap. As he got higher he started to push and poke with his feet to make sure that he could get a proper footing where the pile was less compacted. The job must have tired him because when he reached the top he again sat down. His pushing and poking had taken up a full half-hour. Had by any chance anyone have been watching through an unseen window they would have been thoroughly bored by the spectacle. Four-thirty in the morning was no time to amuse yourself by watching a tramp digging about in a pile of rubbish.

If by some miracle somebody had still been watching they would have been astounded by a sudden burst of energy that belied everything about the broken man in the stinking rags. Suddenly his movements became quick and decisive. He dug hard down into the pile until within a matter of seconds he had cleared a narrow trench. Then he lay down flat and started pulling stuff out of the old bag. That took a further 40 seconds. Then he quickly scooped the garbage back onto himself. 30 seconds later there was no tramp to be seen. The tramp had vanished into the cool of the Gaza night.

The car arrived in front of the house across the street just as the cloudy sky was greying with the light of dawn. Two men got out and carefully scanned the street. They took their time and only gave their signal when they were assured that all was as quiet as it looked. Then a third man climbed out from the back seat and took two furtive glances up and down the street. He then moved quickly across the pavement and darted into the house through a door that had been opened on cue.

The street was still far too dark for anyone to have made out the man's face which has half-hidden by the turned-up collar of his jacket. It was a face that was far too thin and wore a permanently careworn expression. Once it must have been quite handsome, but that would have been years and years before. It was a face that life had treated unkindly. Savagely. It was the face of a man who knew that he lived out his life on borrowed time. It was the face of a 70-year-old worn by a man of 54. Too many strong, unfiltered cigarettes. Too much time spent in rooms far away from the sun. Too much time spent hearing bad news. It was the kind of face that nobody would consider for a minute. Just a thin, tired old man who moved with more agility that you would expect.

Millions of people all over the world would have been astounded to know that this was the face of Mahmoud Bishawa, the man who had become known as The Fox. It was not how such a legend was supposed to look. But it was a face that was utterly familiar to Noah Cohen. He had a perfect view through his night vision glasses as he looked across the narrow street from his hide. He had no more than three seconds to study the quick flash of face, but it was time enough.

He had spent hours over the last days studying every image that the Israeli Intelligence service owned of the man they called The Fox. The last photograph was fifteen years old but the boffins had done their stuff and aged it. In all the basics they had been near perfect. They would have had to make their image a little thinner for it to be perfect. And they hadn't caught the sense of sadness. Not even nearly. But computers couldn't do sadness. They just did wrinkles and bones. But Noah felt it. He felt it because it was something that he knew well enough. He recognised a fellow warrior who had lost the fervour to fight long ago. Now it was a matter of mechanics. A matter of habit. A job of work for men who knew no other.

He felt no sense of the magnitude of what was about to happen. Events would take their course. He would play his part. And then it would be over. It was how it was.

He carefully reached down and took out his mobile phone. His call was answered halfway through the first ring.

"He's in."

There was a very brief pause.

"30 minutes. Zero, six, 35."

"Got it."

Inside there was a small crowd waiting to meet Mahmoud. Some of the older men came forward and greeted him with familiarity. Old comrades. Men who had shared hard times together. The younger men were deferential to the point of being in awe. Like young fans coming face to face with a Hollywood icon or a football hero. And with his usual cigarette in hand Mahmoud was all politician. He smiled easily. He remembered any name that he had known from the past. He asked after mothers and fathers and uncles and sons. He recalled shared events. The atmosphere in the small room lightened. The great man had time for all of them. He smiled and cracked jokes. Food appeared and they all sat around the frayed rug on the floor. Dish after dish came in from the kitchen somewhere at the rear of the house. Thick mint tea was poured.

Only hours before, many of those present had been carrying the heavy load of despair. Every day the Zionists came with their helicopter gunships. Every day there were more and more funerals. Men were being lost. Far too many men. Good men. Tried and trusted men. Men who couldn't be replaced in a hurry.

And all the while the world merely turned its back. The Middle East was all that dominated the hours of news channels all over the planet. Not their little piece of the Middle East. They didn't seem to matter to anyone any more. All that mattered was Saddam. All anyone was interested in was watching American soldiers pretending to be John Wayne. The Zionists knew it of course. They were never men to miss an opportunity. It was their moment and they were taking it with both hands. Every day they came with their helicopters and rockets and machine guns. Every day they gleefully settled old scores whilst the rest of the world shrugged its indifference. And every day the body count grew and the gaps became harder to fill.

But with the arrival of Mahmoud the spirits of the men in the room started to lift. All of a sudden the fight didn't seem to be a hopeless one any more. Mahmoud Bishawa was a last beacon of hope. For 30 years the Zionists had hunted him with all their men and all their technology and all their American money. And yet here he was, still among them. He was almost an old man now, but there was still a light in his eyes, still an infectious smile that was almost youthful. The younger ones in the room had been brought up on the stories of Mahmoud Bishawa. He had become everyone's talisman. Their ray of hope. Living, breathing proof that for all their military might the Zionists were not indestructible.

It had been many, many years since Mahmoud had been anything like active. The last time that he had been involved in the kind of mission that created the legend had been way back in the 1980s. For years his role had become one of motivation. More than anything the organisation needed him alive. So long as he drew breath his people would continue to believe that anything was possible.

Now the leadership of Hamas needed him more than ever. The Israeli Security Forces were taking maximum advantage of the huge distraction being played out a few hundred miles to the east in southern Iraq. The toll that they were extracting was hard to bear. The leadership of Hamas was being picked off one by one in a series of brutal raids. Before the Iraqi adventure the Israelis would never have dared undertake their helicopter assassination missions that guaranteed heavy civilian casualties. The backlash of the world would have been too strong even for Prime Minister Sharon. But now it was different. Every night American bombs wreaked their carnage among the civilians of Iraqi towns and cities. How could the Americans and British criticise Sharon for doing the same?

As a people, the Palestinians had known nothing but crisis for over half a century. Theirs had been a path of more or less endless defeat at the hands of an Israeli nation that massively outgunned them. For years they had tried to break down their enemy's will to resist but had always been futile. The depths of Israeli stubbornness had proved to be endless.

After 50 years of fighting they had become dangerously cornered. All of their sanctuaries had been taken away from them one by one – Jordan, Syria, and Lebanon. Now they were fenced-in and trapped in their two tiny enclaves of the West Bank and Gaza. The might of the Israeli Defence Force held its boot down on their throat. Nothing could move in and out of their territories. Their people were being systematically destroyed. The economy had all but collapsed. For the first time in living memory even basics like food were getting hard to find.

The anger of the people was still there. That was something that would last for ever. But the will to resist was weakening with every murderous attack from the Israeli helicopters. A mood of futility was growing. The old dreams of victory had been lost years before. All that was left was defiance.

In this beleaguered last ditch they had turned to their last and most miserable option: suicide bombers. Like the remnants of the Imperial Army of Japan so many years before, they continued their fight with the only weapon that seemed to be able to hurt their enemy. Every time Mahmoud was summoned for nights like these he felt a small part of his soul rot and fester. The boys in the corner of the room were the same as all the rest. Boys with courageous determination on their faces and sheer terror in their eyes. When he had started his war it had been about politics. A dream of reclaiming what was theirs. A dream of driving the Jews out. But slowly everything had changed. The Holy Men had slowly taken control. The Holy Men created fanatics. Mahmoud found it hard to take at times. It wasn't the war he had known. But he had swallowed down his distaste for the way that they preached young men to their doom.

All the formalities had been completed. Their goodbye videos to their families had been filmed. The training, such as it was, had been completed. All that was left now was death. A few more hours of gnawing tension and then the briefest moment of total agony and then oblivion.

Mahmoud needed no convincing of the military power of the suicide bomber. He could remember clearly the destruction of the US Marine Headquarters in 1983. Over 300 of them killed. He had been in the city that day. He could remember how the ground had shaken with the sheer size of the blast. And the mightiest nation of them all had sailed away over the Mediterranean horizon with its tail between its legs. He needed no military strategist to convince him of the merits of this desperate weapon of last resort. It wasn't just the damage that it caused the enemy in terms of casualties. It was the fear that each one of these actions spread. It gave the Zionists nightmares. None of them could ever feel safe. Not on the bus. Not at work. Not in the cinema. Not in the pavement cafés. It showed them that all their F16 fighter planes and Merkhava tanks and helicopter gunships could never be enough to keep them safe. Because all it took was one young man or woman who was willing to show the ultimate courage. Every attack ate away at their resolve. Gone were the glorious days of Moshe Dayan and the heroic victories over the Egyptians and the Syrians. Now there was just this dirtiest of all wars. A war between billions of dollars worth of machinery and young men and women with high explosives strapped around their young bodies.

This was now his job. His last role for his people. Night after night he was taken to secret places to send these young people off to their deaths. He would touch them on the shoulder. He would speak soft, kind words. He would show them that their courage had brought the respect of the legend. And every time he felt as if he died a little. It was what his long fight had come to. He felt at times as if he had become the embodiment of death. The young faces were beginning to haunt him at night. Sleep was a hard thing to find when there were so many young faces in his mind. Faces that deserved to have all their life ahead of them and yet were down to the last miserable hours. Faces that fought to mask the utter fear that they felt inside. Faces that mapped out the endless failure of his own life. Years and years of the fight and never the taste of victory. Never even close. Condemned to be no more than the hero of a lost cause.

It was time. The feast had been removed and the cloth of the floor carefully folded away. The men were standing up and making ready to leave. The boys in the corner of the room would soon be alone, with only terror as a companion. Mahmoud went to them. He took each of them in an embrace and held on for a long time. Words were of no use. All he could do was to try and show them his love. His sadness. His respect. His resignation. There was no more. If knowing that he was there helped them on their last journey, then that was enough. There was no more that he could do.

He hated himself as they were quietly led into a room at the back of the house to have the explosives wrapped around their bodies. Who was he to send these fine young men to their deaths? What right had he? When he turned to the two old friends who had brought him, his tired eyes were bright with tears. He tried to force a small smile. It was expected that he should never show any doubt. He was supposed to be the one who never wavered from his course no matter how hard the war became. He was expected to be the legend that was Mahmoud Bishawa. He was expected to play the role of The Fox.

"I think that maybe we should leave now. If, of course, you are both ready."

His colleagues were nodding when they felt the air in the room start to gently shake with the beat of an approaching helicopter.

6.33. Two minutes. The sound of the gunships was close now. Noah Cohen had made his final preparations. All was ready. Now there was only the fighting left. He focused on breathing slowly. He drained his mind of all thoughts. This was the time for emptiness. All that mattered was his training, his reactions, his instincts. He had learned long before that there was no need for thought once the combat started. All that he needed was instinct.

The sound was louder now. Probably no more than four or five hundred yards. They would be flying in low, skimming the rusty corrugated iron rooftops of the houses. The men in the house would have heard the sound. For them it would be a time of decision. Should they go? Where the helicopters coming for them? Or were the gunships going to fly over their heads and make towards another target. Maintain cover? Break cover? And only split seconds to decide.

6.34. Almost the moment. Timed to the second. The moment when all the questions in the house would be answered. The next two or three minutes would test out the strength of the plan that they had put together for Operation Fox. Noah felt that it was a good plan. It was the kind of plan that his people had once prided themselves on in the days before the war in Lebanon when fire power and brute force had come to be everything.

They had picked up the intelligence a week earlier. It had been an intelligence dream come true. The time, the date and the place. The exact location of Mahmoud Bishawa in the early hours. The source had been buried away in Gaza City for years and years and now the investment had paid off. They had brought in some of the old men to help with the plan. These were the men who spent their afternoons playing chess in the cafés of Tel Aviv. They were men who could think beyond fields of fire and kill zones. They took the plan a stage further. They took the plan into the realms of what would happen next. What would be the greatest victory? How could the greatest victory be achieved?

Noah had watched them with awe. They sucked at their cigarettes and shouted and bickered and scribbled untidy notes whilst the other officers stood back with looks of disdain. Noah appreciated the beauty of their thought. The modern army had come to rely on rockets, shells and bulldozers. The endless supply of high-tech American weaponry had made them lazy. What was the point of working out how to go round an obstacle when you could just blow it away? Once it had all been so different in the days when his country barely had a friend in the world. Those had been times when imagination and daring had been all that they had possessed. Noah saw these men as the last of the great generation. The thinkers who had helped to annihilate Nassars's mighty Egyptian air force in a matter of minutes on the first day of the Six Day War. These were the men helped the commandos stage their breathtaking rescue of Israeli hostages at Entebbe. And now these same men thrashed out what would probably be their last plan.

Noah saw Operation Fox as a series of straightforward chess moves. If we do this, then our opponent will be forced to react like this. There was a simple beauty to it. It combined huge and overwhelming force with thought and subtlety. It combined the firepower of modern technology with a biblical cunning. Now he would be there to watch it unfold because he was the lynchpin. He was the conductor of the orchestra. He was the quarterback. He would call the plays.

6.35. He heard the hiss of the first rocket. Then the ear-splitting crash of the detonation. Then another. And another. The silence of the dawn was ripped apart as huge pillars of black smoke and dust were thrown into the air behind the house across the street. Now was the time that the old men would be proven right or wrong. He focused on the front door through his telescopic sight. They had known that Mahmoud would travel with his two closest comrades. They were men who have been at his shoulder for years. Good men. Men who would react quickly to the imminent threat of the gunships. What options were there? Two. Stand and fight or risk escape in the car. Standing and fighting helicopters was suicide. Their only hope was the car. They had guessed that this decision would be made in no more than 30 seconds.

The door eased open. Round one to the old men. A figure emerged crouching low, scanning the street, an assault rifle at the ready. Then the second came and checked in the other direction. Textbook. Making sure there were no soldiers before Mahmoud made his dash for the car. The second figure nodded. Noah saw a small movement inside the door. So here he came. Round two to the old men. Now it was his turn. He caressed the trigger and saw the first man's head explode like a burst piece of fruit. Almost lazily he traversed his rifle and squeezed the trigger. This time his bullet tore through the second man's stomach. The force of the shot threw him back into the cracked wall of the house. Slowly he slid down into a sitting position with a look of bemusement on his face.

Mahmoud was out now. He reacted like a soldier. One glance showed him that one friend was dead. Another took in the huge stomach wound. And Noah waited. This was the most daring of the old men's assumptions. They had read all the files. They had argued and assessed. What would Mahmoud do? Would he run? Or would he tend to a friend who had shared years of suffering? The officers had laughed when the old men had delivered their verdict. Bishawa was just a terrorist. Filth. Scum. He would run. Of course he would run. It was all these cowardly bastards knew. But the old men had refused to be swayed. They knew their man. This was The Fox. The only reason that anyone could become such a legend was by sharing compassion with courage. By knowing the truth of comradeship. Here was a true warrior they said. He would behave like a David, like a Gideon, like a Joshua. He would never leave a fallen comrade to die alone and in pain. Not unless there was no other choice. Not unless the armoured cars were already on the street and closing in. Not unless the helicopters filled the sky above him. That was why they had told Noah to shoot one of the bodyguards through the stomach. That was why they had told him to deliver the wound that every soldier feared the most.

Things were very slow now for Noah. The world was down to him and the man across the street. He felt every small movement. He felt the thoughts. He allowed his finger to lay quietly on the trigger. The plan was now down to the vital seconds. If Mahmoud ran, his orders were absolute. Terminate and await extraction. But if the old men were proved right, then it would be different. The seconds passed as

Mahmoud looked up and down the still-deserted street. For a moment Noah thought he was about to go and his finger tensed slightly. The moment passed. Mahmoud slowly crouched down. The wounded man tried to speak, tried to tell him to run, but only blood spurted from his mouth.

A trace of a smile came onto Noah Cohen's face. There it was. Round three to the old men. He eased off another shot that ripped through Mahmoud Bishawa's left leg just above the knee. The power threw him onto his back. For a few a seconds he tried to crawl but soon gave up and lay with his face staring up into the sky.

"Execute phase two." Noah spoke quietly. There was more movement behind the door now as others sought the sanctuary of the street. Noah shot them one by one as they tried their luck. After a minute there were five of them piled in the small doorway. It was enough. No more came. By now the sounds of approaching engines competed with the thump of the helicopters overhead. Three armoured personnel carriers raced to the scene. Soldiers in full body armour leapt out and secured the perimeter. Three moved to where Mahmoud lay and lifted him onto a stretcher. They were not rough. They treated his as if he were one of their own. Noah stood up from his hiding place and clambered down the side of the heap. He waited patiently by the back door of the troop carrier whilst they carefully lifted in the stretcher. Once Mahmoud was inside he climbed aboard. Already two medics were ripping away the shredded remains of his trousers. Within a minute the flow of blood, which was pumping from a ruptured artery, was stopped. The vehicle was moving now. Through the firing slit in the back door Noah could see the other two were following. Overhead the helicopter was an airborne guard.

They crossed the fence five minutes later. From the first rocket to crossing the fence had been less than ten minutes. And Mahmoud Bishawa was with him in the back of the carrier. Mahmoud Bishawa would probably never walk properly again and could easily lose his leg altogether, but he was alive. Alive. That had been the magic word for the old men who had plotted Operation Fox. Alive would mean a huge victory for their people. Killing the Fox would be a small victory. Taking him alive and trying him in open court would be the big victory. And here he was, his face a mask of pain, his leg a bloody mess of cartilage and bone, but very much alive.

There was no expression on Noah Cohen's face as he looked across the back of the carrier to where his enemy lay. Mahmoud focused his eyes and stared back at Noah. There was a small smile for a fleeting moment. His voice was barely a whisper. The Arabic words were easy for Noah to understand. It was a language that he had learnt to speak as well as any.

"So it was you. Of course. It was always to be you . . ."

A massive dose of morphine raced through Mahmoud's body and his head lolled back into unconsciousness. Noah turned away and stared at the groves of orange trees that flanked the road outside.

Mordechai Breslow glanced down at his watch without a great deal of interest. It was almost one o'clock in the afternoon. He wasn't wanting the time because he was in any particular hurry. On the contrary he felt as if he had all the time in the world. After the gnawing tension of the early morning he had thoroughly enjoyed the three hours that he had spent sitting by the bed where Mahmoud Bishawa remained out for the count.

When he had first dug his cigarettes out of his pocket one of the nurses had been about to say something. A snarled insult had stopped her in her tracks. Now the ashtray was beginning to fill up. He was a man who smoked as if his life depended on it. Every drag was taken as if it were his last. Breslow was in his mid-60s and had been chewing through four packets a day since his teens. A pall of smoke hung in the small whitewalled room where he waited.

Every time he looked down at the figure of the man on the bed he felt like pinching himself. The man represented a large part of his life's work. The name of Mahmoud Bishawa had been appearing in the files that crossed his desk for 30 years. Time and time again he had presided over meetings of all the intelligence agencies and the army where they had tried to formulate plans to capture The Fox. Time and time again he had felt the burning acid of failure as The Fox eluded them time and again. He had brought his file with him. Inside was a series of photos that recorded the mayhem that the man on the bed had caused over three decades. There were crime scenes from several countries in Europe, many from Lebanon and even more from the streets of Israel. Bodies on the ground and grim-faced policemen and The Fox nowhere to be found.

RED ZONE

Nobody would ever have said that Mordechai Breslow was a nice man. He wasn't. He never had been. He had never married. He had never really made many friends. All he had ever done with his life was work from the early hours of the dawn until late into the night. He didn't have hobbies. He didn't have even a semblance of a social life. He just worked at the same relentless pace.

His fellow officers tended to avoid him whenever they could. His temper was notoriously short. He tended to be thrown into a total rage by the slightest mistake. He had always been completely unwilling to accept that those around him should not adopt his lifestyle, his near demented commitment, the sour rage that drove him on relentlessly. He had become such a fixture over the years that none of the younger officers bothered to question the source of his all-consuming rage. It was just the way he was, the way that he always had been. Some of the older generation could remember the bright-eyed young paratrooper who had won his medal at the battle of Mitla Pass in the 1956 war. Some just about recalled the story of how his mother and father had both been taken from him by the gas ovens of Treblinka. About how his uncle who had brought him across Europe to Palestine had been murdered in the chaotic fighting with the Arabs in 1948.

Mordechai Breslow's anger came from the old school. He was one of the ones who saw enemies at every one of his country's gates. After what he had seen as a mere infant in Treblinka, he had no qualms about doing whatever it took to protect his people from ever having to suffer a similar fate. He saw no difference between the Nazis and the fighters of the Palestinians. Both sought the annihilation of the Jews. Both would stop at nothing in the pursuit of this goal. Breslow in turn had vowed early on in his life that he in turn would stop at nothing to keep the walls high and the gates bolted. He had no time for the soft-hearted ones who became indignant about stories or torture and state-sponsored executions. What did they know? They had never looked evil in the eye as he had done. They had never been in the presence of the beast. Let them raise the rooftops with their pathetic liberal pleading. They could sleep safely in their beds at night because of men like Mordechai Breslow. If they were incapable of realising it then what did he care? Occasionally he was summoned upstairs for a lecture on human decency. It was never very serious. Mordechai got results. Mordechai made bad guys go away. Nobody really wanted to know the nasty details. He did his work in a twilight world that many of his countrymen preferred to pretend was just a bad dream.

Usually Breslow was a man of perpetual motion. He would jump from his seat and pace the room. Sometimes he would throw things. His hands never stayed still when he talked. His small crinkly face was permanently animated. A Marlboro was always hanging from his lips as he talked. But now he was unusually still. He wore a serene expression that few had ever seen. For once he was in no hurry whatsoever. He relished the knowledge that this day was the highpoint of his life. This day was as good as it was ever going to get. After 30 long years he had Mahmoud Bishawa in his custody. It amused him to see how utterly unthreatening the figure on the bed seemed. Just a small thin man, old before his time. Even in sleep Mahmoud's face was lined by years of pain. He didn't look well. He looked washed-up and worn-out, a miserable pale imitation of the young man from the 1970s with the film star good looks. This man had fought his war with all that he had and in the end he had lost. He had run harder than any of the others, but in the end Mordechai had caught him. Just like he had caught all of them. With this one it had merely taken a little longer.

He smiled contentedly as he lit up yet another cigarette. He was under no illusions about how much this would hurt them. They had set themselves up for this day. All the posters and the murals. All the songs and the stories. As long as The Fox is free there will always be hope. In a way it had always seemed rather pathetic to Mordechai. The fact that one man could hide for so long wasn't much to be proud of. It was a sad excuse for victory. But then it was all they had. They could never come and take on his people face to face on the battlefield. For them to try and do so was unthinkable. Instead they hid behind children throwing stones and legends about a tired old man.

He knew how it would hurt them. He knew how the capture of Mahmoud Bishawa would start to drain away the last grains of their hope. Maybe this would be the defeat that would break them. Maybe.

He sat up straight as he saw the man on the bed start to move. It was what he had been waiting patiently for to happen for three hours. He leaned forward expectantly as Mahmoud eased open his eyes. For a while there was dumb lack of understanding on his face as he gazed up at the strange ceiling above him. He tried to move his arms and legs, only to find that they were securely strapped to the bed. Slowly the memory of what had happen that morning came to his face and his head lolled back weakly.

A dry chuckle alerted him to Mordechai's presence. He slowly turned his face so that he could see his captor sitting forward and watching him. Recognition came to his eyes. For a moment there was a spark of hatred, then his expression softened. When he spoke his voice was small and parched.

"So Mr Breslow. This must be the day of days for you. I hope that it has been worth waiting for."

Mordechai grinned, showing uneven yellow teeth.

"I think I can say that it has. It has been a long wait Mahmoud. Too long. You have been an elusive one. But it was only ever a matter of time. Now is that time. Today is that time. Your war is over my friend. Maybe your people will at last have the sense to realise that their fate is as inevitable as yours."

This time it was Mahmoud's turn to laugh. "What a fool you are Mr Breslow. You are so wrapped up in your own bitter little world that you can never see the real truth. There is no doubt in the war that we both fight. In the end there can only be one winner. In the end there are millions and millions of us and just a few of you. In the end the world will wake up and see that this is our home and it always has been. The only issue at stake is one of time. That is all that men like you and me spend our lives fighting about. Will the day come sooner or later? That the day will one day come is not in dispute. Your success might just add a little to the borrowed time that your people enjoy here. But it will only be a little. You and I are not important. We are just small parts in the big picture. One day you will see this and you will realise what a waste your sad life has been Mr Breslow. No wife. No children. No time in the sun. Just day after day letting the hate eat away at you until there is nothing else."

The calm words twisted at Mordechai. He felt the familiar anger rising up in him. It took an effort not to jump to his feet to strike the man.

"Dream on if it helps Mahmoud. You people like to dream. I suppose it is what you do when you have nothing else."

"I must say Mr Breslow that I am grateful that you are finding the time for this nice little chat. I expect you intend to lull me into a cosy

sense of security before the real conversation starts. I can assure that
there is really no need. You are welcome to torture me as soon as you
are ready. We have heard that it is something that you enjoy. So why
not take the opportunity to round off your day to perfection."

Breslow smiled bitterly. "You need have no fear Mahmoud. You
will enjoy only the best of our hospitality. Those above me have been
very clear on this. They want you to be kept in the very best of health.
They want a well-groomed, well looked-after Fox to show to the
world on the day of your trial. Things are all going to be very
civilised. It is time that us Israelis show the world what decent, law-
abiding people we are."

The words came as a shock to Mahmoud. He had been gearing
himself towards the nightmare of the torture room. It was something
that he had lived with in the corners of his mind for many years. They
all had. And like all of his comrades one fear above all others had
haunted him. How long could he hold out? How long before they
ripped out every piece of information that he possessed? How long
before he gave them the names of every one of his friends? He knew
that it would only ever be a question of how long. He wasn't nearly
foolish enough to believe that he would be able to withhold anything
from them. That was for the movies. He was under no illusions that
when Mordechai Breslow asked questions, the questions were
answered. It was only a matter of time. Time was the only issue.

Instinctively he discarded the words of his enemy. He was
merely being fed false hope, which would only make the reality of
the pain to come all the worse. And yet his brain could not fail to
agree with the logic of Breslow's words. They had all the ring of
Zionist cunning. The whole world would be expecting that
Mahmoud would be about to undergo the torments of hell at the
hands of the Shin Bet torture maestros. How very clever to do the
exact opposite. How very typical. Being nice to The Fox would just
be another useful distraction to keep the eyes of the world's media
turned the other way whilst they fired their rockets into Gaza and
the West Bank.

He closed his eyes for a moment and tried to steady his thoughts.
The morphine felt like cotton wool stuffed into his skull. Somewhere
the wrecked stump of his leg must have been sending messages of
vast pain to his brain. However they were not getting through. The

intravenous drip was feeding the drug into him. All part of the game. Breslow's voice opened his eyes back up.

"We have talked at length about this. It is a good plan. However it has its drawbacks. The biggest drawback is that if we simply announce to the world that we have made the decision to be nice to you then we both know what will happen." A short dry laugh. "Of course we do. Nobody will believe a word of it. So where was the answer? You see, there is always an answer, it is merely a matter of looking hard enough. It was one of our young people who found the solution."

Mordechai twisted slightly in his chair and glanced up to a small camera in the corner of the room. "See that Mahmoud? It is something strange to old men like you and I. This Mahmoud is a web cam. Extraordinary. It sends live feed of what it films to the world wide web. A remarkable thing. It means that anyone from Singapore to Sydney can type in the words www.mahmoudbishawa.com and lo-and-behold there you are, lying quietly on your nice clean bed. Living proof you might say. I must say that I liked the idea straight away. That surprised them. They were sure that I would be the obstacle. But I can see the beauty of it. I see that these pictures will become an object of international curiosity. There will be millions upon millions who will share the same thought. I wonder what the famous terrorist actually looks like? What kind of a man would kill so many? They will be unable to resist it. And what does that make you Mahmoud? A freak show in the circus. That's what. And for 24 hours of every day you will know that the world is taking the chance to take a peek at the freak. You will become an animal in a zoo for children to gawp at and giggle at. And for me that is really rather appropriate, for as we both know, I consider you to be no better than an animal."

It took a lot for Mahmoud not to rise to the bait. It took a lot for him to keep his face quiet and impassive. It took a lot for him not to reel at the shattering implications of their cunning. It took a lot but he had enough.

"I commend you Breslow. I wouldn't have believed that you were capable of such subtlety. It will be nice while it lasts. But you will all look such fools when it ends."

"There will only be one end. That will be the day when we walk you out of here to stand trial as a multiple murderer. If you harbour any thought of some kind of dramatic live suicide then you can forget it. The opportunity will never come."

Mahmoud was more composed now. He was able to smile. "Of course Mr Breslow you would never allow that. No, I am referring to the day when I get out of here. Just imagine how foolish you will all look. Just imagine how the world will laugh at you."

But it was Breslow who laughed. "Get out of here. What fantasy is this? What do you suggest? A heroic commando raid from your colleagues in Hamas. And I took you for a man of some intelligence."

The smile faded from Mahmoud's face. "Oh no Mr Breslow. No commando stuff. Nothing Hollywood. I will get out because Khalil will get me out. He will find a way. Khalil always finds a way."

Breslow was struck dumb for a moment. He could think of no retort. Mahmoud had shocked him deep inside. Khalil Bishawa. A name from long ago. A name from another lifetime. A name that he had barely heard for twenty years. A name of a man who was dead. Who had to be dead. Who had been written off as dead. He got up slowly and left the small room with the white walls.

PART TWO

PART TWO

A journey to the West
Kibya, 14 March 1953

The tension around the family dinner table was tangible. The father sat at one end, mother at the other. On one side were the two sisters. On the other were the two boys. The tension came from the boys. There was tension because a decision was hanging in the air. If the decision were to go in favour of the two boys they would be about to embark on the most exciting night of their young lives. The decision was in the hands of their father and there was nothing in his impassive grave features to give them an inkling as to which way the wind was blowing.

The decision was a straightforward one and it had been coming for the last two days. It had been at the weekend that they had discovered the dead bodies of two of their lambs in the pastures above the small town. They had not been alone. Over the next two evenings there had been three more slaughtered lambs discovered in the small fields of two of their neighbours. An examination of the corpses led to only one possible conclusion. There was a fox, and the fox would not stop killing.

There had been a meeting of those who kept their flocks in the rocky hills that ringed the town. A decision had been reached. They would pool their resources and engage the service of Salim. It had been the job of the boys' father to make contact with Salim. That was an obvious thing because Salim Bishawa was his brother. It was the kind of job that always went to Salim. He was a strange man. He lived alone in a hut three miles outside the town. He never spoke a great deal. He spent his days hunting. But when there were certain

65

jobs that needed doing, the people of Kibya would ask Salim Bishawa to carry them out for a small fee.

They had been the talk of the small dusty town for the five years that had passed since the Bishawa family had arrived in Samaria. Their home village had been close to the sea in the north of the country. It was rumoured that they had been a family of great wealth and had owned many orange groves. Like so many others they had been driven from their home by the Jews in the vicious war of 1948. They had arrived with no more than they could carry. That year the small village of Kibya had more than doubled in size as it accommodated the refugees from what was now known as Israel.

There had been two brothers. The elder brother was Nassir. He came with his wife and four children, the youngest of which was only an infant. Nassir soon became known as the wise one. His education was a thing of wonder to the people of Kibya. Within a matter of months they had asked him to take over the charge of their school. He was soon one of the town's more important elders. His words were respected by all. In the years that followed the war, King Hussein had guaranteed a one-room flat for every refugee who had been driven into his kingdom. For a few months the Bishawa family managed in just such a flat. Then they were able to move into the large house that was reserved for the headmaster of the school. They became central to the life of the town.

The story was very different with the brother, Salim. There was always talk about just how different the two brothers were. One a tall scholar with the wise words, the other shorter, quieter, wilder. Salim was some years younger. He had married only a year before the war. He had rejoiced at the birth of his son in the weeks before the conflict. The boy's life had been cut brutally short when a hand grenade had been tossed into the shed where his mother had been trying to shelter him from the Jews who took away the family land.

Before that night Salim had been a man who was full of life. It had been Nassir who had been known as the quiet one. The serious one. Salim was the life in every room. Nassir had lived out his youth with the books that the holy men passed to him. Salim had roamed wild with the other boys of the village getting into more trouble than his father would have liked. He changed utterly after the murder of his wife and baby son. He withdrew deep inside himself. He showed no interest in becoming a part of the community of Kibya. He found an old, abandoned hut up in the hills and made it his home.

As Nassir Bishawa looked at the expectant faces of his two young sons it struck him that the generation game had played one of its many strange tricks. There was so much of him in Khalil. It was there for all the world to see. The boy was six now and already he was growing tall. His academic abilities were much talked about. He was able to complete work that was usually difficult for boys of twice his age. He was a quiet boy, but never shy. Although he was never to be found in any of the rough and tumble of the playground he was never bullied. It was clear that he would grow into a man who would command respect but find friendships difficult to make. It was something that Nassir knew only too well. It was the way that he had lived out his own life. Though none would ever have guessed it, there had been many times when he felt desperately jealous of the popularity and life of his younger brother. Sometimes it made him sad to see the grave face of his eldest son and realise that the boy seemed destined to follow the same dry path through life as he had walked himself.

His youngest son Mahmoud could not have been more different. How odd it was that he was so much like Salim. He was smaller than Khalil, but he was athletic where his elder brother was stately. Nobody would ever call Mahmoud grave. There was forever the sparkle of mischief in his eyes. At the school he was always at the heart of the playground. Sometimes Nassir would stand and watch him secretly through the window of his small office. A sadness would well up inside him as he would remember how his own brother had once been in the days before they had come, the days when they had farmed their orange groves by the sparkling warm waters of the sea.

Now the two boys shared the same look of yearning, the same silent plea for him to give them the answer that they desired. Tonight was the night that uncle Salim was going to trap the fox. Salim had said that the boys could come with him. Salim had said that they were old enough now and that it was time that they learned to hunt. Nassir smiled to himself without showing it to his family. Outside there was no movement of his serious face. Inside it amused him to see that the boys were so worried as to what decision he would make. Sometimes he wondered what they actually thought of him. Were they really so taken in by the tall headmaster act that had secured the family its place among the elite of the town? Did they really believe that his heart was so very dry and cold? Maybe they did. Everybody else did.

He treasured the relationship that his two boys had built with their uncle Salim. It was the only time that he ever saw a trace of the brother that he had once known. When Salim spent time with his nephews the savage rage seemed to leave him for a while as he showed them how to make catapults or snares. Watching his brother with his two young sons took Nassir back to the days of his own childhood. They were not really so many years behind him. He was by no means an old man. And yet it seemed as if it were centuries in the past. A fine house in the midst of all of those orange trees. He would never forget the scent they gave off in the warm air of the morning. That smell and the smile in his mother's eyes. Theirs had been a happy house. And then the Jewish militiamen had come in the night and murdered his mother and his father and the family of his brother.

So much brutality for a few hundred orange trees by the sea. There were some in the village of Kibya who talked of the return, of the day when those who had been driven from their land would be carried back to the coast to reclaim what was once theirs. Nassir had his doubts. Every year that passed saw the Jews sinking their roots deeper and deeper into the roots of his homeland. It was a day that he doubted he would ever see. Maybe his two sons. Maybe one day they would find the house in the midst of the orange trees and reclaim it as their own. For now all the old home was to his boys was a story told by old men. The only home that they had ever known was Kibya and its dry hills.

The door to the kitchen creaked open and Salim came in. He wore the rough clothes of a shepherd. Once he had considered himself something of a dandy in the coffee shops by the sea. Now he dressed simply. A man of the outdoors.

"Salaam Aleikum brother."

Nassir nodded to his brother and waited whilst his wife poured a cup of mint tea. Salim looked awkward amidst the politeness of his brother's family. He sipped at his tea and seemed nervous to speak. At last he mustered himself.

"My brother, have you given consideration to this night's work?"

It was hard for Nassir not to smile. His own brother was hanging on his decision as hard as his two boys were.

"I have Salim. You may take the boys to help you catch the fox. I am happy that they are old enough to start to learn the art of the huntsman. I trust that you will keep them safe."

As soon as the words spilt out of his mouth he regretted them. Keep them safe. Words that passed a shadow of pain over the eyes of his brother. Keep them safe. Succeed with my sons where you were unable to succeed with your own boy. Salim had been unable to save his wife and his boys from the Jews who had come in the night. There had been no need for the words. He knew that his brother would lay down his life for Khalil and Mahmoud without a thought. The words could not be retrieved. What had been said could not be taken back. Nassir continued.

"If it is possible, the boys should be home for no later than one o'clock."

Salim nodded. "This will be so Nassir."

The two boys leapt to their feet. They nodded to their father with deference. The great night was to be. Tonight they would become hunters. Tonight they would help their Uncle Salim to kill the fox. It would be the greatest night of their lives.

They both chatted excitedly as their uncle led them up the steep path out of the village. It was a bright clear night and a fat moon bathed the hills in a gleaming light. Soon the village was no more than a cluster of dark shapes in the valley below. When they had walked for twenty minutes, Salim called a halt.

"Now you must be quiet. No more talk. Feel with your sandals before you put down your feet. Now we must move without sound. I have found the lair of the fox. It is below the roots of an old tree on the side of the hill over there. We cannot walk there directly. We must make our way round in a circle so that the wind cannot carry our scent to the fox. You must remember how clever he is. He can hear the smallest sound. He can smell the slightest scent. A tiny mistake will alert him. There is no need to hurry. A hunter must know patience. He must have the patience to avoid all sound. He must have the patience to take the time that he needs. The hunter without patience will never outwit the prey. Do you understand me?"

They did. They nodded. And they followed their uncle in a new silence. Walking the long circle to the place where Salim had chosen for them to wait took them over two hours. When they arrived at the place behind some spiky bushes, Salim passed them water and biscuits. He didn't speak. Now it was the time to wait. The time for patience.

About an hour had passed when they heard a sound. It was a strange sound for the quiet of the night. A clink of metal. A sound that could only have been made by a man. The fox heard the sound. It shot out of the lair and was gone from their sight before they had any chance of reacting.

"Khalil, it was you . . ."

Salim shushed Mahmoud and cocked his head to listen. Another clink of metal. And another sound that was slowly growing. Muffled footsteps. Many footsteps. It was coming from the valley over the far side of the hill where they waited where the main track ran down to the village. It was unusual for anyone to be travelling at such a late hour. Salim pushed his face close into the two boys.

"There is someone coming to the village. We will go to look. You must be as quiet as you were with the fox. Before we get to the brow of the hill we will crawl. Do you understand?"

They nodded. "Who can it be Uncle Salim?" Asked Khalil.

"We will know that when we can see." It wasn't far. No more than 70 yards. They crept to the edge of the hill cautiously.

Below was a column of men moving down the track carefully. They were weighing their every step. The moonlight was enough to show them to be soldiers. They carried guns and large packs on their backs. They moved with secrecy uppermost in their minds. They were heading down the track to the village of Kibya.

Salim spat out an angry whisper. "It is the Jews."

"Why do they come Uncle Salim? Why do they come in the night?"

Salim shook his head and watched the column as it shuffled silently past. His brain weighed options. They could not beat the column to the village. Not without being seen, and that would put the boys in danger. Somewhere the Jews would have scouts out at the sides of the column. If the three of them had not been hiding from the fox the scouts would certainly have seen them. What troubled Salim was that he had not seen the scouts as they passed. This could only mean that they were some of their best soldiers. He strained his eyes to pick out a figure near the front of the column. Unlike the others, the man carried neither a large pack nor a rifle. He was a big bear-like man who moved with an air of command.

Unbeknown to his family, Salim had been working with the men who were starting to fight the Jews who had stolen their country. He knew that two nights before a raid across the border had resulted in the death of a young Jewish girl. The Jews believed in an eye for an eye. They believed in twenty eyes for one eye. These men had come in the night to avenge the death of the girl, and now they were heading down the steep road that led to the sleeping village of his family. The facts slowly arranged themselves in his mind. The column was moving quickly but in near silence. The scouts had ghosted past without alerting him. It meant that these were not ordinary troops. These were the best troops. The burly officer identified them. He knew this man. Major Ariel Sharon was something of a pin-up boy for the Jews. He was their movie star. Their John Wayne.

Sharon had persuaded the government to allow him to create his own elite unit. They had been hatched from the belly of the paratroopers. They called themselves Unit 101 and they prided themselves on their daring raids across the border. Sharon loved nothing better than to twist the noses of his enemies in the deep of the night and then return over the border like a ghost. The Zionist papers loved Sharon and his gallant Unit 101. Salim recognised them for what they were. Killers. Killers and they were heading to village where the family of his brother slept. And once again Salim was helpless. It ate at him. If he had been alone, there would have been something he could have done. He could have caused a commotion. He could have forced them to fire their weapons and alert the people below. But he had the two boys in his charge. Their safety had to come first. There was a guard post held by four Jordanian soldiers. Salim knew these men. They would be asleep. They would never be alert to the approach of Unit 101.

As the column of soldiers below slowly faded from sight Salim pulled the two boys close.

"We must follow them. We will stay back on the ridge. You must be silent. Do you understand?"

They both nodded, unsure whether or not to be thrilled or terrified by this new turn of events. They followed the muffled sounds for 45 minutes until they came to the brow of one of the rocky hills that looked down upon the small town. It was hard to make out much below. Occasionally they could pick out the shadowy figures of soldiers as they took up their positions. Salim felt a knot in his stomach. These men were not acting like policemen. This was a pure military deployment. He eased the two boys along the top of the ridgeline so they could position themselves as close as possible to the big house on the edge of the town where their family would all be asleep.

They had only just taken up their new viewing point when the first explosion rocked the still air of the night. Then things below went crazy. Within seconds the deserted streets were filling up with people running from their houses. Many of the men ran down alleys and small streets where the soldiers had not taken up positions. Salim could see hundreds of figures disappearing into the darkness of the hills. It made sense. Despite the murderous reputation of Sharon's Unit 101, it was unlikely that they would do any great harm to women and children.

The explosions were more frequent now. The soldiers were dragging screaming women and children from their houses. Then there would be a pause whilst charges were set. Then the houses would shake with the detonation of high explosives. It explained the heavy packs that the men had been carrying.

Salim only gave half of his attention to this. His main focus was on the house of his brother. He was just beginning to wonder if it might escape the attention of the soldiers when a small squad of six arrived. He strained his eyes and ears. One beat the door, which opened almost immediately. The tall figure of his brother stepped out. The soldiers fell into a semicircle to face him with their guns ready.

There were raised voices. His brother was waving his arms furiously. A sense of utter foreboding filled Salim. The body language was all wrong. Nassir was shouting out his anger when he should have been bowing his head. He slowly drew the two boys close in to him.

It took a moment for the sound of the shot to float up to them. Before the sound they saw the body of Nassir seem to twitch as if it had received a massive electric shock. Then it slowly fell. He sensed that Mahmoud was about to scream and he clamped a hard, calloused hand over his mouth. He stared briefly into Khalil's eyes. They were white with shock but there was control there.

"We must stay silent. There is nothing we can do. Do you understand Khalil?"

The boy nodded. Mahmoud was wriggling like a wild dog but Salim was able to hold him. One of the soldiers had stepped forward from the semicircle. He stood over the tall body on the ground. His arm straightened. Another twitch. And then the sound of the shot. Salim clenched his eyes shut and fought to contain the huge rage that was flooding through him. The soldiers had broken their formation now. One threw the door open. Two others hurled in their packages. They backed off and crouched low for cover. For a few seconds time stood still. Then the sound of two explosions rocked the night one after the other.

Almost immediately there were flames. The shock of what he was witnessing was almost overwhelming for Salim. Beside him he sensed that Khalil was as still as a statue. Mahmoud's fight was fading as the horror climbed into him. The flames were climbing higher now. There was no hope for those inside. Salim silently prayed that the initial explosions had killed his sister-in-law and her daughters. Then to his horror he saw a movement at the door. Two figures. On tall. One small. Wrapped in flames. Emerging from the inferno. Coming out. And then stopping. Stopping dead and falling back inside. The sound of a sprinkling of shots came to them.

There was nothing to say. Nothing to do. All he could do was to keep the two boys down and quiet. They were all he had now. They were all that was left. Below there was the sound of whistles blowing. The soldiers fell in to a group on the edge of the town. They moved out up the same track that they had come down less than an hour before. They left the small town below in flames. They left the night filled the sound of wailing women. They had placed Kibya on the list of small insignificant places that gained their fame through horror.

Salim was cautious. He waited for an hour after the last of the soldiers had disappeared up the hill. Then he took the two boys down to the burnt house that had been their home. The next day they buried Nassir Bishawa and his wife and daughters. Then they left Kibya and walked east. At the top of the hills, which offered a last view of the small town, Salim halted the boys. It was time to try and explain. He was a man for whom words were never easy.

"Our family has all gone now. We are the Bishawa family now. Only three. These murders are beyond all evil. We will fight this evil. One day we will defeat the evil. If you two boys want to join this fight then I will teach you. But now we make a vow. It is a vow that will never be broken. We never leave each other. Never. No matter how impossible it may seem. We make the vow. We keep the vow."

They made the vow. The man of few words and the two boys who had lost everything. They made the vow as the sun climbed high and bathed the land of the Bible in its heat. They made the vow and started their long journey to the east.

Dhahran, Saudi Arabia, April 2003

Outside the night had come. Khalil Bishawa had barely noticed. He stared at the screen in front of him as if he were in a trance. The sounds and voices of the television washed through him without leaving any meaning. They had a few hours before. A few hours before he had digested every word.

He had chosen the BBC 24 news channel. As soon as he had heard. He had made his excuses at work and hurried back to the privacy of his flat. He had sat without moving as the news flowed out of the TV. At first it was confused. Pictures of an angry crowd in the Gaza street. Ambulances loading up corpses covered in rough cloth. Close-ups of pools of blood on the cracked paving stones.

"The raid was carried out before dawn this morning . . . at least one helicopter was involved . . . several rockets were fired . . . there are reports of at least twelve civilians dead . . . witnesses report shots from a hidden gunman at the front of the building . . . he may have been hiding on this pile of refuse . . . at least four men were killed in a hail of fire . . . the army reportedly took one prisoner in an armoured personnel carrier . . . there are unconfirmed reports that the man arrested was Mahmoud Bishawa . . . there are unconfirmed reports that the man arrested was Mahmoud Bishawa . . . there are unconfirmed reports that the man arrested was Mahmoud Bishawa . . ."

The words hammered into him like nails. They were the words that he had been dreading for all these long years. They were words that he had always known that he would hear one day. All these years he had waited. All these years and somehow Mahmoud had always managed to dance his dance just out of the reach of their ferocious grasp. Until now. Until these unconfirmed reports. The elements of the Israeli raid started to slot together in Kalil's mind. These were things that he knew about. This was no small operation hatched by an enthusiastic colonel patrolling the fence. This was massive. This had been put together somewhere way up high.

It was the timing that was becoming apparent to him. Helicopters. Shots. Armoured cars. Then out. How long had they been? It seemed like no more than a matter of minutes. The rockets had been haphazard. The rockets had hit civilians. Why? Why such carelessness in a raid that was so careful, so precise? Because accuracy was not important. The rockets were like the game beaters who drove the pheasants onto the waiting guns. Of course.

And the waiting gun was reported to have been hidden on the pile of rubbish. What kind of a man had he been? He must have come in the night. Alone and on the streets of Gaza where his life would have been measured in seconds if he had been exposed. This wasn't just any soldier. Not just an over-zealous recruit who had volunteered for a crazy mission filled with the indestructibility of his youth. This must have been one of their greats. This must have been a man from their Pantheon.

Planning. Timing. Audacity. Total success. Unconfirmed reports. It was how the Jews had once been in the days when they had made the world gasp. It only left two unresolved issues. Had Mahmoud been there? Had they taken him alive? His mind felt torn to pieces by the dilemma. How could he ever wish his own brother dead? And yet dead was preferable to the unendurable nightmare of the torture room.

The smug face of the army spokesman appeared in the late morning. "This morning the Israeli Defence Force undertook a raid in Gaza. The raid was a complete success. We can report that we now have Mahmoud Bishawa in our custody. Bishawa has committed numerous acts of terror on the people of Israel over many years. He will be tried in the normal manner. This morning's raid marks a major victory in our continuing war on terror."

The TV fell into showing a rapidly patched-up mini biography of Mahmoud's career. There were poor pictures of Mahmoud as a young man. Chaotic scenes in streets reeling from the aftermath of bombs in Germany and Belgium and Austria. The flared trousers and the long hair and the fat ties of the policemen pegged the events to the 1970s. Then yet more mayhem and rubble and screaming women with blood cascading down their faces. This time the images were framed by the war-ravaged backdrop of the flats and apartments of West Beirut that had filled the news of the early 1980s. Then yet more shots of streets filled with broken glass and inert figures and dazed faces from the streets of Tel Aviv during the Intifada years of the 1990s. A terrorist career that spanned four decades. The number one target for the Israeli Security Forces for 30 years. The most important propaganda coup for the Israelis since the commando raid on the hijacked airliner at Entebbe. The most high profile arrest since an undercover Mossad team had lifted Adolph Eichmann from his apartment in Buenos Aires in 1960.

It went on and on. But in between there was more news. There were the pictures of the British Marines staging their night advance up the Faw peninsula towards Basra. There were jumpy images of the tanks of the American 3rd Infantry Division pounding through the empty Iraqi desert.

And then there was an extraordinary story from a place called Sighthill in Glasgow. Seven dead. Huge levels of tension. The worst rioting seen in the city for 30 years. Three boys killed by a knife attack. Unconfirmed reports that an asylum seeker from Afghanistan was being held in custody. A woman and her two daughters from Iraq killed when attackers threw three petrol bombs into their flat.

A woman and her two daughters.

Killed when attackers threw a bomb into their flat. Their house. The house at the edge of the small town of Kibya set amidst the low hills of Samaria.

He hadn't cried for a very long time. Longer than he could remember. He had believed that he had no tears left. But he had been wrong. The city on the TV looked so different from Kibya. Great, bleak tower blocks thrusting up into dark grey skies. Cold, miserable cascading rain. Sullen crowds of youths in sports clothes with twisted angry faces. So different, but always the same. No matter what the calendar said, it would always be the same. 1953. 1982. 2003. There were always those who would throw bombs through the doors where women and their children cowered in their fear.

It had only been the month before that the anniversary of the Kibya massacre had dragged back all the memories. It had been 50 years since the night when the soldiers had murdered his father and his mother and his two sisters. Half a century. Almost a lifetime. His lifetime. He had spoken to Mahmoud on his mobile phone. It had been a difficult call. They had spoken in an awkward code to baffle the Israeli listening posts. No possibility for two brothers to share the grief of a lifetime. No possibility of their meeting face to face. Just an exchange of coded words. It was all that was left to them. The call to Uncle Salim had been similar. His uncle was 80 now but remained miraculously fit. He found the code harder and the call had been short. Not that Uncle Salim had ever been much of a one for words.

Khalil had vaguely considered trying to return to the hill that overlooked the town. It could have been arranged. But somehow there had not seemed to be a point. Maybe if Mahmoud could have shared it with him. But Mahmoud was effectively a prisoner in besieged Gaza. He had barely considered the idea. Anniversaries were artificial things anyway. His family were all dead. They had been all dead for a very long time. What did it matter that the calendar pointed out the fact that it was now 50 years?

He hadn't cried then. It was too far away. Too deeply buried. But now he cried. He cried because the shots of the wrecked flat in a far-away city brought back the reality of the moment.

When the tears stopped his thoughts moved on. He remembered their vow. He had been six and Mahmoud had been five. Just boys. Small boys. Yet they had lived out the vow for half a century. Khalil and Mahmoud and Uncle Salim. It was their article of faith. The rock to which they had anchored their lives.

The vow was no less strong in 2003 than it had been 50 years before. Nothing had changed. They were older now. Grown men. Men long past their prime. Men wearied and scarred by lives that had never yielded victory. It made no difference to the vow.

"We never leave each other. Never. No matter how impossible it may seem. We make the vow. We keep the vow."

He could hear the cracked voice of his Uncle Salim as if the words had only been spoken the day before. Despite the efficiency of the

German air-conditioning system that cooled his expensive flat he could feel the warmth of the Samarian sun. The vow was for life. It was a thing that was straightforward. Simple. There was no reason to change the habit of a lifetime. Unconfirmed reports said that they had taken Mahmoud into custody. We never leave each other. No matter how impossible it may seem.

And the pictures on the TV started to make sense to him. The random jigsaw pieces suddenly seemed to slot into place. The answer came to Khalil like a bullet through the forehead. No matter how impossible it may seem. Oh yes. It certainly seems impossible. Beyond impossible. Here he was. Just one man. Not even young any more. A man of 56 years old who dressed well in suits that were tailored in London. A man who had his silver hair carefully cut once a month by a barber from Calcutta who had once taken equal care with officers from the British Raj. A man who lived quietly and alone in his beautiful air-conditioned flat in the midst of the foreign executives who travelled far from their homes to take the Saudi dinar. Just a man at the gates of old age.

Arrayed against him was the whole angry might of the Israeli State. A huge violent bully that had at last got hold of the toy it had craved for years. His enemy possessed thousands of tanks and soldiers and the most modern fighter jets that the Americans could give them. His enemy had the most efficiently brutal security service on the planet at its disposal. His enemy was convinced of its might. In their offices in Jerusalem and Tel Aviv they would be slapping each other on the back. They had caught The Fox. They had won yet another great victory. They had dealt a crippling blow. Maybe the end was now in sight. They were the supermen. They were the mighty ones.

And with a shudder of excitement Khalil realised that this made them vulnerable. He had a selection of facts. All seemingly unrelated. But he could make them come together. And when they came together he could win. The buzzer from the reception area brought him out of his reverie. He glanced at the clock on the wall. Past eleven. Late for a visitor. He pressed the button for the intercom.

"Yes."

"It's Farouk."

"Come up."

A JOURNEY TO THE WEST

Farouk arrived minutes later. Khalil smiled his greeting as he stood back to allow his old friend to come in. Another man at the gates of old age. But there was nothing crooked about Prince Farouk. Everything about him marked him out as Royalty. It had been carefully bred into him from the day that he had taken his tentative steps as a toddler. Only 70 years earlier the family of Prince Farouk Al Abd al-Rahman had been little more than a gang of thieves who violently defended their patch of desert in much the same way that their ancestors had done for centuries. They were tied to the royal household, but it had been a long time since relationships had been particularly cordial.

Then their empty desert homeland yielded oil and everything changed. The tents and camels became leisure items rather than the tools of everyday life. The family moved into a palace in Dharhan and became part of the world's rich elite. Carrying royal blood in Saudi Arabia wasn't a particularly exclusive thing. There were thousands who carried the title of prince. Many families had frittered away their share of the oil bonanza. Others had gone on to wealth beyond dreams. Farouk's grandfather and father had been shrewd men who had ensured that their family was very much in the latter category. Oil now played a relatively modest part in the family fortune. The dynasty now grew its already huge wealth from investments all over the world.

From an early age Farouk had been earmarked as the prodigal son. He received the best education that his family's money could buy. Prep school in England was followed by Harrow. Slowly, as he grew from boy to man, he became the person who had everything. He sailed. He rode magnificently. He dressed immaculately. He spoke four languages like a native. He enjoyed a procession of glamorous girls on his arm. He developed class. Real class.

The two men who embraced each other solemnly were not dissimilar in appearance. Khalil at 56 was two years senior to Farouk. They were both tall men who had avoided putting on weight. Both were men who took care with their appearances. Neither was ostentatious. Their clothes were of fine quality. They were groomed. They represented quiet money.

When they broke Farouk's face was bleak. "I came as soon as I heard. I was over in Qatar."

Khalil nodded. "I heard. I thank you for your concern. You will have tea?"

Farouk sat and lit a cigarette whilst Khalil prepared mint tea. The news channel continued its remorseless 24-hour-a-day work. Neither man seemed in a hurry to talk. Their silence was that of old friends who had long lost the need to constantly talk to prove their friendship. Farouk watched the pictures from Gaza with an air of detachment. Night had brought the crowds to the street. The mob was half-hearted at best. They had lost their talisman. Their last great hero had been taken from them. It was as if they knew that anything that they did could only ever be futile. Their Fox was gone. They chanted. They shook their fists. Masked men fired their guns into the air. And high above them, the lights of a circling Israeli helicopter mocked their weak rage.

Khalil brought the tea on a tray and set it down carefully on a coffee table. He picked up the remote control and switched off the TV. Still, neither man was in a mind to break the silence that was held in the room tightly by the thick double-glazed windows. At last Farouk was the one to speak.

"I feel sad that we could never persuade him to stop. He had done enough. More than any man could have expected. He took up too much borrowed time."

Khalil smiled. "Could we have persuaded the wind not to blow the grains of sand in the desert?"

Farouk returned the smile. "No. No my friend. We could not."

They resumed their silence. After a few moments it was Khalil's turn to speak.

"Many years ago the three of us made a pledge to each other. We have always lived by those words. Am I right to believe that nothing has changed?"

"There is no need to ask such a question. It is something that will never change. Not whilst I live. Not whilst any of us live. We are men of honour. All of us. Why do you ask this my friend? Is there a way?"

Khalil nodded. "There is a way. It is little more than a huge gamble but there is a way. I will need your help. I will need your money. But there can be a way."

A smile came to the face of the Prince. It was a smile that was familiar to the pages of society magazines the world over. "You know what a weakness I have for gambling, Khalil. As ever, what is mine is yours. It is how it has always been. If there is a way, we will take that way. I have been in debt to your family for 36 years. It is a debt with the term of a lifetime. It is debt that will always be my pleasure to repay. Now. You must pour more tea and tell me about this way that you have found."

Ammunition Hill, Jerusalem, June 1967

The waiting time had been over for two days now. For a while it had seemed as if it would last for ever. The war had been coming for months. It had been coming for so long that people had started to wonder if it would ever come at all. For many of the men who waited in the bunker it had been coming ever since the Jews had taken their homes nearly two decades earlier.

In all there were ten men who had been given the job of manning 50 yards of the intricate defence system that had been built up over a period of years. None of them was under any illusion that the trenches were impregnable. Ahead of them were hundreds of metres of barbed wire, minefields, carefully prepared fields of fire. This sector of the line was held by the men of the Arab Legion. These men had volunteered to fight from all over the Arab world. The majority were Palestinians who had been driven from their homes. Others came from all over Arabia and North Africa. They were a part of the greatest Arab alliance since the days of Saladin. Most were young men filled with the passionate certainty of youth. The commander of the ten was Salim Bishawa. He was the only one who harboured doubt. He drove them on without remorse. Hour after hour he had made then sweat in the heat of the sun to further deepen and strengthen the defences.

The young ones joked behind his back. The defences would be of no importance. The Jews would never be in a position to attack their position. Not this time. Once the overwhelming might of the Arab forces was brought to bear they would be pushed back into the sea. Just like the Crusaders who had dared to come many centuries before. There would be no need for deep trenches. They would soon make their way through the wire and the mines and join the great campaign. It would only be days before they would stand on the beaches by the

Mediterranean. It was as inevitable as the night that would follow the day. But if Salim Bishawa wanted his deep trenches then he would have his deep trenches. Nobody among them had the courage to suggest otherwise. They had no fear of the Israeli Defence Force. They were scared to death by the hard little man who was their commander.

For many years there had seemed to be little hope. After losing their family at the Kibya, Salim had taken the boys to Amman, the capital of Jordan. His position among the fledgling resistance movement ensured that they found a place in which to live. They knew no kind of luxury, but there was always food, always a roof to shade them from the sun. The boys were sent to school. Khalil soon excelled and caught the attention of the Holy Men. He was marked down as one who should receive special attention. His days were filled with study. It was a hard regime imposed by remorseless old men. They pushed him without any consideration to his youth.

Mahmoud received no such attention. He wasn't without ability. He just had no great desire to use it. He learned the basics of reading and writing but not much else. He was happy to allow his older brother to take on the role of the wise one. Mahmoud spent his days with the gangs of other boys who roamed the tracks and alleys of the huge refugee camps that had sprouted up in the wake of the exodus of 1948. He became a boy of the ghetto. By the time he was twelve he was able to fight and beat boys of sixteen and seventeen. His uncle Salim was happy to maintain an arm's-length control. It was clear to him that the two brothers were destined to tread different paths through life. The elders had decided to put Khalil on a fast track. He was to become a leader. A thinker. A planner. Mahmoud would be one of the fighters. Salim saw that the tough streets of the camps were a place where his nephew would grow up hard.

There was never any doubt that the two boys would join their uncle in his war against the people who had murdered their family. It wasn't ever something that warranted discussion or debate. The murder of their parents and sisters was something that was burned deep into the memories of the boys. They replayed the images of the massacre in their minds every day of their young lives. It was not something that they ever wanted to forget. They wanted to remember every detail. Every second. And when the time came they would take their revenge without a second's hesitation.

A JOURNEY TO THE WEST

The hope of their people had started to build when Colonel Nasser took control of Egypt. The Israelis joined with the French and the British to try and destroy him. Although the Allies won the battles, they ended up humiliated by the Suez Crisis of 1956. The Americans and the Russians decreed that Nasser should be allowed to stay and the whole Arab nation believed that it had found a leader who could at last bring them together.

As the years passed, the day when they would reclaim what was theirs came closer for the exiled Palestinians. By 1967 everyone believed that the moment had at last arrived. The tension in the region had slowly been rising to boiling point. Nasser had painstakingly fashioned a mighty Arab alliance to take revenge for the crime of 1948. Countries with a combined population of over a hundred million ringed the three million Israelis with their forces. The Soviet Union had ensured that they had technology and weapons to match the American arms of Israel. It was an alliance that had taken nearly twenty years to assemble. There had been all the usual arguing and bickering amongst the leaders of the Arab world. But by the summer of 1967 all was complete. Hundreds of thousands of troops from Egypt and Jordan and Iraq and Syria and what was once Palestine moved up to the border and waited for the great day.

The men of the Bishawa family were deployed forward from Amman to the Jerusalem sector. They were unsure as to what their exact part in the great victory would be. The main event was set to be played out in the deserts of the Sinai where the massive Egyptian armies would break the main Israeli force. Once the Jews were terminally weakened then the Arab Legion, the Jordanians and the Syrians would take advantage of their enemy's stretched lines and break through from the east and the north. Khalil and Mahmoud had studied an old atlas as they waited on the slopes of what had been known as Ammunition Hill since the days of the British Empire. It was less than 60 miles to the place by the sea where the oranges grew. It would only be days before they would return to the home that had been taken from their family nineteen years before.

Of the ten young fighters under Salim's command, seven were Palestinians who talked deep into every night about what they would do when they reclaimed their old homes. Two had travelled the long road from Baghdad to be a part of one of the Arab nation's finest hours. Then there was a young boy from Saudi Arabia. He was the quiet one of the group. He was seldom part of the banter that tended to find Mahmoud at its heart. He was awkward in the boisterous company. When they all talked about their families and their homes he tended to sit back into the shadows of the trench and stay apart from them. Only Khalil made a connection with the boy who called himself Farouk. Family was not something that the boy wanted to discuss and Khalil was happy to respect his boundaries. Whilst the others talked about girls and the coffee shops by the sea and how many Jews they would slaughter, Khalil and Farouk talked deep into the night about the political shape of the new Arab world that would emerge from the victory that was about to come. As they came to respect and trust each other they shared each other's doubts about the days to come. Both had spent many years studying the history of their lands. The lessons were there for all to see. There had been many times when the seemingly mighty nations had come off second best. Sheer numbers were no guarantee. The Jews were warriors. They always had been, from the long lost days of David and Joshua. They had their backs against the sea and nowhere to run to. They would fight to the last. Neither believed in the complacent confidence of the speeches that their leaders made on the radio.

At last the word arrived that the war had started early in the morning. The mood in the trench changed completely. Where there had been jokes and laughter there was now tension. All attention was focused on the slopes up which any Israeli advance must climb. The hours passed slowly and there was nothing to be seen through the observation slits in the lines. High in the sky the glinting silver of fighter planes left their trails in the deep blue. Occasionally the distant crackle of gunfire floated across the warm air. Otherwise there was barely a sound other than the low hum of flies. The radio poured out news of great victories. To their south the Egyptians were chewing through the Israeli tank armies. They were expected to reach the south of Jerusalem in no more than two days. The Jewish air force was being blasted from the skies. The huge Arab armies were exacting a terrible retribution. It would not be long before it would be their turn.

As night fell on the first day of the fighting they speculated as to when their turn would come. Maybe the next day. Maybe the day after when the Egyptians arrived. Maybe they would secure the southern side of Jerusalem before the Arab Legion and the Jordanians swept in from the east. The young men prayed that there would be no surrender. They had waited for years for their moment to come. They dreaded that it would be taken from them at the last minute. And still the radio played out reports of the great victories that came one after the other. Only Khalil and Farouk seemed slightly withdrawn. A little before midnight Mahmoud became troubled by his brother's unease.

"What troubles you Khalil? You are quiet tonight."

"I do not understand why Nasser does not speak. If the victory is so great, then why does he not speak? Pass the radio please."

Khalil sat patiently and fiddled with the dials until he found the crackly sound of the BBC World Service.

"The long-anticipated war in the Middle East finally broke out at dawn this morning. Fighting is reported on several fronts but is heaviest in the Sinai desert. Reports at this stage are sketchy, however the picture has become clearer through the day. It is reported that the Israelis launched a massive surprise attack on Egyptian air bases in a daring dawn raid. Our reporters saw many Israeli planes attack installations all over Egypt. There have been no sightings of any Egyptian aircraft since the raid. There is widespread speculation that the Egyptian air force has been largely destroyed. There has been no confirmation of this from either Cairo or Tel Aviv. However there has been limited confirmation from Washington. The fighting in the desert is as yet unclear. Our reporters near the front have seen massive activity from the Israeli air force. Throughout the day their jets have been entirely unopposed. Two reporters have moved forward more than 30 miles, which would suggest that the Israelis have already broken through the Egyptian front lines, and are advancing. As yet there are no reports of major fighting on the fronts with Jordan and Syria . . ."

For a while there was a stunned silence in the trench. It was impossible. It couldn't be true. None of them claimed to be expert in modern warfare. However they knew the consequences of the Israeli air force having the freedom of the skies. It was unimaginable. They had all seen the pictures of the rows of gleaming Egyptian planes on Nasser's runways. They had all heard how the Soviets had made sure their allies received the very finest technology. They had read the reports that glorified in the fact that Nasser had ensured that they would have three planes for every one that the Jews could put in the air. Supremacy in the air had been assured.

Now they heard that the air force that had taken ten years to assemble had been wiped out in a matter of minutes. They tried to brush the story aside. How could they believe anything that the British said? The British would lie for the Israelis. It was obvious. They hated Nasser. That was why. Nasser had humiliated them in Suez. These were just pathetic lies. They looked to Khalil. He was the wise one. He would confirm the lies.

"All day we have looked up into the sky. All day we have seen planes. We have not seen any planes fighting. Just planes flying to their destination. There should have been fighting. I wonder why the British would lie? What would be the point? It is not their war. Any lies will be exposed within days. Maybe even in hours. Why would they wish to look like fools? What would they gain?"

His words were poison. His words were ice. His words were the stuff of nightmares. Mahmoud was sombre now.

"What will happen here brother?"

Khalil shrugged. "How can I say? There will be more fighting in the desert. With no cover and no planes it is hard to see how the Egyptians can survive. Maybe there will be quick peace. It is what the politicians in Moscow and Washington will demand. But the Jews will be hungry now. They will want to reclaim the Wailing Wall. That is their dream. It is hard to think that they will stop now. Not when they have us on our backs. I think that they will come. I think that they will come in the next two days. I think that it is good that Salim made us dig the trenches deep."

Salim had said nothing whilst the radio gave out the terrible news. He sat apart from them and patiently oiled the parts of his rifle. They turned to him now. They looked to him for assurance. They wanted him to make things right again. He looked over to them and smiled.

"If they come, then let them come. Our trenches are deep. Our sword is sharp. You are all fine boys. The finest. The Jews who come will pay a terrible price."

Suddenly they were a part of reality. It wasn't about excitement any more. It was about fear.

The next morning the sound of gunfire filled the air around the ancient city. All through the day it came closer. Jets swooped from the sky and ripped up the ground below with their bombs. Men started to stream back from the areas in front of them. On their dusty faces was the despair of the defeated. Some were horribly maimed and burned. Others wore the vacant expressions of shell-shock victims. There were arguments, as Salim demanded that officers make their men stay and regroup in the trench line. Some of the men joined them. All the officers refused and fled to the east.

By the time night fell they were 25. The sky was filled with the streak of tracer bullets and the glow of flames. The ground shook constantly with the impact of high explosives. The firefights seemed to be all around them but still there was nobody to be seen on the slopes below. A little before eleven, mortar shells started to fall on them. Two men were blown into pieces. A third lost his leg and his screams competed with the sound of the bombs as they carried him back to the rear. But still the slopes below remained empty.

Salim moved among them. He urged them to crouch deeper into the cover of the trench. He put courage into them with quick words and a touch to the shoulder. He sent up flares every couple of minutes to light up the barbed wire strewn ground over which they would have to come. His calmness eased their terror. The waiting was becoming an agony. It had been hours that they had waited. Two of them were dead and one was crippled and still they hadn't seen a single Israeli soldier. There was only the endless massive sound all around them

They came a little after two. Toy soldiers far below them. Moving carefully forward. Feeling for mines. Cutting the wire. The boys in the trench fired wildly and the men fell back. Salim did his rounds. "Hold your fire. Save your ammunition. It is too far. You will only waste the bullets. We will need all of our bullets before this night is out. Leave the firing to me whilst they are far away. Mine is a hunter's rifle. My bullets will not be wasted. You must all wait until they are past halfway. Then your bullets will not be wasted."

Below them the soldiers paused. They took cover behind low stone walls. They were planning. And then the air filled with more explosions than there had been before. Mortar fire. Artillery fire. Unendurable. Hell came to Ammunition Hill. The boys cowered low in the trench, as the air around them seemed to turn to fire. Only Salim seemed unaffected. He lay calmly as he aimed his rifle. The toy figures were back now. One by one they fell to Salim's hunter's aim. But they still came. All the time closer. There were several bodies on the ground now. Two were screaming.

Some of the boys panicked and shot wildly only to be yelled at by Salim. His face was terrible to see. There was a rage there. Every one of the men that he cut down had been one who had killed his family. All of them. All these toy figures with their wire cutters had been there when his wife had died. And his infant son. And his father and mother. And his brother and sister in law. And his nieces. All of them. Every bastard murdering Jew. He gloried in the screams and the agony of those he had wounded. Let them know the pain of hell. Let the bastards die a death that was slow. And one by one he dropped the crouching crawling figures as they picked their way across the minefield.

And still they came. Unbelievably they were halfway. What kind of men were these? How could they come forward when death was so certain? Everyone was firing now. More bodies. More screams. And the Jews were firing back. A heavy machine gun raked along the top of the first trench. One of the Iraqi boys was thrown back as a heavy bullet tore through his throat, releasing a fountain of blood.

And still they came. They were remorseless. They were like supermen. How many had fallen? There must have been twenty. 30 even. And yet they still came forward. Close now. Just yards. Close enough to see the smudged black of their faces. Salim took a moment to check his own line. They weren't 25 any more. Only ten now. Some dead. Some wounded. Some had run. He felt no anger at them. How could any young boy be expected to face this? How could any young boy face men like these?

Somehow he managed to pass the order. Fall back to the second trench line. Five would cover whilst five fell back. Khalil, Mahmoud and Farouk held the right of the trench. He held the left with the remaining Iraqi boy. All of a sudden there was a scream of rage. Twenty yards ahead of them the Israelis had risen to their feet and charged.

"Back! Fall back!"

The Iraqi turned to run but the top of his head was blown away before he could take a step. Salim took a second and loosed off three shots. Hit. Hit. Hit. Then he moved. Fifteen yards to the second trench line. From the corner of his eye he saw that Khalil and

Mahmoud were running in a crouch. Thankfully the first five had made it and were laying down covering fire. Just five yards now. He prepared to dive into the cover.

Khalil was also counting down the yards. Somewhere inside him his brain could not quite understand how he had not been hit with all the bullets that filled the air all around him. Ahead Mahmoud was bent low and covering the ground like a cat. Beside him Farouk was . . .

Farouk wasn't there. Where? He stopped and looked back. Yet another flare exploded above him. Farouk was slipping back down into the trench. His face was a mask of desperation. Blood was gushing out from where a bullet had ripped into his shoulder.

"Mahmoud!!" cried Khalil.

It wasn't his voice. He had a deep voice. A calm voice. A voice of learning and reason. Not this voice. Not this shrill desperate scream. Somehow he never even thought about what he was doing. He threw himself back toward the trench, managing to flatten Farouk in the process. They landed in a heap and Farouk howled as his wrecked shoulder crashed into the floor. Khalil fought to get his friend to his feet. He was halfway there when feet landed beside him. Two of them. Three. Eyes filled with murder under their helmets. He had no hands. His hands were under Farouk's arms. Their guns were coming up. And then the first of them fell back as Mahmoud slashed him across the face with a knife. These were big men, strong from the hard work in the fields of their Kibbutz. But in the tight space of the trench they were no match for the vicious speed of the boy from the refugee camps of Amman. Mahmoud fell on them like a demented animal.

But there were more of them now, arriving at the lip of the trench. Suddenly Khalil was tired. What was the point? They would not stop. There were always more. He saw the face of his brother turn upward to meet the eyes of the men who would kill them both. He saw the withering contempt in his brother's eyes. He saw the challenge. And then the men fell back as Salim cut them down with a machine gun that he had collected from an Israeli corpse.

"Lift him Khalil! Get him out!"

A surge of adrenalin blasted away the tiredness. He heaved Farouk onto his shoulder and dragged himself clear of the trench. Behind him Mahmoud pushed him so hard that he almost popped out of the trench like a cork from a bottle. Salim dragged him to his feet and screamed into his face.

"Back! All the way back! This is all over!"

The next five minutes stretched across a lifetime. There were only six of them now and one wounded. Cover fire. Fall back. Cover fire. Fall back. Clear of the last trench. Clear of the edge of the hill and running hard down the far side. And by a miracle the Israelis stopped when they reached the top. They had been bled almost dry by the attack. The top of Ammunition Hill was enough. They stood and watched as the six men of the Arab Legion disappeared into the bushes at the bottom of the hill. Their officer stood for a moment and gave a small nod to the place where the six men had vanished. He spoke quietly to himself.

"Brave men. Too many brave men."

Then he turned to count the cost. It was only later that Salim was to learn the truth about the men who could not be stopped. On the first day of the war a whole Egyptian division had disappeared into the sands of the desert. The Israeli command quickly re-deployed their forces. 300 paratroopers under the command of Motte Gur had been waiting to tear a hole in the Egyptian lines. But the line had ceased to exist. They were re-deployed to the hills around Jerusalem where they were to fight one of the most ferocious engagements of what came to be known as the Six Day War. Never again was the Israeli Defence Force to lose so many men in a single small action. What was unusual about the battle for Ammunition Hill was the bitterness of the fighting. What was not unusual about the battle was the result. The Israelis won.

As dawn broke on day four of the war the remnants of Salim's platoon had become part of the chaos of retreat. All around them the countryside was filled with soldiers fleeing to the east. Overhead the jets buzzed like angry bees, reducing tanks and troop carriers into smouldering wrecks. There was no thought of regrouping and forming a new line of defence. The defeat was total. None could comprehend the sheer violence of the Israeli war machine. It was implacable. It was unbearable. They were completely broken.

In the hours before the dawn Salim had found a deserted car. They had squeezed in and joined the thousands of others who sought the sanctuary of Jordan. Farouk was sprawled across the legs of the three who took up the back seat. The pain of his wound was sending him in and out of consciousness. A little after dawn they found morphine for him and he was released from the pain. The travelling was painfully slow. Roads were blocked every few miles by the wreckage of destroyed vehicles. They constantly had to turn back and try new routes. All the time there was an agony of waiting as the jets swooped down to pick off their targets. It was near dark when they finally drove across the Allenby Bridge.

A few miles on they stopped. It was unlikely that the Israelis would come this far. Crossing the river Jordan would bring on the rage of the world. They could find little to say to each other. They had waited for twenty years for their time. They had shared their dreams of returning to their homes. They had felt part of something that would be remembered for ever. Instead they had been part of a rout. Their dreams had been built on sand. All that they had witnessed was the birth of a new Israel. A mighty Israel. An army that could never be beaten. And men who fought like animals. Men who seemed to know no fear. Men who had come forward when death had seemed certain.

Salim sat a little apart from the others and stared out into the night. He felt a kind of peace that he had not known since the night that they had slaughtered his wife and his baby boy. The rage had eaten away at him for long, empty years. Yet in the depths of defeat he found that the pain had gone. How many men had he killed? Ten for sure. Maybe more. He had shed his rage along with the blood of the Jews who had come forward and laughed at death. He had turned to take one last look at Ammunition Hill before they had fled. He had seen the lone figure of the officer in the hard light of a flare. He could have shot him down with ease. For a moment he had been mesmerised by the stillness of the figure that looked down to where he was hidden. Then he had seen the nod of the head. It was a warrior's salute.

They had fought well. All of them. Mahmoud and Khalil more than any. He felt the tears of pride fill his eyes as he looked over to them. Mahmoud had curled up into a ball and found sleep. Khalil was gently wiping the feverish sweat from the face of Farouk and talking quietly. The tears that trickled down his hard face in the secrecy of darkness were a mixture of pride and sadness. He was proud at how his boys had fought like lions. Proud of how they had stood up to the warriors who had climbed the hill. He was sad as he saw the life that was stretched out ahead of them. Their war was only just beginning. They would spend their lives fighting men like those who had kept on coming. And deep inside he wondered if it was a war they could ever win.

Farouk was becoming a little more lucid. Khalil managed to ease a little water between his parched lips.

"What happened Khalil?"

"You were shot. It is your shoulder. With treatment you will be fine. There is no need to panic. We have morphine. It will contain the pain."

"The battle?"

"The battle was lost. The war is lost. All the armies are retreating. The Jews have won a great victory. It will be many years before we are able to fight again. You need to tell me about your family now. We must get you home where you can recover."

"That is not possible Khalil. I cannot go home."

"You must tell me Farouk."

Farouk twisted his eyes closed as another shot of pain thundered through his body. He shook his head. Khalil's voice was quiet. Soothing.

"Farouk. Do you not find this a little foolish? After what we have shared today there can be no secrets."

There was sorrow in the eyes of the wounded man. "I owe my life to you and Mahmoud. It is not something that I will ever forget. You have my word on that. But please Khalil, do not force me on this, I ask you this as a friend."

Khalil smiled. "And as a friend you are wasting your breath. You are badly wounded and you will need to go home. Problems can be resolved. Have some faith. Share the problem and we will find the solution together."

Farouk hesitated for a few more moments. Khalil hadn't actually said that there would be no more morphine until he spoke. But the unspoken words floated in the air between them. In the end his resolve caved in. It all came out. Khalil's eyes widened as his friend told him story of his life and his family.

He told of the palace that waited for him back in Saudi Arabia. He told of the Prep School and Harrow and the life that he had led amongst the ruling classes of the English. The parties. The polo. The parties for the debutantes. The shooting parties at the huge mansions in the green countryside. He told of how his father had wanted him to attend the London School of Economics. He told him of how London had been in the 1960s, the new ideas, the emergence of a new order. He told of the meetings that he had attended, of speakers from all over the world, of rooms filled with the anger of the young. And he told of how he had felt for the first time the rising rage of the Arab people. For years it had been hidden from him. He had lived apart from so much of the suffering. His family had sheltered him from the whirlpool of tension that eddied around the region. It was in London that his eyes had been opened. He swapped the tweeds of the upper classes for the jeans and the old sweaters of the new revolutionaries. He swapped the gentlemen's club in St. James's that his father had enrolled him in for the smoky little pubs where his fellow students had exchanged their ideas. They were heady days and he had found himself changing.

There had been difficult times when his father had come to visit him. He had been angry at the clothes that his son was wearing. He had been contemptuous of his friends. He had been outraged at his examination results. He had reminded Farouk that he was a prince of the house of Al Abd al-Rahman. When his father came with ultimatums their arguments had got out of hand. Farouk stormed from the room and cut himself off from his family. There was no way back. Farouk had been filled with the full complement of arrogant pride that a prince of the Al Abd al-Rahman was expected to show. He was as stubborn and proud as his father was. Neither man was willing to back down. His younger brothers were sent to London to offer a last chance and were duly driven away. Farouk no longer lived the life of a prince. He became just another of London's Arab community who eked out a living working long shifts in a smelly café.

As the tension between Israel and her neighbours reached boiling point in the first half of 1967 Farouk emptied what was left in his bank account and flew to Amman to join the Arab Legion. He made the decision to take the fight to the enemy with his fellow Arab brothers. He wanted no privilege. He wanted to fight in the front line in anonymity. He had told nobody of his true identity. Not until now with Khalil.

When he was finished Khalil weighed his thoughts carefully.

"It seems to me that you have proved what you set out to prove. You stood shoulder to shoulder with every man who fought on Ammunition

Hill. No man can ever take away the way that you fought. But now the battle is lost. It will be many years until there will be another. It is time to go to your father. I can hear your love for him in the sound of your voice. Never forget just how blessed you are to have a family who love and respect you. It is something that Mahmoud and I have had to learn to live without since they wiped out our family. Mahmoud and I will take you home. I will speak for you. No father can maintain anger when a son returns home from the battlefield."

The words burst a damn of emotion that had welled up inside Farouk. He had missed his family more than he could bear. All of a sudden the blinding pain from his shoulder merged in with the yearning to be reunited with his family and the gnawing shock of the horrors he had seen on the battlefield. Khalil held him to his chest as he wept it all out.

The next day they made it back to Amman. The city was in sombre mood. The streets were filled with broken men bearing all manner of wounds. The sound of mournful wailing seemed to pour from every other doorway. The speed of the massive defeat had taken everyone by surprise. The consequences were almost too much for anyone to face up to. It had seemed as though their victory was so sure. Twenty years of hope had been obliterated in a few short hours.

Farouk had hidden five gold sovereigns in his belt as his emergency fund. They were able to cash them in for sufficient to have his wound dressed and treated and to buy air tickets to Saudi Arabia. Two days later the taxi from the airport stopped outside the huge gates to the palace of the Al Abd al-Rahman family. Mahmoud stayed in the car with Farouk whilst Khalil took the long walk up the drive that ran straight as an arrow along an avenue of palm trees. The guards outside the great wooden door watched him with interest as he approached. He had grown as tall as his father and walked with a straight back. When he arrived at the steps the sergeant of the guard moved forward and raised an eyebrow.

"I come from Farouk. I wish to see his father. I bring news."

The guard's eyebrow raised another couple of millimetres. They instructed Khalil to wait in the shade of the porch. After a few minutes he was ushered inside. Farouk's father waited behind the desk in his study. His face betrayed not a trace of emotion. When he spoke his voice was cold. Dismissive.

"They say that you bring news of my son. I bid you speak."

Khalil kept his back straight. He refused to be intimidated. Why should he? Only days before he had faced the wrath of the Israeli guns. There was nothing to fear in this fine room.

"Four nights ago it was my honour to fight beside your son Farouk on the slopes of Ammunition Hill in Jerusalem. There were 25 of us when the Jews launched their attack. There were only six when we were forced to retreat. I stood with men who fought with the courage of lions, none more so than your son. Even when he was wounded he never flinched. There was no shame in our defeat. No men could have given more. No men could have fought harder. Over these last weeks I have become a friend of your son Farouk. He has told me of the rift that has grown between you. It is a wound to his heart. I vowed to speak on his behalf. The Jews at Kibya executed my own father when I was just a boy. I know what it is when a father and a son are divided. I will never be reunited with my own father. This does not need to be the case with you and your son. Four nights ago he honoured the name of your family by the way he fought. For the rest of our lives those of us who were there must live with what we saw on the slopes of Ammunition Hill. We must carry the memory of those who fell. I beg of you, do not force Farouk to carry his burden away from those that he loves."

Even when he was barely halfway through his speech Khalil knew that he had won. A fierce pride lit the old man's eyes when he heard the part that his son had played in the doomed fight against the Jews. His dignity demanded that he waited for a time whilst appearing to give deep consideration to the words that had been delivered. Khalil in turn played out his part in the game. He maintained his stiff stance and looked down to the marble floor with proper deference. At last the head of the Al Abd al-Rahman family made his pronouncement.

"You speak with wisdom that is surprising for your years. You never gave me your name young man."

"I am Khalil Bishawa."

"I thank you Khalil. Life is nothing for an old man who has lost his son. Farouk will lead our family when I die. It is not an easy burden to carry. At times I have been impatient with my son. At times I have pushed him too far. It is something that is easy for a father to do." All the hardness had gone from the voice now. Now there were only the words of a father. "There is no need for this to happen again. Farouk has become a man in the hardest way. In my position a man is expected to act in a certain way. It is a tradition. It doesn't mean that the behaviour is the true measure of the man inside. I may be a prince but I am also a father. I rejoice at the return of my son Khalil. I thank you for bringing him back to me. I am in your debt."

Khalil bowed his head slightly to show his appreciation of the words. "There is no debt sir. Farouk is my friend. Helping a friend is never a distasteful task."

"My son is lucky to have found such a friend. Your brother too. I will ask for them to be brought to me. I insist that both of you stay and enjoy the hospitality of my family."

Farouk's reunion with his family was an emotional time. Mahmoud and Khalil stayed in the palace for two weeks and were discouraged from leaving when the day came. That morning the two brothers walked out into the desert with Farouk as the sun was rising. For days Farouk had tried to persuade them to stay with him in Saudi Arabia. Why return to Amman? The war had been lost. What could they do? He would ensure that they lived comfortably. Then they could stay together. Once again he tried. In the end Khalil cut him short with a smile.

"Farouk. My friend. We appreciate all that you offer us. But you must understand that we have no choice in our destiny. All choice was removed in 1953. Our people have just lost a battle. It has been a terrible loss. Maybe the greatest loss that we will ever have to endure. But a battle is only a part of a war. Our war will go on. Maybe it will go on for the rest of our lives. There can never be any change to this path."

They walked quietly for a few minutes. Farouk had accepted how things would be. He considered his words before speaking.

"I hear what you say Khalil. Maybe I have been a fool. I have thought of our defeat as something that is final. But of course you are right my friend. The war will go on. When the time comes when we must fight again you must call me. You must know that I am also unwilling to accept defeat. Please believe that."

Khalil smiled and gestured for Farouk to sit.

"If we take in the lessons of what has just happened, then next time things can be different. Let us look at Ammunition Hill for a moment.

We were there. We saw exactly what happened. No man can ever say that we fought with any less courage than the Jews. Every man who fought showed more courage than could have been expected. There was no difference between Arab and Jew. Our traditions are built on stories of courage and belief. But this war has shown us that mere courage is not enough. We live in a modern world where the battlefield has changed. We had the men. We had the belief. We had the courage. And we lost. We were slaughtered. Why? That is the question that we must now ask. We lost because they were better organised. We lost because they carefully planned every move that they took from the moment that they destroyed Nasser's planes before they could take off. We lost because their American equipment was superior to ours. We lost because the units of their army were more closely bonded and the links between their officers and men were stronger. We lost because they were better than us in the art of war.

"So. Who were these men who defeated us so easily? Well, of course there were the men at the front. Men like the ones we faced at Ammunition Hill. Men with determination and bravery. Warriors. And we also have our warriors. Salim is a warrior. Mahmoud is a warrior. But what about the men that we did not see? What about the men who were far away from the blood and noise of the battle? The men who made the plans that were their greatest weapon. We must have men who can match the Jews in these skills. I must try to become one of these men. I will serve my people better with the book and the pen than I ever will with a rifle.

"And what about the men in Europe and America who sourced the weapons that ate up our armies? The men who financed their fight? The men who engineered the diplomacy that gave the soldiers the opportunity that they needed? Your family, Farouk, has great power. Great wealth. Soon you will be responsible for all this. It will give you great power. This is how you can be a dangerous enemy to the Jews. You will be able to use your power to help us. To be truly dangerous the world must see you as no more than a rich prince. Only a few will know that you are still one of our warriors. Do you understand these words?"

Farouk nodded. The logic was impossible to avoid. It meant travelling a road that he had little taste for. But he had seen at first hand the might of the Israelis. His people were a simple people. They had never been like the Europeans and Americans. To defeat the Jews they would have to become like them. They would have to match all of their strengths. He could not dispute that his position made him important. After watching the ultimate sacrifice of his comrades living a lie was little enough to be asked of him. He nodded.

"I accept your words Khalil. There is wisdom there. I will always be guided. You will always see things more clearly than I ever will. It is how it shall be."

Mahmoud had been very quiet. He had been quiet since the night of the battle. A rage had consumed him. His rage had made him kill several times. It had frightened him. He felt the cold grip of guilt. Unlike Khalil he had never properly seen just how brutal their life was going to be. He had been naïve. He had believed all the stories of glory he had been told. But there had been no glory on Ammunition Hill. All there had been was chaotic violence. And in the midst of the violence he had been one of the strongest. His brother had been right. He was a warrior. He was a killer. And he would have to kill many times more until their fight was complete. Never again would he know how it felt to be a man who had not killed. There was no turning back. There had never been a chance to turn back. Fate had dealt them their cards. For the first time since they had walked into dawn light of the desert he spoke.

"We will make a promise to each other. We will fight until we win. We will always be comrades. When one of us needs help, the others will come. Always. That is our promise."

They made their promise. They were three young men fresh from their first sight of death and they made their promise in the shadow of a great sand dune. They made the promise that would always shape their lives.

It took over an hour for Khalil to run through the plan that had started to form as he had watched the pictures on the news. Farouk passed no comment. He sat very still and digested each element piece by piece as Khalil scribbled lines and arrows on sheets of paper. When he was done he looked up and gave a shrug of his shoulders.

"So? What do you think Farouk?"

"Where do I start? Crazy. Lunatic. Rather brilliant in its way. I worry that you are being impetuous Khalil. Things are still very fresh. I know that your thinking tends towards the unconventional, but this? This is nothing but a colossal gamble. Are you sure you want to take it?"

Khalil frowned. "Not just me Farouk. What about you? I must know how you feel."

"You know already. I will back your decision. I always have. Besides, there is no risk to me here. The gamble is not mine. It is yours Khalil. You are sure?"

Khalil lit a cigarette and blew at the glowing tip.

"Over the years I have spent many hours studying the game of chess. I have done so because it is a game that our enemy holds in great esteem. Many of the men who formulate their plans are expert at the game. It seemed to me that if I could understand the game, then maybe it might help me to understand them better. Maybe I could learn how to predict some of their moves. I don't believe that it has ever really worked, but I have become very fond of the game. When I am unable to sleep I play against my computer. There are times in a game of chess when you find yourself in a position that is almost impossible. Almost. There is only ever one course of action available when you find yourself in such a position. You have to take an outrageous gamble and hope that your opponent has become complacent in his supremacy. Such a tactic never works with the computer. Computers do not know the meaning of complacency. However we do not face computers. Our adversaries are mortal men. I have seen the triumph in their faces. They see themselves as supermen. They may just be complacent. Of course it is a gamble Farouk. But it is all we have left."

Farouk nodded. "Then we must proceed. We both have arrangements to make. We shall start right away?"

Khalil nodded. "Indeed. Right away."

Mordechai Breslow looked at his watch. It was approaching twelve. The celebration was on course to last for hours yet. The songs were starting now. And the wine was flowing faster by the minute. It was a mixed crowd that filled the room. There were men and women. There were young and old. There were those with the skin of Europeans and those with the olive complexion of the Mediterranean. There were senior politicians and lowly clerks. There were high-ranking soldiers and the men who drove tanks and helicopters. It was how they were. A team. Their whole nation was a team. They could bitch and argue with the best of them. They could scream at each other like fishwives. They could throw tantrums. They could crash phones down so hard that the plastic would split. But when it counted, really counted, they always dropped easily to the instincts of the team. When a victory was won there were no distinctions of age, gender, class or rank to subdue their celebrations. They would get drunk together. They would dance together. They would sing together. Even a man like Mordechai who had problems being remotely nice to anyone would have let his hair down if he had any.

His head told him that he had probably had enough whisky. He thrust yet another Marlboro into his mouth and hung his arm around a man of his own age who was much worse for wear than himself.

"So. Avi. Where is he? He will come?"

Colonel Avi Bloom grinned with dreadful yellow teeth.

"Sure. He'll come. He always comes. Never stays, but he always comes. Never drinks. Never smokes. Barely speaks. He'll become that because it is expected, then he'll go. The man's a fucking machine."

Breslow chuckled. "But he's our machine Avi. He's our machine."

At that point a silence slowly slid through the sweating revellers. In the doorway stood the utterly unimposing figure of Noah Cohen. He seemed diffident. Shy. He looked like the man from reception who had come to inform one of the guests that their taxi had arrived.

The big red-faced colonel stepped forward with a booming voice.

"Noah! At last. Come here my boy. Come so we can raise our glasses."

He half-dragged Noah to the centre of the room where a space cleared for them. Bloom swept a pile of empty glasses and plates full of half-eaten food from a table with a swing of his arm. There was laughter as the crowd hopped and jumped to get out of the way of the spilling drinks and smashing glassware. Bloom then scrambled up onto the table like an unsteady bear and nearly wrenched Noah's arm out of its socket as he heaved him up alongside him. They were surrounded by grinning, bright-eyed faces. Eager. Filled with the adrenalin of a great victory. Fresh from a killing.

"OK. OK. So shut up will you. No big speech. Just a toast. Comrades I give you our new David, our new Gideon, our new

Moshe Dayan, our new Arik, our greatest fighter, comrades raise your glasses, raise the fucking roof, I give you NOAH COHEN!!"

More a roar than a cheer. Veins stood out from the sweat of brows. It was an animal roar with fists held high. Noah met it with a small smile and took a reluctant sip from the glass of champagne that Bloom had forced on him. As soon was it was possible he stepped down and endured the backslapping all the way to the door.

A young woman stood at the back of the crowd. Deborah Hammerstein was no more than a bit-part player in the great drama of Operation Fox. Not that it mattered. The night was for all of them. The greatest and the smallest. The fighters and those from the back rooms. Deborah had the unenviable task of occasionally having to cover for Mordechai Breslow's secretary. Sometimes this was when the long-suffering woman was ill. Other times it was when she almost dropped from exhaustion. For three days the secretary had been struck low by a bout of food poisoning. As a result Dorothy had endured three miserable days of Breslow's ill temper. She hated him. He represented everything that she despised about the way her country was changing. Her family had escaped the clutches of Hitler in the nick of time and found their way to the Promised Land in the early 1950s. Her grandfather had been a famous musician who had shared the twin passions of Beethoven and socialism. Her mother had followed in his musical footsteps and had married a philosophy lecturer. She had been raised by gentle, kind, cultured people who carried the dying dream of Israel. Her Israel was not the land that was dominated by violent bullies like Breslow and Bloom and Sharon. Her Israel was not the land where young men were ordered up into the skies in helicopters and jets to slaughter the innocent civilians below in the name of security. Her Israel was about equality and justice and freedom and art. Her Israel was a haven for those who treasured peace, not war. Her Israel had died many years before.

She kept her face neutral as she slipped from the room. She played the part of a young woman in need of some air. She allowed the breeze to gently dry the sweat on her face as she checked that there was nobody there to see her. She took the mobile phone from her bag and dialled the number.

"Yes."

"It was him. Again."

End. A message sent. A betrayal to assuage her guilt. She would throw away the phone later.

Roland Keeley was enjoying a quiet morning. He had allowed himself to sleep in until after eight, which was unusual. He had dressed in casual clothes and strolled down to the Indian deli on the corner. He had slowly devoured the papers along with boiled eggs and toast. To have nothing planned for the remainder of the day was another thing that was rare for him. The endless options that were available lifted his good mood even higher. He was in the process of weighing these options when his phone rang. He briefly considered allowing the answer machine to act as a secretary. It was tempting. The call would almost certainly limit the options that he was just beginning to treasure. Reluctantly he resisted the urge and picked up the receiver.

"Keeley here."

"Hello Roly. It's Farouk."

A smile at the voice. "Bloody hell Farouk you old bastard. I thought that you must have died or something."

"Alas no. And as far as I am aware my house isn't on the list of your marines as yet."

Keeley winced slightly. It was unlike him to be so clumsy. "Ouch. Bit below the belt that old man. Sorry. I was forgetting that things were getting a bit warm down your neck of the woods."

A chuckle. "Don't be so daft. I'm a bloody Prince remember. I live in a palace with a pool. I don't get bothered by minor inconveniences like allied invasions."

"So life goes on much as same as ever for the man who has everything then."

"Some and some. This bloody war is no good for business. The sooner that it is over the better. And how about you Roly? You're still ducking and diving for your living I presume."

"But of course. I'm too old to think of getting a proper job. There are always people out there who will pay a shilling or two for the services of a man like me."

"An unscrupulous bastard you mean."

Keeley grinned. "Something like that. So to what do I owe this honour? I sincerely hope it is business. I always welcome any chance to lighten you of even the merest fraction of your obscene fortune."

"Actually, there is something. I rather think it might fall within your territory. Perhaps we could meet."

"Just name the where and when. I'll be there."

"I thought that we might talk over golf. Why don't we meet halfway? Valderama in Spain. Tomorrow. Tee off at two. I have arranged tickets for you to collect from your club."

"Always so organised Farouk. You were always the one with the tidiest room at bloody school. Never change do you?"

"Tomorrow?"

"Of course. See you in the bar."

Keeley's grin was even wider. Sacrificing his options in favour of a game of golf with Prince Farouk Al Abd al-Rahman was more than acceptable. His life was all about contacts. Acquaintances. Recommendations. For the first twenty of his 56 years he had been a fully paid-up member of the idle rich. His family had owned three copper mines in Northern Rhodesia and life had been just fine. It had been Harrow and Sandhurst and not a care in the world. Then it had all changed. Northern Rhodesia became Zambia and the new government nationalised all copper mines. It was at this point that the sheer miserable depth of his father's alcohol and gambling addictions had come to light. Daddy had killed himself to avoid the shame and the gravy train had pulled out of the station.

For the first time the dreadful prospect of working for a living raised its ugly head. The Guards suddenly became a career opportunity rather than a three-year hunting and shooting jaunt. Once he turned his mind to doing well as a soldier he soon began to surprise himself. By the time he was 25 he had risen through the ranks at a more than respectable speed to become a Major in Intelligence. Soon after his thirtieth birthday he transferred across for a ten-year stint within MI5. All the way along he met people in bars and tents and sports events. His charm was legendary. He always remembered names. He always remembered family members. He always knew someone who could help with a problem. In the end he decided to retire from the service and make a living from being a man who knew people.

It soon turned out to be wise decision. Thatcher's London of the 1980s was a perfect playground for a man who knew people. He helped people who wanted property. He helped people who wanted advice on stocks, which may just have come from the wrong side of the financial pages. He gave budding businesses introductions to venture capitalists. And every time there was a modest percentage payable. Introduction fees. Commissions. And soon he was able to live his life in the style that he had always intended.

He had drifted out of touch with Farouk Al Abd al-Rahman for many years. In fact they hadn't seen hide nor hair of each other since the years after leaving school. They had gravitated into different areas of London life in the mid-1960s. Roland had carried on with the Balls and the drinks parties whilst Farouk had entered his radical phase. Once Farouk returned to his desert roots they more or less completely lost touch. Farouk had tracked him down in 1984. He had heard whispers. He had heard that Roland might be able to help him with his family's property portfolio.

Now the commissions became very serious things indeed. Roland had been lucky. He had been given the big money to play with at exactly the right time. He made a fortune in a very short time for the Al Abd al-Rahman family and they rewarded him handsomely. It had meant that he had never really needed to work properly again. As he passed his half-century in 1997 he had more or less adopted a life of leisure. But he never failed to respond to a request from Farouk.

However, an invitation to Valderama was unusual. Meet halfway? Not usually an issue for a man with a private Lear Jet. Maybe he had just been particularly impressed with the look of course when it had staged the Ryder Cup. He shrugged to himself as he packed his things. Outside, the rain was hammering away at the windows. If Farouk wanted to treat him to a round of golf in the Spanish sun, why on earth should he wonder about it?

When they met the next day they fell into a familiar bonhomie. Their small talk took them through the progress of numerous friends and acquaintances. They laughed over all their familiar school memories. They considered the economy. They debated the war. By the time that they reached the small bar at the back of the ninth green Farouk was one up.

"Let's stop a while. It is quiet here. A good place to talk."

Keeley took a cold beer. Farouk espresso. They sat out in the sun, which wasn't particularly hot. By now Keeley's curiosity was getting the better of him. What the hell was all this cloak and dagger about?

"Come on Farouk. You're bloody killing me here. Spit it out for Christ's sake."

"OK. I have had to consider this meeting carefully Roly. I know that we have known each other for many, many years but our friendship has been a light one. I have had to consider whether or not I can trust you. Really trust you."

There was a hardness in Farouk's voice that Keeley had never known before. There wasn't much to say. "I see."

"Don't look so glum. We're here aren't we? I have decided that I am willing to take the risk. I will tell you a story now. It is a story that you will no doubt find extraordinary. When I have told you what I suppose is the real story of my life, I will offer you a job. It is a job unlike any you have ever taken before. It will involve some risk, but nothing over serious. It will make you a hugely rich man. Shall I continue?"

"Of course." Keeley was riveted now.

Farouk told his old friend of the years after they had lost touch. Of his brief estrangement from his family. Of three young men and the battle of Ammunition Hill. Of a vow taken in the dawn light of the desert. Of years of secret work supporting and funding the work of the PLO and Hamas. Of his part in a war that he had now been fighting for 36 years.

"We have kept our vow. Always. Myself and Khalil and Mahmoud. Now our vow will once again be tested. I am sure that the news will not have escaped you. Three days ago Mahmoud Bishawa was arrested in Gaza by the Israeli Defence Forces. They are convinced that they have secured a massive victory. They even have pictures of Mahmoud strapped to his hospital bed posted on the Internet for the world to see." There was an edge to his voce now. He had been furious about it. However, Khalil had taken the web cam images philosophically. Of course it was clever, he had said. The whole world expected that the Israelis would treat Mahmoud appallingly. Instead they had pulled a rabbit out of the hat. Look what decent people we are. We can even prove it. What a difference between us and the terrorist murderers who send their suicide bombers to kill our women and children. Khalil had been impressed by the elegance. He had been aware that it was another victory for the enemy. He had been happy to shrug his shoulders at the consequences. At least they knew that Mahmoud was OK. That was all that really mattered. All would change soon enough.

Farouk continued. "Our vow still stands. We will help Mahmoud. No matter what it takes. Khalil thinks that he has found a way. This is where we need you."

Keeley nearly spat out a mouthful of beer. Up until five minutes before he had always known his old school friend as a jet-setting playboy. A fully paid-up member of the super rich club. Never in his wildest dreams would he have ever guessed any of this. Funding the PLO. Fighting in the Six Day War as an anonymous foot soldier. It all took a lot of digesting. And now Farouk was wanting to tie him into this most dangerous of all worlds.

"Bloody hell Farouk. I do property. Share deals that might be a bit insider. But you're talking about the fucking Israeli Defence Force. That's out of my league. Miles out."

Farouk spoke sharply to stem the flow. "There will be no need for you to visit Palestine. You get no nearer than where we sit today. I would require you to work in the UK. In Scotland. The job will take no more than two months. The pay is five million dollars. I can transfer half of it when we return to the hotel. The other half will be payable when your part of the work is complete. Shall I continue?"

Five million dollars. Five bloody million dollars. Continue? Not bloody half.

"Actually, I think that you should. Let me get some more drinks in."

Farouk spelt out the way that Khalil had found. Keeley absorbed his part and considered the risks. And then he considered five million dollars. And then he said yes. Just like Farouk had known he would. The money worked as a serious distraction to his golf game. Farouk beat him on the fifteenth hole.

Crossing the border into the occupied West Bank had been a risk. It wasn't the first time that Khalil had done it. He had slipped into his old homeland on three occasions in the last decade for clandestine meetings with Salim and Mahmoud. It was a journey that would have been near suicidal for a man alone with no knowledge of the ground. However like so many things in life it became a great deal easier when you had money and access to the right contacts. Smuggling in and out of the locked down territories still went on. There were small groups of men who knew every rock, mine and trip wire along the border. They could always get a man in and out for a price.

The rough clothes of the impoverished traveller felt strange to him. He had spent many years in the uniform of an executive. He had become accustomed to suits and silk shirts and hand-made leather shoes. Now he wore a tired woollen jacket, cheap nylon trousers and plastic sandals over his bare feet. His identification papers marked him as a builder from the north of the West Bank enclave en route to visit relatives.

The dusk was just beginning to gather as the small bus bounced down the rutted road to Kibya. The small town had changed little since 1953. There were some new buildings, but not many. The charred shells of the houses blown up by the soldiers of Unit 101 had never been touched. They remained as a bleak reminder of the night of killing that had guaranteed Kibya a place in the history books. An air of decline hung over the town. For hundreds of years its main economic role had been to serve the travellers who moved from east to west and back again. This was no longer the case. To the east the border into Jordan was locked tight. To the west the border to Israel was locked even tighter. There was no passing trade for a place like Kibya. The main road had become a cul-de-sac. It had become a town in the wrong place at the wrong time.

Khalil found a small coffee shop on the square and sat to kill an hour of time. The sprinkling of customers stared with morose interest at the Al Jazeira news channel on the TV mounted high on a peeling wall. There was an air of resigned shock as one report after another highlighted the lightning speed of the American and British advances. The drained gloom of the faces of his fellow customers reminded Khalil of the days in Amman in the wake of the Six Days War. His people were very good at persuading themselves that each time it would be different. For weeks the Arab world had taken to the streets to howl out its defiance at the imminent allied invasion of Iraq. The more they had shouted, the more they had started to believe that maybe a miracle might be in the air. Maybe Saddam could emerge as their new Saladin and send the men from the west running back to their far-away homes.

It was the tragedy of his people, thought Khalil. There were always those who would fill the hearts of fine young men with wild dreams of impossible victory. What use would shaking fists ever be against F16 jets and Bradley Fighting Vehicles? Over the years he had spent plenty of time in Iraq whilst carrying out Farouk's business. He had seen the threadbare hold of the regime. Take away the naked terror of the torture rooms and there was nothing there. Just a corrupt shell of a nation that was unfortunate to sit on top of the last great untapped lake of oil on the planet.

He bitterly considered the consequences that his own people were already paying for Saddam's greed. The 24-hour television war had the world watching with rolling fascination. It had become the ultimate reality TV and the networks couldn't get enough of it. It provided the Israelis with a cloak that they had been craving for years. They had shut down the Palestinian enclaves, and the journalists that they had expelled were happy to leave anyway. The big story was to be found in the east. They had achieved a blackout. They had prepared their killing field. And now they were taking full advantage of their window of opportunity whilst the backs of the rest of the world were turned to watch the fireworks in Iraq.

He checked his tatty digital watch. It was time. He paid his small bill with a brief nod. Outside it was dark now and the streets were all but deserted. There was nobody to notice the rather tired-looking man who made his slow progress to the edge of town. There was nobody to see him pause for a few minutes outside the overgrown shell of the big house where the headmaster of the school had once lived. He was allowed to pay his respects to his long dead family in silence.

The track into the hills was still familiar after half a century. No doubt the hooves of goats and sheep had been setting the shape of the path into the hills from the days of the Old Testament. The gradient was much harder on his legs now. Around him the night was similar to the night of the killing. Only this time the moon was smaller and it was the dim light of the stars that guided him. He had no trouble in finding the place where the fox had once made its burrow. He sat down and waited. Strange that the fox had also escaped its fate that night. If the soldiers had not come then the fox would have died whilst his family would have lived. It was how fate seemed to work. Some lived whilst others died. Some had freedom and justice whilst others knew nothing but oppression. How long did foxes live anyway? Five years. Maybe ten. Maybe it had bred and a whole generation of its ancestors now hunted the dry hills of Samaria because Ariel Sharon had brought his men across the border to commit murder in the night.

He was far too deeply wrapped in his thoughts to sense the approach of his uncle.

"Salaam Aleikum Khalil." The voice had broken down and cracked a few more notches. In the dim light he sensed that his uncle had become stooped. When they embraced he could feel how the bones had become brittle and the flesh was stretched tight.

"You are well, uncle?"

This brought a derisory snort. "Well? How can an old man like me be well? I am tired and I am old. I live in one room and I am of no use to anyone any more. How can a man be well in such times?"

Khalil smiled. Old age had made his uncle constantly grumpy. "And yet I still hear that those in the movement talk of you as a man of importance. I hear that your hand still guides the younger ones. I hear that you were there in Jenin when our people fought so well."

"You can always hear things. People always hear things. Maybe I am of small use. Maybe not. You come about Mahmoud?"

"I come about Mahmoud."

"Mahmoud is lost. Don't believe those pictures that they show the world. They will have him in the Russian Compound right now. They will never stop until he is dead. Mahmoud is lost. There is only you and I now. Soon there will only be you Khalil. And then the Bishawa family will be finished. It is how things are."

The old man's words dripped with anger.

"I believe the pictures uncle. The Jews are not fools. We know this. They gain much by showing the world that they treat Mahmoud well. So much of our war is about propaganda. Over recent years the world media has turned against the Jews. They have been branded as brutal and violent. They cannot afford this. They need the Americans to keep sending them their tanks and planes. They need the Europeans to keep buying their oranges. They cannot afford to be hated. Already their economy is beginning to fall apart. They have shown cunning to treat Mahmoud well. I believe the pictures uncle."

Khalil sensed a small surge of hope ripple through the old man. However he refused to allow it into his voice.

"He is still lost to us. Even if they treat him well, they will still try him. And once they have found him guilty they will kill him. He is beyond our reach now."

"I don't think so. I believe that there is a way. It is why I have come. I will need help. Your help. Shall I tell you of the way that I have found."

The hope was growing in the old man now. He knew that his nephew never spoke words that were frivolous. If Khalil said that he had found a way, then maybe there was a way. He poked about in the dust with a stick whist Khalil spelt out the plan which he had now started to shape and refine. Salim heard it in silence. In the end he passed his judgement.

"A crazy plan. But yes, there is a chance. I give it about one in ten. But one in ten is enough. What do you need me to do?"

"Two things. You need to find a place for Mahmoud when he comes back to us."

Salim nodded. "That is easy. The other thing?"

"You must find a man in Syria. He must be from our people, about the same age as me. He must have spent many years in the prisons of the Syrians. He must be free now but still under threat from the secret police. You will make an arrangement with him. Give him a new identity. Take him to a new home somewhere safe. Take his family with him. Do not worry about the cost. Money is available. All that I want is his name. His identity. His life. He must disappear in two weeks time."

Salim nodded. "It can be done. It is not long, but it can be done. For such a man this will be a great blessing. He will feel that Allah has smiled on him. And you will become this man for your journey into the west?"

"I will become this man."

"Then it shall be done."

They talked for another two hours. When it came time to part they were sad. They both knew that it was unlikely that they would ever meet again. In the way that Khalil had found, there was no way back. They would part on the hill where they had come to hunt the fox all those years before. For both of them this would be their last engagement in the war that had stolen their lives. When they walked away from each other having embraced for a last time, neither man looked back. The silence settled back over the low rocky hill in Samaria where once a fox had taken lambs from the sparse pastures.

A JOURNEY TO THE WEST

As he took his seat in the departure lounge of Manchester's Ringway airport, Zaheer Khan mused that the last two days had most surely been the strangest that he had known in his young life. He had received a call on his mobile phone whilst he was manning his uncle's clothes stall on Blackburn market. It was from one of the Mullahs who occasionally preached at the Mosque in Burnley where Zaheer said Friday prayers with his family. The Mullah had requested a meeting. He had given Zaheer an address in Oldham. Would that very evening be convenient?

The family who lived in the small terraced house that was the venue for the meeting made themselves discreetly absent from the front room where the Mullah waited. Tea was served and the old man started his speech. He told Zaheer that his work had been noticed. The work in question was the Young Moslem Defence League that Zaheer had been instrumental in founding in the wake of the race riots that had set alight the mean streets of his home town of Burnley.

Zaheer was very much one of the new generation of British Muslims. Their parents had escaped war and poverty to come to Britain in the 1960s and 1970s. They had come from the misery and catastrophe of places like Pakistan and Bangladesh and Uganda. They had been grateful to have been given a home and shelter by their old colonial masters. They learned to be meek. Deferential. They put up with the mocking comments and casual bullying with stoic silence. They gathered together in poor sides of towns such as Leicester and Bradford and Burnley. They bought the cheap houses that nobody else wanted. They worked the long hours that nobody else was willing to work. They did what they did best. They traded. They worked. They sank their roots into the hostile soil of their new home.

Zaheer's generation was different. They enjoyed a level of education that was beyond the dreams of their parents. They took up places in the many new colleges that had been built to accommodate the baby boom kids of the 1960s. They lost patience with the way that their parents were always treated. They grew frustrated. They grew angry. And all over the country groups of young Muslims decided that the time had come to fight back.

Within six months Zaheer's group boasted over 150 members. They were ruled by the mobile phone. One call from a family being threatened by the local hoodlums of the British National Party would bring an immediate response. Because all the members of the group worked for the businesses of their own families there were seldom any consequences to be faced for downing their tools. They prided themselves at being able to deploy at least twenty bodies to any street in the their East Lancashire territory within fifteen minutes of receiving a call. There was seldom a need for fighting. They always took a video camera to ostentatiously film the event as it unfolded. The BNP lads generally could not deal with being filmed by a group of fit young men who had them outnumbered. It was the rule that they would beat a grudging retreat accompanied by a torrent of abuse and the occasional thrown stone.

The system proved to be far more effective than any of its young founders could ever have dreamed. There were soon appreciative noises from the elders. There were visits from community leaders from as far afield as Bradford and London.

Now the Mullah told Zaheer that their work had been noticed beyond the shores of Britain. He said that there was a man who wished to meet Zaheer. He said that the man was a person of great importance in the Muslim world. He said that the meeting needed to be an absolute secret. Could Zaheer keep this kind of secret? Zaheer had told the Mullah that he could. And when the Mullah had produced the return ticket from Manchester to Frankfurt he had agreed that he would go.

More or less as soon as he left the house and got into his car to drive over the bleak grey moors back to Burnley, Zaheer was starting to regret his decision. For a while he had been mesmerised by the words of the Mullah. Of course he had been. The man after all was a professional when it came to the art of persuasion. And like a silly young fool he had fallen for the flattery. But now, as the inefficient wipers battled against the sleet that was trying to blot out the view of the road ahead, he felt an icy dread. It could only mean one thing. Al Q'Aida. How could it be anything else? And he had said yes to the Mullah. And now that he had said yes there could be no turning back. He had been brought up to always honour his word once it had been given.

He glanced up at the departure board. The flight was on time. It was time to make his way to the gate. He felt as if the eyes of hundreds of watchers were all over him. He felt as if he were stepping out into a great ocean of freezing water. He was about to join the most dangerous game on the planet because he had been foolish enough to say yes.

Once he arrived in Germany he followed his instructions and took a taxi to a discreet hotel in the countryside. The girl at the front desk was fully aware of his arrival and politely led him up to his room on the second floor. He again followed the instructions and killed time for an hour by watching highlights of Bayern Munich thumping some team that he had never heard of four nil. When an hour had elapsed he went into the corridor and found room 301 and knocked.

A voice requested that he should enter. Inside, the man was alone. He was a man in the later years of middle age. He was dressed casually in slacks and a cotton shirt. His smile was easy. His English was perfect. He was unlike anything that Zaheer had expected.

"Zaheer. Good of you to come. How was your flight?"

"Fine." The man spoke the English of the rich. Zaheer was suddenly conscious of his thick East Lancashire accent.

"Please, sit down. Tea? Coffee? Anything stronger?"

Anything stronger! Had he really said that? No way he could be Al Q'Aida if he asked if Zaheer would like anything stronger. As it happened Zaheer had never drunk alcohol. But lots of his friends did. "Coffee please."

The older man made himself busy making them coffee. When he had completed the task he sat opposite Zaheer and crossed his legs.

"I am so glad that you have come. I didn't know if you would. These are troubled times. You must be very worried about our meeting today."

Zaheer nodded. "Yes. Yes I am."

"Of course. Well let's get things clear before we go any further. I can assure you that I am not Al Q'Aida. Of course there is no way for me to prove this. There are times my young friend when we have to trust each other. This is one of those times. I have met with Osama Bin Laden many years ago. There are many areas of his work where I have nothing but the greatest admiration. But I see Al Q'Aida as a mistake. He has brought down the wrath of the west on our people. Has that made things better? No. Has it improved the lot of those who find it hard to find food for the family table? No. Has it brought victory any nearer? No. You must carefully consider whether or not you believe me when you leave tomorrow. If you do, then maybe you will be willing to help."

"What kind of help are you looking for sir?" Zaheer surprised himself by calling the man 'sir'. It wasn't what he normally did. He had been dressed down on many occasions for not showing sufficient respect to his elders. There was something about this man that commanded a respect that was natural.

"I am afraid that I cannot give you my name. I have worked for our people for many years. The work I do is not a public thing. It is important that it always remains discreet. I hope you understand this."

"I do sir."

"Tell me. Does it surprise you that the work of the Young Moslem Defence League has been noticed in countries far from your own?"

"To be honest, yes it does."

"You see, Zaheer, what is so good about what you are doing is that it is simple. You are not trying to change the world. You are merely dealing with problems that arise in your own part of the world. You are making sensible use of technology that is cheap and easily available. Your members simply have to follow a set of simple instructions. Because it is simple it works, and you have thrown your enemies back in confusion. It is something that others can build on and I feel sure that they will. I have asked for this meeting because I need the help of your group. May I tell you why?"

"Of course sir." Zaheer was thoroughly intrigued now. The fear had left him. He knew that he was in the presence of someone who had been fighting for many, many years. Farouk poured more coffee.

"We receive intelligence, Zaheer. We receive intelligence from all over the world. Our people are under threat everywhere. Our enemies are hugely powerful. There are many times when we can do nothing to protect those who are in peril. And then there are times that we can do something. Often it is not enough. Sometimes we can make a difference. Like in Bosnia. Like in Chechnya. Recently we have received intelligence from Scotland. You will have seen what happened at the place that they called Sighthill a few days ago. It will not stop Zaheer. We have some links into the BNP. They have targeted the area. They see the asylum seekers as their ticket to their next level of political acceptance. I gather you have some experience of the BNP, Zaheer?"

"Lots. They are why we started the group. Things are getting serious where we live. They have four councillors now. They keep gaining ground. I have read their magazines, looked at the website. What you say about the asylum seekers doesn't surprise me any. I can see why they would want to escalate things up there."

Farouk nodded. "When the Afghani killed those three boys he couldn't have done a bigger favour to the BNP. They are claiming that this is exactly the kind of thing that the British people can expect from these savages who claim to seek asylum. And there will be those who believe them, Zaheer. There will be plenty. We have made some enquiries. It seems that the man in question had been a member of the mujahidin. He was no stranger to fighting. The three boys were by no means angels. It would appear to be a case of three young thugs picking a fight with the wrong man. But the media will not be interested in that. All that will matter is that the boys were all fifteen years old and he slashed their throats. Things will get a lot worse before they get better. There are about six thousand asylum seekers in Sighthill, many of them Moslems like you and I. Many are women and children who have lost everything. They are from Iraq and Iran and Kosovo and Afghanistan. Their situation is perilous. They speak different languages and have no unity."

Zaheer nodded. The threat was one that he found familiar. "So what do you plan to do sir?"

"We are sending a man. He will arrive as a refugee. His task is to bring the people together. He must make them discover unity. Only with unity can they make themselves safe. If the BNP are allowed to win up in Sighthill, there will be consequences for our people all over Europe. Sighthill is where we must try to draw a line. It is where we must stop them."

"I can see that sir, but you say that you are sending only one man. How can one man make such a stand?"

"It only takes one man to become a leader. If they can find a leader then the people up there can remember that they are six thousand. Now these people are frightened. They hide behind their doors. One man can persuade them to come out and stand together. One man can do much. But he must be the right man. The man that we are sending is such a man. He is a great man. But when he gets there he will need some help. He will need people who know the language and understand the enemy who they must confront. Your group knows this enemy. You have fought them with courage and guile. And you have forced them to take a step back. I ask that you take some of your group up to Sighthill to help the man that we have sent. I want you to have your group ready to go when he calls. I want you to take 50 of your best men."

The prospect made Zaheer feel almost dizzy. It wasn't Al Q'Aida. It wasn't what anyone would ever call terrorism. It was defending people who were vulnerable and friendless. It was a task that he knew that his fellow volunteers would take on with relish.

"Fifty of us will not be a problem. It is work that we will be proud to take on. All your man must do is call me. We will be there the next day."

Farouk smiled. "You are a fine young man. All that I was told is true. When you arrive there will be places for you to stay. We do not know how long it will take. Our guess is no more than two weeks. We know that most of you work alongside your families. It will be difficult for them to run their businesses whilst you are away. You can tell every man that there will be five thousand pounds to compensate their families for their absence. Dedication deserves reward. I am not willing to negotiate on this point. It has been decided."

Zaheer was astounded. A quarter of a million pounds tossed out like a twenty-pence piece. Who on earth was this man? Not that he cared. He was a man that Zaheer was willing to follow. That was all that mattered. Farouk continued.

"Do we have an arrangement Zaheer?"

"We do sir. We do."

It was agreed with a shake of hands. Contact details were agreed and Farouk said that he had to leave immediately. The money would be left in a left-luggage locker at Manchester Airport. He gave Zaheer the key. When Farouk had left, Zaheer went for a long walk through the pretty German countryside whilst the thoughts swirled around his mind. Farouk travelled back to the airport with a small smile playing on his lips. So Khalil, now you have your army. Soon you will have your war.

Campbell Swann felt as if his arteries and veins were filled with some kind of acid. There seemed no other logical explanation for the way that the pain flowed to every corner of his body. He had been in hospital for a week. The consultant had told him that he was a very lucky man indeed. Because he was young and fit, his body had dealt better than could have been expected with the beating it had received. The only real structural damage was two cracked ribs. Otherwise it was a case of the most extensive bruising that anyone working on the ward had ever seen.

He had never imagined that the simple act of getting dressed could involve such complete and utter agony. He had already had his argument with the ward sister who had told him that he was not allowed to get up under any circumstances. After much ado he had established his rights and suggested that she save her breath. Instead she had made a call and his inspector had arrived.

"Not a good idea Campbell. Don't be a pratt. Just accept that you've had ten bells of shite knocked out of you and do as they say."

Inspector Donaldson had been in to see him the day before. He had explained that they had finished the initial internal enquiry into what had happened. They had concluded that PC Swann had made difficult choices under intense pressure. They had concluded that his decision to get the Afghan suspect clear of the area as soon as possible had been fully vindicated by the events that had followed. He had let Campbell know that a commendation for valour was in the pipeline for his decision to return immediately to the area to try and stabilise the situation. The news had not been the weight off Campbell's mind that he had thought it would be. After what he had seen he had developed grave doubts about his wish to continue with his career. For months he had been dutifully filling in intelligence reports about the situation in Sighthill. He had described the growing influence of Tac Brennan and his cohorts. And the reports had been dutifully filed away and forgotten. What had happened had been coming for months and months. The police had been caught with their pants down around their ankles. And the Khan family had been burnt alive whilst hundreds of policemen ran around Fountainwell Avenue like headless chickens.

He hadn't said much to Donaldson. He hadn't let him in on the fact that he could shove his commendation somewhere where the sun wouldn't shine. The only thing that held him back was Nicky. She had been in to see him every day. The events of the night seemed to have ripped her into pieces. The weight had fallen off her and her eyes were black-rimmed with fatigue. The school had given her compassionate leave.

Campbell had tried to help her with the grief that was tearing at her but he didn't really know how. After all, what could he say? What could anyone say when people are burnt alive? He had been having to deal with his own nightmares as images of Madiya Khan and her two children floated out from the corners of his mind, their faces contorted with blinding agony. Instinct had told him not to even try persuading Nicky from returning to Sighthill. It would be utterly pointless and could drive a wedge between them. The moment he had regained consciousness in the A & E ward she had been there at his side. Images flashed into his head like strobe lights. Images of Nicky defending him like some demon. Images of the look of confusion on the faces of those who would have probably succeeded in killing him. There was no woman like Nicky on the whole planet and there was no way that there would ever be a wedge between them. She had obviously been expecting him to fight her.

"Are you not going to argue Campbell? I was expecting a fight."

He had managed a smile which hadn't been easy. "I've seen you in a fight. No thank you."

Today was the day of the funeral and nothing was about to stop him from attending, certainly not Donaldson or the ward sister. The inspector looked big and awkward with the task. It wasn't something that had been covered in the manual. Campbell actually felt quite sorry for him.

"Honestly sir, I'll be fine. It's only bruising. Nothing terminal. I'm going to the funeral. It's final. Non-negotiable."

Donaldson shrugged. "Fair enough. I had to come when they rang. Just don't overdo it. OK?"

Campbell nodded and tried not to show just how much it hurt as he pulled on his right shoe. Nicky arrived five minutes later. The sight of her made his heart sink. The black of her clothes emphasised the dreadful pallor of her skin. All the flesh seemed to have been dragged from her cheeks. She looked like a ghost. She helped him to stand and immediately registered his pain.

"Campbell, you shouldn't be doing this. You're not well enough."

"I have just put up with a whole morning of bollocking from the ward sister and a lecture from Donaldson. Please don't you start Nicky. I'll be fine. It's just bruising. No way am I not coming."

It took him a long time to make it to the front entrance of the hospital. He had to lean heavily on Nicky and soon felt as if he had run a marathon. He collapsed onto the back seat of the taxi and had to lean his head back to stop the spinning sensation. The funeral was to be held at a crematorium. It would only be a small affair. What family the Khans still had were thousands of miles away. They probably didn't even know. They had bigger fish to fry anyway. Their main concern was not getting themselves bombed by the Americans. Their neighbours in Sighthill were all too scared to move from their flats. Only Rosemary would be there, along with her son Moses. Campbell had smiled when Nicky had told him. Rosemary would have still been there if the crematorium had been ringed with machine-gunners. When the taxi arrived in Sighthill he waited in the back whilst Nicky went up to collect them.

Outside, the streets were still filled with the mess of the riot. There was nobody about to speak of. He had clocked five police cars as they had made their way to Rosemary's block. They were just parked up. Visual Presence he thought bitterly. And how long would that last? How long before a bean counter would present the management with a bill and a worried shake of the head. And then it would be back to business as usual. He knew that there had been no real attempt to investigate Tac Brennan's part in what had happened. Brennan had played a clever hand. He had spoken to every tabloid journalist who had found him. He had posed for their photographs. He had played the role of the devastated father for all that it was worth. The daily perusal of the tabloids had been the worst part of Campbell's stay in the infirmary. Every day brought a new spin on the Hero's son butchered story. Maybe Tac had even got himself some kind of an agent; it certainly seemed that way. There were lots of pictures. There was Tac in dress uniform. There was Tac with three comrades by a Union Jack in the Falklands. There was Tac in Ulster. There was Tac at home in Sighthill. Tac Brennan the warrior. Tac Brennan the peacemaker. Tac Brennan the beleaguered divorcee. Tac the man who had done his bit for Queen and country only to see his only son butchered. There was no mention of Tac Brennan the cold-hearted gangster. Somehow the medals on his chest and his sombre dignity made that politically incorrect. All of a sudden every journalist in town wanted to hear Tac Brennan's view of the world.

Two days earlier Kevin Brennan's funeral had been the greatest event that Sighthill had ever seen. It drew in the media from all over the world. Tac wore his medals and played his part. Polls revealed that middle Britain was beginning to see his plight as symbolic of the plight of a crumbling country. And in the midst of all the hysteria the Khan family seemed to get forgotten. It was almost as if there was a feeling that they deserved what they had got. It was as if they had personally slit Kevin Brennan's throat as a part of some pagan ritual. How dare they? How dare they abuse the hospitality that had been shown to them? Nobody actually came out and said it, but it was always hinted at in the spaces between the lines. The whole issue of asylum seekers needed to be re-addressed. Who were these people? How many more murderous monsters were hidden away? Ministers did their best but public opinion was sliding away from them. Liberal values were out of favour.

When the taxi arrived at the crematorium it became immediately apparent that the media had the mourners outnumbered by ten to one. They pushed their cameras in close as Nicky helped Campbell out of the back of the taxi. Reporters yelled questions. Microphones and fake tans and gleaming white teeth. Campbell gritted his teeth and allowed Rosemary to carve a path through the throng. Inside the chapel of rest was a dismal place. There were only the four of them. The service was a miserable affair. He gripped Nicky's hand hard as the bitter tears of loss streaked her ashen face. And then it became too much. The sobs climbed up from deep inside his chest. His ribs felt as if they were being clouted by a madman with a crowbar, but still the sobs came.

The half-hearted service drew to a close and the coffins disappeared. None of them could face the idea of what waited outside. The sight of Nicky was almost more than he could stand. Her neck seemed barely able to support the weight of her head. She had lost all of her colour and her eyes were ringed with the grey of sleeplessness. In her eyes was the desperate confusion of a happy person confronted by all the miseries of the world. It made him feel helpless and inadequate. It made him feel like striking out and howling. It made him feel like breaking everything within reach.

It was Rosemary who took control. She gently helped them to their feet. She wiped the tears from Nicky's cheeks and straightened her hair for her. She spoke quietly in her deep sing-song voice of Africa. She spoke about pride. She urged them to stiffen themselves and led the way outside. Despite himself Campbell could not help a small smile at the sight of the tall woman in the bright colours of the homeland that was lost to her. She positively blazed. God help any of the journalists outside who dared to cross the line. And then his eyes fell onto the face of her son and the smile fell from him. Moses had grown fast in the months since he had arrived in Sighthill with his mother. He was tall for seventeen and his shoulders strained at the fabric of his suit jacket. His face was completely impassive but his eyes burned with a fury that sent a shiver through Campbell.

The plane bounced gently as it dropped through the clouds. Khalil stared out of the window and waited for a view of the land below. At last they broke through and the bleak flatness of the countryside came into sight. It had been so many years since he had first gazed down on the same view. He had been a young man then. He had been 27 and embarking on the greatest adventure of his life.

In the dark years that had followed the catastrophe of 1967 he had become one of the Movement's rising stars. The genocidal fighting of September 1971 had passed him by. He had been in Cairo whilst the Jordanian army had evicted his people from their country like a hated tenant. It had been a time when his people had come to terms with being alone. The war of 1973 had gone better for the Arabs. For a few heady days it had even seemed as if the Jews might be broken. But it hadn't lasted. In the end the armies of Egypt and Syria had once again been thrown back. There had been an element of pride this time but it was also clear that they would never try again. Israel had become too strong. The moment when it could be destroyed by its neighbours had passed. The talk in Cairo and Damascus and Amman was all about peace. And his people were on their own again.

They had shaken the world when they kidnapped the Israeli athletes at the Munich Olympic Games. It had all ended badly as the German police slaughtered everyone in sight, but the world had been forced to wake up to the fact that his people had not disappeared. It was the war that they knew that they would have to learn to fight. All of a sudden the Jews had become the elephant and they had become the fleas. They could never throw the forces of occupation from their lands on the battlefield. Instead they had to make the occupation as uncomfortable and miserable as possible. They had to make the Jews pay a price of blood and fear for the land that they held.

Khalil had been one of the ones who had driven the new policy forward. Many of the older men had been dead against it. This was no way for their people to fight. Theirs was a decent people. An honourable people. How could it help their cause if they become terrorists? They would bring on the hatred and contempt of the whole world. Part of Khalil had agreed with them. He hated the new path every bit as much as they did. But he had argued that it was the only path open to them. He never bothered with the rhetoric and flowery language that some of the leaders of the Movement favoured. He tried to be cold and logical. He explained that they all needed to accept that they now faced a long war. Maybe 50 years. Maybe 100 years. The Jews had become strong. They would stay strong for many, many years. Victory would not be possible for decades. What was now important was to ensure that his people were not allowed to be forgotten. He pointed out the fate of the American Indians. They had tried to fight it out on the battlefield. They had shown courage and ferocity but they had been overwhelmed by superior force. In the end they had been destroyed completely. In less than 100 years they had lost all claim to the lands that were once theirs. His people had to learn lessons from their fate.

The path of terrorism was distasteful, disgusting even, but it was the only path that was open to them. Every time they hijacked an airliner or bombed a café they forced the world to remember that they were still there. Khalil became a planner. In the early 1970s he helped put together several operations that saw targets bombed within Israel. Unlike other similar attacks, his tended to be successful. The fighters who undertook the raids were always properly briefed and trained. He was noticed. At the same time Mahmoud was making his own name. Five times he successfully crossed the border and returned leaving dead bodies on the streets of Israel. The impact of these attacks was good for his people. By this time hundreds of thousands of Palestinians were eking out miserable lives in refugee camps all over the Middle East. Many years had passed since they had been thrown out of their homes. With every year that passed their hopes and dreams of a return faded. By now there was a whole new generation that had never set foot on the soil of their homeland. The bombings kept the dreams alive. They were a mere fleabite on the hide of the great Jewish elephant. From a military perspective every attack was a disaster. Every time they left the bodies of civilians on the dusty pavements they brought on the rage of the Jews. For every Israeli killed there would be ten of his own people wiped out in retribution as the American-made jets took out their revenge on the refugee camps. But the war was at a stage when success could not be measured in pure military terms. All his people could do was to hang on, to keep the flickering flame of their hope alive, and to try and live to fight another day.

The attacks on Israel worked wonders for the morale of his people, but they were soon ignored by the rest of the world. A few dead people on the streets of Tel Aviv soon lost their appeal to the world's media. The world was a place that was full of dead bodies on pavements. There was Ireland and Vietnam and Central America and any number of countries in Africa. It was a time when terrorists had to compete hard with each other for column inches. Khalil started to argue that the campaign needed to be taken further afield. A bomb in Tel Aviv would only do so much to remind the rest of the world that his people were still alive and kicking. A bomb in London or Rome or Berlin counted twenty times more heavily. He demanded that they took the war to their enemy in Europe. It was much harder of course. It would involve funding and careful planning and alliances with other terrorist organisations. And it would involve the Movement employing the services of only the very best of its fighters. Arguments raged amongst the leadership throughout the early months of 1974. There were those who feared that the hatred that such attacks would bring would never go away. Others saw it as the only way. In the end the men who advocated the hard line had won the day. They chose their people. They chose Khalil Bishawa as the man to plan and co-ordinate the attacks. They chose Mahmoud Bishawa as the man to lead the teams to deliver blows.

But there was more to be done first. New skills needed to be learned. New alliances and contacts needed to be forged. The decision was taken that Khalil should be sent to the world's foremost school of terrorism. They arranged for him to attend the Patrice Lumumba University in Moscow. At 27 years old he was a man in his prime. The leaders of his people had listened to his words and had accepted the way that he had showed them. He and Mahmoud had been given the task to lead the fight against the enemy that had slaughtered their family.

Now he could still remember the thrill of excitement that he had felt as the Aeroflot plane had cleared the runway of Cairo International Airport. It had been his first time away from the Middle East. The prospect of spending time in the Soviet capital had been a fantastic one.

The reality had been altogether different. Within weeks he had become more depressed than he had ever been before. The cold of the Russian winter seemed to have climbed into his bones and there was nothing he could do to drive it away. The city was a place of monstrous grey buildings and slushy snow that leaked through his inadequate shoes. The people were uniformly dismal. Their unhealthy, pasty faces wore a perpetual scowl. In their eyes was a constant flickering fear. He found himself in a cold place where there was no joy to be found. He yearned for sunshine, for the dusty streets where children chased around and played their crazy games. He yearned for the food that he had grown up with as opposed to the miserable lukewarm fare that was served in the canteen.

He found little in common with most of his fellow students. Many of the Europeans, Africans and South Americans seemed intent on drowning every waking hour in a lake of vodka and screwing each other like rabbits. Others were besotted by the teachings of Marx and Lenin and hell-bent on twisting these words to fit all situations. He became tired of arguing with these men. They refused to grasp that his war had nothing to do with the ruling classes exploiting the workers. They would never listen to the truth of any situation. They pretended to be warriors when all they wanted to do was to show off in front of their grim-faced Russian lecturers. After four months he felt isolated and lonely. He was learning nothing that could possibly be of any use to his people. He completed the exercises that they set for him. He generally got top marks in his class but it gave him no satisfaction. He felt as if he were living out a charade. He yearned to be back at home.

And then he met Sergei. The summons came in the form of a note left one morning in his pigeon-hole. He was ordered to attend a one-to-one session with a new tutor. He went along with little enthusiasm. He was becoming disillusioned with the arrogant way that the Russians ordered them all around with their barely concealed racism. As soon as he entered the room he had sensed that here was a man who was different. This instinct was confirmed when the man behind the desk asked him to sit down in fluent Arabic and offered him an American cigarette. The man was young, maybe even younger than he was. He wore an impressive uniform and chatted easily as he prepared tea. He was quite unlike any of the other Russians that Khalil had met during his brief stay. He had manners and class and the good looks of the soldiers and factory workers who stared down from the massive posters that were plastered on the side of every one of the great grey buildings of the city.

Sergei Mikhailovich was as near as it was possible to get to Soviet aristocracy. His father had commanded a tank division that had broken through the Nazi lines at the great battle of Kursk. He had received a bullet through the shoulder and the Order of Lenin for his feats that day. The long and brutal road to Berlin had brought many more medals. He had become a hero of the Soviet Union and had been lucky enough to avoid a bullet through the head, care of Stalin, once the hostilities had ended. Instead he had been rewarded for his efforts. Sergei was the only son and grew up amidst the trappings of luxury that the Soviet leadership were happy enough to award themselves for their supreme sacrifices made on behalf of the masses. There was a big flat in the centre of Moscow with a clear view to the domes of the Kremlin. There was a dacha in the pine forests on the edge of the city. There was a home amidst the olive trees by the warm waters of the Black Sea. There were passes to the shops that sold the treasured goods of the west and there was the best education that the system could provide. Father and son had endured a sticky patch when Sergei had refused to follow the family tradition and become a tank commander. Instead he had chosen the KGB. He had risen through the ranks like a meteor. By the time he was 26 he commanded a small section of the Fourth Directorate that was responsible for co-ordinating the efforts of a variety of Arab terrorist groups who were taking the fight to the Soviet Union's joint arch enemies of America and Israel. It was a plum posting, one of the hottest fronts of the Cold War. There was twinkle in the deep blue of his eyes as he stared across the desk at Khalil.

"So Khalil. I expect that you will be tired by now. Confused. Yearning for home. Wondering why it is that you are here. Am I right?"

What was this? Some kind of test? The university was a place where you had to choose your words carefully.

"I am quite content sir."

Sergei laughed. It was a rich sound. A warm sound.

"Please, let us try to avoid all this nonsense. I know you are sick of this place because we do all we can to make it so. We need to know, you see. We need to sort out the ones who have no other interests than vodka and women. We need to know the ones who are no more than walking text books. And we need to know the ones who are serious. We watch quietly. We make our notes. We are careful men you know. Very careful men. We dislike wasting our time. I have been watching you Khalil. And I have been impressed. Very impressed. And I have seen a man who I feel that I can work with. From now on you will work with me and I hope that you will come to feel the same. Your apprenticeship is over Khalil. Now the real work starts."

The real work was everything that Khalil had come for. During the course of the next year he became one of the world's foremost experts in the art of modern terrorism. He was given the tools. There were contacts with like-minded men from Germany and Italy and France. There were contact points all over Europe where he could access help and equipment from the KGB. There were communication techniques. There were surveillance and counter surveillance techniques. There were bomb-making techniques. There were escape and evasion techniques. Planning. Cell structures. Lectures on the counter terrorism departments in all the countries of Western Europe. Studies of past attacks, both successful and catastrophic.

By the time that his year was complete Khalil was ready for the war that he was to fight. Over the next two years he and Mahmoud had gone on to stage six successful attacks on Jewish targets all over Europe. They had become two of the world's most wanted men. The media filled page after page with stories of their atrocities. They became the bogeymen and the legend of The Fox was born. After each attack Khalil would meet with Sergei in different locations all over Europe. They became a close team, bound by mutual respect and an unlikely friendship that grew from the bleak little war that they fought together.

A JOURNEY TO THE WEST

As the tyres of the plane bounced and bit on the runway Khalil allowed himself a small smile. How long had it been? Twenty years. Twenty years since the nightmare that had been Beirut. He had always followed Sergei's career. His rise up the ranks of the KGB had only been halted by the dramatic collapse of the Soviet State in the early 1990s. For a while he had seemed to have dropped off the map. Khalil had feared that he must have met with the traditional fate of a bullet through the back of the head. But his concerns had been unfounded. Sergei had reappeared in the late 1990s as a new man. He was often in the papers that Khalil browsed on the Internet. This was a new Sergei and yet in many ways the same. He had become a man of Italian designer suits and shiny Mercedes cars. There were all sorts of rumour and innuendo about Mafia connections and high level corruption. The stories made Khalil smile. They would never catch Sergei out. They would never even get close. The newspapers he read as the years drifted by told of a great fortune made from a chain of hotels and nightclubs. There were also strong rumours of arms trading. In 2001 there was blanket coverage of the opening of the Rose Bowl Club which immediately became the number one place to be seen in Moscow. A tanned and beaming Sergei looked easy and relaxed as he posed for the cameramen with stunning blondes hanging on his arms. The photos had brought a smile to Khalil's face. His old friend had simply taken his skills and used them in a different field. World revolution or organised crime, it must have all been much the same for Sergei Mikhailovich.

It was a very different Moscow that Khalil stared out at through the window of his taxi. No longer were the streets of the night barely lit. Now there was brash neon everywhere. The brands of western capitalism had replaced the posters of Lenin. Once empty roads were teeming with traffic. Hordes of beggars had replaced the queues at the government food shops. It seemed almost unbelievable that it had only been a quarter of a century earlier when these people had believed they were about to conquer the whole world. Instead they had laid down on their backs like a Labrador puppy and allowed their tummy to be tickled by the likes of Nike and McDonalds. Just another defeat. Just another lost cause. Even with all their submarines and MiG fighter planes and SS20 missiles they had still lost, just like all of those who his people chose as allies always lost. There had been the Egyptians and the Jordanians and the Syrians and the Iranians and the Soviets. In the end they all lost. In the end his people were always left to stand alone.

The staff at the front desk of the hotel were just the same as their colleagues the world over. He was a well-dressed businessman with matching luggage and a wallet full of credit cards and a ten-dollar bill at the ready to show his gratitude. His suite included Internet access along with a minibar and a selection of Finnish porn to go with the usual Hollywood offerings. He made himself a coffee and logged on. It had become habit. A daily ritual. He found Mordechai Breslow's site and spent a few moments gazing at the figure of his brother. The straps had been taken away now. The cell certainly seemed comfortable enough. Mahmoud was sitting rather awkwardly on the bed. He was clearly unused to finding a comfortable position. It was the stump where his leg had once been that was the problem. Khalil wondered how much the amputation was hurting his brother. Was he on heavy medication? There was no way of telling. Even if he was suffering the agonies of hell he knew that Mahmoud would never give his captors the pleasure of seeing it. Instead he spent his days reading quietly. He must have known that the camera on the wall was sending his image all over the world. He must have known that he had become the prize exhibit in the new Israeli zoo. All he could do was to maintain as much dignity as he could. As ever, Khalil felt his eyes moisten with tears at the pitiful sight of his younger brother. As ever, he felt a cold knot of hate in his stomach. The pictures were a gift. The pictures would drive him on.

The Rose Bowl was all that it had seemed in the paper reviews. The place dripped with money. Fat, red-faced businessmen pawed impossibly beautiful girls whilst their hard-faced minders scanned the room with disinterest. A singer gave a more than decent Sinatra tribute with a backing group who must have been poached from the National Opera. The surroundings were outrageously opulent. Lenin must have been turning in his mausoleum.

Sergei allowed a redhead with a thousand dollars worth of teeth to show him to a table. She pouted when he insisted on coffee instead of the champagne that she suggested. There was the merest flash of loathing in her sparkling green eyes when he politely explained that it was because he was a Muslim. Some things hadn't changed then, he thought. More neon, more consumer goods, same old Russian racism. She made a startling recovery when he slipped her a 50-dollar bill and asked to see the manager. When he came over, the manager dripped smoothness. Khalil reckoned that he had modelled himself on Humphrey Bogart's Rick in *Casablanca*. The beaming smile faded somewhat when Khalil spoke to him.

"I would like to see Mr Mikhailovich please. You can say that it is Khalil."

The manager was about to express his utter contempt at the idea when Khalil calmly counted out three 100-dollar bills.

"Please. There is no need to be concerned. Your job will be perfectly safe. Sergei and I are old friends. Very old friends. I am sure that there are cameras. You need not worry. Sergei will check me out first. He will be pleased with you. Here, take it. Go."

He sipped his coffee and smoked whilst the Sinatra sound-alike demanded to be flown to the moon. He was surprised at how quickly the manager returned. This time the beaming smile was once again wedged in place.

"Please sir, you can come now. Mr Mikhailovich is waiting."

Corridors and huge men in ill-fitting suits. He was frisked three times. Sergei must have made a few enemies along the way. Nothing new in that. All that was new was the lack of anonymity. Nobody ever knew who was behind all the dirty little operations his old friend had set up during his time in the Fourth Directorate of the KGB. That had all changed. Sergei Mikhailovich was now a face on satellite TV.

His office showed a remarkable lack of ostentation. Sergei leapt to his feet like a man of half his age. The photos had done him no more than justice. He was lean and tanned and fit. Life was treating him well. He took Khalil in a hard embrace which he held for half a minute. When he released him his handsome face clouded in concern.

"My old friend. The years have treated you hard."

Khalil smiled, more than anything relieved at the genuine warmth of his welcome.

"Unlike you Sergei. Capitalism suits you I see."

Sergei gave a very Russian shrug.

"Maybe. All this . . ." He took in the room with a lazy sweep of his arm. " . . . all this. Just things. Just American stuff. Sure, it's OK. It's comfortable. No more than that. If I could turn the clock back, I would.

I miss those days Khalil. Truly. No bullshit. We were worth something then. Now? Now it is only money. The fucking god of the dollar."

Khalil gave a quizzical frown and Sergei laughed.

"Hey. Sorry. I forgot. These days I swear too much. We all do. We have no fine words any more. So we swear. I apologise my friend. It will not happen again. So. Come on. Sit down. I have told my man to make tea. Real tea. Like we used to drink in Damascus. I told him if it wasn't right I would have him shot. The damn fool believed me! So sit. Tell me. I thought you were dead. Everyone thought you were dead. Are you a ghost? Are you real? Who cares? You are here. Nothing else matters. If you were a Russian there would not be enough vodka in the building. Instead we will toast each other with tea. Why not? We will toast the old days when we lived in a world that we could understand. We will talk until the dawn. We will pretend that we are young again. What do you say, my old friend from the grave?"

"I say that your Arabic is still superb."

Another big shrug. "Why not? They say languages are like riding a bike. I practise sometimes. I get my men to bring me Arabs to talk to. It makes me feel young again. I miss those days. You know, I always thought that we would win. Always."

Khalil sat and stirred the glass of tea that had been brought. He took a sip. It could have been served in a café in Damascus and nobody would have complained. "I think that you man should be allowed to live. The tea is fine."

Some of the vigour seemed to drain from Sergei as he sat and poured himself a glass. "So I talk and talk like some old washer woman because I avoid what I must say. It is because I am getting old and weak Khalil. Once I would have looked you in the eye and been straight. Twenty years and I think that your are a dead man. Twenty years and then you come to me here in Moscow. And still I talk and talk and pretend that this is some kind of social visit." He lowered his head and stared down at the antique coffee table. "Of course you come because of Mahmoud. It was a bad day when I heard. A bad day. And now. To see him on the Internet like some animal on show . . . I can't find the words Khalil. Mahmoud was one of the best of us. Maybe the best of all. Is it true? Is it because of Mahmoud that you come?"

"I come because of Mahmoud."

"But what can I do? I am no longer KGB. Those days are long gone. All I am now is a jumped-up gangster. Sure I have money. Nothing more."

"There are some things that I need. I can pay whatever the price."

"Like?"

"Guns. Not many. Four handguns. Four semiautomatic. Tear gas. Smoke grenades. Some gas masks. A satellite communication system with anti-jamming. And Semtex. 500 kilos. I also need the electric riots sticks developed by the American police."

Sergei nodded absently. "All of this is nothing. All of this can be done. All . . ."

"I will need it all to be delivered to an address in Glasgow, Scotland within a month. I will inform you of the address within ten days."

Now there was raw interest on the Russian's face. "Again, it is nothing. It will be done. So. Let me assemble the pieces. You see Khalil, there are things that I never quite understood. Maybe now I have clues. When the Syrians took you we all thought you were gone. We tried you know, we really did. You were one of ours. We cared. They gave us nothing. They had started to hate us by then. That day when the Israelis shot 87 of our jets out of the sky without losing a single one of their own. That was when they started to hate us. They blamed us. As if we had done it all deliberately. They couldn't see that it was the end for us too. We had ruined our whole country to build up our armed forces. For what? So that the Americans could laugh themselves sick as their planes shot 87 of our most modern planes down as if it was a fairground stall. But I digress. You disappear into the deepest darkest prison in Syria. You disappear so deep that even the Soviet Union cannot find you. And yet here you are. You got out. How? There could only have been one way. Money. And here you are in your English suit, throwing hundred-dollar bills at my manager and telling me that ordering thousands of dollars worth of hardware is nothing. Money. Somewhere there is money. Somewhere behind you is a backer. I always felt it in the old days. Nothing I could put my finger on. Just something. Maybe you can tell me now?"

Khalil smiled and shook his head. "Remember what you taught me Sergei. Seared units. Cell structures. Need to know. Optimum security procedures . . ."

"Enough! Enough. OK. So. This is why you have come? To place an order out of loyalty to an old friend? Maybe not. Maybe there are many men who could get you these things. Men who would be much easier to find than me."

"Not men that I could trust like you?"

Sergei nodded. "OK. Sure. That is right. You can always trust me Khalil. We both know that. And I will do what I can for Mahmoud. Of course I will. So is that all or is there more?"

"There is more."

Sergei filled their glasses with more tea. "So. Come on. Tell."

"I have a plan. If the plan works then Mahmoud will walk free." This made Sergei sit up very straight. "It is an ambitious plan. Maybe a crazy plan. Maybe a doomed plan. But I must try. You know this. I have to try. It is my plan. Just me. There is nobody else. You were my teacher Sergei. You were the best that there was. I would like you to help me with my plan. Find the holes. Find the places where I have been careless. Try to help me to find perfection."

"Now we are talking. My God Khalil you come in here like the first warm day of the spring." He jumped to his feet and clapped his hands. "A plan for Mahmoud to walk free. This I have to hear. If you do this you will give them more than a bloody nose. You will throw them to the ground. They act as if they are supermen. They act as if nobody can touch them. You do this and they become vulnerable again. You do this and you bring back the hope."

Now it was Khalil's turn to smile. "I see my friend that you are still a believer then."

"Old habits die hard. Even for a jumped-up gangster. There is one thing you must tell me. Before we start. One thing." Suddenly his face was filled with all the old hardness. Once again he was the man who had sent so many out to kill and be killed. "Is it still Breslow?"

"It is still Breslow."

"Good. Very good. For many years I have dreamed of destroying that Jewish bastard. We need coffee. Lots of coffee. And you can tell me now. All of it. Every detail. Mordechai Breslow. Suddenly you make me feel young again."

It was different to when Khalil had told Farouk. Sergei pulled apart every element. He worried at the detail, the timing, the thought processes, the assumptions. By the time that Khalil was done he felt as if his idea lay in pieces on the 50-thousand dollar rug on the office floor.

A silence hung in the air. The longer it went on the more dejected Khalil felt. Maybe he had just been dreaming. Maybe he was just too desperate. Or too old. Or too long away from the game that they had both played with such ferocity. He slumped back and stared up at the ceiling. Maybe it would be all over before it had even started. But it was why he had come. He had come because Sergei would see the truth. If the whole thing was madness then it was better that he should know. It took a long time for the Russian to speak.

"So OK. It's crazy. But you know that. Is it worth it? Sure. Of course it is. For Mahmoud it is worth it. The odds? Five-to-one against. No better. Good enough. So we need to improve the odds. It can be done. We can move the odds to three-to-one against. But no more than that. It will still be crazy, but Mahmoud is worth crazy."

"Tell me."

"This is a fighter's plan. Of course it is. Because you are a fighter. It is all that you know. You rely on complete surprise. Plant the bomb. Boom. And away. You do not need to try and guess what your enemy will do. There is no need. You need to evade him. Trick him. Get in under the fences that he has erected. But you don't need to guess how he will react. You know that. He will go crazy and he will try to hunt you down. You're with me?"

Khalil nodded.

"This is different. You were right to call this plan a chess game. It only works if your enemy reacts as you anticipate. If at any time he reacts in a way that you have not predicted, then the plan will start to fall apart. There is no plant the bomb, boom and away here my friend. You need to make your enemies behave like puppets on your string. So, can this be? No. Never. It is the first rule of planning. It never works out how you think it will. Never. Your problem is knowing what your enemy will do. How he feels. How he is thinking. How is his frame of mind? What kinds of people are around him? It is called intelligence my friend. Knowledge. So. Let us see here. There are two enemies. Two opponents across the chess board. First there is Breslow. Can we get close to him? No. Of course not. He is behind high wall. So all we can do is guess. But this other man, this Tac Brennan, he is different. He is behind low walls. He is a man that we can get close to. I can suggest two things. I still have access to people in Britain. They are men from the old days. Good men. The ones that they never managed to catch. I can use these men to get some surveillance onto Brennan. We can bug the hell out of the bastard. We will be able to hear him when he takes a shit in the morning. These men will tape everything they can and send it to me. I will do the analysis and report to you. All you need is the hard information. You will have no time for analysis. You will be under too much pressure. Let me do this for you."

Khalil was astonished. It was much more than he had expected. "You are a true friend Sergei. I thank you."

The Russian brushed the words aside.

"This will take the odds down to four to one. There is more. I am surprised that you haven't seen the next move. I can see why. It is because you don't have a good enough understanding of how things are in Britain. In Scotland in particular. Why should you? It was never important for the war that you fought. I know these people. I was working in this area for five years in the late 1980s."

"Go on."

"You are quite correct about the kind of people who will come to support Brennan. The Far Right. Splinter groups. Losers. Just thugs mainly. We spent a lot of time looking into them. We thought that there may be something there that we could use to destabilise the British. It was all a waste of time. They have no unity. No brains. They just like to fight each other at soccer matches and listen to idiotic music. However there is one group that is made up of more serious men. Tell me Khalil, do you know much of Ireland?"

"A little. Nothing really."

"OK. We of course were very interested. The war in the north of Ireland was something of an Achilles heel for the British for 30 years. Most of our attention was focused on the IRA. We helped them when they would let us. It wasn't very often. I have often wondered how it might have been if they had allowed us to give them proper assistance. However, the IRA were not the only terrorists in the mix. The IRA were a Catholic group determined to unite Ireland and to end the British occupation. In many ways they were similar to your own Movement. They faced two enemies. There was the British army of course. But there were also the Loyalists, men who were determined to stay in Britain whatever the cost. In terms of brutality they were every bit as dangerous as the IRA. As the war ground on they became more radical. To start with they were just shopkeepers and postmen defending their communities. Once the army took effective control most of the reasonable men drifted back to their normal lives. Many of those who maintained the fight went beyond mere Loyalism. They moved into organised crime. They became affiliated with the Far Right. I will show you websites. They are part of a network of crazy men all over the world. Neo-Nazis in Germany and Eastern Europe, Ku Klux Klan in America, BNP on mainland Britain."

Khalil shook the cobwebs from his brain. It was getting late and his brain ached. "Sorry Sergei, but I don't understand."

"When Brennan starts his fire many of these men will come to feed the flames. It is only a short ferry journey from Belfast to the West of Scotland."

"I still don't understand."

"I have met these people Khalil. The men of the IRA and the men of the UDA and the UVF. They all come from the same towns, the same streets even. They are the same colour. They share the same workplaces. They catch the same buses. To look at them and to listen to them you could not tell them apart. In fact they find it incredibly hard to tell each other apart. If an IRA man were to share the company of ten UDA men and they were all strangers to each other it is unlikely that they would suspect anything."

"Oh now I can see. You say that there will be some of these UDA and UVF supporters who will join Brennan."

"Without doubt. Their war is all but finished. They crave action. They are bored. It will be irresistible to them."

Khalil was smiling now. "And you feel that an IRA man could easily masquerade as one of them, yes?"

"Yes."

"Which means that you are thinking about Declan, yes?"

"Of course. He can be your man on the inside. The man to tell you of the moves that your enemy is about to make."

They talked for another hour until it was time for Khalil to go. He sensed that there was something else that Sergei wanted to say. He had wanted to say it from the minute that Khalil walked into his office. Once Khalil left it would be too late. Both of them knew that they would never see each other again. When they stood, Sergei placed his hands on the thin shoulders of his old comrade. "In those days, the last days, the dark days, I never saw you at the end my friend."

Now Khalil knew what it was. "No. Things were too crazy."

"I never had the chance to share my sorrow. Fatima was a terrible loss. Fatima and Palestinia. She was a great woman Khalil. I cannot imagine how it must have been for you. Is there anyone else?"

"No. There was only Fatima. There will never be anyone else. And you my friend?"

"I have a wife. A fine woman. Rosina. I named this place after her. And I have my boys. Two boys."

"I am pleased for you. You must enjoy your life. Family is everything. All I have now is Mahmoud. All that matters is Mahmoud."

"Then you must win Khalil. This time you must win."

Donald Kelly had a furtive look about him when Roland Keeley walked into the small Italian restaurant in Soho. It was a little past three and the lunchtime rush had run its course. The waiters were lazily talking football at the counter, at ease after the daily race to serve their food quickly enough to avoid complaints from customers with vital early afternoon appointments. Only one other table was in use and the two lunching middle-aged ladies were nearing the end of the coffee stage of proceedings. Keeley worked his trademark big smile.

"Donald. Marvellous. So sorry I'm running late. Busy as buggery as per got a drink? Great. Eaten have you? Sure? OK."

Kelly was a rather shrunken-looking man whose small eyes flickered around the room compulsively. He was now in his early 50s and he wore clothes that had seen better days. He was the sort of man who never was not going to be noticed. Once upon a time there had been a wife called Sheila and a semi-detached house in Maidenhead. Somewhere there were two children who must have arrived into adulthood. For 30 years Donald had been a low-grade civil servant. He arrived in work at 9.00 and left at 5.30. He took holidays in France. He had used the same Tupperware box for his lunchtime sandwiches for the last fifteen years. No doubt it would travel with him all the way to retirement. His 30 years in the service of the Crown had seen a mere two promotions up the pay scale ladder. There wouldn't be another. All they wanted now were bright young people who are at one with their computers. All Donald Kelly was doing was counting down his days. He had become a dreary fixture that nobody ever noticed.

Except somebody had noticed. Roland Keeley had noticed during his time at MI5. Roland had noticed because he had been looking. He had used all his charms on the sad little man from the clerical office. And soon he had discovered the reason why the wife called Sheila had moved back home to her mother's house in Reading. He found that the love of Donald Keeley's life was racehorses, and it was a love that he indulged every day. It was a love that he indulged with every spare penny that he could find. There could never be enough money for Donald for there was always another race, another sure-fire winner, another windmill to tilt at. When Roland had left the Service he had used Donald on several occasions to access information from the mainframe of the MI5 computer. The fees were always generous and paid in cash. Every time Donald had told him that this time would have to be the last time. But there was always a next time. There always would be so long as sleek horses were raced through the countryside.

A waiter brought them both coffee and Roland continued his good-natured banter whilst Donald looked ready to burst into tears with nerves. Finally Roland tired of trying to put his man at ease.

"So Donald. How have you got on? Goods as usual I hope?"

Kelly nodded. "The army file wasn't a problem. It's in a carrier bag under the table. The other stuff was a little tricky. You were right, they have upgraded him. I got bits and pieces. That's all."

"BNP?"

"Yes. I found something. He only attended one meeting. Back in 2001. Never said anything. Just sat at the back and listened. Never went back. It seemed like he had gone along with a friend. Our operative put him down as a day tripper."

"And now?"

"We showed a bit of interest after what happened when his boy was killed. No surveillance. Just questions. Enquiries. I couldn't get the findings. It would have been too risky. I may have left fingerprints."

"Don't worry. I don't really need that. You have the stuff I really wanted. As ever Donald, I appreciate your help. I can assume that you still hold an account with the same Turf Accountant?"

Kelly looked down and nodded rather miserably.

"I will make the payment as usual then. Must be going now, Jolly good to see you again. Keep well old man. Get lucky."

Keeley tossed a ten-pound note onto the table and came easily to his feet with the carrier bag in his hand. He got the taxi to stop by a bookie in Islington and made a cash payment of five thousand pounds into Donald Kelly's account. When he arrived home he made a pot of coffee, kicked off his shoes and settled down to read the file that Kelly had brought him. It was a much thicker file than would have been generated by the average British soldier.

Tac Brennan had joined the British Army in 1976 at the age of seventeen, except it hadn't been Tac then. Then it had been George William Brennan of Sighthill, Glasgow. He had passed the test to get into the Parachute Regiment with flying colours. For five years every file entry was exemplary. He was mentioned in dispatches in the wake of a brief and vicious gun battle on the outskirts of Newtonhamilton in South Armagh in 1980. By the time the battalion was shipped out to the Falklands he had been promoted to corporal. He received a Military Cross for his efforts at Goose Green when he had led his men to glory as they followed Colonel H. Jones's lunatic charge without a second's hesitation. An Argentinean bullet through the shoulder that day had ended his personal interest in the battle to retake the islands.

By 1983 he had made it to sergeant. It was impressive. Not many made sergeant in the Paras at 23. By 1985 he was back a corporal. The details of his demotion were sketchy. Keeley smiled as he read between the lines to sense a cover-up. The Battalion had been taking part in a major NATO exercise in Germany. They had done well. They had slipped three companies through the lines of the German Division that were opposing them in the war game. 300 men had materialised out of nothing to surround and capture the German command and control centre. Complaints had been made by the German officers about the way the Paratroopers had behaved. The British had taken no notice.

That night, when the exercise had drawn to a close, Brennan's company had been out celebrating. A Company of German Grenadiers had wandered into the same place. A fight had broken out. A German sergeant was hospitalised for three months. Tac Brennan was demoted to corporal.

It was the last blemish for many years. By 1988 he was promoted back to sergeant. Throughout the 1980s and early 1990s the file was full of Ireland. Brennan must have got to know West Belfast and South Armagh as well as Glasgow. There were a couple of enquiries for two shoot to kills. Neither had any criticism of Sergeant Brennan or any of the members of his platoon. Things were similarly impressive following the Battalion's time in Kuwait during the Gulf War.

By the mid-1990s it was clear that Tac Brennan was within an inch of making it to Regimental Sergeant Major. He was very close. Then came Kosovo. The men of 1 Para were sent over as part of the peacekeeping force. An incident happened during the third week. Brennan's company were sweeping a small village. There had been a shot and one of his privates had taken a bullet in the leg. There had been a brief exchange of shots and the attackers had fled into the wooded slopes that surrounded the village. Brennan had ordered that all houses should be thoroughly searched in order to fully secure the area. His men were well used to searching property. They had all done it time and again in Ireland. It wasn't something that they did with any great care and attention. They got into every nook and cranny and they did it quickly. If that meant breakages and damage then so be it. They weren't Pickfords Removals. They were 1 Para and some joker had just shot one of their own through the leg. As far as they were concerned it meant that the village was hostile and they searched it accordingly. Apparently there had been some kind of commotion. An old man enraged at the way that his front room was being wrecked. The men on the search had called Brennan on the radio. When Brennan arrived there had been an incident. The old man was felled by a blow from the butt of a rifle. The old man had a weak heart. The old man died where he fell. It would have probably have all been brushed away under one of the army's favourite carpets, but this time it was different. This time there had been a Norwegian film crew to capture the whole incident.

Even then it might have all being different if the incident had happened in Ireland. Phone calls would have been made. There would have been deals done. The film would have been quietly recovered and disposed of. Tac Brennan would have had a proper bollocking, but that would have been the end of it. Tac Brennan had earned a bit of leeway. For twenty years they had sent him into the shittiest situations they could find and never once had he flinched. He was owed. It was something that the British army understood. When the chips were down they expected the Paras to behave like ultimate savages. It was only fair to cut them a bit of slack when they went over the top a bit at the wrong moment.

But this time it was different. This time it wasn't the British Army on the streets of Ulster. This time it was an International Peacekeeping Force on the streets of the Balkans. The PR men demanded that there was only room for the Serbs to play the role of the baddies. And so Tac Brennan had to take the fall. All the army could do was to ensure that he didn't have to serve any time. It was dishonourable discharge and back to Sighthill.

Roland sat back in his old leather chair and blew a smoke-ring up towards the ceiling. The file had been worth every penny. From afar he had sensed the rage inside Tac Brennan. He could feel it when he watched videos of the interviews that he gave in the wake of the killings. He had been convinced that there was more than the loss of his son. And now he knew. He had known many a Tac Brennan during his time in the army. They were hard men from hard places who lived and breathed their regiments. None were more proud than the Paras. He could easily imagine how Brennan must have felt. All those places that he had been. Belfast. Goose Green. Kuwait. Crossmaglen. Always sent in to fight against bad odds. And after all that, twenty years of it, they had hung him out to dry to appease the media. No wonder he was an angry man. It was anger that Keeley could easily understand. It was an anger that he could use.

The next morning he took a train from Euston to Blackburn. He had always been a fine mimic. It had been something that he had first used in the dormitory at Harrow. It had come in handy at times during his time in military intelligence and MI5. On several occasions he had favoured the accent of an East Lancastrian whilst playing out one role or another. It had been a while and he was a little rusty. Three nights of practice in numerous small pubs on steep, terraced streets soon put that right. On the third morning he carefully adopted the persona of Mr Burton before leaving the Motel. He wore a wig of thick ginger hair and matched it with a moustache. His clothes were rigorous Marks and Spencer. Checked shirt. Brown slacks. Robust shoes. A grey windproof jacket. He smiled to himself in the mirror. Roland Keeley had vanished without trace. John Burton came from a different planet. He left the key in the latch of his room and arrived in plenty of time to make the one o'clock train to Glasgow.

Johnny Hendon was in the process of dozing off in front of a regulation Bruce Willis film when the doorbell snapped him awake. Automatically he checked his watch. Eleven-thirty. Strange. He wasn't expecting anyone. He pulled himself to his feet and went to the intercom.

"Yeah?"

"Is that John Hendon?"

"Aye." He had no idea who it was. English. North country somewhere.

"Benson. John Benson. I'd like a chat."

Cheeky bastard. Half past eleven at night and he would like a chat. But in the end Johnny Hendon was a journalist and you never slammed a door until you were sure.

"What kind of chat?"

"As far as you are concerned a £500 chat."

"You what?" What the hell was going on down here? It was usually him who laid out the cash.

"Like I say. I want a chat. I'll pay 500 quid. I'll put it under the door if you like. You can count it and that. Then you can make your mind up. How's about that?"

Johnny couldn't think of anyone in particular who was in the market for giving him a kicking. Things had looked up considerably since the Sighthill killings. All of his debts were cleared, at least all those that carried the threat of baseball bats and big men with bad breath. Even so, 500 quid was 500 quid.

"Go on then. Third floor. Money under the door. Like you said."

A few moments later a brown envelope slid under the front door. Inside there was five hundred pounds just as the man had promised. He checked him out through the peephole. Seedy-looking bugger. In his 50s somewhere. He looked like a train driver due for his retirement clock. What the hell. He opened the door.

"Thanks ever so much Mr Hendon. I'm obliged. I can come in can I?"

"Aye. Through here. Take a seat. The place is a tip I'm afraid."

"Oh that won't bother me any. Here OK? Grand."

Who was this guy? All smiles and black puddings and good old Lancashire bonhomie and 500 quid in a brown envelope. Weird.

"You want a drink? I haven't got much. There's scotch I think."

"Aye. Smashing. It'll warm the cockles. Bit parky out tonight. Should've put on a thicker coat. That's Scotland for you."

"Aye. So it is. Water?"

"No thanks. Best not drown it. Don't want to upset the natives."

Johnny poured the drinks and tipped the junk off the armchair that faced Benson.

"OK Mr Burton. Put me out of my misery. What the fuck is happening here?"

"A proposal Johnny. Plain and simple. A proposal. A real belter. You hear me out and you can say yes or no. Simple as that. Sound fair enough?"

"Aye. Fair enough. Make your pitch."

"OK. You can have the choice of stories. There is the real one, which you are about to hear. It's probably just about the daftest tale you'll ever hear. It would make a cracking read in any paper you managed to sell it to. But there is a problem. A big problem. No bastard would believe it in a million years. My name isn't Burton. I don't suppose you ever thought that it was. You will never find out who I am or who the people that I represent are. That's a promise. You might as well take my word for it and save yourself a lot of wasted time and effort. You with me?"

"No, but carry on. I'll catch up at some stage."

"Things are going to happen Johnny. Big things. Front page news every day of the week things. They are going to happen in the near future and they are going to happen up the road in Sighthill. How do I know this? I know this because the people that I work with have paid me to make them happen. It's what I do Johnny, and I'm bloody good at it. So what is about to go off? Local hard man Tac Brennan is going to declare war on six thousand asylum seekers. That's what. Nothing new in that. Maybe he already has after what happened to Kevin. But it won't be a handbags-at-five-paces type of war. Oh no. It will be a proper blood-in-gutters type of war. How do I know? Because I am going to make it happen, and like I said, I'm good at making things happen. However, this where things will start to get interesting. Because the asylum seekers aren't going to just lie down and take it. Nope. The asylum seekers are going to fight back. How do I know this?"

A theatrical raising of the eyebrows. Johnny played along. He was fascinated now.

"Because you're going to make it happen."

Burton roared with laughter. "Ten out of ten lad. Move that lad to the top of the class. The people I work for are sending a man. Not just any man. A special man. A one in a thousand man. A leader. He's a been there, done that, got the T-shirt man. He will organise the resistance. He will make them stand their ground. He will lead the fight. Can you picture it Johnny?"

Could he ever. The whole thing was the purest madness, but even so.

"I can a bit. So where do I fit in?"

"This whole thing is about news Johnny. All of it. It is a real time, real lifeblood and guts battle played out for the media. It is a means to an end so they tell me. I don't know the ending. Neither do you. We just play our part, you and me. I make it happen, you report it how my employers want it reported. I can put you next to this man that they are sending. Imagine it Johnny. He will be the new Che Guevara. How big is that going to be? Huge Johnny. Massive. Big, big bucks. Bigger than a close-up photo of Princess Di showing her twat. And it will be all yours Johnny. Exclusive to Johnny Hendon. You can be the man on the inside. The man at the heart of the biggest story out there. Can you see it Johnny?"

"Aye. I can see it. Is that it then? The chance of tapping the papers for a quid or two in the unlikely event that you make this fairy tale come true?"

Another joyous laugh straight out of the rainy valleys of East Lancashire. "Of course not you silly bugger. We'll pay you. We'll pay you stacks. Anything you can make on top is just luck money."

"How much?"

Burton grinned like a fisherman about to reel in a big fat trout.

"Stages Johnny. Stage one comes tonight. You help me with a small piece of information and I pay you five grand. Here and now."

"What information?"

"I need to meet Tac Brennan. Where and how?"

"Rogan's Bar. Any night after nine. You can't miss him. He's got his own seat at the bar. Right-hand side. You've seen pictures. That's it. Money please."

Burton reached into the inside pocket of the Marks and Spencer golfing jacked and pulled out another brown envelope, which he duly tossed across the room to Johnny. Johnny opened it and counted the money. It took all he had to play it cool.

"Thanks Mr Burton. I'm obliged. Stage two."

"I keep you informed as to how things will pan out. When the man arrives I will put the two of you together. That is when things will start to happen. You report it. No spin needed. Just tell it like it is. The media will be crawling all over you. The man won't talk with anyone else. Just you. Only you. You will be the man in charge. For that we will pay twenty grand. You will quadruple that with what you earn from the rest of the media. I have an account open for you. Here's a cheque book and a card."

He placed them on top of the clutter on the coffee table. Everything's done. Signature the lot. There's twenty grand sitting. You can do what you like. Draw it in cash. Buy Premium Bonds. Move it overseas. Up to you."

"What signature?"

"Yours of course."

"But how . . ."

"Don't ask. Just accept. It is how things need to be. I tell you what will happen and it will happen. Don't go worrying about how it happens. OK?"

"OK." Johnny had a sudden feeling of having jumped into very cold water that was already up to his chest. This was no bumbling buffoon. This guy was a player. A bigger player than any he had come across before.

"Good lad. That's the spirit. OK. Now to the big bucks. The serious money. You had a mate at school who has done rather well for himself. Daniel Morrissey. Am I right?"

"Aye."

"When the time comes we will want you to put him in touch with our man. It will be when things get really hairy. He can play the part of the knight on the big white horse who comes in to save the world. We don't think that he will take much persuading. It will suit him.

144

Very ambitious man is our Daniel. Wouldn't you agree Johnny?"

"Maybe."

"We will want more than maybe Johnny. We will want him there on the appointed day. We will want him right in the middle of it. And we will want you to make sure that it happens. And when you do we will drop a hundred thousand quid into your account."

It was too much. What the hell was happening? Nearly midnight on Tuesday night and this abject weirdo was starting to talk telephone numbers. No way. It was sheer bloody madness. He couldn't keep the laugh back.

"Oh come on, what is this? This is all just a fucking wind-up."

"Actually it isn't. Strange as that may seem. There is no need to make your mind up tonight Johnny. In fact I would be both surprised and disappointed if you did. You think about it for a day or so. Look at it this way. You've done OK so far. We've had our chat and you've got five hundred quid. You gave me details on how to meet up with Tac Brennan and you have a further five grand. Even though you probably don't believe it right now you will find that the cheque book and card will both work for you in the morning. So there you are Johnny. 25-and-a-half thousand quid for a wind-up. Not bad. Not bad at all. So think about it. Not here though. It's a grim place in which to think. Try this."

Burton tossed over a hotel key and continued. "Try here. Nice suite. Champagne in a bucketful of ice. A bag of a certain white powder that you have a fondness for in the bathroom cabinet ... ."

"How the fuck . . ." Burton just carried on regardless of Johnny's attempted interruption.

" . . . and a friend Johnny. A good friend. A friend that you have been missing. She's waiting for you Johnny. The lovely Lena. She has heard that things have started to pick up for you Johnny. She has heard that the good times are about to roll again. And she has decided that she really wants you after all. And she's there Johnny. Waiting. Waiting just for you. Think about it Johnny."

Burton had got to his feet and was clearly ready to leave. Johnny made a half-hearted effort to form a sentence that would ask things like How did you know, but it died in his throat. What was the point? The water was up to his neck and he couldn't care less. Sure, it was all a fairytale but fairytales sometimes came true. Burton grinned at the look of utter wonder on his face.

"I'll ring you tomorrow Johnny. Give my regards to Lena. Have a good think. Don't wear yourself out lad."

And then he was gone.

As the enigmatic Mr Burton made his way out into the Glasgow night Daniel Morrissey MSP was trying to polish up the keynote speech that he would deliver to the Scottish Assembly the next day. He owed just about everything that he had to his ability to speak. He would never have guessed it as a boy on one of Parkhead's estates. Then he had always been one of the lads to be found on the edge of the crowd. He had always been accepted but had never been in the centre. He was a tag-along boy. Not bad at football. Hardish, but never a top dog. Fairly popular, but never one of the favourites. He was always rooted firmly in the middle ground at school. He got into trouble occasionally but it was never anything very serious. His work was always adequate. Had his mum and dad ever bothered to turn up at a parents evening they would have been told that Daniel was doing OK. Daniel could do a bit more, but all things considered . . .

Then one day he had been more or less frog-marched by his English master into taking part in a debating competition. And it had been like some kind of miracle had happened. After living out the whole of his short life on the edges, the very minute that he nervously got to his feet and started to talk he found that he was in the centre. Instead of stuttering his way through his prepared notes he found that he was throwing his voice around the room with the glee of a baseball pitcher. Within seconds he could sense the change in the small audience. They sat up a little straighter. They stopped checking their watches. He had started to ad lib and it worked. He made them laugh. He had them and he had no idea whatsoever how. He just knew that for a few brief moments they all belonged to him. He had found a way to the centre.

Once he had made his discovery his life became simple. He left school as soon as he could and an uncle got him a job on the railways. By the time he was twenty he had won himself a junior position in the union. At 22 he made his big breakthrough when he had stood up to make a speech at a conference that had the audience baying for more. Over the next few years he moved steadily up the ranks. Next it was the TUC National Conference and then the biggest of all at the Labour Party Conference in Brighton.

He was noticed. He was marked out. They bought him drinks. They patted him on the back. They told him that he was the kind of guy that they were always looking for. A young firebrand. Sure, a bit rough around the edges, but that would soon be sorted out. They could find a place for him. A chain-smoking activist from Putney called Linda told her friends that he was a bit of all right. She claimed him that evening and confirmed her opinions the next morning over breakfast. Daniel had been picking away at his cornflakes and wondering how it was that his life had started to move so fast when he was joined by two spic-and-span officials from the Scottish Labour Party. Cards were exchanged. Two years later he was elected to represent a constituency of Glasgow's South Side.

The Scottish Assembly was a culmination for Daniel. Soon he was more often the one who was pushed forward as the party's attack dog. He effortlessly took apart more senior men from the Conservatives and SNP alike. His wit was savage and the opposition feared to cross him. His South Side roots gave him a cutting credibility, which he exploited to the full.

Soon the perks of his new role started to pile up. There was a new flat in Morningside. There was a shiny Audi. There was a weekly newspaper column. Life just kept getting better. And then the big promotion had arrived as he entered the Cabinet as the Junior Minister for Justice. The Party were pretty cute with the appointment. They had chosen their man carefully. They sent Daniel out into the front line to speak about all the hard stuff. He was the spokesman for the Party's efforts to tackle a number of Scotland's more desperate problems – drugs, prostitution, child abuse. He was often back in the kind of places that he had come from. The audiences got tougher as he carried the message to meeting halls in the hard parts of hard towns all over Scotland. For a while he had favoured an image of Italian suits and expensive grooming. All of a sudden this didn't really fit any more. He made a radical change and started to favour the jeans and donkey jacket of his union days. He started to turn the angry audiences around. He proved to them that he was one of theirs. They believed in him.

His masters were alarmed at first. There were a few words spoken, but Daniel stuck to his guns. The donkey jacket brought back nightmare memories of Michael Foot and Derek Hatton. But the press lapped it up and his masters relaxed. There was talk of him being the politician that the people had been waiting for. At last here was a man who wasn't out of touch. And Daniel Morrissey became a pin-up boy of the New Left.

Then along came the greatest test in his young career when a man from Afghanistan sliced up three young Scottish boys on the sprawling Sighthill Estate and the fireworks started. There was never any doubt who would be sent in to fly the flag. Daniel had arrived in Sighthill the next day and had started the nightmare task of trying to put his government's toothpaste back in the tube. The world's press had wanted to know how any government could be so crazy as to put six thousand asylum seekers into such a small area. The police wanted an answer to exactly the same question. As did the groups who represented the local residents. As did the groups who represented the asylum seekers. Daniel found himself on a tightrope and the drop below was horrendous. For three weeks he had picked himself along and much to his own surprise he had somehow not fallen off.

The government message had been as predictable as it had been dreary. They had taken the short-term option of piling policemen into Sighthill to settle things down. Nothing had remotely settled down of course, but with so many coppers and journalists milling around everybody had their style cramped. Everyone realised that it wouldn't go on for ever. It was a quick fix designed to give the government some breathing space. After a week Daniel had returned to Edinburgh to make his report. The recommendations that he made to his bosses were simple. Get these people out of Sighthill as soon as humanly possible. Send them out to all four corners of Scotland. Break down the numbers and do it quickly. It was the only course of action that the locals would accept. Leave them there and the place would go up in flames.

They had told him no way. Not now. Not ever. Not in a month of Sundays. Not till hell froze over. Who would accept these people now, after what had happened? Nobody. Wherever they tried to send them there would be uproar. There would be local pressure groups sprouting up all over Scotland. It would be a nightmare in the planning applications. It would be a nightmare in the local press. It would be nightmare full stop. And it would mean lost votes all over the land. It wasn't an option and it never would be. They would have to stay exactly where they were and hopefully it would soon blow over. Better they lose votes in one part of Glasgow rather than the whole bloody country.

They told Daniel that they would commission an enquiry. They said that he could promise that it would all be done quickly. They said that he could promise that they would take heed of the findings and that they would act on them. They said that he could tell the Assembly that they were appalled at what had happened and that they would make sure it would never happen again. There would be more money spent. Lots more. There would be more training and better facilities. And Daniel knew that he had been given the shortest of short straws. They were asking him to sell beer at a tenner a pint. No matter how he tried to dress it up, everyone was going to hate it. And that meant that everyone was going to hate him, all because some maniac from Afghanistan had decided to completely lose the plot on a rainy night in Sighthill.

He was finding it hard to really focus on practising his speech. He had been striding around his flat practising earnest passion. He would make frequent stops at the mirror to check that his best grave look was working well enough. His audience was his researcher Roseanne who had been sitting on his leather couch smoking and sipping at a glass of wine until she had grabbed him as he passed, dropped his trousers and taken his dick in her mouth. This made the grave look even harder to find. For a moment or two he had played the role of the dedicated politician and tried to keep going. But William Gladstone would have been hard pressed to put political dedication ahead of the divine Roseanne. He tossed the speech to the floor and leapt on her.

Of all the perks that had come with his burgeoning political career, Roseanne Clement was by far the greatest. He had chosen her within ten seconds of her entering the interview room. The red hair, the lilting East Coast accent, the glinting green eyes and the well-cut suit were everything that the Parkhead boy craved. Her dad was a doctor and her mum was captain at their golf club. She was product of a posh school in Stirling and Edinburgh University. She had seduced him and claimed him as hers on her second day in the job. She was ferociously good at her job and he was putty in her skilled hands. Not that he cared. It was no kind of problem. He wasn't married and it was the twenty-first century. Were the tabloids ever to discover that he was fucking the living daylights out of his research assistant they would have undoubtedly granted him bucketsful of Brownie points. Soon it was Roseanne who did most of the speech-writing and as a pair they were formidable. She had an innate understanding of the words that would have the good and the great nodding their heads in approval and he knew how to play the people. Roseanne saw that there was no reason why he shouldn't make it all the way to the top and she claimed him as her own. Daniel Morrissey was more than happy to be claimed.

A while later they lay on the floor amidst a mess of clothes. His mind wandered back to his keynote speech.

"There is no winning this one. Every which way you look at it. It's just a complete bastard from top to bottom."

She nuzzled his ear. "But that is the very point my dear. Everybody knows that is exactly what it is. There is no grey area here. Every person in the chamber tomorrow will share exactly the same thought. Thank fuck it's him not me. Nobody is expecting a miracle. There isn't one. They know that you're fucked. They will be looking forward to it. Gagging for it. And so the issue isn't solving the problem. The issue is looking good. Stand tall and take it on the chin. Look fabulous in defeat. Shine with defiant pride. You need to be General Custer out there. Who gives a shit if it is all bullshit. Just make sure you look the part when you tell it. That is all that they will be looking for. The mark of a truly great politician is the man who can look and sound sensational whilst peddling a ton of shit."

Daniel adopted a rather miserable expression. "The people won't see it that way. They will be really pissed-off. When kids get their throats cut they expect a bit of action."

"Oh bollocks Daniel. The people will forget the story the minute they turn the page to have a look at the tits of the day. Don't go all Glasgow man of the people on me. The people can do nothing for you. Your career is made by the old bastards in that chamber tomorrow, not the bloody people. Fuck the people. The people are wankers."

This brought a laugh. "What a charmingly liberal view of the world you have."

She was mildly angry. "Anyway, tell me what it is that your wonderful caring people of Glasgow actually want. You've had to listen to enough of their whining drivel over the last week."

"Oh that's easy. They want the asylum seekers stuck on a fleet of jumbos and flown away. It doesn't matter where. Just anywhere but Sighthill. I would say that goes for about 98 percent of them."

She grinned. "So they are almost as liberal as me then."

"Oh aye. If Heinrich Himmler stood to represent Sighthill on the council next week he'd win by a landslide."

They were quiet for a while. Roseanne got up and went through to the gleaming chrome kitchen whilst Daniel watched her with a lazy grin and devoured every inch of her nakedness and wished he had a camera. When she returned he reached for her but she gently pushed him away.

"No. Not for a sec. You've not asked me about all this yet, which is fucking stupid to be frank. You've not asked me because all of this stuff has gone down in your old stamping-ground which means that you think that you know best. The problem is that you don't. You are looking at this thing through the eyes of a Glasgow boy. You are thinking that it might have been you or one of your cousins or one of your mates who had their throats cut. Well that's no good. You're about to fall off the fence on the wrong side."

This brought a frown to Daniel. He never much liked being contradicted. "Why?"

She noted the frown and stepped carefully. "Look. I'm not saying that you aren't playing well in the pubs and launderettes of Glasgow. Of course you are. You always do. They love you. But you are forgetting about the bigger picture. The issue of asylum seekers is not up for debate. The government is locked into it by all kind of statutes and treaties at the UN and EC. It has quota to fill and obligations. Simple as that. And at the moment the only place to put these people is Sighthill. Now try taking a look at the top brass in the party. Not just here. London as well. Where do these people come from? What were they doing 25 years ago? They were marching to free Mandela. They were marching to ban the bomb. They were marching against racism. It is inside them. All of them. So whose side are they all on in their heart of hearts? The asylum seekers of course. The underdogs. The victims of torture and repression. Can't you see it Daniel? The party has always been embarrassed by the uncouth side of the working class. The leaders are about the *Guardian* and a new play at the Royal Court whilst the voters like pie and chips, hate Pakis and watch strippers and football. The voters are Nazis waiting to happen, who vote Labour because their dad and granddad did. See it?"

"Maybe."

"Well you need to. You need to get yourself out there and bat for the asylum seekers. Speak up for the oppressed. Tell of the miseries that they have suffered. Remind everyone that they are people too. Adopt a world vision. Cry if you can manage it. Look at the tradition. Barbara Castle. Wedgy Benn. Kinnock. Even Tony Blair before he became a twat. It goes down the ages. It goes to the heart of the party and all it likes to pretend it stands for. See it Daniel. Sure, it might piss-off a few idiots in their high-rise flats in Glasgow but the party will love you for it. They will envy you. They will treasure you. You can be their misty-eyed memory of a time when things were clearer. You need to trust me on this Daniel."

"I am one of those idiots from high-rise flats in Glasgow."

"Want to go back? Fine. Go back. Go and be a fucking councillor if you like. But don't waste my time."

"Christ you turn me on when you get pissed off."

"Going to listen?"

"Don't I always?"

"Come here then."

The electricity within the chamber was slowly growing. There were no empty seats. It was something that they had all been looking forward to. The Government had been panned from all quarters following the Sighthill Riots. The press had been merciless. The polls had made grim reading. The opposition parties had been having the time of their lives. And now the day of reckoning had arrived. It was time for the rising new star to take the stage and try to stick Band-aids over the gaping, festering wound. Today Daniel was middle of the road in his attire. He wore green corduroy trousers and a well-worn tweed jacket. No tie. He started in a suitably sombre manner. There was little flourish. Just facts. Just a summary of the nightmare that everyone in the chamber was intimately familiar with. Almost pathetic. Then he started listing his government's response. Nobody could quite believe it. He was being boring. He commended the police for calming the situation. He praised community leaders for their efforts. He paused for a moment like a man with a pain in his back. Then he passed on the Government's commitment to a full and frank enquiry.

For a moment there was a stunned silence. Was this it? Was this the best that the supposedly great Daniel Morrissey could come up with? Awful. Pathetic. And there was an uproar of abuse from the opposition.

For a moment Daniel surveyed his attackers looking for all the world like a rabbit in the headlights facing imminent demise. Then he burst into action. He hurled his papers to the floor and started to shout

"Listen to you. Go on. Shut up for a moment and just listen. You're all like a bunch of kids. This isn't a game you know. Are you capable of understanding that? Where have you been for the last week? Come on. Anyone volunteering? No. Of course not. You've been here. You've been in Edinburgh giving nice cosy interviews in nice cosy studios. What a treat. Well I haven't been here. I've been in Sighthill. And I've been talking to people. I've been talking to my own people. In case any of you don't know, this is where I come from. That's me. A Glasgow boy. So when they tell me how they feel when three young Glasgow boys are slashed to pieces I know just how they feel. But it is not just my own people that I have been talking to. I've also been talking to the other people who are involved in all this. The asylum seekers. You lot might be having lots of fun with your schoolyard games here but I would like to remind you that three people were burnt to death last week. A mum and two kids. Burnt to death in my city. In our country. In 2003. Has any one of you even stopped for a moment to imagine the unimaginable pain that those people went through in the last seconds of their life? Well have you? Why not take a few seconds? Why not try to imagine how it must have felt when the flames climbed all over their bodies? Try it. I challenge you. All of you."

The chamber was very quiet now. Daniel had them. Absolutely had them. The sweat was pouring from him but he didn't care. There was a gleam of exhilaration in his eyes that looked for all the world like burning passion. There was some nervous shuffling. Every face was rapt. Where the hell was Morrissey going to take this? Only minutes before they had believed that he had been found out. No way. He had reeled them in. He had given them false signs of failure. And he had slammed them to the floor. He allowed the silence to hang as he allowed his fierce eyes to slowly roam the seats of the chamber. At last he spoke. His voice steadier now.

"Better. A bit of respect at last. I would like to take a moment or two to talk about asylum seekers. They are becoming a dirty word aren't they? Bad people. Nasty people. Smelly people. Madmen. Zealots. How do we know this? Because the papers tell us. The tabloids have decided that we should make them bogeymen. And so when a man from Afghanistan goes stark, staring berserk we all take the opportunity to brand every single asylum seeker in our country as responsible in some way. Have any of you taken the trouble to consider who these people are? Where they come from? Why they are here? Have any of you, God forbid, taken the time to actually talk to any of them? Well maybe it is time that I reminded you. These people come from places where nightmares are the reality. They come from rape and torture and murder and hunger. They come from places where life is of no more value than a packet of crisps. They come from the places that we only read about. They come from horror that we dare not even think about. They have lost their mums and dads and brothers and sisters and daughters and sons and wives and husbands and lovers. They come from pain and terror. They come here. Why?"

Again he paused and allowed the silence to eat away at the ranks of MSPs.

"I'll tell you why. They come because they have been told that Scotland is a safe place. A place of truth and justice where people do not disappear in the night to torture rooms or summary execution. They become because they see our country as a sanctuary from the horror that they have known. They come because from the time when they were young they have been brought up on stories about how our country is a cradle of freedom and compassion where people can feel safe. Safe. Try to understand how beautiful that word can be to a person that has known only fear and danger. And let's face it, we are all very good at bleating on about the beauty of our old democracy. Well we are, aren't we? We love it. We go on and on and on about freedom of speech and truth and justice and doing the decent thing.

And believe it or not people actually listen to us. And they believe us. And that is why they come to us in their darkest hour."

Daniel paused and wiped the sweat that was pouring down his cheeks. He was almost conversational now. The atmosphere was easing.

"So. What are we doing here? The papers are basically inciting our people. Let's not be too polite about it. That is what is happening here. And what do we do? We play our silly little games and score points off each other. So what do I have to say? A simple message. Forget the reports and commissions of enquiry and careful talk. I say to you this. It isn't good enough. Again. It isn't good enough. IT ISN'T GOOD ENOUGH!

These people have come to our country to feel safe. Sanctuary from fear. It is a tradition of these Islands that goes all the way back to King Alfred. It is a tradition that every single one of us should be proud of. I don't care if a few voters might not like this tradition. It is something that makes me proud. And it is something that should make every single one of you proud. All of you. Proud of the long and decent history that we all share. So what does it mean? Well the press might have decided to throw all decency out of the window and sell their papers on the back of prejudice and hate. That is their decision and they should be ashamed. It is not a way that is open to those of us who sit in this chamber. We have a responsibility to every tortured soul who comes to our country to escape the nightmares they suffered. If we haven't the decency and the guts to stand up for these people, then who can they turn to? I will never accept that guests in my country can be burned alive. Not again. Not if I can help it. And I expect every single one of you to support me. This is an issue that goes way beyond party bickering and point scoring. This is a very old-fashioned issue. This is an issue of conscience."

There were those who felt that the prolonged applause and cheering that was awarded to Daniel Morrissey was the greatest that had been seen in the short life of the Scottish Assembly. He was no longer a rising star. He was a star that had risen. And that night the risen star screwed his research assistant with a vigour that she had never imagined that he possessed.

Two thousand miles to the east two new recruits sat across the desk from Mordechai Breslow in Tel Aviv. They were both young, the older of the two was just 24. They were new graduates. Fresh from fabulous grades at university and into the security business. It was their first experience of working for the legend that was Breslow. They had burned the candles endlessly for three days to compile the report that he was now reading. The occasional twitch on his ugly face betrayed his ill temper. The minute he completed speed reading the final page of the report he threw it across the desk. It hit the young woman of the two-person team on the bridge of her nose leaving her with a look of hurt bewilderment.

"Shit. Worse than that. Fucking shit. Total, utter, useless absolute fucking shit. I ask for good people and they give me morons wet behind the fucking ears. What is this? Go on. Speak if you can. What?"

The young man took on the responsibility of speaking for the team. It seemed like the chivalrous thing to do.

"With respect sir, you asked us to go over all the information that we had on Khalil Bishawa. It is what we have done. Every report. Every one. I can assure you."

Breslow slammed his hand down on the desk. "Why the fuck would I want that? I know what was in those reports. I was here when those reports were written. I helped to write those reports when you two were shitting your diapers."

By now the young man was beginning to wish that he had chosen a career in the army. He gritted his teeth.

"It appears that we have not understood our task fully sir. Maybe you could clarify the precise nature of what it is that you want."

Not bad, thought Breslow. Quite a cool one. Not a flicker of temper but not backing-down either. He lit-up and calmed down.

"OK. We'll start again. Every single piece of information that we have ever received confirms that Khalil Bishawa disappeared into Tadmur Military Prison in 1983. We know he was subjected to intense and prolonged interrogation. Then nothing. Nothing for twenty years. Conclusion. He's a dead man. Obvious. Matter closed. Case closed. Everything closed. Then his brother looks me in the eye and says that Khalil will come to get him out. Bullshit? Maybe, but I don't think so. Mahmoud isn't that pathetic. Think about it. How pathetic is it to threaten me with a big brother who is twenty years dead? I don't believe it. Just watch the bastard in his cell. This is no pathetic broken man. He has lost most of his leg and he faces the death sentence and yet he is still proud. There is something here. I know it. I can feel it. That is what I want. No matter what it takes, that is what I want. Is that clear enough? Find it. Do what it takes and find it."

A sense of relief filled the new people. It had seemed for a moment as if their careers had been over before they had begun. Once again the young man was the one to speak.

"I think that we will need some guidance here. How would you like us to go about this task? It is clear that the answer can only lie in Damascus. How do we go about finding it?"

Breslow grinned at their naivety. "Money of course. Always money. Go to the Syrian section. I will call them. They have people. Get them to find people who were working in Tadmur in 1983. And pay them. Pay them whatever it takes. If Bishawa got clear of that place then there must have been money. Someone must have taken a pay-off. They always do. Pay what it takes. Bring me the truth. Bring it fast."

Khalil had cancelled his flight. The revised plan meant another destination. It meant another day to kill in Moscow. Sergei had promised to ring him at his hotel in the evening. When he had been with his old mentor he had been able to keep his emotions under control. It had been hard, much harder that he would have anticipated. But he had managed it. He had noticed the glance from Sergei of course. He had seen that his friend had guessed at the pain that the name must have brought.

Fatima.

Just a word. Nothing more. A popular girl's name chosen by millions of Arab families. Fatima. Just seven letters that started with F and ended in A. And yet it was a collection of letters that could still hit him harder than a sledgehammer. As he wandered the once familiar grey streets he realised that it was more than just mere mention of her name. It was the city itself. It was the Moscow that was dragging the memories out of all the places where he had buried them for so many years. And it hurt. It hurt like the worst kind of terminal illness.

It had been three months after his fateful first appointment with Sergei that he had first seen her. It had been from a distance across the cheap tables of the canteen at the university. To start with it had been no more than a glimpse. An impression. Raven-black hair. Animated hand-gestures. Lips that always seemed to carry a smile. Eyes that reminded him of the sun and clean air of his home. She was holding court to a small group of Arab men who hung on her every word. There would have been many at home who would have been livid at the way she was dressed. She was casual and easy in a green army jacket and baggy pants. Her hair was loose and wild. They would have said that she was a disgrace. That she had no respect. That her family should be ashamed. But Khalil was fascinated at first sight.

It took him days to summon the courage to ask Sergei about her. When he did his new friend beamed at his painful embarrassment.

"Ah, the fair Fatima. She is of your own people Khalil. A rich family. Very rich I gather. Once they owned land all along the coast north of Tel Aviv. Then it all went in 1948. They escaped to Cairo and went into business, very successfully from what I can gather. She had two older brothers. One died in 1956 and the other in 1967. She wants to be a doctor. I don't think that her family approves but she seems to be able to twist her father around her little finger. Well I don't suppose that is all that surprising. She's all he has left. So. As you can see. Daddy has stumped up and here she is. She's nothing to do with our side of things. She's a Med student. Rather a fine one from what I can gather."

The weeks had passed and Khalil's courage had shown no signs of improving. All the time he watched her from afar. He tried always to co-ordinate his visits to the canteen with the times when she would be there. He caught glimpses of her rushing across the snowy courtyards to her lectures. And every night he would lie awake trying to find the courage to speak to her. And every morning the courage would remain elusive.

It had been Fatima who had bridged the gap. One morning whilst he was picking at the miserable stodge that was the university's excuse for breakfast she had come to the table where he sat alone.

"May I sit here?"

He had almost choked on the dry piece of bread. "Yes. Yes of course."

She hit him with a smile that nearly put him onto the floor. Then she held out an elegant hand across the table. "I'm Fatima."

A JOURNEY TO THE WEST

He took it and felt a shudder run through him. "Khalil. I am Khalil."

"Oh I know that much. Khalil Bishawa. Man of mystery. An apprentice to the supposedly great and dashing Major Mickhailovich, another man of mystery. I ask everyone and nobody knows you Khalil. They all say that you are quite brilliant. They say that you were the top of all your classes until the Major whisked you away. They say that you have been ear-marked. For what ask I? Who knows they reply. And day after day I see you sitting alone in here carrying your sadness like a heavy cloak. And sometimes I feel your eyes on me but when I look up you look away. Well I am an inquisitive woman Khalil. I always have been. So I think it is time to ask. Who are you Khalil?"

He wanted the ground to open up and swallow him. His life had been about books and guns and bombs and death. There had been no time for girls. Certainly no time for a girl like this one. She was killing him with the sparkle in her eyes and the slightly mocking smile that hung on her lips. He felt as helpless and as trapped as he had done all those years ago in the trench on Ammunition Hill.

"Who am I? A big question for so early in the day. I am no more than me. I am none of these things that they say."

"And are you so alone?"

" No. There is my brother Mahmoud. There is my Uncle Salim. Other than that, yes, I suppose I am alone. Here I am alone."

"You have no other family?"

"No. They killed them all. The Jews. In 1948 and then at Kibya in 1953. There are only the three of us now."

The sparkle was gone now. "They took my brothers. One was a pilot. The other was in tanks. Both gone now."

"I know." She raised her eyebrow, amused again.

"So. It would seem that I have not been the only one to make enquiries."

For the first time he smiled, found out. "No. I too have been asking. Our families must have once lived quite close. Our village was a little further north. We had nothing like your family of course, but we grew oranges too."

After that morning they became inseparable. For two years they found their own paradise in the cold grey city. Khalil had learned the art of killing and maiming whilst Fatima had learnt how to heal and save. The opposite directions that their lives were bound to take did not matter. They shared the dreams of their people. One day they would grow their oranges again. There had been many times when Khalil had wondered at the idea of love at first sight. It would never have been a thing that he would have ever given a second thought to. His had always been a cold mind. It had always been the disciplines of logic and science that he had been drawn to. He would have instinctively rubbished such fanciful notions. And yet from the moment that she had sat down on the cheap Soviet plastic chair, from the moment that she had taken his hand, from the moment she had spoken . . . The wonder of it never left him. And now as he wandered aimlessly around the same streets where they had once walked hand in hand and huddled close he found the memories flooding back. He hadn't realised just how far he had buried them. He had buried so much. How strange that it was all coming creeping out now. He hadn't felt the pain of the Kibya massacre for years until he had returned to the hill to meet his uncle. Now he realised that he had also hidden the memories of Fatima far from the light.

Life was a strange thing. There were millions of people all over the world who had the chance to quietly live out their lives. Nothing much ever happened to them. Their days were filled with basic problems. A school for a child. A leak in a roof. A problem with the crop in one of the fields. Small hurdles to overcome. There were millions who were angry that their lives were so mundane. They craved excitement. They wanted to see how it was to stand on the edge. Not so Khalil he thought. Khalil who has known nothing but the edge for all his life. Khalil who had watched so many fall off it. Khalil who could only make his life bearable by burying away the memories of all those that he had loved.

The emotions that were suddenly all over him forced him to sit. Once again his eyes had misted over with tears. He was in the huge square of the Kremlin. All about him there were fresh-faced tourists taking pictures of each other. Young Russian couples laughed with each other. Children ate their ice cream. All around him was the joy of life on a sunny spring day in a city that was glad to say good riddance to yet another endless winter. He realised that for years he had done more than live out an excuse of a life. He had been comfortable. He had worn nice clothes and lived in his luxurious flat.

He had read his books and made money for Farouk's family. He had stepped away from the fire. He had found some kind of comfort in cold, ordinariness. All he had done was exist and he had turned his back on pain and love and grief and pain. He had taken all that he could. His soul had cried enough. He had been in hiding.

Now in the city where he had once known true happiness it was all coming back. The walls that he had surrounded himself with were collapsing and there was nothing that he could do to stop it. He wiped angrily at the tears that he could not stop. He fought to control the sobs that were climbing up from his chest. Damn Sergei. Why had he had to say her name? Why hadn't he just left the memories where they lay? Why did he have to bring it all flooding back? Fatima and Palestinia and Declan. Names from a different life. A different era. The dark time.

Sidon, Lebanon 1982

Declan Connelly was in pain. He couldn't quite believe just how much pain. Every inch of the outside of his body felt as if it had been rubbed raw with sandpaper. The muscles on the inside of his body felt as if they had been beaten with metal rods. The sweat was cascading down into his eyes. He would have never believed that it was possible to quite so hot. His foot caught an exposed root and he tripped. He hit the hard dusty track hard and managed to roll. The momentum of the roll was enough for him to scramble straight back to his feet.

He took a second to wipe the sweat from his eyes with his forearm and to glance back up the track which wound down the rocky hillside. They were only 40 yards behind him now and coming on fast. He had left them far behind on the way up. He had forced himself forward up the steep track scrambling up and over the rocks like a determined terrier. The pack on his back was filled with 100 pounds of sand and every step had seemed to make it weigh 20 pounds more. The hill was just over a 500 feet high. There had been many hills that were far taller that had surrounded his hometown of Derry. As a boy his dad had taken him out most weekends for bird-watching. The long tramps across the moors in sun, wind and rain had instilled a natural stamina into Declan, which he had never lost. Now was the time to draw on every last drop.

RED ZONE

Twenty recruits had started their run in the heat of the summer's afternoon. Declan had been the first to the top by well over 100 yards. He had paused for a moment to see who was closest. The other runners were strung out for 500 yards. The way that some of them were floundering he wondered if they would make it to the top at all. Their problem. Not his. It came as no surprise to see that the three bearded Iranians were the closest to him. Nothing new in that. The bastards had dogged him from the moment that he had arrived at the camp. They were moving up the hill mechanically. Sticking together just like they always did. Moving like machines. Bastards.

They were coming on faster on the way down. He had glanced back on three occasions and each time he saw that the gap was smaller. Going down with the big heavy pack and legs that were ruined was a nightmare. He felt as if his knees were about to pop clean out of their sockets every time he landed a step. The Iranians didn't seem to care. They were simply running headlong down the steep slope and falling and rolling constantly. The pain didn't seem to matter to them. Nothing seemed to matter to them. Bastards.

Once the sweat was out of his eyes he could more easily gauge the distance that was left. Not far now. 500 yards. Maybe 600. Come on Declan you soft piece of shite. Make it. Jack the pain. Don't let those bearded bastards have the pleasure. He forced himself forward.

After 300 yards the track flattened out. It was just a small distance through the olive trees now. He was running like a drunk. The easy, fleet-footed steps of the beginning of the race were nowhere to be seen. Now he was lurching from pace to pace like a man running through marshmallow mix. And all the time he could hear the thumping footsteps of his pursuers. Come on Declan. Hang on. Just 50 yards now. He could see the tall, stately figure up ahead. Waiting with a look of mild amusement on his face. He forced himself not to look round. Jesus they were close now. He could hear their rasping angry breathing. They were bound to get past him. There was nothing left in his legs. Nothing. Not even a memory of anything. Only stubbornness. Only sheer Irish bloody-mindedness. Fuck the bastards. Fuck them all. And he was there. Crashing to the floor in a heap a mere couple of yards ahead of the Iranians. And he started laughing hysterically as they stood over him with hate and contempt written across their hard faces.

It was hard to find the breath to speak. It was hard to stop the manic laughter that had taken a hold of him. He figured that he must have looked pretty comical, as he lay sprawled in the dust. At last he managed to put a sentence together.

"Guys. Nice to see you made it. Just a bit late I'm afraid. Like usual. Nice try though. I'll give you that. Give you ten for effort. But you've not got it yet have you? You lads will never beat an Irishman. No way. Nobody beats the Irish . . ."

A wave of coughing and laughter took hold of him and he fell back onto his back taking in air in huge gulps. The biggest of the three Iranians stepped forward with anger etched across his face. The other two followed suit.

Khalil spoke with quiet authority. "OK. Enough. Go to the showers. We start our next class in twenty minutes. Leave this."

They hesitated for a brief moment. They met Khalil's eyes and found only calmness. The moment passed and they moved away towards their tents.

Declan grinned and held out a hand. Khalil took it and hauled him to his feet.

"It is foolish, Declan, what you do. I cannot watch all the time. They will hurt you. They are men who enjoy inflicting pain. You should be more careful"

Declan grinned. "You know, Khalil, all my life people have been telling me to be more careful. My ma, my da, teachers, priests, coppers, everyone . . ." He took in the expanse of the dusty camp with a generous sweep of his arm. " . . . do you seriously think I would be where I am today if I had taken the advice. God forbid I might have been married with a couple of kids and a nice house and a job with the post office and my Sunday dinner waiting on the table. Instead? Instead I'm here at the Khalil Bishawa university for Freedom Fighters with scenic jogging and tender loving care from bearded nutters care of the Ayatollah. Now what incentive is that for a boy from Derry to be careful?"

Khalil shook his head. The red-haired man from Ireland never ceased to amaze him. It didn't matter how hard things got, there was always a mischievous smile glued to his impish face. Not for the first time as he watched him hobble towards the tents he felt a mixture of amusement and downright amazement. The pack full of sand must have weighed more than half Declan's body weight and yet he had managed to leave the rest of the runners straggled out behind him. The sun had burnt his white skin raw and the straps of the pack must have given him the very purest of pain and yet the smile was still firmly in place.

It was the first time that he had worked with one of the Irish fighters. In fact it was the first time that he had ever met an Irishman at all. There had certainly been none to be found at Patrice Lumumba University. It was unusual for the fighters of the IRA to come to the Palestinians for training. If they went anywhere it was generally to the camps in Libya. Khalil was more than familiar with their cause. He had spent many hours studying the ways and means that they had used to fight their war for so many years. They were without doubt a perfect role model for his own people. Their effectiveness was outstanding. At any given time their army was made up of little more than 300 volunteer fighters representing a community of just over half a million. Ranged against them were the might of 50 million Britons and their army of over a third of a million. For over ten years the British had been forced to station over 20,000 troops in the tiny corner of Ireland where the IRA fought their war and still they were no nearer to victory. There was no escaping the fact that his people faced much easier odds in their own war and yet they were not nearly as effective. They had much to learn from the Irish, and the sooner their leaders accepted the fact the better.

It had been Sergei who had sent Declan Connolly to the training camp in Sidon where Khalil had been in command for two years. The PLO leadership had brought the shutters down on the European bombing campaign in early 1979. Khalil and Mahmoud had become too well known to the security forces. It was getting almost impossible to move. Khalil had been ordered back to Lebanon to take on a training role whilst Mahmoud led small raids across the border into Galilee. Khalil had been delighted. He had requested that he should work at the camp at Sidon so that he could live with Fatima who now worked in the small hospital that fought to keep up with the needs of the huge population of Palestinian refugees. They had married in 1978 having at last overcome the strenuous objections of her family. Her father had lined up an impressive queue of fine upstanding Cairo businessmen who would have given his treasured daughter the life that he yearned for her to lead. A well-paid post at a fine hospital also awaited. Her life was planned and unlike his boys he vowed that her life would be happy and safe. Her choice to marry Khalil and work under the threat of the ever-present Israeli jets nearly broke the old man's heart, but in the end he had given in.

Their daughter Palestinia had been born in 1980 and was soon the centre of Khalil's world. Married life and fatherhood softened him. Even Mahmoud was often to be found spending hours on end on the balcony of their flat coo-cooing to the newly arrived infant. To start with Khalil had numerous run-ins with the East Germans who oversaw much of the training regime in the camps all over Lebanon. They had complained that Khalil's regime lacked proper discipline. They said that he was lax. They said that volunteers needed to be broken before they could be made into effective fighters. Khalil saw the war through different eyes. Volunteers deserved respect. He had learned first hand on the slopes of Ammunition Hill that men never fought well because of fear. They needed pride and comradeship and absolute belief. The Israelis who had come at them had not been broken. They fought for their families and their people. The officers fought for their men, and the men would have followed their officers through the gates into hell. These were the kind of fighters that Khalil knew that his people would need. In the end Sergei had intervened and the East Germans had disappeared in a Teutonic sulk.

Sergei had arrived one afternoon with a file. He had asked that Khalil find a place for a man from Ireland. He said that the man needed some time and some space to refocus. He said that he was too good a man to be lost. He said that he had suffered a bad time and that his soul was damaged. Khalil had tried to get more details but Sergei had merely shrugged and told him to read the file.

Declan Connolly had been born in Londonderry in 1955. His father was a postman and his mother worked in a small shoe factory. He was the youngest of three brothers and was raised on the Catholic Creggan estate that overlooked the town by the sea. By the time Declan entered secondary school the town had become the centre of the growing tension that was sweeping across the north of Ireland. The minority Catholic population was becoming increasingly militant in its demands for proper equality. Nowhere was the inequality of the small Province more evident than in Londonderry where a two-thirds Catholic majority never were able to elect more than ten percent of the town's councillors due to careful rigging of the electoral boundaries. By the time he was fourteen the whole thing had exploded onto the world's television screens. It seemed like the whole of the Creggan estate and the neighbouring Bogside joined in a three-day pitched battle that eventually set the whole of the Province alight.

Declan's father would have none of it. Theirs was a respectable family and always would be. He had grounded his three sons and there was no negotiation. Throwing stones at policemen was not part of the plan that he had for his boys. Declan's older brothers were incensed and tensions grew daily in the house when night after night they would escape down the drainpipe to join in the battles with the British soldiers who now held the line. Declan was never much interested in any of it. He had always been the one who was closest to the father. He preferred to escape at weekends to the countryside with his dad for long walks where they watched birds.

He was viewed as something of an oddball at school. His prodigious abilities and enthusiasm for maths and science would normally have had him marked down as a swot and guaranteed that he was subjected to endless bullying in the playground. Similarly his love of bird-watching and disinterest in throwing stones and petrol bombs were hardly designed to endear him to his classmates. However Declan had always been able to make people laugh. He did it to everyone that he met; fellow pupils, teachers, the local priest, local shopkeepers. They forgave him everything for his sense of humour. He was allowed to grow up in his own little world whilst all around him was consumed by the hate and killing of the Troubles.

Everything changed during the course of two months at the beginning of 1974. Unbeknown to Declan his two brothers had volunteered to fight for the IRA in the wake of the Bloody Sunday massacre in January 1972. An informer had alerted the security services that they were to be part of an operation staged by the North Derry Brigade to stage an armed robbery on a post office across the border in Donegal. The army had known about the arms cache in the hills for several weeks and they had mounted a surveillance operation. Nobody ever really knew exactly what happened on the evening when the two brothers went to pick up the guns that would be needed for the armed raid. The bare facts were that there were six soldiers involved in an ambush, which resulted in two IRA corpses with a total of 21 holes in them. The Army swore blind that the lads had opened fire first. The Republicans pointed out that most of the holes were in the lads' backs and that six against two were pretty rotten odds. As a follow-up to the execution of the two older sons of the family, the Army undertook a mob-handed raid on the Connelly household. At the point that the front door flew off its hinges the family were unaware that they were now a family of three instead of five. As far as Declan's father was concerned the presence of soldiers from Yorkshire in his living room was a disgrace and an outrage and he let the squaddies know as much in no uncertain fashion. When one of them up-ended a table that held his collection of RSPB replica British birds and sent them crashing to their doom on the stone hearth he lost his cool altogether. He dragged the young soldier away from his treasured collection and received a blow from the butt of an SLR to the side of his head.

Maybe in a way he was lucky. He never made it out of the coma that he descended into. And therefore he never had to deal with the crushing news that his two eldest boys had been executed. The specialist at the hospital said it was because he had an unusually thin skull, almost like that of a bird. He said that 99 out of 100 could have stood the blow with nothing worse than a thumping headache. Declan's dad was just unlucky. The Army saw no need to apologise. After all here was a man who had sired two volunteers of the Provisional Irish Republican Army. What the hell did he expect?

Declan fell into a twilight world. For a while the residents of the Creggan Estate had to do without his cheeky smile and his seemingly endless supply of jokes. He vanished for days at a time to find solace amongst the grey rainy hills where he and his father had shared so much of his young life. He had won a scholarship to study Maths at Bristol University but he never took it up. Like so many of his school friends he signed-on and eked out a living care of the State that had killed his father and his brothers.

There was complete confusion among the ranks of the North Derry Brigade when a Land Rover carrying an officer and two squaddies was blown to pieces one evening in May. Everyone was delighted of course but they hadn't the first clue who had actually done it. The IRA was nothing if not pragmatic and claimed responsibility anyway. Why the hell not? It was almost a case of finders-keepers.

A month later Declan walked into a pub in the Bogside and asked to be taken to see the local commander. He explained that the bomb had been down to him. He told them that it hadn't been all that difficult. It was no big deal for anyone who had a decent grasp of physics and chemistry. He wondered whether they might have any use for his services. No one could ever accuse the North Derry Brigade of dithering over their decision. Within 48 hours he was sworn-in and part of the team.

Over the next five years he became one of the legends. He was the man who made bombs that worked. There were those who at times found him to be over choosy. No matter what, he always refused to be involved in any operations against sectarian or civilian targets. He had no axe to grind with civilians. His war was a simple one. He merely wanted to make the British Army pay as heavy a price as possible for what they had done. He was more than happy to leave the politics to others. He wasn't a political sort of guy. He considered himself to be a straightforward scientist who preferred to keep things simple and logical. The British Army had murdered his dad and brothers. He would make them pay. Simple. No need for politics and fancy theories. Others could worry about that.

After two years his services were being used by Brigades all over the Province. In 1978 he successfully produced a bomb that killed two soldiers on sentry duty at a base on the outskirts of a small town in the Rhineland. And then in 1980 it all went spectacularly wrong. He was working with the South Armagh Brigade on a small country road a few miles out of Newtonhamilton. A local farmer had reported that an army Land Rover had taken to using the road every other day or so. It was unusual. Careless. Idiotic. But that wasn't Declan's problem, it was a problem for the soldiers who were ignoring procedure and taking the quickest route back to the bar at the base. In the end he had waited on a cold hillside with two local volunteers for three days until the Land Rover came into view. At this point everything was down to the pressure of the wheels and the weight of the vehicle. He instinctively braced himself as the Land Rover covered the last few yards to the bridge. Four . . . three . . . two . . . one . . .

Nothing happened. The Land Rover bounced over the bridge and made its way up and out of the valley. Declan stared down in complete disbelief. For a moment he was utterly dumbfounded. Such a thing had never happened before. He had never even considered it. What on earth had gone wrong? He was trying to rerun the assembly of the detonator in his mind when one of his colleagues spoke in a harsh whisper.

"Come on sunshine. No point in moping. It's a fuck-up. Time to go."

And then there was the sound of another engine floating up the valley on the breeze. Declan looked up and his heart turned to ice. The school bus. The afternoon run. Yellow and going along steady and slow. Just 400 yards to go. Oh Jesus. Sweet Jesus. Please Jesus. Please make the detonator completely faulty. Please make it a bad wire. Please don't let it be a mistake with the weight calculations. The man was pulling hard at him now.

" . . . come on. We're out of here. Move!!"

He couldn't. He was frozen. He was stone. Just 100 yards now. No time. No wire to cut. No warning to give. Just desperate hope. Just 50 yards now. Just 24 . . . three . . . two . . . one . . .

Boom.

He had not stinted on the explosive. The bus was lifted clean off the bridge. It twisted gently in the air before crashing down into the stream below and landing on its roof. The horror was absolute. Complete. Beyond all comprehension. He was being dragged now like a disobedient dog. Somewhere angry savage words were pouring into his ears. There were blows but he barely felt them. Halfway up the hill his legs started to work like they belonged to someone else. The walk to the car was a dream. A nightmare. The nightmare of all nightmares. A drive. Just numbness. The small farmyard. Just numbness. The chipped Formica kitchen table and shouting from all corners of the dark little room. Just numbness. His brain was a sponge. His body was suet. His eyes were raw with tears. Voices were fighting to get to him but there was a wall of cotton wool.

Much later he had come back. The horror only grew until it filled him like a great cancerous growth. He blinked away tears and looked across the table to the scowling face of the local Brigade commander. No sympathy there. Not a shred. Just boiling rage at an atrocity that would never be forgiven. There had been seven children on the bus.

Just primary kids. The youngest had been six, the oldest ten. All of them were Catholic. The driver was Catholic. They were all from their own community. It had been a catastrophe almost beyond any of their comprehension. All because of this ginger-topped twat from Derry.

"I need to give myself up. I need to do it now." Declan's voice was flat, drained of everything.

The Brigade commander moved with a speed which belied the middle-aged spread of his belly. He hit Declan with a strength that had slowly grown over 25 years of laying bricks. The younger man flew backwards over the back of the chair and cracked his head on the concrete floor. Before he had a chance to get to his feet he was pinned down with angry raging words and spittle raining down on him.

"What the fuck do you think this is you wee piece of skinny shite? Thinks it's the fucking boy scouts? This is the IRA. You are a soldier. You've just fucked the whole thing up more in one day than the fucking Brits have managed in three years and you want to give yourself up like some twat of a choirboy. You stupid, stupid, stupid little fucker . . ."

Each "stupid" was backed up by a heavy punch to the face. The last blow put Declan's lights out. When he awoke he was gagged and bound in a world of darkness. It took him a while to realise that he was in the boot of a car. He managed to force down the panic that gripped him. Maybe this was it. As the big man had said, it wasn't the fucking Boy Scouts. The infamous "Nutting Squad" usually only put a bullet in the back of the heads of informers. Maybe blowing up a bus full of school kids rated as bad. Maybe he deserved it. Maybe it would be for the best. As the car sped along he allowed a resignation to take hold of him.

After an hour the analytical side of his brain started to assert itself. The car was clearly driving fast. How fast? Had to be 60. Maybe even 70. And yet it kept bouncing through potholes. Fast speed. Straight road. Poor road surface. It had to be the Republic. They had to be going south. If they were planning a bullet through the head it would be done in South Armagh. It would be public. His body would be left somewhere where it would be quickly found. His corpse would be the IRA's gesture of atonement for what had happened. There would be no logic in killing him quietly. So they planned to let him live. Then what?

He was dragged clear of the car after four hours. All he knew was that it was dark. He was frog-marched into a windowless room and tossed to the ground. The blindfold was ripped off and a thin man of about 50 gestured to some tired-looking corned beef sandwiches and a carton of milk, then slammed the door. The next day the blindfold was back on and he was trussed up into another boot. Just an hour this time. He emerged into a warehouse that looked like it had been deserted for years. There was a wooden crate on the floor. Two men shoved him into it. There was just about room to stretch out his legs. Inside were more sandwiches, bottles of water and some empty Tupperware containers.

"You're going to Spain. In here. There's plenty of food and water. Try to piss and shite in the plastic boxes. It will be two days."

They nailed down the lid. Later he discovered that the Army Council had been in a flap about what to do with him. The nightmare that they found themselves in would only be compounded if he were to be caught. They were under no illusions as to his woeful mental state in the wake of the massacre. In the end they had called in a favour with the ETA group in the Basque region of Northern Spain and had shipped him over to them in a crate on a Dublin wagon, laden with cheese.

He was kept under lock-and-key in an isolated farmhouse for several months until he came to the attention of Sergei. The Russian had patiently reconstructed his career and had decided that he was a person worth investing in. It was very much Sergei's job to bring along anyone who had a track record of being a major thorn in the side of the Soviet's handbag wielding nemesis, the dreaded Margaret Thatcher. He sensed a man with a fractured soul. He had shipped him over to Khalil for rehabilitation.

The Irishman was very much in Khalil's thoughts as he made his way across the camp to the shabby old building that he used as an office. To start with he had been dangerously withdrawn. Khalil had kept him apart from the other fighters and their hard daily routine. He had left him in his tent for a day before going to see him.

The man who lay sweating on the rusty camp-bed seemed to be little more than a shell to Khalil. He had seen men in a similar state many times before, but never this bad. He could almost feel the desperate guilt that was eating away at him.

"I am Khalil. I am in command here."

Declan never looked away from the canvas wall of the tent.

"Nice to meet you."

Khalil took a seat on the unopened wooden box that contained the Irishman's few meagre possessions. He continued in a quiet businesslike tone.

"I have studied your file. You are rather more educated than most that are sent to me. I gather that the sciences have always been a strength."

"Aye. That's true."

"You will work in the hospital. You will work with my wife Fatima. There is much to do; we need people to administer the medicines and supplies. It will be easy for a man with your skills."

Declan rolled over with a look of mild interest on his face.

"I thought that this was a training camp. For terrorists. A place where men learn to kill. To murder."

Khalil smiled in the face of Declan's cynicism.

"Oh we are rather more than that. Of course training fighters is part of what happens here. Only a small part. Once Sidon was a small town. Just a sleepy place unnoticed by the world. Not any more. Now we have thousands and thousands of refugees. My people. The ones who live from suitcases. Shelter is a problem. Sickness is a problem. And on a regular basis the Israelis send their American planes to attack us. And then we have more problems. Lost limbs. Phosphorus burns. Shrapnel. It all keeps us on our toes."

"I'm no nurse. My people didn't send me here for that. They want me to learn to kill. You know that."

Khalil nodded thoughtfully. "Oh yes. I know that. But a man with no heart who kills is just a murderer. I do not teach murderers. I train men with heart. With soul. They sometimes go on to kill. Of course they do. But they kill as soldiers. Right now I see a man with no heart. No soul. An empty glass. Before you can fight you must learn to love. To heal. To care. To cry. My hospital will offer ample opportunity for you relearn these things. I believe that you are a good man Mr Connelly. I can sense it. We must make you believe the same of yourself. You will report to the hospital at seven tomorrow morning. You will take your instructions from Fatima."

In the end Declan was to work for a year in the hospital. Khalil was proved right. He soon learned all the skills required to make him an excellent medical orderly. Fatima made him work with the children. They had a whole ward filled with those who had lost limbs and eyes and parents to the Jewish bombs. First he learnt how to cry again. And by crying he began to find his old strength. After three months he was able to laugh. Soon he was the camp clown. No matter how dire things became, Declan was always on hand to make the children laugh. No matter how desperate their suffering, somehow he would manage to make them smile. It was a bitter moment when Khalil informed him that the healing process was complete and it was time to move on.

Declan brought a manic energy to the training. Now matter how hard the task, he kept a smile on his face. He was the best at everything. He excelled on the firing range. He easily mastered even the most complicated weaponry. He showed calm efficiency at unarmed combat. He was everyone's favourite. His infectious good humour overcame all language and geographic difficulties. And when the training day was over he was like the Pied Piper. Wherever he went amongst the dust and smashed buildings of the teeming camp there was always an entourage of laughing, skipping children in his wake. After six months Khalil knew that the time was fast approaching when he would have to inform Sergei that the man was ready to return to his world. He spent long hours trying to find the words to persuade the Russian that Declan should be allowed to stay with them, that he had done his part, that he deserved the chance to stay and heal rather than return home to kill. In his heart he knew it was pointless. Sergei was a man without sentiment. His masters were without sentiment. Declan was no more to them than a killing machine that had required a service. He wasn't a man to them. He was merely a weapon which was now primed and ready. All Khalil could do was to put off the inevitable day.

Things had started to sour when the three Iranians had arrived. Khalil had not wanted them. He found their extremism to be alarming. He found nothing in Islam that he had followed faithfully all his life to justify their hate and violence. They took against Declan within two days of their arrival at the camp. He was all that they detested. They hated his humour and the popularity that he enjoyed. They hated his irreverence. They hated his pale skin and red hair and green eyes. They hated his Catholic faith. To them he was an infidel from the West. To them he had no place in the camp. The problem was that Declan met their unfettered hostility with mockery and jokes. He never missed an opportunity to show them up or to poke fun. Surely he must have sensed their mounting rage. Khalil could see it only too well. He had met these kinds before. They were killers hiding behind a curtain of faith. They claimed to be the soldiers of Allah when he suspected them as being no more than violent men who yearned for blood. Dangerous men. Men who would kill for simple pleasure.

As he sat down at the tired old table that he used for a desk he knew that things were coming to a head. The incident following the cross-country run had been close. The Iranians had held back, but only just. He had seen the boiling rage in their eyes. They would not hold back for much longer. Declan was in mortal danger and he seemed completely immune to it. It was time for him to leave. There was no way the moment could be put off any further. With a sigh he pulled a writing pad from his drawer and started to pen a letter for Sergei.

He was interrupted by a wild-eyed youngster of no more than ten years old. The boy was so agitated that he could barely speak between rasping breaths.

" . . . Sir . . . you must come. Quickly. Now . . ."

They crossed the camp at a run to the ruin of an old tannery. The walls had been deemed to be unsafe and the building was never used. There was a small group at the door peering inside. Khalil forced his way through.

In the main area of the warehouse Declan stood very still with a Kalashnikov levelled at the three Iranians. Two were standing. One crouched on the floor with his trousers around his ankles. In front of him was a naked boy of eleven years old. Khalil recognised him as one of the many orphans. His face was a mask of terror. There was trickle of blood between his thin buttocks.

Declan's voice was like ice. "I would like to kill them Khalil. I really would. They were about to take turns. If you give the word I will kill them. If you give the word."

Khalil sucked in his disgust. Part of him yearned to give the word. Part of him wanted to see them cut to pieces as Declan poured bullets into their foul bodies. He swallowed down the anger.

"No. No don't do that please. We must be better than them. Keep them covered please. You. Get up. Make yourself decent." He turned to one of the little boys whose eyes were wide with the scene before him. "Go and bring Fatima please. Now. As quickly as possible."

He took off his jacket and wrapped it around the small shaking boy who was covered in the grime and dust of the floor. Soon other men arrived. They led the Iranians away at gunpoint. Declan sagged as if all the air had been forced from him. He tossed the gun to the ground and sat down heavily next to Khalil who was cradling the boy to him.

"I nearly did it Khalil. I nearly lost it. I wish I had."

Khalil's expression was bleak. "We have been forced to walk a terrible path, you and I. We live amidst ugliness and hate. It is the world that we have been given. All that we can try to do is to be better. It is all that we have."

Fatima arrived and took the boy away, her face a mixture of fury and sadness. The crowd at the door drifted away leaving the two men sitting alone. They shared an easy silence. Khalil was the first to force himself clear of the moment.

"Mahmoud returns tonight. You will join us for dinner I hope."

"Aye. Of course. He is well?"

"It seems so." Khalil looked straight into Declan's eyes. "The time has come for you to leave us now. I think that you know this."

"I do. Maybe it should really have been some time ago. Maybe you have been putting off the moment Khalil?"

Khalil smiled. "Maybe I have."

Once again they shared their silence until Khalil spoke again.

"We can never escape from the wars we have chosen. We can only go forward. There can only be one way. I think we both understand this my friend."

"I think we do."

Mahmoud looked tired. There was little spirit in him. It was almost as if he had shrunk. The raid had been a qualified success. They had managed to fire off ten rocket-propelled grenades into the living quarters of a kibbutz ten miles across the border. The Israeli reaction had been even faster than usual. Only three of the twenty-man raiding-party had made it back over the border alive. They had killed a 70-year-old grandfather, two infants and a mother of three.

Seventeen men dead to kill innocents. Khalil could see that the shame of it was cutting deep into his brother. It was the war that they fought. Ugly. Brutal. Without even a semblance of honour.

The talk over the dinner table was of the border. Reports had been coming in for weeks of unusual levels of Israeli troops. For all the world it seemed as if they were preparing an invasion. And yet it was unthinkable. The Israelis prided themselves on the fact that they had never been the aggressors in any of the many wars that they had fought in their short history. Of course they were livid at the constant attacks that the PLO were launching over the northern border. But in the end they were suffering little or no damage. Each attack was little more than a fleabite. Surely they would not jeopardise their fragile position in the world by responding to these fleabites with massive force.

"I just can't see it" said Khalil. "Where would be the logic in them invading? They would be attacked from all quarters, the UN, maybe even America. I find it inconceivable that they could do something so stupid."

Mahmoud picked at his food with little interest. "Maybe you are right brother. I hope that you are. But there are things down there that cannot be explained. When we were running after the attack we had to lie up for a night on a small hill. I watched tanks driving north. Not just a few. Many. Maybe even 100. They were using no lights. Sure. Maybe it is just a manoeuvre. I don't know."

All but Palestinia fell silent. Fatima started to get to her feet but Mahmoud waved her down with a smile. He took the youngster onto his knee and started to bounce her up and down. The look on his face told them that the silent column of Merkheva tanks was forgotten. Declan had shared Mahmoud's sombre mood all evening. For him the cause for his gloom was different. He was coming to terms with how much he was going to miss the vibrant life of the dusty camp. It had come to be his home. Soon he would be forced to leave it behind and rejoin his own bleak little war. All the talk troubled him deeply.

"Khalil, let's just assume that they are going to do it. Invade I mean. Forget all the political stuff for a minute. What will happen if they let the tanks roll? What will the PLO do?"

"What do you mean?"

"What I say. Come on Khalil. We have been training for months on how to fight a guerrilla campaign behind enemy lines. Fair enough. We're all in the same boat on that one. So what happens when you face a full-scale invasion from the Israeli Defence Force? Fall back? Run for the hills? Concede ground? What?"

Khalil shook his head sadly. "Oh, I see now. Will we be sensible? That is what you are asking? Of course not. Our leaders have let our position in Lebanon go to their heads. There will be a lot of talk about not giving an inch and throwing them into the sea."

"Then it will be a massacre."

"Yes. It will be a massacre. Just like it always is."

"And you Khalil? And Fatima, and Palestinia and Mahmoud?"

Khalil shrugged. "What can we do? We cannot run and desert those who stand and fight. Fatima and Palestinia will get away to Beirut, they should be safe there . . ."

"Excuse me." Fatima's voice cut through his sentence.

"You must, Fatima. We are just a few miles from the border. It will be too dangerous. You must go. There is no choice."

She met this idea with a sharp derisory laugh. "Oh that is just fine. The men can stay behind to play their silly games whilst the women are whisked away. You think that it is OK for you to stay and fire your little peashooters at the Jewish tanks and planes. To achieve what, may I ask? To give old men something to get tearful about in their cafés in years to come? At least when I stay I will do something that does have an effect. I and all my staff will be here to try and put back together the broken bodies that are always the result of your idiot games."

"But Fatima you can't . . . and Palestinia, what about Palestinia . . .?"

"She is of our people. She will stay. I will stay. There is a very large red cross on the roof of the hospital. Even the Jews would never stoop that low, not on purpose. We will stay and we will do our work. It isn't something that I am willing to discuss. Now I will make some coffee."

She stormed off into the kitchen and made more noise with the pots than was warranted by the task. Declan and Mahmoud did their best to hide their amusement. Khalil tried hard to remain stern but couldn't keep it up.

"They always said that your Muslim women knew their place" chuckled Declan. "I'm glad to see that you have your wife under total control. If it happens Khalil, if they come, I will be with Fatima. She is right you know. Another idiot in the front line will make no difference one way or another. Another pair of hands in the hospital will save lives. It is where I want to be."

"Then so be it. I am glad. It isn't your war my friend."

"It wasn't. Not before I came here. But things change, Khalil. This bloody place feels like home now. I think that it is my war now."

Khalil looked at him for a long time whilst Mahmoud just smiled and pulled faces at the giggling Palestinia.

They came two days later. They came with no warning. They came with massive irresistible force. One minute it was just another slow dawn in the camp. The air was filling with the smoke of a thousand cooking fires. The sun was a deep red as it eased itself over the rugged mountains in the east. Stray dogs were shaking themselves awake. Mothers were yelling at sleepy children to go and fetch water. Stallholders were carefully arranging their meagre wares for sale. The mournful voice for the minaret of the mosque called the people to prayer through a tinny tannoy system. Just another day in the life of thousands of people who had forgotten what their homes looked like.

And then the jets came. They came in low out of the deep blue of the sky. Within seconds the whole camp was engulfed with smoke. It wasn't a new thing. The Israelis had been raiding the camps for years. The people scrambled to put out the fires. There would be casualties. There would be dead and wounded, but they would put out the fires and rebuild the damage and life would go on. But this time it was different. This time it was not just one wave of jets. This time the jets kept on coming. And coming.

Within half an hour the camp at Sidon was a chaos of smoke and flames and corpses and horrific injuries. Khalil fought to maintain some kind of order but it was impossible. Reports from the south were sketchy and panic ridden. It was clear that the Israelis were advancing with hundreds of tanks. They had done it. The nightmare was under way.

Mahmoud had been gathering men with a view to trying to set up a defensive position to the south of the town but Khalil stopped him.

"No brother. We are needed here. We need to organise every man to help the wounded. It is all that we can do. If they get close we will fall back to the north. Resistance is just stupid. We do what we can for as long as we can. Then we go."

A JOURNEY TO THE WEST

The next three hours were beyond anything that either man had ever imagined. In comparison Ammunition Hill had been a noble, clean affair. The jets poured their fire down from the sky and brought hell to the dusty alleyways of the camp. The injuries were horrific. The dust seemed clogged with blood. There were chunks of obliterated bodies every few yards. And still they came. Always graceful, their silver wings glinting in the warm sun of the late morning, sleek and elegant. The smoke was everywhere now. Black. Choking.

By eleven, every corner of the small hospital was filled with screaming victims. Fatima's white coat was soaked a bright red. Her eyes seemed to have shrunk back into her sockets. She worked like a machine. Her brain forced itself into an automatic mode. She made judgements over life and death like some bloodstained goddess with nods and shakes of her head. The ones with no hope were filled with morphine and left to die. The ones where there was hope she worked on. And all the time she inwardly cursed the smiling man from Ireland whom she had come to love. Where was he? Was that all he was, a coward who had run as soon as the bombs fell from the sky? All morning she had waited as the endless conveyor belt of injured and the dying came to her. At first she thought that he must have been held up. She made excuses. She had trusted him. Relied on him to be there when she needed him most. But he had run. All those fine words and he had run.

She saw her husband come into the operating area. His face made her heart twist. In his arms was the tiny body of a girl who had lost both of her legs. Her little face was twisted in pain and her screams were losing their power. She left the table and went to him. His eyes were bright with the horror.

"Give her to me. We will do what we can."

His Adam's apple jumped as he tried to force words from his parched mouth.

"How can they do this? What kind of men can do this? The children, Fatima. All the children. How can they."

He was so helpless. So wretched. So broken. She wanted to take him to her and hold him and help take the horror away. There was no time for softness. She took the wrecked little body from him and laid it on the table.

"Be strong. They need you. All of us need you. You mustn't break Khalil. Not now. Be strong. For me. For Palestinia. For all of us. You must go now. Leave the little one with me. We will care for her."

For a moment it seemed that he could not move. He was shaking with emotion. He held onto her eyes like a drowning man clinging to driftwood. Then he turned and went back out to the living hell that was Sidon.

The smoke was so thick that he could barely see twenty yards. Where should he go? What should he do? What on earth could he do? He slumped down to the pavement and took long breaths of the filthy air. A hand grabbed a piece of his jacket and yanked him to his feet. It was Mahmoud. His eyes were alight and burning with rage.

"Come. Now. It's Declan. They had to open up the cells in the jail when it was hit. The Iranian bastards are out. They have Declan. The boy knows where." He pointed to the ragged urchin by his side. "We must be fast."

They had to ignore the cries for help as they ran through the alleys and wrecked streets. They crossed the camp to the old warehouse where they had found the Iranians a few days before. Khalil found it ironic that the building that had been too unsafe to use had escaped the attention of the jets. The sky overhead was oddly quiet and the mayhem of the streets suddenly seemed far away. They told the boy to stay outside. They kicked in the door and charged in.

Declan was spread-eagled on the floor. His arms and legs were stretched wide and tied. He was naked. His pale flesh was covered in bruises. A fresh cut across his chest was oozing blood The utter stupidity of the scene paralysed Khalil. Here they all were under attack from the Israeli air force and these three maniacs from Iran had decided to torture a man from Ireland. It was lunacy. Utter, utter madness. What was wrong with people? The events of the morning had numbed his senses to the extent that his brain received no great warning signs when the three men sprang to their feet and reached for the guns that were on the floor. There was no surge of adrenalin. No sense of danger. Just a dull feeling of outrage.

This was replaced by confusion as the bodies of the three men started to jump and twitch like puppets held by an alcoholic in dire need of his next drink. Then the deafening sound of gunfire hammered into his head and the smell of cordite filled his nose and his brain started to catch up. For a few brief seconds spouts of blood splashed out of the jumping figures until one by one they collapsed to the floor and silence filled the tired old space of the disused building.

Still his feet felt like lead. Mahmoud tossed his weapon to the ground and started to untie the prone figure. Declan sat up with an expression of pain and naked relief. His voice was shaky and weak

"Thanks."

"How are you?" Mahmoud was all business. He was taking the horror of the morning better than his brother. The horrors of the front line were nothing new to him. It was his domain.

Declan ran his hands across his body tentatively, wincing every time his fingers touched the numerous bruises. "I'll live. I don't think there's anything too serious. They were saving that for later I suppose. Hurts like a bastard, but I'll patch up. I best get myself to the hospital. I expect that Fatima is about ready to finish what these bastards started."

The brothers helped him to dress and had to support him for a while until he could walk on his own. Once again Khalil was astonished at the depths of determination within the bony man from the north. Once they were outside Declan gasped at the mayhem that had engulfed the camp.

"Holy Christ Almighty." For the first time in many, many years his right hand traced the shape of the cross across his chest.

The journey back to the hospital was even harder than it had been on the way out. The fires seemed to be everywhere now. The wounded seemed to be everywhere, clawing the air, looking for loved ones, crying for mercy. The situation had drifted far out of control. Those who could walk were streaming out of the town and making their way north to try and find sanctuary from the Israeli guns. For a moment Khalil cursed himself. They had got lost. How could they get lost? Sure there was smoke and fire, but how could they get lost? Where were they? He looked about for a landmark. He had no idea. They should have already arrived at the hospital by now. Instead they were lost in part of the town that he didn't even know. Stupid.

He felt his brother's hand on his shoulder. He saw sorrow and pain in his eyes. What was this? Why did his brain refuse to work? And now Declan too. Green eyes overflowing with tears. And words. Words he couldn't arrange in the right order.

" . . . you stay here . . . we will look . . . maybe they were not inside . . ."

With a blinding agonising flash his brain became aware of the huge mound of rubble in front of him. It was covered with what seemed like hundreds of people picking up rocks and throwing them to the floor. And now the sound hit him. Screams and wailing. Shouting. The crackle of flames. The crash of falling masonry. The approaching roar of yet another jet. And the worst truth in the world fell on him. The pile of rubble was the hospital. Under the rubble were the bodies of his wife and his daughter. They had done it. There was a huge red cross on the roof and they had done it anyway.

They were gone. His mind brushed aside the words of optimism. It listened only to his heart. And his heart knew. They were gone. Gone with his mother and his father and his sisters. Taken away. Everyone he loved was always taken away. He had been stupid enough to think that this time it might be different. He had allowed himself the daydream that his life could be like millions of others. He had taken a wife that he had loved and they had brought a beautiful child into the world and now they were gone. Buried. Broken. Mangled. Destroyed in the stone and the dust and the smoke.

Taken.

They joined the crowd that hacked away at the debris. They worked through the night until their hands were raw. In the morning the guns of the advancing tanks could be heard no more than two miles away. Khalil had given up all hope hours before. He had worked because there seemed like there was nothing else to do. Now in the smoky light of the dawn it was time to kill the last flickering flame of hope. Mahmoud led him away gently. His voice was low, soothing.

"We must go now brother. We must go north. They are nearly upon us. Can you hear the tanks? They are close. We must run now. Do you understand me brother?"

"I understand."

They were three men covered from head to toe in white dust as they left Sidon and joined the thousands who tramped up the highway towards Beirut.

A JOURNEY TO THE WEST

Moscow, 2003

Khalil dragged himself clear from the pain of the memories. A bent old lady in little more than a collection of rags was pushing a rusty tin at him. She was talking to him in a keening, imploring voice. He reached into his pocket and put a few Kopecks in the tin. She studied the offering, wrinkled her nose in disgust and shuffled off across Red Square muttering to herself. Another triumph for the great god of capitalism. The old Soviet system by and large had given the people of Moscow a roof and basic level of miserable calories and nothing much else. Nobody starved, everyone looked miserable and lots disappeared without trace. Now things had moved on. Now only the majority looked miserable whilst a few flaunted their new-found riches like spoilt teenagers. Now there were many who starved and froze to death on the streets. Now the Mafia who had taken over the role of the KGB happily gunned down their enemies in the glare of the public gaze. They didn't feel the need to send them away to labour camps thousands of miles to the east where the dirty work could be done quietly and discreetly.

Systems. Ideals. Dreams. Prophets. New dawns. False dawns. He had seen all of it. He had been a part of it. Then his light had died in the midst of a pile of rubble on a warm afternoon in 1982.

Only now did he really feel the weight of Sergei's parting words. This time the Jews mustn't win. This time they must be deprived of their killing. This time it was his turn. He rose from the bench with a new purpose. There was a note from Sergei waiting for him when he checked out of his hotel. The old cold warrior had acted quickly. As of ten o'clock the previous evening Tac Brennan's flat was bugged from ceiling to floor. The first shot had been fired before he had even set foot on Scottish soil. The first skirmish had been won and Tac Brennan hadn't even known that there had been one. It felt like a good omen. He was smiling broadly as he gave a generous tip to the doorman and jumped into the taxi. He made the airport in plenty of time to catch the five-fifteen flight to Dublin.

Daniel Morrissey stole another look at his watch and cursed himself. A mere minute and a half had passed since he had looked the last time. This was pathetic. he was acting like a third-former about to read the lesson out in assembly for the first time. Why on earth was he so nervous? It was crazy. Since his big speech in the Assembly things had gone spectacularly well. It had been a non-stop media round – the *Today* programme, *Newsweek*, even *Frost on Sunday*. He had thrown open the doors and walked straight into the big boys league and the general consensus of opinion was that he looked comfortable in it. Here was a young man who seemed to be heading for the top slot. Maybe Edinburgh wouldn't be enough for him, they said. Maybe he would be persuaded by the party to move south to Westminster. There had been lots of phrases like 'a breath of fresh air in the stale corridors of British politics'. He had even started to receive fan mail from teenage girls.

But whichever way he looked at it, tonight was different. The new Daniel Morrissey was groomed for the TV studios and interviews with glossy journalists in short skirts in the lobbies of plush hotels. This one the other hand was no place at all for the new Daniel. This was a haunt of the old Daniel. And he wasn't at all sure how the audience who were filling the Sighthill meeting hall would take to the new Armani Daniel. They were sensing betrayal. He could almost smell it. He could almost feel it seeping under the door that separated him from the gathering crowd.

The meeting hadn't been his idea. The chairman of the local party had made the suggestion and the First Minister had taken it on. Daniel's boss had been astounded at how things had turned around. The Sighthill killings had been yet another blow to an already floundering administration. They already had problems enough with a flat economy, the idiot war in Iraq and the seeming desire of an ever-growing number of Scots to become junkies. Getting the world on message about Scotland was a tough job. The Government tried to paint a glowing vision of sunlit glens and superb education. All too often the rest of the world chose to see endless rain, bleak estates and discarded needles. Adding racist murder into the mix was hardly going to be good for trade. The emergence of the Daniel Morrissey factor had been a gift from the gods. He had played like a dream in Brussels where his old-fashioned emotional liberal views were still in vogue. Even the Americans took to him because he reminded them of Richard Gere in a film about the kind of good old-fashioned liberal views that Hollywood occasionally tried to push at a population that had voted for Bush. It seemed that everybody liked him. And if they liked him it could do no harm for his party.

The idea of putting Daniel on his white horse and riding him into Sighthill had an icing-on-the-cake feel to it. It was guaranteed to make great television. How could his wit and charm and raw emotion fail to win over the people there and shepherd in a bright new dawn of racial harmony? It was sure fire. It couldn't fail. The only problem was that Daniel knew the people who were gathering in the hall much better than his boss. They were not the types to be easily swayed by fine words and a boyish grin. They knew that the man in the flash suit had once been one of them. They had set him on his path, and without their help there would be no nice Edinburgh flat and fancy clothes and lovey-dovey with Jeremy Paxman. Maybe he had forgotten that he owed them. Maybe he had got carried away with his own PR and forgotten where he had come from. He hadn't let on to any of these concerns to the First Minister. Of course he hadn't. He had smiled modestly and agreed that the whole thing was a jolly good idea and had promised to do his best for the party. And now as he checked his watch yet again he knew that he was about to jump into a very large bucket of shit. Bastards.

"I'm just going to use the bathroom. Won't be a sec."

The corridor was two bulbs short and the stacks of cardboard boxes along the wall made it treacherous going. The Gents was a sorry affair lit with bright blue neon to make it impossible for even the most determined smack user to locate a vein. He dived into a cubicle and lit up. He heaved the smoke down into his lungs and closed his eyes for a moment. Come on Danny. You can do this. How many times have you done your stuff in rooms like these? Tons and tons. So stop being such a twat. He nearly jumped out of his skin when there was a tap on the cubicle door.

"That you Danny?"

"Aye. Who's that?"

"Old school mate of yours. Johnny Hendon."

Daniel opened up the door. "For fuck's sake Hendo. You jumped me out of my skin."

Johnny smiled at how easily the newly groomed accent had disappeared in the familiar environment of a Glasgow community centre toilet. He raised a quizzical eyebrow.

"Crafty fag before the off is it?"

"Aye. Not politically correct any more. The Parliament is like being back at school. The only difference is that it is the spin-doctors you have to watch out for instead of the teachers. What you doing here anyway?"

"Come to see you of course. The rising star. The Nigh Bevin of the twenty-first century and all that. Nice speech by the way."

"Christ I forgot. You're still a reporter then? I heard that things . . . well, you know."

"I know. And yes. Still a reporter. Just a freelancer now. None of them want rampant cokeheads on the books any more. They like to have us at arms' length. I'm not moaning. It's still a living."

"You were there on the night weren't you. You took that picture, when the copper got his head run over."

Johnny nodded and lit up himself. "Aye, that was me. The newshound on the spot. Bit of a best-seller for me that one. Nothing like one of our boys in blue spreading his brains across the floor to get the redtops into a bidding war."

"Is that what you are down to these days Johnny. Just a few quid?"

"Maybe. Maybe we all are. Don't you go judging me Danny. The new choirboy act might wash with all the twats in the suits but we go back, remember. I know you for what you are, just a pretty Glasgow boy with a silver tongue. Come on, admit it. You always were an ambitious wee twat."

Daniel grinned and took a proffered cigarette. "So what's wrong in that?"

"Not a damn thing. Just so long as you remember to admit it to your old mates. This thing isn't done you know Danny. Not even nearly."

"What thing?"

"This thing. Sighthill. Trouble. It hasn't even got started."

Daniel was silent for a while. "What makes you say that?"

"Because I know Danny. Remember, I never took the golden road to Edinburgh. I stayed here. I know this town better than most. Don't go believing all the shite from the council and the cops. They have drenched the place in coppers for a while, that's all. It won't last. In fact I hear that they have been quietly moving them out over the last few days. You'll know better than me."

"What choice is there? We can't keep that many here permanently. We're already seeing an upsurge in crime in other areas."

Johnny laughed. "Hey. Don't go justifying yourself to me. Save it for that lot out there. I'm just stating a fact. When the coppers go then watch this space, that's all I'm saying."

Daniel shook his head. "No it isn't. You've got an angle Johnny. That is why you are here. This isn't just a bit of friendly advice from an old mate. What's the play?"

"Very good. Very on the ball. Let's just say that I am well connected. Things are going to blow and when they do the players will emerge. I know these guys, on both sides. The other night will be nothing. When this place goes up you will be able to smell the smoke in Aberdeen. When it happens it will be make-or-break time for you Danny boy. That nice speech of yours has placed you right at the end of a branch. There are only two ways to go. You can come out of this the hero. Or you can come out of this the sad twat. No middle way. Not after your speech. I can help you. To be the hero you will need to talk to the big men who are making it all happen. I can get you in there. You work the miracle and I'll write it up. I win whatever happens. You win if you can keep the balls in the air. It can be a partnership."

At that moment the door opened and a flustered-looking Roseanne burst in.

"Daniel, you really will have to come now, they are all . . ."

She stopped mid-sentence and took in the sight of the two men sharing their conspiratorial fags. "Oh . . . sorry . . . didn't mean to . . . it's just that they are ready . . . sorry."

She backed out with some embarrassment. Johnny once again raised an eyebrow.

"My researcher" said Daniel as he ground out his half-smoked cigarette. "Better get moving. My public awaits. Got a card Johnny. Here's mine. We'll stay in touch. Maybe we can help each other."

They exchanged cards and Daniel gave himself a last inspection in the greasy mirror. Roseanne's perfume hung gently in the air.

"I can see that the Assembly has its perks then."

"Fuck off Johnny." Daniel swept out into the corridor and marched away between the boxes of donated toys like a true leader of men.

The applause that greeted Daniel as he took the stage having been introduced by the local party chairman was rather muted. It was hard to properly judge the size of the audience as he had the strong TV lights in his eyes. There were no empty seats to be seen. It was a big event for Sighthill. Outside were three TV vans, each with the driver keeping a careful watch on the groups of kids who hovered hopefully. The faces that stared back at him held little warmth. They hadn't much liked his speech. As far as most of them were concerned, three young lads had been slashed-up by a nutter. That was the issue. If there had been no asylum seekers then there would have been no nutter. It was clear-cut. They didn't want any high and mighty Edinburgh bullshit. They wanted to hear what was going to be done about it.

Daniel paused for longer than he really needed to and waited for the moment to be just right to start. Just as the moment arrived a member of the audience grabbed it instead.

"Get on with it you Paki-loving bastard."

There was a mixture of shock and sniggering. For a brief moment Daniel was horrified. His brain raced into overdrive on how to address the comment in a proper statesmanlike way. And then common anger kicked in. It wasn't hard to identify the speaker. He sat on the end of the second row. He wore a baseball cap and tight T-shirt designed to show off just how many hours he had put in on the weights machine. Around him was a small entourage who were all grinning with delight at their man's intervention. For a moment Daniel hesitated and then decided to let the anger have its head. He jumped down from the stage and waved at the astonished TV crew.

"Come on. Light. Let's have some light."

They reacted quickly and within seconds Daniel was bathed in light as he marched along the front row towards the heckler whose expression was losing smugness by the second.

"OK. Got this?" The TV crews nodded eagerly. Had they ever. "One. Two. That OK? You all hear me at the back?"

He checked that heads at the back were duly nodding.

"Fine. Excellent. OK people. Let's get one or two things straight. You lads in particular." He was standing right next to his tormentor now who was looking distinctly uneasy. "Right boys. See those big things over there? They are called television cameras. Good aren't they? That means that people all over the world are watching us. They are wondering what kind of people we are, what kind of a place we live in, what are we like? Now most of you will know that I am a Glasgow lad. I'm proud of it. I'm proud of my city. I always have been. And why not? It's a great, great city full of great people. So what does the rest of the world see? They see this young poet here making his inspired philosophical comments. Seven people died here the other night. Seven. That is why we are all here tonight. To think about it. To talk about it. To make sure it doesn't happen again. And what does this gentleman have to contribute? Paki-loving bastard. Brilliant. Outstanding. Is that really what we want the rest of the world to think about us? Well, come on, is it? Hands up all those who agree? Let's get it out in the open shall we? Let's just be straight for once shall we? Easy question. Hands up all those who think I'm a Paki-loving bastard."

He stopped and theatrically swung his gaze around the room. Inside his heart was nearly thumping its way out of his chest. This was the moment when the wheels could come off. If they all rose up as one and yelled at him he was a goner. They didn't. Instead they sat still as stones with their hands very much down. He turned back to the man in the baseball cap who was by this time wishing more than anything in the whole world that he had stayed in the pub. Daniel grabbed his arm and pulled it up.

"Come on now. You have to put your hand up. You said it. And what about you lot? Not going to stick with your mate? Come on. Not even one of you?"

They didn't. They gritted their teeth and stared ahead with arms folded.

"OK. So there we have it sunshine. All these people and only you have your hand up. Where I come from that means that you are in a hopeless minority. I think that the best thing is if you leave now, don't you. We don't need you here. We don't need your views."

Daniel wrenched him up out of his chair and gave him a solid push up the gangway. For a second the man spun round with his fists bunched. Maybe he might have given it a go, TV cameras or no TV cameras, but Campbell had quietly made his way down from the back of the hall to lay a hand on his shoulder.

"Come on Tully. Best you go out don't you think?"

He led the lad out with a minimum of fuss. Daniel made his way back onto the stage and started his speech. After the fireworks of the beginning it was something of an anti-climax. The applause at the end was rather warmer than had greeted him at the beginning but it was by no means an ovation. Questions were invited but nobody was keen to follow the unfortunate Tully down the road of humiliation. Eventually it was Nicky Jennings who rose to her feet.

"We have all listened to what you have had to say Mr Morrissey. Not just tonight. For days. It all sounds very good. Fine words. Worthy thoughts. But that is all there is. Fine words. May I point out that over the last few days the police presence on the streets here is more or less back to normal? That is a fact. After the riot you flooded the area with police and they have kept a lid on things. So what happens now? Do you really think that fine words will be enough? This isn't a small problem Mr Morrissey. A family that I cared for very deeply were burned to death a few days ago Mr Morrissey. And the people who did it are still out there. I would like you to explain exactly what it is that you are doing to make sure that this doesn't happen again."

Daniel did his best. He talked about reports and enquiries and commitment. The trouble was that the bloody woman didn't sit down. She stood there and stared at him with accusation in her eyes. What did she expect? Tanks on the bloody streets? He bluffed it out and gave a discreet signal. The chairman took the cue and brought the meeting to a close. Daniel felt frustration that the wind had been taken out of his sails right at the end. As he shook hands at the local dignitaries he took a last glance out into the hall. It was emptying fast. The woman was still stood exactly where she had when she asked her question. Still there was accusation in her eyes. He felt as if she was looking straight through him. The tall policeman who had guided Tully from the hall went over to her. They exchanged words. She nodded and bent to pick up her bag. She gave him one last look and she turned to leave.

Suddenly Daniel felt cold. He remembered the words of Johnny Hendon. This thing isn't finished. This thing hasn't even started yet. He hadn't really considered the words then. He hadn't had the time. Now they came back to him. He had a feeling that he was getting in over his head. But it was too late to do a damn thing about it. He had bought his ticket to ride. Now he would just have to hang on tight.

Tac Brennan wore a thoughtful expression as he made his way out of the hall and out into the night. The three cronies who had accompanied him to the meeting knew the expression well enough to keep their distance. He walked slightly ahead of them. He had to admit to himself that he had been rather impressed. Like many others he had turned up with the confident expectation of watching the cocky bastard from the Government brought down a peg or two. Instead he had come out fighting. He had enjoyed every second of the humiliation of Jimmy Tully. He had always been of the firm opinion that Tully was a complete wanker. For years he had been trying to worm himself in and Tac had never given him house room. There was no doubt that the politician would have got away with a clean pair of heels but for that girl. Again. Every time he saw her he was struck by the plain and simple fact that she was bloody fantastic. Was there nothing that would faze her? It didn't seem so. No matter how rough things got, she just waded straight in. If ever there were the equivalent of a female Para then Nicky Jennings was it. He would have had her in his platoon any day of the week. Christ, she would have been some woman in Ireland. They could have sent her into the hardest bar in Crossmaglen and she wouldn't have batted an eyelid. She would have had every secret they possessed over two or three pints. He shook his head in admiration.

More to the point, it appeared that the massive police presence was at last being wound down. It wasn't much of a surprise. There was no way that they could keep up the numbers. It was all PR. They had to keep a lid on things for a respectable period. Then they would ease off. It was about time.

There had been an awful lot of talk and debate about the night of the killings. Hands had been wrung. Concerned expressions had filled the TV screens. Oh yes it was tragic, terribly tragic. Truly dreadful. But it had to be seen as a terrible one-off. An appalling, freak chain of events that would never happen again. And nobody had the bottle to state the obvious truth that if there hadn't been 6,000 bastard asylum seekers dumped in the middle of his community then none of it would have happened in the first place. Nobody was making the point of last in, first out. The asylum seekers were the last in. The asylum seekers should be the first out. Nobody had bothered to ask his community if they wanted them. Obviously they hadn't. Because if they had they would have been told to fuck right off. It was the answer that none of them dared to consider. No asylum seekers, no problem. Give Sighthill back to the people who had always lived there. Move the fuckers out. He didn't much care where. Just out. Somewhere else. Back home preferably. If not there, then in the nice leafy suburbs of Surrey and Midlothian where the bastards who made the decisions lived. Fat chance. They wouldn't like to see their treasured house prices take a hit because of some smelly Paki bastards being moved in up the road. No chance. Bastards.

He had come to the conclusion that there wasn't a snowball in hell's chance of any politicians making the decision to get them out. Fair enough. He would never have expected any different. If they wouldn't, then he would. He knew that he would have the people behind him. Everyone was sick of it. Now the coppers were away he would be able make a start. Then there would be some action.

He gave a nod as he took his seat at the bar and his drinks were duly delivered. He wasn't much interested in talking to anyone. His mind was running hot. There would be no General Staff to pussy-foot around with things this time. No fucking politicians to shit themselves every time a shot got fired. This time it would be his show. This would be a sergeant's operation. In hard, and fuck the niceties. Set a goal and reach it by whatever means available. Use whatever force was required. He turned with mild anger when he felt a tap on the shoulder. A stranger stood at his side. He frowned slightly as he searched his memory. The man with the red hair and blue anorak smiled.

"You don't know me Mr Brennan. We haven't met. My name is Burton. John Burton."

Reporter? Possibly. The thick northern accent and shabby coat suggested otherwise. There was nothing wide about the man.

"What do you want?"

"Just to give you this. Take it as a gesture of good intent. You'll find a mobile number inside. I would like to meet for a chat. You can choose the time and place. And the conditions. There are no strings. You will see how serious I am when you open the envelope Mr Brennan. I work for some people who admire you, who would like to help you. We all believe that we share a great deal of common ground. Give me a call Mr Brennan. You won't regret it. I can assure you of that."

He handed over the envelope and left without ceremony. Tac nodded to one of the lads who followed Burton out of the door. He slipped the envelope into the inside pocket of his jacket and took a sip of whisky. The lad returned after fifteen minutes. Burton had made his way to the Kirkintilloch Road and taken a taxi. Tac was intrigued. He had been a steady one, that was for sure. He knew his name and must have known something of his reputation. And yet there hadn't been a flicker of nerves about him. Everything pointed to the fact that he was a pro. The question was what kind of a pro and who was paying his bills. He didn't want to show any undue interest in the brief conversation. He could tell that those around him were every bit as intrigued by the appearance of the stranger. He sat for a further hour watching the TV with little interest. Then he headed home. Once he was inside his flat he opened the envelope. Inside was five thousand pounds and brief note.

'Call me. Your choices, time and place. 07762 871 236.'

Stranger and stranger. Big money, no doubt about that. Big money delivered by a pro. Had to be serious people. Surely not the police. They would never get authorisation to toss around that kind of cash on a wing and a prayer. Not a chance. So who? It didn't seem like the media. No need for any cloak and dagger stuff if it was the media. So who? Only one way to find out. He picked up the phone and dialled. It answered on the second ring.

"Good evening Mr Brennan. Thank you for getting back so promptly."

Knew it was him. The phone must have been just for the one call. Brennan said, "I'll call you tomorrow. Be in the city centre somewhere. In a hotel room. I'll let you know which. Then you can come. OK with you?"

"Fine with me. I look forward to hearing from you Mr Brennan."

The next afternoon Tac booked his room and made the call. Burton arrived twenty minutes later. Once again there seemed no nerves about him.

"Good afternoon Mr Brennan."

"Aye. You need to strip now Mr Burton. Hope you don't mind. A man needs to be careful. We live in an electronic age. There is a robe over the chair. Put your clothes in the bag."

Burton nodded. Again, not a flicker of surprise. He stripped-off carefully flooding each garment and putting it in the bag. Once he was naked he held out his arms and turned around slowly before putting on the robe. Brennan made a brief call on his mobile and the door opened for one of his men to come in and collect the bag. He gestured Burton to a chair.

"Sorry about that. You want coffee or anything?"

"No thanks. I'm fine."

"So talk to me then."

"The people that I work for have sympathy for your situation Mr Brennan. A great deal of sympathy."

Tac lit up and sat backcrossing his legs. "And what situation might that be Mr Burton?"

"A son butchered by an asylum seeker. A neighbourhood stolen. A career tossed onto the scrap heap. They think that you have been treated over-harshly Mr Brennan."

"Aye. Well. Life's tragic isn't it? What's fresh about that?"

"Nothing Mr Brennan. Nothing whatsoever. Only we feel that you might not be inclined to take it lying down. We feel that your record suggests that you are the kind of man who will be inclined to fight back."

"And what might you and your employers know about my record Mr Burton?"

Burton smiled. "Oh, more than you might think. Goose Green. Ireland. The Gulf. Kosovo. All of it probably."

So what, thought Tac. Most of it had been plastered across the tabloids anyway. "Kosovo you say. Why don't you tell me about Kosovo then?"

Burton shrugged. "Regular patrol in a potentially hostile environment. Shots fired. Man down. You did things by the book. You went house to house and you went in hard. Not a time to fanny around. Do the job first, worry about the niceties later. We learned that the hard way in Ireland didn't we? Do the Snow White bit and you get shot. A man acted aggressive and you neutralised him. You didn't shoot him. You used appropriate force to ensure the safety of your men. Again. By the book. The problem was that they had left the book back in Aldershot. The TV changed everything. You acted according to the Para manual. You got the job done. You ensured the safety of the platoon. They knew that. Everyone knew that. But you weren't expected to be a Para. You were expected to be Dixon of Dock Green. You acted in the way that they had trained you for twenty years. Except they had moved the goalposts without telling you about it. The media got their teeth into the brass and you were history. For me that is no way to treat a man who followed H. Jones at Goose Green. That's how I see it. That's how my employers see it."

Brennan nodded thoughtfully. "You have good access Mr Burton. I'll grant you that. Tell me. You said something about 'we' when you were talking about Ireland?"

"Yes."

"Were you in uniform or out?"

"Both." So. The picture was getting clearer. Ex-soldier. Ex-spook. Well enough connected to pull the classified Army files. Interesting. Very interesting.

"Go on."

"The people that I work for are patriots Mr Brennan. It's an old-fashioned sort of idea I know. Maybe they are old-fashioned men. They are not remotely politically correct. They hate Europe. They want to keep the pound. They believe that this country of ours is still special. They believe that if we concentrated a bit more on looking after our own then we would all be the better for it. They don't like asylum seekers. They see them as the thin end of the wedge. Anyone with a brain in their head can see it. The world is not going to become a better place over the next 30 years. Resources are beginning to run out. Food. Water. Oil. Everything. There will be more wars as developing countries scrap it out for what they can get. And there will be refugees. Refugees the like of which the world has never seen before. Millions and millions and millions of them. And unless something changes quickly they are going to be headed right here. We are the number one destination. We feel that this is something that needs to change. Let someone else have the number one slot. Not us. We need to change perceptions. We need to make our country the kind of place that will make these people shit themselves. No more tea and scones and cosy English classes. Instead there needs to be a bit of stick. Broken heads. Broken legs. A clear message. You are not welcome here thank you very much. Not now. Not ever. See where we are coming from?"

Brennan nodded, increasingly fascinated.

"This is why my employers have taken such a close interest in Sighthill. There are many things that make it special you see. Number one: there are so many. Six thousand in a few blocks of flats. Number two: the locals are not happy about it. They weren't before three kids were killed; now we feel that they are ready to do something. All the conditions are in place Mr Brennan. What we want to do is to move things along. So what do we do? Invest money in the BNP? You must be kidding. They are just a bunch of mouthy plumbers and clerks who like to act big and shave their heads. Morons. No. We would prefer to invest in a professional. You Mr Brennan. Your CV is all that we desire. You have the training, the skill and the motivation. You can set the place on fire Mr Brennan. We merely want to help you to buy the matches."

Unbelievable. Absolutely unbelievable. Who the hell was this guy? "So, Mr Burton, I presume that you don't actually want me to literally set Sighthill on fire. I expect that you have something a little more subtle in mind."

"We do."

"Well . . .?"

"We want them out Mr Brennan. Use fear. Use intimidation. Violence. Bullying. Whatever. We want them queuing up demanding to be re-housed. We want them to find life in Sighthill unbearable. We want the Government to be given the task of finding somewhere to put 6,000 of them."

"It sounds a little like ethnic cleansing to me Mr Burton."

"That is exactly what it is. Why beat about the bush? You either want it or you don't. There is no middle line here."

Tac got to his feet and went over to where he had left the whisky bottle. He poured out two glasses and handed one to Burton. "You talk about help. What do you have in mind?"

"Money basically. Lots of it. We have some ideas on how you will want to do things. You will need good men to run things. They are not in short supply. We feel sure that you will have plenty of ex-comrades from the Paras who would come and help if the price is right. We thought maybe ten of them at 50 thousand pounds. How long? Probably a month at the most. Half in advance. twenty-five thousand pounds. Other costs? We thought maybe a million. On account. Maybe you won't need that much. Maybe you will make a profit out of the operation. Why not? All we want is to see the job done. We also hope to have a man for you. He is from Ireland. Once upon a time he was in the UVF. One of the best. Not happy now that he is kicking his heels. He is a dab hand with explosives. We can give you what you need Mr Brennan. The tools. If you want them."

"The money. How?"

"I assume that you have some kind of offshore facility?"

"Yes."

"250 thousand pounds can be deposited tomorrow. We will make payments in instalments of 250 thousand pounds as and when you need them, assuming of course that we are happy with the results that you are achieving."

"It's a very generous offer Mr Burton."

"I hope so."

Tac swirled his whisky around in his glass. "I will call you. I won't need long. You will be available this evening?"

"Yes."

"OK. You'll here one way or another by then. I'll get them to bring your clothes."

The bag was brought in without ceremony and Burton started to dress. "There is just one more thing Mr Brennan."

"Aye?"

"Tac? How come 'Tac'? It wasn't in the files."

Brennan smiled. "It was back in 1985. Germany. We were on a big NATO exercise. Up against a bunch of Krauts. Grenadiers. Thought they were God's gift. Anyway. 1 Para went through their lines at night as if they weren't there. We took their command centre. Gave them a bit of a kicking. They weren't happy about it. That night we were celebrating in this bar when about 50 of them came in. They had this big sergeant. Huge fucker he was. He wanted to defend the reputation of his poxy regiment. Well I was the champion at the time so they all pushed me forward to take him on. I was whacking it to be honest. The bastard was about eight feet tall and about the same across. If we had been in a boxing ring I think he would have probably killed me. But we weren't. We were in a bar and I got a glass into his face before he knew what had happened. I went a bit nuts to be honest. I was a wild fucker in those days. He went to hospital for three months and I lost a stripe. Anyway all the talk in those days was about tactical and strategic nuclear weapons. Tactical meant wiping out a Sov tank army and about 50 miles of countryside. Strategic meant wiping out a whole Sov city. Bollocks really. Anyway, one of the lads said that was what I was like in the bar. Fucking tactical battlefield nuclear weapon. We all had a laugh and tactical became Tac and it still is."

Burton nodded and grinned as he pulled on the blue anorak.

"Better days eh?"

Brennan nodded and tossed down the dregs of his drink. "Aye. That they were. It has been interesting Mr Burton. I'll be in touch."

They shook hands and Burton left. Tac grinned as he poured another Scotch, much bigger this time. He had said that he needed time to think about it. As if. Only the night before he had been planning his own sergeant's war. Now he would fight it with a proper armoury. He waited until ten that night and then he made the call.

Khalil was in his room in Belfast's Europa Hotel when his mobile phone rang.

Keeley's voice had lost the Lancastrian twang. "He's agreed."

"Good. Will he accept our man?"

"He will."

"OK. Goodbye."

Another piece of Khalil's jigsaw was nicely in place. Not many more now. Then it would start.

John Burton pulled off his red wig and became Roland Keeley. A huge smile was plastered across his face. Brennan had done more than just bite. He had more or less taken his arm off. He had never met the man who was responsible for the plant. At first he had harboured one or two doubts about it. It all looked feasible enough on paper, but he had always been worried about the human factor. Everything depended on the men they had chosen reacting predictably. It only ever needed one to behave out of character for the whole thing to come apart. But they hadn't acted out of character. They had fallen neatly into line just as the planner had predicted. Who was this man? There was clearly a bond between him and Farouk. A hell of a bond. The money that was being thrown around was little more than loose change for the Prince but he wasn't generally extravagant with his cash. On the contrary, Keeley had always found that he counted every penny like a born-again Yorkshireman. But there seemed no upper limits on what he was willing to spend in this plan.

He opened the door to the room service waiter who brought in an elegantly laid out tray carrying a fillet steak and an outrageously expensive bottle of champagne. The lad's eyes nearly popped out when Keeley gave him a 50-pound note and clapped him on his back. Well why not? He had more or less played out his part and now he could live out the rest of his days in more or less whatever style he chose to. Unbelievable. Bloody sensationally unbelievable. He poured himself a glass of champagne and savoured the cold bubbles hitting the back of his throat. Halfway through the steak the feeling of elation was fading. Three-quarters and he pushed the plate away and poured a glass of Scotch which suddenly seemed more appropriate. It was ridiculous to feel this way. He was pushing 60 and he had just pulled of the coup of his life and bagged a fortune. It was all he had ever wanted. It was what he had worked for more or less the whole of his adult life. He knew that he should feel complete. Over the moon. Happy as a pig in muck.

Instead he felt like the boy who hadn't been invited to the party. The man was coming. Already on his way. A man whom Farouk would unlock the family treasure-trove for. A man who was about to march into utter mayhem without a second thought. A man who had come up with the most outrageously audacious plan that Roland Keeley had ever seen. And he had seen a few. Without really knowing it he was talking to himself.

"So what are you about to do Roland? Ride off into the sunset? Spend the cash on some girl half your age on a beach in Nevis? Play poker with sweaty Texans with their boring stories about oil? Watch a bit of bloody cricket somewhere with palm trees . . .?"

He suddenly realised that he was walking around the room waving his glass of Scotch and ranting. It made him grin. Getting old you silly old sod. Well, maybe not that old. And he realised that he wasn't ready to walk out of this particular story. Not yet. For the first time in his life he managed to admit to himself that it really wasn't about money after all. It was the life that counted. He wasn't ready to retire just yet. And once the truth had fought its way into his head he felt 30 again. He grabbed the phone. Farouk picked it up after three rings.

"Hello."

"Farouk. It's Roland."

"Roland. Hi. I heard about Brennan. Bloody marvellous work. The balance of the money will be transferred tomorrow. I thank you my friend."

Keeley took a deep breath. "Farouk. Stuff the money. Don't want it. It would be the death of me. There would be nothing left to get me out of bed in the mornings. I don't know. Look. I'm in this thing now with you guys. The Israelis are behaving like utter bastards. There must be some charity helping all the kids that they are blowing up. Give it to them. I'll leave it to you Farouk. You'll find someone worthwhile."

There was a stunned silence on the line. "Have you gone mad Roland?"

Keeley chuckled. "No. I've just gone sane. Life would be no fun without wondering where the next ten grand is coming from. Anyway, bugger it. The decision is made. That's not really why I am calling. I want to stay in on this Farouk. You've always been a mate to me. There were plenty of others you could have used over the years. They would no doubt have been cheaper."

"I have always trusted you Roland. That is all that is important. Besides, you have made my family many, many times the amount of what we paid you."

"Well, I suppose it is always nice to be trusted. Not always the case with a man like me. I appreciate it. The thing is, well, this all means a lot to you doesn't it?"

"It does. It means nearly everything."

"Well that's good enough for me old chap. I'll stay in if you don't mind. I have rather hit it off with the gallant Mr Brennan. I'll stay close to him. You can never have enough intelligence. That OK with you?"

Suddenly it was very, very important to him that his old friend said yes.

"Roland, I am quite honestly lost for words. You are indeed a true friend. Of course the answer is yes. How could it be otherwise?"

"Good. Then that's all sorted then. Tell your man that I will pop over to see him. He's at the Europa I believe?"

"He is. I will tell him. When will you be there?"

"Tomorrow evening. Tell him to call me on mobile when it is convenient. Got to go now. I need to have a chat with my hacker friend. Speak soon."

"We will. And once again. I thank you."

Keeley couldn't wipe the smile off his face. He had just handed over five million pounds to a bunch of kids in the Gaza strip who he would probably never meet and he felt better than he had in years. The next call took much longer to answer.

"Yeah."

"Rufus. It's Mr Burton here. Can you talk?"

"Yeah, it's cool. Talk away."

"We're ready. You can do it now."

"Sure. Buzzing. No probs Mr B. Give me an hour and I'll have it wrapped and packed."

"I need to remind you of something Rufus. If a single penny goes astray I will personally dig you out and castrate you with a rusty razor blade. You DO know that, don't you Rufus?"

"Hey chill it man. That's no game of mine. What Rufus says is what Rufus does. You know that man. You're paying me plenty. No need for all the heaviness man. You got the destination details then?"

Keeley gave him all the details of Tac Brennan's account in Nassau.

"OK. I'm cooking. Give me 60 man. Later."

Keeley picked up the discarded champagne and poured a glass. The mysteries of computers never ceased to fascinate him. It was quite outrageous what one could achieve with a head case like Rufus. As he sipped his drink the man in a basement flat in Islington would be working his magic. 250 thousand pounds of electronic cash would be bouncing through several shell company accounts that Farouk had set up all over the world. Then it would plunge into a Croydon branch of a high street bank for the merest of seconds before jumping straight back out again and winging its electronic way across the Atlantic to Tac Brennan's account in the Bahamas. The Croydon account was a more or less moribund account that belonged to a sleepy branch of the British National Party. It was their travel account. A few years ago a zealous leader had harboured dreams of sending the youth of South London to summer camps to learn how to be good bigots in the bracing air of the British countryside. He had been inspired by a History Channel documentary about the Hitler Youth in the 1930s. The problem was that the youth of South London did not have the remotest interest in good old-fashioned boyish fun in the fresh air. The great idea died a miserable death and the budding Hitler was forced to resign from the BNP a year later when the local paper carried the story of him being caught in the act with a fourteen-year-old smackhead called Terry in some Gents toilets close to Wimbledon Common. Nobody ever got round to cancelling the account. In fact it was pretty unlikely that anyone even realised that it existed. Keeley had found it care of his gambling pal at MI5. His old colleagues probably knew more about the financial health of the BNP than any of its members. They would know that a quarter of a million pounds slipped through the sleepy branch whilst the account holders would probably never find out. It would take them a day or two to link the Nassau account to Tac Brennan but they would get there in the end. They would have hours of fun trying to fathom where the cash had come from. In the end they would give up. What did it matter anyway? What mattered was that the BNP had wired 250 thousand pounds to the account of ex 1 Para sergeant Tac Brennan. And that would keep their candles burning late into the night.

West Beirut, 1982

The journey north from Sidon had taken them two days. It had seemed endless. The whole of Lebanon was already sliding down the slope into the abyss. There were refugees everywhere. Roads were clogged with a mixture of civilians and fighters all sharing the common goal of getting away from the charging Israeli tanks. There was no hint of any kind of organisation. The Palestinian forces had fallen apart. Now they seemed to face enemies on all sides. On the ground there were the hundreds of tanks which ate up the dusty soil. Above were the glinting jets which wreaked their havoc. And all around were the Lebanese who were taking the opportunity to settle festering sores with the Palestinians who had taken over their country.

It was Mahmoud who drove them on. Khalil had descended into a twilight world of grief. He never spoke. Never showed a flicker of emotion. He went forward like a machine. Twice bombs had dropped just a few hundred yards away and his eyes had never flickered. They walked through the horror of the debris of the bombing raids and Khalil's eyes never seemed to register the carnage. Mahmoud and Declan talked to him soothingly, patiently. They tried to bring him back slowly. They instinctively knew that there could be no hurry. Khalil's brain had thrown a blanket around everything. Inside his mind maybe there was some kind of peace. Maybe not. He just wasn't with them for a while. Declan was in trouble by the afternoon of the second day. The cut that the Iranians had lanced across his chest was turning septic. Delirium was only hours away. Mahmoud managed to find a doctor who was able to disinfect and dress the wound. The old man passed no comment. There was no comment to pass. The world had gone quite insane. The pavement outside his house was filled with smashed-up people. Young and old. Rich and poor. Shredded limbs. Raging burns. Embedded shrapnel. He had no training for anything like this. But he was there. His eyes had died through the night when they had put the body of a five-year-old on the old desk that he was using for an operating table. A huge ragged piece of shrapnel had chewed through the boy's stomach and wedged itself against his spine. There was only the merest fraction of life left in the child. The doctor had been able to do no more than stare as the last remnants of life flickered like a dying candle through the small, destroyed body. And still in their madness these Israelis poured down their death from the sky. An Irishman with a cut that festered was nothing. Just another mad thing in a world that had gone completely insane.

Mahmoud found an old car whilst Declan was being treated. All night they crawled forward without lights through the mass of people trudging away from their fear. Dawn brought their first view of the outskirts of the city and by now the sound of the Israeli tanks was all around them. Khalil had been sleeping and his eyes slowly registered the utter mayhem around him. He shook himself awake and sat up.

"Where are we?"

Mahmoud breathed an inward sigh of relief. "Nearly in Beirut. Khalde I think."

The building ahead of them suddenly seemed to crumple like a screwed-up piece of paper. The sound followed hard. The shadow of the jet flew past just a few feet above them followed microseconds later by the roar of its engines. The explosion filled every centimetre of air. Dust. Flying stones. The car buckled as the debris of the explosion slammed into it. The windows shattered and the dust cloud came at them. Another huge bang. Somewhere behind. Then one ahead. Their ears were worthless as they staggered out of the car.

There was a beach ahead of them. People were running in all directions. Somewhere close was the growl of the tanks.

They found young men on the beach. Hundreds of them. Young men with eyes blazing with hatred. They had guns and anti-tank rockets. They had crossed some kind of line. Death had become unimportant. It had become the norm. It had lost its terror. The tank engines were close now, their sound filling the air. Instead of running the young men were digging foxholes. There was madness in them. One or two had ripped up pieces of white cloth and tied them into headbands. There was a Mullah there, his eyes filled with zeal, telling them of the paradise that was waiting for them. All of them. Just a few moments away. Allah loved those who gave their lives to hold back the infidel. Allah was waiting. He was close. He was with them on the beach. Mahmoud saw it in their eyes. A new kind of resolution. Life was unimportant. The 40 or 50 tanks that were just minutes away mattered nothing. Odds mattered nothing. They had run and run and now was the time to turn and fight. Martyrdom would be their escape. They had all lost people. Mothers. Fathers. Children. Friends. They had all seen horrors enough for their lives. Now they would fight. Now they would turn the tide. They were Palestinians and Lebanese. It mattered nothing any more. They were with Allah now. All of them. And all the time the young Mullah fuelled them as the shells from the tanks started to chew up the sand of the beach.

Mahmoud couldn't move. He was thrilled by them. Thrilled by their total belief. Thrilled by the courage that had filled them. Khalil pulled at him and shouted as the shells in the air thickened.

"Brother. We need to go. Now. This is just madness."

The gleam in his younger brother's eyes stopped the words. Mahmoud bent down and picked up a ragged piece of cloth and tied it carefully around his forehead. There was an oddly peaceful smile on his lips. He was a man who had found the place that he had always known was waiting for him. So many times he had placed his bombs and run away. Streets that were far from his home in Dusseldorf and Antwerp and Lyon. Never had he seen the faces of his enemy. Never since Ammunition Hill had he faced them. Now was the time. Now, as the first shambling tanks rumbled into view. Now was the moment to show the world that his people would fight for ever. Death no longer mattered. The Jews had called them cowards and terrorists.

The media all over the world had said that they lacked the courage to stand and fight like men. Criminals. Madmen. The scum of the earth. And now it was about to change. Here on the beach at Khalde under the heat of the afternoon sun. Here was where the tide would turn.

He laid a hand on Khalil's shoulder. "No. I will stay. Here is where we will fight them. It is time. You go. Take Declan. Get him out of this place. He has done enough."

Khalil knew his brother well enough. He had known him all his life. He knew that there was no point in argument. Nothing would divert him now. He merely nodded. As he and Declan reached the modest cover of the flats that bordered the beach the Israeli guns started their crescendo. They took cover behind the low wall that surrounded the garden of a hotel. A few feet away a small group of press photographers were firing off shot after shot. One by one the huge tanks lumbered onto the sand. Massive. Impregnable. Arrogant. The snapping light of their machine guns lit up. The bigger light of shellfire from their guns lit up. The beach churned under the weight of the fire.

Then it happened. A tank near the middle of the advancing line was covered by a huge sheet of flame. The hatches started to open. Tiny figures wrapped in fire tried to scramble out before the turret was blasted clear into the air by the exploding ammunition within. The cameras went into overdrive. This was different. This was news. A Merkhava tank was no more than a smoking twisted ruin. Unheard of. Unthinkable. Then there was another. A few yards to the left. Great columns of black smoke billowed up into the rich blue of the sky. A jet screamed over the beach like a bad-tempered wasp but nothing happened. Declan started to laugh. Like a crazy man.

"See that Khalil. Couldn't do a damn thing. Too close. He would have hit his own tanks. Stuffed."

Boom. Another tank was in flames and the advance ground to a halt. It was impossible, but they were reversing. The mighty tanks were seeking sanctuary. They could not abide the losses. They couldn't face death. Not like the men on the beach who had held their ground. Khalil was stunned. There had never been a moment like this. Not in the 34 miserable years since they had stolen his country. Like strange dusty ghosts the figures on the beach were coming to their feet. With their weapons held high they jumped and screamed in triumph. Mahmoud was one of them. A crazy figure with his arms held aloft. The machine guns started up again and several of the figures were picked up and thrown backwards as if they were as light as pieces of paper. The man next to Mahmoud seemed to almost disintegrate as five heavy-calibre bullets almost cut him in half. The scream was only just forming in Khalil's mouth as the next bullet in the line took Mahmoud in the shoulder and threw him backwards. Without thinking Khalil was on his feet and about to leap the wall until Declan pulled him back hard.

"No. Wait here. Wait for me. Understand?"

Khalil was fighting and wriggling against the Irishman's firm hold. Declan pulled back his arm and thumped Khalil hard in the face, splitting his nose open.

"Understand? Fucking wait. OK?"

Khalil nodded and seemed confused at the torrent of blood that was running down his chin. Declan gave him a last look and satisfied himself. He vaulted the wall and jogged to where the photographers were intent on capturing every second of the action on the beach. He pulled a revolver out of the pocket of his jacket and pushed it hard into the earlobe of the nearest one. The man's eyes seemed about to pop out of his head.

"Hey, cool it. I'm Press. Look. Look at my jacket. Here."

"I know you're Press you clown. Now give me the jacket before I give you a fucking earache. Now. Come on. Jacket off." The cameraman wrenched off the jacket with the miserable expression of a man who had just realised that he had wet himself. Declan pulled it on. "OK. Camera. That one. Give. Take the film out if you like. Come in. Now."

He pulled the camera over his head and grinned. "Good lad. Now I need the car keys and you might just live to tell the grandchildren about this." There was no fight in the man now. He dug in his pockets and tossed over the keys. Declan pulled Khalil to his feet and propelled him towards the 4x4 vehicle that was parked in the side street behind them. It was a white Toyota with word "PRESS" emblazoned over every square inch. Two bamboo poles were wedged in the back and carried ragged pieces of white cloth. Declan pulled off one of them and jumped into the passenger seat. He threw the keys to Khalil.

"Can you drive a 4x4?"

"Yes I think so."

Declan's eyes were gleaming with adrenalin. "Well let's go and pick him up then."

The tanks had moved back into the cover of the shattered buildings at the far end of the beach and were laying down a withering fire. As soon as the white vehicle bounced onto the sand it attracted their fire like a magnet. Declan was standing up and jumping up and down in the open-topped vehicle frantically waving his white rag above his head. The firing seemed to stutter, then ease. As they raced across the beach to where Mahmoud lay it ceased. They stopped right next to him and both of them leapt out. Astonishment was painted all over his face as they lifted him and threw him into the back. Declan once again turned to wave the flag at the bemused tanks. He was gambling that the sight of a red-haired white man in a press car would be enough to make them hesitate. So far it had worked. How they would view them collecting one of the wounded would be another matter. He jumped back into the Toyota.

"Go Khalil. Go like fuck!!"

They were halfway there when the tanks ran out of patience. The shells rained down all around them. But they were too late. The white vehicle managed to tear off the beach and down an alleyway into sanctuary.

Khalil yanked on the handbrake and laid his head back against the seat. Suddenly he was laughing. All the misery and grief of the previous days miraculously dropped away for a few moments. Declan stared at him as if he were mad as a hatter. The sight of the Irishman's bemused face covered in white dust only made it worse. Khalil flapped a hand at him and his laughter doubled. Declan was never a man for whom laughter was very far away. It wasn't long before he was infected and in turn Mahmoud who was sprawled out in the back joined in. The photojournalists were with them now. Three of them were firing off shots of the crazy men of the beach. And within seconds they were laughing too. The strange sights and sounds brought faces to the doorways and windows. Alice and Wonderland had followed the Israeli Defence Force to Khalde. A couple of hundred yards away the shells ripped into the sands where only a few short weeks before children had played and lovers had walked arm in arm in the sunset. Khalil had tears streaming down his face as he clambered into the back to start to attend to Mahmoud's wound. One of the journalists pulled a half-full bottle of scotch from his camera bag and shared a few healthy gulps with Declan. The only quiet member of the scene was the photographer who had donated his camera, jacket and keys at gunpoint.

Declan tossed him the scotch then pulled off the jacket and passed over the camera. "Sorry about that mate. Needs must I'm afraid. Can't give you the car back just yet. We need to get my man here to a hospital. Let me know where you're staying and I'll drop it back later."

The man just nodded. Who was this crazy red-haired guy? Who were any of them? He took a long slug at the bottle. It was his first proper war and none of it made the slightest bit of sense. The others he was with seemed totally unconcerned by it all. Later, in the bar of the hotel when they were all steaming-drunk, one of them hung an arm over his shoulder and explained that they had all done Vietnam. Crazy was how it was. No point asking what it was all about. Just point and shoot and point and shoot again. The next morning he had a head that felt as if it had spent the night on the beach at Khalde. The man at the desk shouted him over as he made his groggy way towards the breakfast room and coffee. A man had left things for him. There were his car keys. There was a litre bottle of Jamesons whisky. There was a dog-eared collection of the poetry of W. B. Yeats. Crazy was how it was.

Two days later Khalil and Mahmoud and Declan went their different ways. In the midst of the chaos of the PLO command centres Khalil had found a phone that worked. It took half an hour to make contact with Sergei. Later that afternoon arrangements were in place. Declan headed out of the city in a battered minicab and was taken to the Turkish border where he was met and smuggled onto a cargo ship leaving Istanbul for Hamburg. Mahmoud was ferried out to a Russian ship and given medical treatment. A week later he was in Moscow to convalesce. Khalil was ordered to Damascus to act as liaison officer with the Syrians.

As he had stood with Declan in the bouncing light of the hundreds of fires that blazed across the city, the weight of his loss was once again upon him. Yet again everything was loss. His wife. His son.

And the strange man from Ireland who had become as good a friend as he would ever have. Now they were both leaving to take up their separate roles in their doomed wars.

"I would like to stay here you know" said Declan.

"Yes. I know."

"It's nicer fighting in the sunshine and the beaches are terrific."

Khalil forced a smile. Declan felt a prickle of tears and pushed them back.

"There is no choice for you and I, Khalil. Or Mahmoud. We go where they tell us. And one day we might just win. It's what we do. It's what we'll always do. Until they kill us. It has been good knowing you my friend."

"You too. Maybe there will be a day when we will meet again."

"Aye. Maybe. I'll be seeing you."

Khalil had stood and watched as the dented minicab had picked its way between the piles of rubble that littered the smashed-up street. He had stood even when the dirty red taillights had disappeared from view round the corner. He had said that one day they might just win. Might. For a while on the beach at Khalde it had seemed that anything was possible. But the euphoria had soon vanished as wave after wave of bombers had hammered away at the city. All around was turmoil and pain. They had thought their tactics so carefully. They had assessed and considered. And they had fatally misjudged their enemy. They had considered the Israelis to be hard but decent. They had been so convinced that they would protect their position in the world above all else.

Like naive children they had pulled and pulled at the tiger's tail. They had believed that the tiger would be sensible and restrained. They had been absolute in their assessment that the tiger would never do anything so stupid as striking out in rage. And they had been wrong. Completely, utterly, catastrophically wrong. The tiger had come at them with a killer ferocity that they hadn't imagined in their very worst nightmares. And now tens of thousands would pay the price of their misjudgement. Fatima had paid the price. Palestinia had paid the price. Yet another generation of his people would pay the price. Of course Sergei would point out how in the long-term it was a great victory because the Jews had given up the moral high ground. He would calculate the strategic significance of every pint of blood spilt into the dry Lebanese soil. Sergei was an expert in the political value of sacrifice. But Khalil had seen the reality of sacrifice too many times. The reality was mangled little bodies and phosphorus burns. The reality was the screaming of mothers who had lost their little ones. The reality was the lost stares of old men. The reality was the iron ring of Israeli tanks that had closed the city up tight and were bombing the Palestinian problem into a bloody oblivion.

Deep inside he knew that Khalde would change everything. For 35 years they had fought their war along political lines. They were fighting to return the land to the people. It was a simple war. One that he had always understood. Khalde had changed everything. Young men had thrown their lives under the tank tracks to earn their place in paradise. Khalde was the beginning of the Holy War. Maybe it had always been coming. Maybe it had always been a matter of time before the Mullahs declared their Jihad. And now the war would become unspeakable. Men would stoop to more or less any depths of savagery if they were made to believe that they were doing God's work. Slowly but surely the men of reason would be moved to the sidelines. Khalil knew that his part had been played out. He had seen the fierce gleam in the eyes of his brother on the beach. Even Mahmoud would be lost to him. Khalde would be the place when they would take their different roads. Mahmoud would take his fight to the depths of the pit of darkness. He had found his way.

He sat down on the cracked stone of the pavement and stared out at the burning street and felt more alone than he had ever felt before. He was a man out of step with the times. The world had moved on and left him behind with nothing and nobody. He felt every bit as broken and ruined as the city that surrounded him.

The memory of that moment of total despair came to Khalil as he drove his hire car north out of Belfast. He felt as if no more than a few days had passed rather than 21 years. For a while he had been able to keep tabs on Declan. Sergei had kept him informed. There had been a bomb outside a barracks in a place called Portadown. There had been another at a British Army base in Cyprus. And then in 1984 Declan had been caught. The security forces had been guided to him by an informant in the East Tyrone Brigade. A squad of soldiers had stormed into a barn on an isolated farm near Dungannon and caught him in the process of putting together another bomb. The last he had heard of Declan was that he had been sentenced to serve 30 years in a prison called Long Kesh. Then nothing more as Khalil himself had in turn disappeared.

Sergei had explained that a kind of peace had broken out in Ireland. The prisoners had been released as part of the Good Friday Agreement. Declan had been set free in 1999 having been locked away for fifteen years. After that there was nothing. The Russians no longer had any interest in the Irish. Times had changed. Everybody was the best of friends now. Old hatreds had been cast aside. Mandela was out. The Berlin Wall was gone. McDonalds seemed to open up a new restaurant in Moscow every week. Even Castro had grown old and cuddly. Only the Israelis and the Palestinians seemed to hang on to their vicious fight like possessive children. Sergei had told him about a pub. In the old days they had always been able to leave a message behind the bar. It would probably still be the case.

Khalil took his time with the drive. He chose side roads and stopped frequently to study the map provided by the hire company. He found the countryside relaxing. It was all so green. Field after field of cows and sheep bounded by stone walls and hedges. It seemed so quiet, so peaceful, and yet Declan's people had been fighting their war with the British for 700 years. Would his people have to fight as long? Could they? Could it be true that they still had another 650 years of suffering to endure? Maybe.

He arrived in Derry in the early afternoon and parked up in a multi-storey car park. He took an hour to stroll about the city. It was a perfect warm spring afternoon and he sat for a while drinking coffee from a cardboard cup. The bench that he had chosen was on the top of the old walls of the city and the map from the tourist information office confirmed that the warren of small streets below was the Bogside. It was where it had all started for Declan all those years ago. It was hard to imagine now as the sparrows twittered about picking up crusts tossed by young children. Then he realised that a visiting Irishman would no doubt have the same feelings about the sleepy streets of Kibya. No doubt there would be kids running around and laughing on the beach at Khalde. Picnicking families would be sitting on blankets and enjoying the panoramic view afforded from the top of Ammunition Hill. Each place had its own brief moment in history and then the world had a habit of moving on to the next place leaving memories and old wounds. This time things were different. If history had been left undisturbed Sighthill should have already played out its own notorious part. But this time Khalil was about to manipulate history rather than go with its flow. This time he would set the timetable.

He couldn't help but wonder who had been sitting in this spot 30 years before when the paratroopers had murdered fourteen civilians on Bloody Sunday. They would have enjoyed a view not so different from the place on the hill where he and Mahmoud and Salim had witnessed the execution of his family. Old wounds. Wounds that could never, ever heal. Events that took just a few minutes that affected the lives of generations. But for Kibya he would probably have become a teacher, maybe even a university professor. But for Bloody Sunday Declan would probably have been a scientist. They would have never met each other. Their paths would have been thousands of miles apart. Maybe they would both be happily married men with families and circles of friends. Instead their lives had been thrown off-course. Instead they had been sent into the darkness. Fate had dealt them both a cruel hand of cards. A small shiver ran through him. He was spending far too much time dwelling on the past. Once he would have been able to wipe his mind clean of all superfluous thoughts. Then there had only been the task in hand, the mission. But he had been young then. Young and still filled with belief. Now he stood at the gates of 60 and he was too tired for certainty. He had blocked away the past for too long. It was good that he was at last facing it.

He found a taxi and it took him to Logan's Bar which lay at the heart of the Bogside. The driver seemed intrigued that the smartly dressed man from the Middle East should wish to be taken there. It wasn't exactly a standard destination for visitors. Inside the place was more or less deserted, which was exactly what Khalil had hoped. There was only a single customer, an old man who sat in the corner with the racing section of the paper open on the table. His chin was resting on his chest as he dozed. A lady in her 50s was polishing glasses behind the bar. The TV was off and no music played. The place was very quiet. Just another place from which the world had moved on. Khalil was greeted by a warm smile.

A JOURNEY TO THE WEST

"What can I get for you love?"

"Do you have coffee?"

"Aye. Of course. I'll just be a moment."

He sat down on a bar stool and lit a cigarette as she disappeared through a door behind the bar. The walls were festooned with photos and flags. A small smile came to his lips as he spotted the Palestinian flag among them. It had been something that he had also seen as he had driven through Belfast, the flag of his people hanging in the midst of the flag of the Irish Republic. A good omen, surely.

The landlady bustled in and placed a mug of coffee on the bar.

"I made it strong love. You look like a man who is used to strong coffee. I'm like that myself. Can't abide the dishwater that most of them round here drink."

He smiled at her tact. "Indeed, strong is how I prefer it. Thank you."

She collected a pint glass and started to polish. "Is there anything else love?"

"Yes. I hope that you might help me. I would like to leave a note for an old friend. He told me that if I ever wanted to get in touch I could leave a message here."

There was an amused look in her eyes. "Is that so. And what might he be called this old friend of yours?"

"Declan. Declan Connelly."

"Oh, so you're a friend of Declan are you?" She looked him up and down another time. "Aye well, maybe so. A note you say."

"Yes." He reached into the inside pocket of his jacket and passed an envelope to her. She studied for a moment then pushed it into the pocket of her apron.

"I'll see he gets it. Coffee all right for you?"

"It is very good thank you."

She resumed her careful polishing whilst he finished his drink. Outside the sun still washed down onto the tired terraced streets. He decided to walk back to his car. He drew occasional glances from groups of children and women who talked with each other on the front steps. There were a few short conversations and then he was forgotten. He was back at his hotel in Belfast in time for dinner.

Declan was surprised by the knock at the door of his flat. He wasn't expecting anyone. It was one of the boys from Logan's.

213

"Got this for you Mr Connelly. My ma sent me with it."

"Good lad. Hang on a sec." He dug in his pockets and found a two-pound coin. "Here you go. Don't spend it all at once."

The boy's face lit up. "Thanks Mr Connelly."

Strange. It had been a long time since he had received a note via the bar. Another lifetime. He opened the envelope with a mild sense of trepidation. It wasn't a lifetime he had any wish to return to. There were only a few words on the page. But there were enough to put a wide smile on his face.

> *Remember riding a Toyota on the beach?*
> *Remember a street full of fire?*
> *We said one day we would meet again.*
> *Call me. 07770 657 129. K.*

A voice from the grave. He had tried to find Khalil when he had been released. It had been hopeless. Nobody had known anything. Nobody wanted to know. Eventually he had been give terse word that Khalil Bishawa was dead. He had been dead for many years. It had been no more than Declan had expected. Through his years in Long Kesh he had read of the Intifada years and the increasing brutality of the Israelis. The were occasional mentions of Mahmoud. He had become something of a "Last of the Mohicans" figure to the men behind the wires in Long Kesh. But Khalil had disappeared off the face of the earth.

It seemed amazing that the letter had arrived now. For days Declan's mind had been filled with memories of his time in Lebanon. The Mahmoud Bishawa story had dominated the media for a few days. Like millions of others he had logged onto Breslow's site and had been shocked by how old his comrade had become. It was incredible. First Mahmoud and now this. He thrust a cigarette into his mouth and reached for the phone. Then he stopped. Idiot Declan. Coincidences like this didn't happen. Not ever. They capture Mahmoud and Khalil gets in touch after 21 years. The smile faded a little. Not coincidence. Not a chance. It was something more. Something that guaranteed that using his landline was a very bad idea.

He threw on a jacket and took the stairs to the street two at a time. Ever since his release he had convinced himself that he was blessed to have another chance. He had got a job as a lab assistant and had once again taken to the hills at the weekends. His life was quiet and simple and it suited him just fine. The old days were far behind him. He had done his bit, and what was left of the poison had drained away during fifteen years away from the sunshine. It was enough. But this was different. This was a friend, a friend that he had been sure was lost to him.

He used a phone in a busy pub on the edge of the town centre.

"Hello."

"Is that you K?"

"It is. Hello my Irish friend." They were both far too experienced to give out any of the keywords that might interest a listening computer.

"Holy Christ but it's good to hear you. I had given you up. Want to meet?"

"Of course. Could you get to the Holly Bush Restaurant in Newcastle for lunch tomorrow?"

"Ay, that I could. One o'clock, shall we say?"

"We shall."

He went to the bar and ordered himself a double Jamesons to celebrate. It seemed that his life was about to get exciting again.

Khalil put the mobile back on the table. Roland Keeley raised a quizzical eyebrow. Khalil nodded. "He will be there."

"And do you think that he will be with us?"

"Oh yes. Declan will be with us. There are some men who you know will always be with you."

"Will you tell me about it?"

Khalil looked at him with interest. This was all so out of character for the man that Farouk had described. It was strange how men discovered their causes. Why not? He had proved himself. He sat down and quietly told of the days in Lebanon when his world had gone dark. By the end he could see that Keeley understood. He didn't say anything. He knew enough to realise that there was no need. Instead he reached into his briefcase and pulled out a folder.

"I have another file. Got it from my man in London. There's a chap here called Bland. In fact he likes to go by the name of Frankie 'The Pitbull' Bland. Thoroughly nasty piece of work. He hails from the Rathcoole estate here in Belfast. Grew up into the UDA. Became reasonably senior in the early 1990s. They pulled him in for directing terrorism and gave him ten years. He got out in 2000. He isn't much more than a gangster these days. Drugs. Prostitution. Protection. The usual stuff. The interesting thing is it would appear that the Pitbull fancies himself as something of a Nazi. Apparently he has a swastika flag on his living-room wall. The file says that he has been spotted a time or two at discreet BNP rallies. He has also popped up in Pretoria and Alabama. I thought that I might have a wee chat with him."

"Is it safe?"

Keeley laughed. "So what's safe about any of this?"

"I suppose so. I am happy to go with your judgement. He would take men with him you think?"

"Yes. I would expect so. There are lots of them who go across the water every fortnight to watch Glasgow Rangers. Football. It is too complicated to explain the niceties. Basically you take lunatic Loyalism, raging sectarianism, a generous handful of racism and you come up with a lunatic fringe of idiots who sing their songs together on the terraces of Ibrox Stadium. All in all there are lots of deluded idiots who would love to do a bit of asylum seeker bashing. The Pitbull is something of an icon for them. Here. I have a picture."

Khalil studied it. The Pitbull was about 40. He had no hair and no neck and a T-shirt that was about four sizes too small. His arms bore testament to many hours pushing weights and the pale skin was almost invisible beneath an impressive array of tattoos. His small piggy eyes exuded malevolence. Such men had always been an utter mystery to Khalil. No matter how crazy things got in his homeland, they never got crazy enough to produce men like The Pitbull. It was quite beyond him how such a man could ever become an icon to anybody. He shrugged. It wasn't his country.

"I can see no reason why not. Are you sure you can handle this man?"

Keeley chuckled. "Like putty my friend. Like putty."

Declan was waiting when Khalil walked into the restaurant the next day. Fifteen years of prison had obviously treated him well enough. He had filled out a little but still looked fit enough. His thick red hair was cut short and his face was as pale as ever. As soon as he saw Khalil he leapt to his feet and crossed the floor to meet him. They embraced whilst a waiter stood with a menu looking rather embarrassed. Declan led the way to the table, talking animatedly.

"Christ it is good to see you. I'd given you up. For sure I had. Asked everywhere, got nowhere. You were just gone. Vanished. Anyway. A drink? Something? What is it to be? I suppose you're still teetotal."

Khalil grinned. "I see that you can still talk Declan."

"Aye. I suppose I can. And why the bloody hell not. It's a great day. A day to celebrate for once and there are too few of them."

"Of course." Khalil smiled up to the waiter. "I will have coffee please. I think that perhaps we should find a bottle of champagne for my friend, don't you?"

The young waiter nodded eagerly. Champagne was a rarity. A better than usual tip tended to follow in its wake. Declan tried to keep the concern off his face at the appearance of his friend. The young man that he had left on the kerbside in Beirut was long gone. Across the table sat a man who was close to being old. His clothes were good enough, expensive, tasteful. But the skin was stretched far too tight across his face. He had grown brittle. The same old careful smile played on his lips but it did nothing to hide the overwhelming sense of sadness that seemed to wrap itself around him. Suddenly he felt rather awkward.

"I'm sorry about Mahmoud, Khalil. Well, you know I am. Well, well you know."

"I know."

"It's why you're here isn't it?"

"It is."

"And?"

"I am going to set him free. And I need help. Your help Declan. I know it is a great deal to ask after all these years. I don't expect anything really."

Declan leaned back, more relaxed now that he had confirmed his thoughts. "Don't be daft. You have it. You should know that. The two of you saved my life. It is the sort of thing that counts with me."

"If I remember correctly you repaid that particular debt on the beach at Khalde."

"Ah bollocks. That was just a wee bit of joyriding. Come on. Let's order some grub."

They filled their lunch with pleasantries, carefully avoiding anything that might be too painful. The champagne fuelled Declan's humour and soon they were both laughing at old memories. Outside the weather was once again postcard perfect. "I thought that you said that it always rained here?"

"Just a lie I'm afraid. It's Irish propaganda to keep the tourists from cluttering the place up. It's always like this. Never a drop of rain. Come on. We'll walk along the beach."

For the first few hundred yards the sand was busy with families kicking footballs and organising picnics. As the crowds thinned there were couples lying close together and looking out across the unusually blue Irish Sea. After half a mile they were alone save for distant dog walkers. They walked for several minutes in companionable silence. It was Khalil who broke it.

"You were many years in prison Declan. You were OK?"

"Aye. No bother. I was lucky really. A few years before it would have been harder. That was the time of the Blanket Protest and Bobby Sands. You remember?"

"I do."

"By the time I got there the Brits had conceded most of the things the hunger strikers had fought for. We had our own wings. We could do much as we pleased. We wore our own clothes, our cell doors were never locked by the end. The only hard thing was dealing with the boredom. How about you? What happened? After I left?"

Khalil did not reply for a while. When he spoke his voice was slightly tight. "The leadership sent me to Damascus. A liaison role. Things were turning bad between the Syrians and us. They lost just about the whole of their air force when the Israelis attacked. They soon saw that as being our fault. Then our people started calling them cowards for running away from Beirut when the going got too hard. It was foolish. Very foolish. The Syrians became angry. Soon things became very bad for all the Palestinians in the country. They came for me one night. No trial. Nothing. Just prison for ten years. It was the ways things were at that time. In the end a friend discovered where I was. Everyone else had given up. Only my friend and Mahmoud and my Uncle Salim had kept any hope. My friend is a man of great wealth. He paid for my release. Since then it seemed sensible to remain one of the disappeared. I have lived quietly for the last ten years."

Declan could sense the unease in the words. He wondered if he should say any more. In the end he was tentative. "And the time in the prison. It was bad."

"I never talk about it. Never think about it. Never."

Khalil closed his eyes for a few seconds. Maybe he was asking the impossible. If all the other memories were coming back to haunt him how could he expect the ten years of Tadmur Military Prison to stay buried? But not now. Not here. He took a long slow breath and opened his eyes again. "Sorry about that. Too much fresh air I think. I'm not accustomed to it."

Declan saw the raw pain in the eyes. Almost terror. What the hell had they done to him? "No. You're fine. So come on then. Even the Brits couldn't manage to bug this beach. Maybe you should tell me about this plan of yours. To be honest I'm getting a bit impatient."

They walked and Khalil talked. The others had listened to the plan in stupefied silence, Declan repeatedly burst into fits of laughter. Only when it came to the part that he would play did he become serious. At one point he interrupted.

"Bloody hell Khalil, it's a good job that you're a mate. If anyone else suggested that I should imitate one of those murdering UDA bastards I would give them a good thumping."

When Khalil had finished he said "Well?"

"Hey. Don't go asking me. You were always the one with the brains. I'm just a get-it-done sort of guy. Sounds OK as far as I'm concerned. If you reckon it stands a snowball's chance in hell, that's enough for me. My bit? Can't see a problem. Sure. I'm there. Just let me know when you want me. Just so long as you know that I won't hurt any civilians. Not even for Mahmoud. You know that don't you?"

"Yes. I know that. I respect that. I would never ask you."

"Then we're on. What next?"

"I will leave you with a colleague of mine. He will change your appearance and train you in your new identity. It should take no more than a few days. Then you can wait with him in Glasgow. There are a few arrangements to complete. From here on you will be working with my friend. There will be no contact between you and me."

"I disagree. You will need good people with you for the final stage. People you can trust. That is when it could all go wrong. I'll be there then Khalil. We see it through together."

Khalil found it hard to find any words. "You know the consequences?"

RED ZONE

"Sure. Remember, I never wanted to leave in the first place. That was down to you and Sergei. Well this time you're stuck with me. I was there Khalil. I saw what they did in Sidon. I saw the kids with their legs blown off. My fight too. All the way. And that my friend is non-negotiable."

Clouds had slowly been wandering from the west. They now blocked the sun and the evening darkened. A gentle breeze slid its fingers between the sand dunes. All along the now empty beach oystercatchers hopped and let out their metallic call. The men spoke little as they made their way back.

The welcome that the Loyalist estate of Rathcoole afforded to Roland Keeley was less than cordial. Once again he had become the non-descript Mr Burton. From one o'clock in the afternoon he was shoved in and out of cars and doorways by a selection of thugs. It was just after three when he was taken into the back room of a club with a canvas bag on his head. When the bag was removed he was rewarded with the sight of Frankie "The Pitbul" Bland holding court at the end of a long table laden with bottles and well-used ashtrays. There was no doubt that he was the king of his little castle. The ten shaven-headed acolytes gave him the deference of serfs.

"Well Mr Burton. This had better be good. Better be fucking good. I'm not sure that I like Brits waltzing onto my turf and asking for an appointment as if I was a fucking dentist or something."

This brought a predictable bout of chuckling from the audience.

"OK if I take a seat?" said the clearly unflustered Burton.

"Hell. Why not? Make yourself at fucking home."

Burton sat somewhat primly and viewed the in-house thugs with thinly disguised distaste. "I think it would be better if we talked alone Mr Bland."

Bland made a big show of laying on his best mocking laugh. "Oh do you now? Well isn't that just jolly hunky fucking dory. And exactly what gives you the idea that you can swan in here and start giving the fucking orders?"

All around the room muscles that had been worked for hours in the gym tensed in anticipation. Maybe the Pitbull was about to knock ten bells out of the Brit shite.

"Just ten minutes. I can assure you it will be worth it. If not then do as you wish."

220

Bland's face was interested now. "A cool fucker aren't you. OK. Why not? Go on you lot, fuck off out."

They obediently filed out with an air of resentment.

"You have the floor Mr Burton. So talk."

Burton looked about the shabby room. "Do you carry out anti-surveillance?"

"No. Why should I?"

Burton sighed. "It would be best if we took a walk outside. Just in case."

Bland looked for a moment as if he was about to blow his top but then he shrugged instead. "Come on."

He pushed open the double fire doors and they emerged into a back yard enclosed by high walls topped with broken glass. "Happy now?"

"Yes. I will be brief. I have a proposal for you."

Half an hour later he had reeled in his fish and dropped it into the keepnet. Farouk was £100,000 poorer and Frankie "Pitbull" Bland had committed himself and twenty of his finest to the coming fray as and when Mr Burton required them.

Tac Brennan was in his element. He had felt more alive in the last few days than he had in years. Night after night he had turned up in the wrong end of cities up and down the country to look up names from the past. There had been hard drinking sessions in pubs and clubs and flats where resentful wives had taken themselves off to bed early. None of the boys had been thriving. Four had been working in security. Three were bouncers. Three were unemployed. To a man they found civilian life a lousy replacement for the Regiment. They had kids under their feet and bills filling drawers and wives nagging from dawn till dusk. They hadn't needed much persuasion. They hadn't really needed any persuasion at all. The money was for the wives. New wide-screen tellies and lounge suites. Maybe a holiday in Spain at the end of the summer. Playstations and X Boxes and BMX bikes were brought home in triumph. The money was just a bonus. Being back with the lads was what counted. Tac Brennan had asked ten and all ten had said yes. They had arrived in Sighthill in dribs and drabs. Now they were all with him. The living room of the flat was a fog of smoke as old war stories were shared.

Tac said little. He sat back in his favourite chair and sipped at his drink. To many, the men in the room would have looked like any randomly chosen bunch of middle-aged British men. They weren't noticeably big. Three were rather heavier than they would have liked to be. Five were small men under five-nine. There were no bulging biceps or sunbed complexions. There wasn't one of them who would have looked out of place behind a desk in the job centre or driving a bus. Their clothes were everyday. Just regulation guys in their middle years who could be found in the betting shops and working men's clubs of Britain. Tac knew the story behind the ordinariness of their appearance.

These men were the bedrock. These were the ones who held it together when everything was falling apart. These were the men whom the government had sent to the worst places in the world without batting an eyelid. When things got really nasty, really ugly, really brutal, then these were the men who were sent in to sort it out. Riots in Ireland, impossible odds at Goose Green, genocide in the Balkans and Africa. In the days when the Red Army had been at the gates in Germany their regiment had been given an expected life expectancy of less than half an hour had the tanks ever rolled. And if it had ever happened not one of the men in the room would have flinched. They would have kept their cool, kept grinning with their poor teeth, kept cracking lousy jokes to keep up the spirits of the lads. And they would have kept it going for 30 minutes until they had been blown into a thousand little pieces by the Soviet guns

He smiled as he remembered the old banter. 30 minutes? Big fucking deal. Never happen because the commie bastards knew only too well that in that 30 minutes they would lose 30 for every Para. It was just how things were. If you don't like the idea of a 30 minutes then don't join the Paras. Easy as that. If you join, then don't moan about it. Simple as that. It had always been the same, ever since Arnhem. Every time a tonne of shit got spilt on the floor they would send in the Paras to clear it up. And for a while everyone would fall over themselves. Hey, they took Mount Longdon when we hardly had any bullets left. And for a while everyone would love the Paras. But it would always pass. And then it would be not in this pub thank you, not in my nightclub. And when it was all over and they were pensioned off nobody wanted to know them. Paras were nutters, head-bangers, just give them the shitty jobs, security night shifts, club bouncers, builders, taxi driving.

Tac knew that he had been lucky. He had been able to come home and been able to write his own script. He had respect. Nobody had messed him about. Most of the other lads had it much harder. For them it had been the job centre and polite smiles from girls half their age. Giro cheques and wives who would never let up on them. It made him sick. They were the ones who had held the front line whenever the country had asked. When it was all over they were tossed to one side like something that smelled nasty. Well now it would be their turn. Now they would make the toffee-nosed bastards who had turned their backs sit up and think. Now they would show them what it was like to have these guys on the other side.

It was time to fill them in on the detail. He tapped his glass on the wooden coffee table to gain their attention.

"OK. Enough of the mother's union lads. Time to get down to it. You all know more or less what is involved here. The money's good. There will be no officers and politicians to fuck us about. This is our show. Nobody else's. Just how it always should have been."

There were murmurs of agreement. Brennan continued.

"The objective of the op. is simple. We have 6,000 asylum seekers here in Sighthill. We want as many as possible out. All of them if we can. They have been put here because the bastards in Edinburgh and Westminster don't want them where they live. They don't want to spoil any nice areas. They chose Sighthill because it is a shit-hole as far as they are concerned. The people who live here don't matter. So they decided to screw us. 6,000. Just like that. And we are expected to put up and shut up. Well it is our job to change all this. As you know we have backing. Big backing. The guys behind us will pay the bills. No limit as yet. As to planning and strategy, it is all down to us. There are no rules of engagement here. OK so far?"

More nods. Faces were animated now.

"Good. Now we look at this in two ways. One. Consider the advantages of being able to get the job done on our terms. Remember all those times in Ireland. We all had the conversations didn't we? All the politicians had to do was to give a list of the players to the Regiment and we would have been through them like a dose of salts in a fortnight. All we needed was permission to take the gloves off and we would have wrapped the thing up. Well there are no gloves this time lads. Think about it.

'Two. There are just eleven of us. No battalion behind us this time. No radio to call up fire support. No choppers to come and lift us out if it gets a bit hairy. Not this time. It is just us. Eleven. So how will this work? Well we know how to make it work don't we. We have all seen how it is done. We throw away our book and we read someone else's. Who? The IRA. That's who. We played the game against the bastards for long enough. Now we need to learn from them. Agreed?"

Again heads nodded.

"So what have we got? One, an urban area of high-rise blocks. The police get nowhere here. Never have. Nobody talks to them. When they come they have to bring 50. The community will be behind us. Even if they are not they will be too shit-scared to say anything. This place is a rabbit warren. Our rabbit warren. Two. I can put the lads on the streets, hundreds of them, to throw the stones and the petrol bombs. They will be the shield. They will keep the coppers occupied whilst we do our work. Can you see it lads? This place is the Lower Falls and the Bogside rolled into one. This time we are the players. This time the difference is that we aren't a bunch of Mick toe-rags on a Giro. We know what we are. How would any of you have fancied patrolling the Bogside knowing that the eleven of us were up there somewhere behind the curtains?"

This brought general laughter. They could see it all right. They could see it in Technicolor.

"Good. I want you all to take a few days getting to know the ground. You will work in five teams of two. We will need to work across the city. Maybe out of town too. We'll need to stretch the cops as thin as we can. It will be too easy for them if they can concentrate everything on Sighthill. I want to give it a week to get everything drawn out. Then we'll make a start. Now I want all the ideas that I can get on this. We all know each other. We do this together. Simple as that. Now. Let's get pissed."

As they did exactly that the violence in the room was as thick in the air as the smoke.

A JOURNEY TO THE WEST

A week later Nicky felt a feeling of deepening foreboding as she drove to park up outside Rosemary's block. Every day there seemed to be more graffiti. To start with it had just been a couple of walls. 'Pakis Out', 'Send them home', 'Sighthill for the Scots'. Each day had brought more. Now it seemed that there was barely a square inch of concrete that had escaped the attentions of the artists. More alarmingly was the increasing violence of the slogans. 'Burn the bastards out' in particular sent a chill down her spine. Campbell had told her that the police were doing what they could but it was like pissing in the wind. He had been as mad as she had ever seen him the night before when they had eaten out in a Thai restaurant.

"We got one this afternoon you know. Spotted him as we came around the corner. He tried to leg it but he slipped and cracked his head on the pavement. Couldn't have been any older than eight or nine. I picked him up and dusted him down and got him in the car. The little sod was in floods of tears. He had nearly finished his little work of art. 'Kill the Paki fuckers'. That was his contribution. I asked him what the hell he thought he was playing at. Well his guard slipped for a moment. He said that some bloke was paying all of them a tenner each for everything they wrote. He was even doling out the spray tins. When I asked him who the bloke was he clammed up. I took him home and got a screaming fit from his mum for my troubles. No prizes for guessing who is behind it."

"Brennan I suppose."

He had nodded and taken a sip of his beer. "I had a right old ding-dong down at the station. You can't prove anything they said. You're letting what happened cloud your judgement they said. They explained how sensitive things were. It's because the bastard got his face in the papers. All the brass are laying eggs after what happened. All they seem to care about is PR. Christ Nicky I've got a bad feeling. A really, really bad feeling."

It was a feeling that she shared as she locked her car. A small group of teenagers were hanging around in the doorway to the flats. They smirked as she approached and moved to block her way.

"Where do you think you're going you Paki-loving bitch."

"Inside if you will excuse me."

The largest one of them pushed himself in close and gave a mocking imitation of her voice. "And what if we don't excuse you.

And what if we decide to stove your fucking head in instead. What about that?"

She pushed him back. "I suggest you have a word with Mr Brennan before you do anything that you might regret. He and I have an understanding. Now, unless there is anything else I suggest that you all piss off."

The mention of Brennan worked its usual magic. She pushed through them and went through the main door with her heart thumping with adrenalin. It infuriated her that the only way she could feel remotely safe any more was by mentioning the man she despised. As usual there wasn't a police officer in sight. For a few days she had given Campbell a hard time about it until she had realised that it wasn't fair. He pleaded with her to let him know when she was coming to Sighthill so that he could keep an eye on her but she always refused. She wasn't concerned about herself. It was all of them. Where was their protection? It was a disgrace. Finally she had realised just how unfair she was being. It wasn't Campbell's decision. If it had been, then things would have been very different.

He was doing his best. More than that. Every day he begged for more officers to be deployed only to be told that it was impossible. She hadn't been at all happy when he had insisted on returning to work. It had been far too early. His face still bore the marks of the beating he had taken. He had brushed the concerns aside. Normally his superiors would have refused him permission point blank. And then they would have posted him far away from Sighthill. But it was a situation that was far from normal. The press gave great coverage of the gallant PC as he returned to his beat a few short weeks after nearly being beaten to death. It was about the only decent bit of PR that the Strathclyde force managed to get in the wake of the riot. They also realised that more or less the sum total of their intelligence of what was going on up in Sighthill was down to PC Campbell Swann.

She had felt the fear in him as he had got himself ready to return for his first day back. He was too artificial in his high spirits. She felt torn inside as he gave her a wink and walked out of the door of her flat. The only reason that he was returning was that he could try to be there for her when she visited. If she had told him that she wouldn't go any more then maybe he would have stayed clear too. She hadn't been able to. She felt quite unable to leave the friends that she had made, particularly Rosemary. She knew with a cold certainty that she would never be able to live with herself if she ran away. And so every night after school she had got into her car and driven to Sighthill. Every night she had to fight a little harder to push down the fear that crawled up her throat. The place was like a great ticking bomb and nobody in authority seemed willing to accept it. Thursday night was an English class night. Before the riot Rosemary's lessons had been growing more popular every week. The night before the killings the room had been filled with 32 students from nine different countries. The following week there had only been ten and the evening had been a sombre affair. When Nicky walked into the meeting room only Rosemary and her son Moses were waiting for her. The African woman was almost shaking with rage. She was talking at Nicky before she had time to take her jacket off.

"Look at this. This is why nobody is come here Nicky. Everybody they get one of these. Last night. Everybody in the building. Everybody in Sighthill. You read Nicky. You read it good."

She thrust an A4 photocopy into Nicky's hand.

Take this as a final warning. It is time for you to leave Sighthill.
Go now, and you will be safe. Stay and you will suffer.
Go before we burn you out. Go home. Go anywhere.
Just go or pay the price. You are not welcome here.

The words chilled Nicky. Again there was the talk of burning. She tried to show bravado. She tossed the paper to the table dismissively.

"Come on now Rosemary. Don't take any notice of this nonsense. It's probably just kids. It is the sort of nonsense I see every day at school."

She didn't believe a word of it and hated herself for the silly breezy lie. She could see that Rosemary didn't buy it either.

"I too saw these things at my school Nicky. In Bulawayo. They came from Mugabe. It is no joke Nicky. You know this."

Nicky knew it well enough. She gave up on the pretence and nodded. "That is why nobody has come?"

"Everyone is scared. Real scared. They queue all day asking for a transfer out of here. People are staying in their flats. They not come here tonight Nicky. They not go anywhere."

Moses stood up from where he had been sitting quietly. He had shot up in the months that Nicky had known him. Now he stood well over six feet. Nicky had been growing concerned at the boy's state of mind. When she had first met him he had shared his mother's sunny personality but he had changed in the days after the riot. Now his face was a mask. Outwardly he seemed calm enough, but there was something lurking below the surface. For a moment she met his eyes and her feeling of disquiet deepened. What was it that she saw there? Rage? Hate? Nothing good, that was for sure. "I think that nobody is coming to this place now. I will go mother. I will see you later in the flat."

Rosemary watched him leave and shrugged her huge shoulders. "I not know what is happening with this boy. New friends. Two boys are from home in Zimbabwe. There is one from Kosovo. Two from Iraq. I tell him be careful but he is no listen to me."

"I'm sure he'll be fine. He has always struck me as a sensible boy."

The African woman let out a booming laugh and slapped the table. "Sensible! No sensible. Moses is a Matebele boy. He is his father's son. No Matebele is ever sensible."

"Would you like me to get Campbell to have a talk with him?" Campbell had taken to Moses. He had taken him to the football at Celtic Park on two occasions and had been trying to persuade him to join a team.

"Maybe. It will need a man to talk with him. Matebele men never listen to their women. It is why they always fight."

"Not just Matebele men" chuckled Nicky. It broke the tension and the two women fell into their normal familiarity. They allowed 30 minutes just in case any pupils were running late. They weren't. It was fruitless. Nicky was furious that Brennan had undone months of patient work with a simple piece of photocopied A4. "Come on. No point in us waiting here. Let's go find Campbell. He needs to see this, though I doubt if he will be able to make anyone listen."

They drove about the estate for ten minutes until they spotted Campbell's car. He was talking with a group of eight youths on the pavement. They started jeering as Nicky and Rosemary climbed out of the car. Campbell sent them packing and they strutted off shouting comments at Rosemary as they went. Campbell looked rather embarrassed. "Sorry Rosemary."

A JOURNEY TO THE WEST

She beamed a huge white smile. "You not worry about me Campbell. Little words are like flies on an elephant to a big woman like me. You watch if they dare come close in to say these things. I think no."

"I think no too."

Nicky pulled the sheet out of the pocket of her jacket and handed it over. "Have a look at this. They were delivered last night. Every asylum seeker in Rosemary's block got one last night. Maybe everyone in Sighthill. I don't know. This is getting worse Campbell. Surely you can feel it."

He read it with disgust etched over his face. "Course I can. But nobody will listen. I am beginning to sound like a stuck record at the station. They are even sniggering as I walk in. I'm sick of it. Look. I'll pass it on. Of course I will. But don't get your hopes up. Nobody dares rock the boat at the moment."

Rosemary shook her head. "Someone going to have to die before people get interested. That is what it is. Someone going to get killed."

He wanted to argue and to say of course not but he couldn't because it was true. Somebody was going to have to die and it was only a matter of time until they did.

The same A4 sheet of paper arrived through Johnny Hendon's letterbox the next morning. He had been expecting it. The previous evening he had received a call from the enigmatic Mr Burton.

"Hello Johnny. Mr Burton here. How are you?"

"Fine and dandy."

"And Lena? How is Lena?"

"She's good." That was the understatement of the year. Of the century. Of the bloody millennium. Lena was better than good. Lena was fantastic. Lena was a miracle. Lena was perfection. And Lena was back in his bed sipping champagne and waiting for him to finish his phone call.

"Excellent. I'm pleased for you Johnny. I think that it might just be time for a bit of copy. Have you been up to Sighthill this week?"

"No."

"You should go. The graffiti artists have been hard at it. I've heard that there is barely a square inch of wall that isn't covered. They seem to want our friends the asylum seekers to be on their way out. All very choice from what I can gather. I have heard that someone is paying the kids a tenner a go for every bit of artwork. Beats a paper round I suppose. And there has been a little mail-shot sent round. Not very pleasant. Along the lines of 'Get out or we'll set you on fire.' I think that a lad of your talent will come up with some decent copy Johnny. I look forward to reading it."

Johnny read the A4 sheet and felt a prickle of excitement. Part of him had been unable to believe Burton's crazy story. Sure, the money was real enough. Lena was certainly real enough, but even so, it just all seemed so bloody far-fetched. His sense of reality hadn't exactly been helped by the newly-affordable mountain of cocaine that he had been shovelling up his nose. But there was something inescapably real about the sheet of paper in his hands. It was accompanied by a brief note. "Is this the BNP? Maybe. Raise the stakes."

He spent the morning wandering around Sighthill snapping photographs. The onset of the graffiti artists had been astounding. Someone must have shelled out a hell of a lot of tenners. The local economy must have had the greatest boost that it had seen in years. He talked to a few people that he knew. Nobody was saying much. Nobody was saying nearly enough, which meant more than if they had said a whole lot. Something was brewing for sure. The whole place felt like a tinderbox. He captured several images of walls where "BNP" appeared besides violent messages.

He hit his word processor as soon as he got back in.

LETTERS OF HATE: STREETS OF FEAR

The Government tells us that things are fine up in Sighthill now. The police say that things are calm. Obviously neither have taken the trouble to go and look for themselves. In the last seven days every spare inch of wall has been covered in the messages of hate. It is an open secret that someone is paying the kids £10 for every message they spray. There must have been many, many ten-pound notes handed over in the last seven days. If anybody knows the source of the payments they certainly are not telling. The estate is clamped into a vice of fear. It is impossible not to notice that the slogan BNP has appeared on every street. The far-right organisation has always struggled to gain a toehold in Scotland. All that seems to be changing in the wake of the Sighthill riot. A new and ugly racial hate has come to the heart of Glasgow.

Two nights ago a letter was hand-delivered to every asylum seeker in Sighthill. You can see it below. Who is behind it? Nobody knows, but it isn't hard to guess. The police are adamant that the situation is calm and everything is under control. This begs the question of how on earth do they know? In the week following the riot the streets of Sighthill were filled with police officers. Now they are nowhere to be seen. Nobody is willing to admit that the dark forces of racism are growing in strength in the middle of Scotland's largest city. It is quite impossible not to draw the conclusion that time is beginning to run out on Sighthill's streets of hate."

He emailed the story to his old editor on *The Recorder* and received a call back minutes later. They haggled happily for a couple of minutes and then shook on a price. The piece appeared the next day.

Daniel Morrissey spat out his mouthful of cornflakes as he turned over the front page of *The Recorder* to be confronted with the photo at the top of Johnny Hendon's story.

"For fuck's sake."

Roseanne wandered into the room stark-naked from the shower rubbing at her wet hair with a towel. She chuckled.

"Dear oh dear. What kind of language is that for a Minister of State to be using at such an early hour?"

For a moment the joint impact of his research assistant's sensational nakedness and the spray-painted message *"BNP – Burn the bastards out"* left him utterly lost for words. His disorientation wasn't helped when she sat in his lap and took the paper from him. Despite his onerous Ministerial duties in the face of a major crisis on the streets of his home city, he couldn't help but allow his left hand to caress her nipple as she read. When she finished the article she tossed the paper down and kissed him vigorously before getting up to switch the kettle on. "Excellent. Don't you think darling?"

He dragged his eyes away from her bottom. "Excellent! What the fuck do you mean, excellent! They're talking about burning people alive here. Can't you fucking read?"

She was perfectly unperturbed. "Of course I can read darling. You know that full well. I hate to point this out, but 'fucking' in this contest is a more or less wholly worthless adjective. I do wish you would stop it. Just imagine if it popped-out at the wrong time."

Now anger was mixed in with consternation and frantic arousal. "Don't go all posh on me Rosy. Can't you see this is serious? I mean fuc . . . damn serious. They will expect me to say something."

She grinned and put a coffee in front of him. "Better darling. Much better." She sat down opposite him and he wondered whether he should ask her to put a robe on. She was wreaking utter havoc with his ability to concentrate. The Junior Minister of Justice in him was on the verge of asking her cover herself up, but the lad from the South Side was enjoying looking at her majestic tits far too much and won the day.

She gave him a mocking look, fully aware of the effect she was having. "Quite right Daniel. You will indeed be expected to say something. Of course you will. And that is why I say that it is excellent. An excellent opportunity. What we must decide is what you say, how you say it, where you say it and when you say it. And we must be quite sure that you milk this opportunity for all that it is worth. Yes?"

At times her brazen attitude to everything knocked him sideways. Here she was sitting at his kitchen table stark bollock-naked all chuffed because some maniac bastards in Sighthill were threatening to burn some other poor bastards to toast. At times she was frightening and there wasn't a single damn thing he could do about it. "What do you think? Call a Press Conference at the Assembly this afternoon?"

"Oh no. Far too boring. We can do better than that. You must go. Now. This morning. Shoot from the hip. Man of action and all that."

"Go where?"

"Sighthill of course. We can be there in an hour."

"Sighthill! Are you bloody mad!"

She just smiled. She loved getting him going. "No I am not. Think about it. When do politicians ever go and get their hands dirty? Not often. And what happens when they do? Everybody thinks they are wonderful. Remember Heseltine in Liverpool after the Toxteth Riots? It was the making of him."

"But I can't just go like that. There need to be arrangements. Police. Press. Lots of stuff."

"Maybe not. Maybe this can be the clever part. From what you tell me this dreadful man Brennan calls the shots. Isn't that what your little journalist friend told you?"

He nodded. She lit up her first Silk Cut of the day and continued. "Well he is clearly nobody's fool. No matter what ghastly plans he has in mind for Sighthill, I am sure that bashing up a Minister of State isn't one of them. After all, where would that get him? No, what you must do is ring this Johnny Hendon and arrange to meet him in a couple of hours. Have a walk about. Talk to a few people. Get him to take your picture. Can't you see it Daniel? Just one journalist. Not a whole gang of them. The Minister who doesn't care about the publicity, yes? Man of the people only interested in getting to the root of the problem. Yes?"

One by one the pennies dropped into place and he could see it. All of it. Like a long view over wheat fields on, clear summer day. And a smile spread over his face. Roseanne went over to the window and looked out. "Even better. It's cloudy."

"Why does it being cloudy make it better?"

"Because, my love, it means that you can wear your donkey jacket and you know how much I like to see you in your donkey jacket."

Johnny waited in his car. He could still barely believe it. He had always realised that Danny Morrissey had something about him, but he would never have expected anything like this. He had to give him ten out of ten for bottle, no doubt about it. It was ten past. Maybe he had changed his mind. He couldn't have blamed him if he had.

At that moment a blue BMW pulled up next to him. Morrissey was in the passenger seat. The knockout research assistant was at the wheel. There was something about her. Maybe she was the power behind the throne. It wouldn't be a first if she was. He jumped out and shook Morrissey's hand.

"Good to see you Danny. And thanks for this."

The easy smile of the successful politician was firmly in place.

"Hey, us lads form the South Side don't get many opportunities to have an old boys network. Got to grab the chance when it comes around. Why give a good story to all those twats on the tabloids. Did you get hold of Brennan?"

It was the line that Morrissey had drawn. The only way that he was going on a walkabout around Sighthill was if Johnny managed to get the nod from Tac Brennan.

"Aye. Nae bother. He thinks that you're a mad fucker but you'll be fine. So. What's it to be? Walk or ride." Daniel was on the verge of choosing the car when Roseanne chirped in.

"Oh I think we should walk. We could both use some air after being cooped up on the M8. Let's go shall we."

Johnny looked to Morrissey for confirmation and received an ambiguous shrug by way of a reply.

Rosemary marched out of the front door of her block and set out at a determined pace for the supermarket. Her body language was that of an angry woman and the set of her face challenged anyone to get in her way. She was fresh from a big row with her son. Ever since the riot, Moses had taken to escorting her wherever she went. This morning had been the final straw and she had erupted. She didn't need no son of hers to follow her around like some guard dog. She wasn't about to be frightened by any skinny kids and she didn't need a chaperone. She had given it to him with both barrels and shaken the walls and all he had done was sit and smile at her with an annoyingly patient expression. What really fuelled her anger was that she realised that they were already beyond a crossroads in their lives. Moses was not a boy any more. The days when she could be the one in charge had passed. Now he was nearly a man and she was getting older in a cold place far from home and her husband was in the ground. She had thrown on her coat and stormed out into the corridor whilst he had locked the door and followed.

Her anger was slowly fading but she wasn't ready to let him know. He followed her at a respectful distance whilst she marched along the pavement. It came as no surprise when a group of figures emerged from a doorway 50 yards ahead to block the pavement. It was an everyday occurrence now. It had become quite impossible to simply walk to the shops and return without confrontation. The shopping list that she had in her pocket was huge. None of her neighbours dared to leave the block and they had all accepted her offer to pick up their provisions. Secretly she had been happy enough to lose the morning argument. She was damned if she needed her son as an escort, but he would be more than useful as a bag carrier.

The taunts started up when they were 30 yards short. Five of them. What was it with some kids in this country? They had no respect. It wasn't just the asylum seekers. It was everyone. She had heard them screaming their abuse at fathers and mothers and passers-by. They needed a good beating. All of them. They had needed a good beating from the day that they had learned to walk. She would have loved to see how cocky they would have been after a few whacks across the backside with a good firm stick.

They arranged themselves across the pavement in a tight group. It was usual. They would part once she got close enough. She thrust her chin up and stared into their pale faces with all the ferocity that she could muster. They were all shouting now. Faces twisted.

Ten yards and still the line held. There was no doubt that they were getting bolder. The riot had changed everything. Before there had been something to hold them back. Now the string had been cut and they were on the edge of letting loose. The whole of Sighthill was like a great game of chicken. Who would be the first to go over the line? Who would be the first to turn threats into violent reality? Five yards and still no movement. A small flutter of fear in her stomach. What was she doing here? She was a middle-aged woman. What chance would she have against five of them? She shook the thought from her head angrily. What was there to be frightened of here? They were just boys. Pathetic skinny boys who could only be brave in a gang. She marched straight into the one in the middle who didn't step aside.

For a moment they were all as confused as each other. Rosemary couldn't quite believe that the boy had stood his ground. The youth couldn't quite believe that the black woman had actually marched straight into him and almost knocked him flat on his back. The other four struggled to work out what they should do next. It was the lead boy who was suffering with a near mortal injury to his pride that reacted first. He jumped forward and started screaming.

"You fucking black bitch. Think you can push me do you? Fucking slag."

He reached out and pushed Rosemary hard in the chest. He had expected her to topple backwards. Instead he had completely underestimated her size and strength. She swotted his hand away and started shouting back at him in a voice that swallowed up his and spat it out.

"You take your hand off me. Lay one hand on me and I beat you like a dog. Get out of my way. Get away."

His pride was almost in shreds now. There was nowhere to go. If she had only backed off then he would have had options. But she hadn't. She was leaning into him. Pushing him back. Humiliating him with the sheer volume of her anger. He had to do something. If he didn't he would have the piss taken every day for the next ten years. He drew back his fist and made to punch the black face that was yelling at him. Then the lights went out.

Moses had stepped forward and floored him with a single huge punch. The boy went down like a burst bag of cement. He was actually nearly a year older than Moses was but in terms of build and strength he was an infant. Blood gushed out of his wrecked nose. The boy's friends took an instinctive step back as they reeled at the sudden intervention. Rosemary was every bit as stunned as her son took a slow, careful step towards them. Suddenly he seemed to be about three feet taller. To the boys he was just a huge scary black lad and each of them was ready to run like hell. To Rosemary he was more. She could feel the fighting madness that was gushing through him. How many times had she seen it before? It was bred into the men of her tribe from the moment that they took their first steps. Fathers and uncles and grandfathers put it into them with their tales of great battles from the past. It was a madness that did not know when to stop. It was a madness that would kill.

"You boys want to die? OK. You can die. You come near my mother and you die."

His voice was just as quiet as it always was. He was right on the edge. She laid a hand on his shoulder and spoke evenly.

"Moses. You leave this thing now. You leave these boys now."

At that point a police car skidded to a halt and the four gratefully took the excuse and ran. Campbell Swann climbed out and watched them as they disappeared down an alleyway. He took in the situation on the pavement and sighed. He turned over the unconscious boy onto his side and shook his head.

"This one's out for the count. What happened Rosemary?"

"They block the pavement. Not let us go past. This one he push me and call me names. He about to hit me. Moses hit him."

Campbell nodded. He had seen as much from the far end of the road. He pulled the radio out of the car and called for back-up and an ambulance. A few residents were collecting on the edges of the scene now and nobody was very happy. Campbell had an awful sense of déjà vu. Another Sighthill lad on the pavement in a pool of blood and a crowd gathering. Oh Christ, not again.

The crowd was still barely a cluster when Johnny turned into the street.

"Aye aye, what have we got here?"

He drew nearer slowly. The picture slowly became clear. One lad on the ground. Big black boy looking like Mount Rushmore. Tall black woman. Probably the mother. Constable Swann looking like a man with toothache. And a crowd that could become a mob in about ten minutes. Not good. Not good at all.

"Danny, this looks a bit hairy. I don't think it's a very good idea that we stop."

But Roseanne was way ahead of him. There had been something immediately familiar about the tall policeman. Then it clicked. It was Swann. The one who had been in all the papers after the riot. She along with all her friends had decided that they fancied the pants off him. This was too good to be true.

"Hey. No. Stop."

Johnny half-turned in his seat. "You what?"

"I said stop. This is what we've come for. That's Swann. The one from the riot."

"I know it's Swann. So fucking what if it's fucking Swann?"

She was mad now. "So it's a blinding fucking photo opportunity you dickhead. So stop the fucking car and let's get out!"

Now Daniel turned with the face of a man with earache and toothache and a boil on his backside. "Look Rosy, this isn't a good idea. The situation . . ."

"Oh shut up Daniel and stop being such a bloody wimp. Just get out."

For a moment Johnny had shown an instinctive concern for the up and coming Deputy Minister for Justice and the very real chance of him being embroiled in a very real Sighthill riot. But the concern didn't last. It only took seconds for him to see the situation through the eyes of the blazing research assistant. She was dead-on right. This was about to be one hell of a photo opportunity and he was the only man in town with a camera. He thanked his lucky stars that it was the lady who was wearing the trousers.

"Come on Danny. Cometh the hour, cometh the man and all that. Out you get. Time to see if you've got what it takes."

The Junior Minster for Justice could come up with nothing more profound than "Oh fuck it" as he reluctantly opened his car door.

Campbell had to do a double take. No. Couldn't be. No bloody way. But it was. Ten yards away Daniel Morrissey MSP was climbing out of the passenger side of a shabby VW Golf. Who was the driver? Something familiar there. Of course. The reporter. The one who took the pictures of Teague. What the hell was he doing here with Morrissey? What the hell was happening, full stop, period. The politician had forced his public image into place and approached the policeman with a firm confident smile.

"Good morning constable. Everything in order?" He spoke with the voice of a man meeting a work colleague on the tenth tee. Campbell was utterly lost for words. Was the bloody man stark raving mad? Everything in order? What kind of Disneyland did he think this was? The best he could come up with was the single word that had served junior ranks so well down the ages whenever they were utterly staggered by the rampant idiocy of their superiors.

"Sir."

Heads in the crowd were turning now. The word was spreading. It was Morrissey. Remember. That jumped-up bastard from Parkhead who had given them all a lecture. That wanker. Grinning like a bastard in his donkey jacket with his posh tart behind him. It was a 56-year-old divorcee called Mary Higgins who rode onto the attack first fresh from the first double vodka and orange of the day.

"Don't you come down here with your smug fucking smile and think you can tell us what to do. Ah ken you Morrissey. Just a jumped up wee prick from Parkheed who thinks his shite doesn't smell any more. Well look there you bastard. Look at this lad on the floor. Another one. When's it going to stop? When are you going to get these smelly bastards out an send them . . ."

He missed the last part of Mary's considered thoughts on the problems of Sighthill because the rest of the growing crowd joined in with her. The hard face framed with a violent halo of peroxide hair bore in on him, showering him with spittle. She jabbed him hard in the chest with thin nicotine-stained fingers and backed him up. As he retreated inch by inch to the car his mind was filled with a single train of thought. He didn't care how much he fancied Rosy, he didn't care how good she was in bed, he didn't care how much he enjoyed watching her flounce naked around his kitchen, he didn't care about any of it. If he ever got out of this she was fired, fired and fired again. For the moment she was pinned between himself and the car. He didn't hear any smart words of political wisdom coming from her pretty lips now. Welcome to the real world darling. Welcome to my town. From the corner of his eye he caught the grinning face of Johnny Hendon as he reeled off the photos. Bastard.

Then the pressure of the crowd eased as Swann pushed his strong body in the way. To his astonishment he saw that the tall black boy was with him, forcing back the press of the crowd. A man in the front kicked out at him only to be felled conclusively by a short ferocious jab to the face. A crazy part of Morrissey's brain remembered Brando saying how he coulda been a contender. Beside him Swann's raised voice betrayed growing panic as the situation started to spin out of control.

"Moses! Easy! Take it easy for Christ's sake!"

And then by a miracle there was no pressure from the crowd. They backed off. They fell silent. A cool blissful river of relief flooded through Daniel. Behind him he could hear Roseanne taking on board oxygen in short, panting breaths. The crowd, which had now grown to over 50, fell back into a semicircle around the figure of a middle-aged man in a light blue golf jacket.

Tac Brennan smiled warmly to the Minister. "Very sorry about this sir. Things are a little excitable round here at the moment. You OK?"

No he wasn't. His heart was thumping at four times the legal rate and he was sweating like a pig in the donkey jacket, which had turned out to be too warm after all, cloud or no cloud. Thankfully his political instincts were made of stern stuff. He pulled himself up to his full height and strode over to Brennan to take his hand in a firm confident grip. Tac's eyes flickered with mocking amusement as he registered the clammy sweat of fear on the politician's palm.

"I'm fine thank you. Too whom do I owe thanks?" As if he needed to ask. He knew full well who it was, the hard looking bastard.

"Brennan. I'm Brennan."

"Good lord. Of course. You lost your boy. May I say how terribly sorry I am for your loss."

Smarmy bastard thought Tac. Just an overblown lad from Parkhead and he thinks he can offer me condolences. Instead he merely nodded. He seemed to notice the crowd for the first time.

"OK people. That's the excitement for the day. I saw what happened. Those idiots had a go at the lad's mum. We don't do that round here. There are rules. This pillock deserved all he got." He casually gestured to the still unconscious figure on the floor. Then he turned to Swann. "I don't think that there is any need for anything formal constable, do you? Just a bit of fisticuffs. Youthful high spirits. Nothing wrong with that."

He challenged the younger man with a mocking smile. One day, thought Campbell, one day I'm going to split your ugly face in two like an over-ripe peach. But not today. He was under instructions. Maintain calm. Keep a lid on things.

"Aye. Maybe it is best if everyone just goes home. Let's not have any more trouble."

The crowd knew that the show was over. Sirens heralded the approach of two squad cars and an ambulance. The people melted away. With a soft click Johnny Hendon got one last shot. The next day it would appear alongside one of the frantic crushed figure of Morrissey as Moses and Campbell held back the mob. It was a picture of four men. A grinning Tac Brennan. An uneasy looking Daniel Morrissey complete with rumpled donkey jacket, a scowling Campbell Swann, and Moses Mdanga looking every inch the young warrior.

Brennan strolled away down the pavement leaving the others not really sure what to do. Campbell went over to the injured boy and waved the ambulance crew over. Roseanne dragged a Silk Cut out of her handbag and wrenched off the filter before lighting-up. Daniel Morrissey didn't have a clue what to do next and looked over to his old school friend for inspiration. Before he could speak the black woman was upon him.

"I hope you can see now how it is here. So you do something. You do something quick before people get killed. You do something Mr Politician. Come on Moses. We got shopping things to get."

As they started down the pavement Daniel jogged forward and tapped Moses on the shoulder. The boy turned and Daniel took his hand and shook it.

"Thanks. Thanks for the help. And . . . Well. Best of luck."

Moses nodded then turned and followed his mother as she continued her head-high swaggering walk to the shops.

Johnny put his camera away in the bag and joined the Minister.

"Enough fact-finding for one day?"

"Aye. I think so."

"Fancy a pint?"

"I fancy about thirteen but one will do."

The next morning Daniel's star rose even further into the firmament. Johnny's story told of a deeply committed politician who had walked into the heart of danger without a second thought. And Rosy kept her job.

Khalil glanced up at the airport clock. Still plenty of time. Two hours until check in. He felt as if he had spent enough time in airports to last a lifetime over the previous week. He had flown to Amman from Belfast via London and Paris and had met with his Uncle Salim in a small town a few miles across the border. The old man had brought along his new identity. He was now Ahmad Mansour. Mansour who was born in Jenin in 1950 and fled to Syria with his family ahead of the Israeli tanks in 1967. Mansour who had studied at university in Damascus and become a teacher. Mansour who had risen to the post of deputy head by 1984 when the secret police had come for him and thrown him into Tadmur prison for sixteen years. His family hadn't even known where he was until 1991. He had received a belated trial in 1993 and had been sentenced to twenty years for crimes against the state. His crime had been the same as many in those dark days. His crime was that he had been a Palestinian. It was a crime that Khalil had shared. His only son had followed his father into the teaching profession and in 1988 he followed him into Tadmur. He never followed him out. His weak heart gave in after a particularly energetic beating in 1990. Mansour was now starting a new life in Cairo with his wife. Care of Farouk he had a new name, new papers, a new house, a new bank account with enough to live out his life, and a new job in a local school. He hadn't needed to think for very long before relinquishing his identity.

From Amman, Khalil had flown to Cairo and then on to Paris. Now he was whiling away the time before the Ryan Air flight to Glasgow's Prestwick airport. He had worked his way through most of the material that he needed to cover before catching the plane. Sergei had come up trumps. The transcripts from Brennan's flat gave him chapter and verse. The ex-sergeant was taking things at his own pace. He had started with the graffiti campaign and the leaflet drop. He was allowing things to escalate in his own time. He certainly seemed more than confident that he enjoyed the full backing of his community. That was good. It had been one of the many imponderables that Khalil had been nervous about. His plans needed Tac Brennan to be followed.

The morning papers made fascinating reading. Another of the imponderables was firming up to perfection. It had been Keeley who had read Daniel Morrissey MSP like a favourite old book. Khalil had been sceptical at first. However, he had seen enough of his own leader Yasser Arafat over the years to be only too familiar with how far politicians would go for a few headlines. Morrissey had swallowed Johnny Hendon's bait without a second's thought. Perfect. Absolutely perfect.

He finished the last of his reading and walked over to toss his papers away in a bin. There was no more to do. All the preparations that had seemed so impossible and daunting were now complete. His team was in place and ready to be called from the dressing room. Now it would be just a matter of a short period and things would be resolved one way or another. He felt no great fear as he sipped expresso coffee and waited to take a plane to his last battle. Only anticipation. One more time and it would be over at last.

Three-and-a-half hours later he waited until last to get off the plane. As the couples and families and businessmen made their way through passport control to collect their baggage he made his way to an immigration officer.

"Excuse me. I am Ahmad Mansour. Please. I would like to claim asylum."

He had arrived in the West.

PART THREE

Red Zone

Darkness had come to the skies of Tel Aviv hours earlier, but Mordechai Breslow worked away mechanically. He seemed to go home less and less as he got older. All through his life he had never regretted for a second his decision not to marry. His work had always been everything to him. It had always been more than enough. Only now was he beginning to feel the emptiness. Almost every one of the colleagues with whom he had fought his long war had now retired. Half of them had died. He was the last of the old guard. A relic. And he knew that there were whispers in the corridors that the time was fast approaching for Mordechai Breslow to retire.

He had no home kibbutz to return to where he could live out his days on a veranda. There were no grandchildren to bounce on his knee to make him feel young. There would be no ardent young patriots to sit and listen with awe to his stories of the days when their people had faced the abyss. Instead there was just a small flat on the outskirts of Tel Aviv. A living room. A bedroom. A kitchen. A bathroom. A balcony that overlooked a cement factory. Inside he always felt like a prisoner entombed by his loneliness. He could never find the heart to stay for long in the flat. The empty hours made him question everything.

The last time he had been there was when he had staggered in after the party that they had thrown to celebrate the capture of The Fox. His head had been spinning as it hit the pillow and even though he had been awake for 48 hours straight, sleep had refused to come. As the ceiling slowly revolved above him he could not erase the words of Mahmoud Bishawa from his thoughts. The man had been so utterly certain. But had he been right? Was it really true that all the efforts of men like him would be ultimately futile? Was the tide of history really set against his people? He had paced his room, feeling the tightness of the walls. He refused to accept that his whole life had been wasted. It was outrageous. They were winning. So what that the rest of the planet had come to hate them? That didn't matter. What mattered was that they could still take out the enemy's best men whenever they wanted. They had them fenced-in and bottled-up. They had seen them kicked out of Egypt and Jordan and Syria and Lebanon. One by one they had taken on and beaten all their enemies. Smashed them. Destroyed them. Now even the big mouth Saddam was gone. All that was left was the ragtag remains. The Fox had been the last of their great ones and now The Fox was in a cage. It was crazy to feel such a sense of foreboding. But still sleep had refused to come.

That had been the last time that he had been to his flat. Ever since he had preferred to use the camp bed in his office to catnap for a couple of hours at a time. Grudgingly he had admitted to himself that he had grown to fear the flat. It was like a giant mirror on the misery of his life. Within its walls he felt small and old and lonely. It was better to remain at work where even in the early hours of the morning there was always life around him. He realised that he had been day dreaming when there was tap on his door.

"Come."

It was Rachel, the girl that he had thrown the file at in temper. Suddenly he felt bad about it. She was nervous in his presence. Frightened even. He attempted a smile. Careful Mordechai. That will probably make her worse.

"Please. Sit down."

She perched herself on the chair opposite. So young. Young and vibrant and brim-full of hope. How old was she? 22? 23? If he had married he could have had a granddaughter like Rachel. How proud he would have been to watch her graduate and join the fight. She would have invited him over for lunch with her husband and their friends. She would have beamed with pride to introduce all of them to her Grandfather who had been there on the walls with Moshe Dayan and Motte Gur. He pulled himself out of his thoughts.

"Sorry. I was drifting. Tired. Far too tired. You are too young to know what it is to feel really tired."

She nodded without a trace of understanding.

"The other day. When I threw the file at you. It was wrong of me. I apologise."

"No need sir."

He lit up the 73rd Marlboro of the day. "But there is. Sometimes. Sometimes I behave more badly than I would like." My God Mordechai what was this? Rambling. Rambling like an old man. He snapped himself out of it.

"Anyway. You have news? About Khalil Bishawa?"

"Yes sir." She offered him the file in her hand.

"No. Tell me. My eyes are too tired for files."

"You were right sir. He got out of Tadmur in 1993. There was money involved. A great deal of money it seems. There were bribes paid all the way up the chain. He was taken through a side door at four o'clock in the morning. There was a Mercedes waiting. That is all there is I'm afraid. After that, nothing."

"How did you discover this?"

She smiled nervously. "I did as you suggested. I went to Damascus and spent money. I found one of the guards. He told me all of it. He remembered it well. Apparently Bishawa had a bad time but they never broke him. He talked of course but he hung on for long enough to make the information worthless. They tried to destroy him, but it seems they never could. In the end he said that many of the guards actually came to respect him. Many were glad when he got out. He said that he was in very bad shape physically. Maybe he is dead sir. He is hardly a young man."

Breslow shook his head slowly, a look of bewilderment on his face. "You went to Damascus?"

"Yes sir. I posed as a French student."

It was astounding. Year after year these young people threw themselves into harm's way without hesitation. God alone knew what would have happened if they had caught her. He closed his eyes as images of her young body being abused by unshaven soldiers filled his mind. Why? Why did his mind always turn to things that were foul and ugly and evil? All his life it had been there, ever since the nightmare visions of his childhood in Treblinka which would never leave him.

"You are a very brave young lady. Very brave."

"Thank you sir."

All of them were brave. Rachel was brave. Khalil Bishawa was brave. His brother in the cell with a stump of a leg was brave. The young soldiers in the tanks were brave. The kids who threw their stones at the tanks were brave. They were all brave. Brave to the point of lunacy for year after endless year.

"Do you think that he might be dead sir?"

"No. I don't. His brother knew something. I could feel the truth in his words. Khalil Bishawa isn't dead Rachel. He is out there. Somewhere over the wall. And soon we will be hearing from him."

He leaned back in his chair and blew smoke up at the ceiling. She didn't really know what to do. Should she leave? He was in a strange mood. So sad. When he started speaking again it was almost to himself.

"I wonder if we will still be fighting when you are old Rachel? Will we ever be allowed to stop? It has been so very, very long and still we fight. Maybe we will always have to fight. Maybe it will never end." He slowly sat up in his chair and it took an effort to arrange his thoughts. "Find the old pictures of Khalil Bishawa. Get the artists to come up with how he might look now. Tell them that he was over ten years in Tadmur. Such a time will change the appearance of any man. Such a time will have changed him greatly. Damaged him. Can you even begin to imagine what it must have been like to spend ten years in Tadmur Rachel?"

She shook her head feeling awkward. "No sir. I don't suppose I can."

"I can Rachel." He undid the button on his shirt-cuff and rolled up the sleeve. The arm that emerged was as white as the belly of a dead fish on a cold beach. He turned his arm so that she could see the small tattoo that they had given him on the day that the train had arrived at Treblinka. Her eyes widened slightly. "Once upon a time there were many of us who wore the mark of the beast. Not any more. I am one of the last. We are now only a few hundred out of all the millions. We know what it is to see the face of the beast. Maybe it is why we have come to share that face. It is why we have always fought the hardest. It is how we are able to harden our hearts. But we are people too. So yes. Yes I can imagine how it must have been for Khalil Bishawa for all those years in Tadmur. And yes, I can feel my eyes prickle with tears for him and all the others. But when I find him Rachel I shall kill him. I shall kill him without a second's thought. I shall kill him without a trace of remorse. I shall kill him because I will never allow any more of my people to wear a tattoo like this one. Never Rachel."

Tears crept down over her fine high cheekbones that were a genetic gift of a Hungarian grandfather who had perished in Belsen in 1944. The tears flowed because she had joined in with all the rest of them in the canteen as they joked about the old man and his impossible moods.

Tac Brennan was in as good a mood as he had known in years. His plans were running far more smoothly than he could have ever anticipated. The incident with Morrissey had been an absolute godsend. The next morning his phone was again ringing off the wall with calls from the tabloids. His campaign was a little over a week old and ridiculously enough he was being portrayed as the voice of reason in the midst of chaos. The papers were painting a picture of a Glaswegian Kissinger. Then it had got even better. Daniel Morrissey had called to ask if he would come to Edinburgh for discussions on the situation. He had even sent a car. The Chief Constable had sat in on their meeting, which had been very friendly and cordial. At the end the photographers had taken exactly the kind of photos that Roseanne had envisaged. She was particularly pleased with the contrast between the thousand-pound suit from Milan that Daniel wore for the meeting to the photos of the embattled, fearless Daniel in his donkey jacket from earlier in the week. For her, Tac Brennan was incidental. She considered him a dreadful weasely man in his cheap, nasty sports jacket and hideous fawn trousers. Lord alone knew why the papers were making such a big deal about him. She thought he even looked like a rat-faced little runt in the stock picture from the Falklands that they were so fond of using. It was quite beyond her to understand why Daniel treated him with such deference. Glasgow stuff. At times she got completely pissed off with Daniel's Glasgow stuff. The sooner they both made it down to London the better.

Tac had called his team into the pub for a meeting. It was before ten in the morning and the doors were closed. They all knew better than to ask for the bar to be opened up. They sat on the tired old stools that accompanied chipped, wobbly tables and sipped at the dreadful coffee.

RED ZONE

"OK. So far so good. All this press stuff is a huge bonus and we need to cash in. As of today we move up a gear. We raise the stakes. Teams one and two. Here." He passed out sheets of paper. "These are lists of numberplates for cars belonging to the wogs. Blow them. Spread it out over four nights. Teams three, four and five. You will start burning a few of them out of their flats. We'll start at the edges of the estate. I have three addresses for each of you. I'll leave the how and the when up to you. Night time is obviously best. I want the flats empty before they burn. Got that? Empty. That is essential. We aren't ready for any casualties. Knock the door in. Check every last inch, and I mean every last inch. Get the wogs out. Torch it and away. No frills."

He dug into two bin liners and started pulling out black boiler suits and balaclavas.

"Here you go. Check them out for size. Time we started looking like a bunch of Provies. Any questions?"

There were none. The mission could not have been any more straightforward. It was a matter of delivering fear. Pure and simple. They passed the boiler suits around between them and tried them on. There was less joking now. The real business was about to start. None of them were under any illusions about the seriousness of what they were about to do. Cocking-up and getting caught would mean a minimum of ten years. None of them was unduly concerned. They were well trained and they had all been tested in the hard places. Nobody worried about anybody else's bottle. They knew that they would always follow the same basic set of rules. Keep it simple. Keep to the plan. Keep it calm. They packed up their boiler suits and balaclavas and drifted out into the sunny morning.

Tac was reading yet another article about himself when Terry stuck his head round the door behind the bar. "Someone here for you Tac."

"Who?"

"Dunno. Irish. Won't give a name."

"Aye. I'm expecting him. Send him in Terry. Cheers."

Declan didn't look anything like himself as Terry showed him in. The red hair was gone. In its place was a severe crew-cut died black. A pair of glasses seemed to change his whole face. In place of his usual smile his features were set in a sullen expression. When he spoke his tone was flat. Disinterested. The Ulster accent was much harder than usual.

250

"You Brennan?"

"Aye."

"Burton sent me. He said you're expecting me."

"Aye. He did. Take a pew. Want a brew?"

"Tea. Just milk. No sugar."

Declan could feel the eyes of the older man on him as he took a seat. He in turn studied Brennan. Nothing much to look at. Keeley had said as much. Hard though. A real through and through little hard bastard. He had seen plenty of Tac Brennans in his time. Long Kesh had been full of them. They were never men to be underestimated.

"So what's your name then?"

"No need to know that" said Declan indifferently.

"What do I call you then?"

"Not bothered. Anything. Call me Nathan."

Tac was making his own judgements. He liked the feel of this man. Good age. Late forties probably. A cold fucker. No doubt about that. Lots like him where he came from. He was the type would as soon as kill you as offer you a fag. The sort where he would have told the lads to shoot first and ask questions later in the old days.

"Burton tells me that you were UVF."

"Maybe."

"He tells me that you know how to blow things up."

"True enough."

He wasn't the chatty type. Fair enough.

"Have you got the stuff you need?"

"Aye. Burton got it. It's stashed in the city."

"Where is it from?"

"A UFF dump. It will all trace back to them. It's how he wanted it."

"OK. Good. Here are some addresses. Three are in the city here. One is in Dundee. We will be stepping up things here in the next few days. The temperature will start to rise. These are places where they house asylum seekers. Blow them up. We need to stretch the coppers. Stop them piling in here with everything they've got. No casualties. That needs to be clear. Not yet. Later maybe. How you do it is down to you. Try and hit all four in the next week. Fair enough?"

"Aye. Fair enough. I'll be seeing you then."

Declan got up and left. Brennan thoughtfully lit a cigarette. So Sergeant. Now things start to get interesting.

Khalil sat patiently in the waiting area. A secretary with pink hair was giving all of her attention to composing a text message on her mobile phone. He had been waiting for nearly an hour now and her closely bitten nails had never stopped their fluttering over the buttons. On five occasions a bleeping sound had heralded the reply to her latest message. He wondered idly whether she ever suffered from cramp. He had leafed through a couple of well-thumbed magazines and studied the various notices on the wall. Now he was wishing that he had brought a book. It seemed somewhat ridiculous, but he was beginning to fidget. He thought of the endless hours and days and weeks and months that he had sat staring at the same bricks on the wall of his cell in Tadmur. Then he had learned the art of patience. A patience as endless as the desert that surrounded the prison. He had learned how to drain his mind of every single thought and to sink himself into a near coma.

Later he had read books from the east about Buddhism and yoga and meditation. He had managed to discover many of their disciplines through his own trial and error. By the end he could have stayed in there for ever. He had found a place of permanent nothingness. His emotions had been eroded away completely. He had learnt how to live without hopes or dreams or company. He became a human being locked into sleep-mode. He slept. He woke. He completed a basic exercise routine. He ate what they gave him. He drank what they gave him. He spent endless hours writing vast rambling novels in his mind. By slowing down his breathing to virtually nothing, he could induce an almost hallucinogenic state where the stories became a reality and the hours would drain away like rainwater in the sand.

He had always wondered how on earth he had managed to hang on to his sanity. Lots of those around him hadn't. Night after night their crazed shouting would echo up and down the stone corridors. Everything about Tadmur was madness. Most of the victims whose lives were wrecked beyond all help had done nothing more than to be born in the wrong place. By the mid-1980s Asad's regime had descended into a pit of paranoia. They saw enemies everywhere and the secret police were urged to pick up more and more of their perceived enemies. They called them spies and saboteurs. In fact most were teachers and engineers and clerks. There were no bounds to the brutality employed in the torture rooms. At first maybe there had been some kind of purpose to the torture. Maybe the men who applied the pain really had believed that they would uncover a plot to destroy the country. But they must have soon learned that it would never be the case. How much could a schoolteacher divulge? He could tell them how much homework he had been setting. He could tell them that more than half of his class were struggling with their long division. He could even let slip that he had little faith in his headmaster who drank in secret. What he couldn't do was to give up the name and location of a Mossad agent who was about to smuggle a small nuclear device into the heart of Damascus.

Somewhere along the line all sense of reason had vanished. The men of the torture rooms lost their own sanity. The torture stopped being a job and started being pleasure. Their lives revolved around dispensing pain. They never tired of it. They fed off it. They became consumed by the general madness of Tadmur.

For the first few weeks Khalil had been quite sure that he would die. Every morning they would come and drag him to their room. First it was just beating. They stripped him and simply laid into him with fists and boots. Then they tied him to a chair and interspersed their questions with blows to the face. He had passed out after two hours. He knew that he had to hold on for three days. His routine was to ring the leadership every afternoon. If he missed two consecutive calls they would do all they could to ensure that any information he gave up would be out of date. He woke on the second morning in a woeful state. His ribcage was pure white agony. He was bruised all over and could not find any position on the bare stone floor where he could ease the pain that ran all through his naked body. His spirits fell lower than he could ever have imagined. The sheer hopelessness of his situation was overwhelming. Outside the metal door there were the sounds of screaming. Terrible, awful sounds. The sounds of agony beyond all belief. The sounds that he too would be making in a few short hours. He had started to cry, and once started he couldn't stop. He cried for everything. For Fatima and Palestinia and his family and the pain that was too much to stand. He cried because he couldn't even begin to understand what he could have possibly done for his life to be so terrible. He cried because it was his brother Arabs who would torture him and drive him to the worst depths of human misery, and not the Jews whom he had fought against for his whole life. He cried because he wanted to be tougher and stronger and able to spit in their faces and smile at their leering and give them nothing. He cried because he knew that when they came for him he would tell them everything because he had no strength left. He cried because he couldn't face it, couldn't stand it. He cried because they had broken his spirits in less than 24 hours.

It was typical of the madness of Tadmur that they left him for four days. No food. No water. And some of the wounds had started to fester. But with each day his strength had grown. Each day that passed meant that he could never betray any of his comrades. After three days they would have moved on. Changed addresses. Changed cities. Somewhere along the line they had muddled up their paperwork. Here he was, a genuine in the flesh senior man in the PLO, and the men in Tadmur thought he was just another schoolteacher. By the fourth day they had missed their chance. He would have told them anything and they would have struck gold. He would have had to live with the screams of his comrades living in his dreams. Instead they had waited too long.

When they started again it was all pain. He told them everything he knew. He even made things up. He invented. He embellished. Until the truth and the fiction became a mad jumble of facts and figures that were barely any use at all. After a fortnight they told him not to bother any more. They weren't interested in what he had to say. He was just a plaything. They half-drowned him. They plunged his head in buckets of shit. They hung him from the ceiling upside down and beat him with thick electric cables. They pummelled the soles of his feet with iron rods. They attached wires to all parts of his body and drilled him with electricity. They twisted his broken body in all directions in the hated German Chair. And then after a month they just stopped. By this stage he was so weak that there was no fun in it any more. He barely had the breath to scream and writhe. He was used up. A game that they had grown bored with. A toy to be consigned to the corner of a cupboard and forgotten about. There was never a shortage of shiny new toys in Tadmur. They came in every day, eyes wide with terror, bowels loose, new boys on the block of nightmares.

After that there had only been occasional beatings. Otherwise it was endless empty hours of nothing. Somewhere the paperwork must have stipulated that he should only ever know solitary confinement. Sometimes they allowed him an hour's exercise once a week. Other times he would have to wait for over a month. Sometimes there would be no food for three days. In the summers the cell was baking-hot. In the winters it could be icy cold. The seasons passed. A year became five. Five years became ten. And then Farouk had found him and had taken him away from Tadmur.

Strangely enough, from the very minute he had climbed into the back of the Mercedes he found the experience almost impossible to deal with. During the years in the bare cell he had become fully adjusted to the inevitability of his eventual quiet death. Life had simply stopped. It was merely a case of living through a kind of netherworld for a few years until death brought along the ultimate quiet.

Freedom shone a harsh light on the sheer desperate misery of his ten years in Tadmur. He couldn't take it. He crumbled completely. Farouk flew him to a sanatorium high in the Swiss Alps and little by little he was able to put himself back together. The only way he found to handle the nightmare images that he had witnessed was to completely blank them out. Slowly he had achieved it. Mahmoud was able to visit on three occasions and after many hours he managed to persuade his brother that he had done enough for his people. And so instead of returning to play out his part in the continuing fight of his people, Khalil had flown to the kingdom of Saudi Arabia to take up a post in Farouk's huge business empire. For years he had lived out a dull but safe existence. With every day that passed he was able to push his time in Tadmur further to the back of his mind into the same place where he kept pictures of the flattened hospital in Sidon and the executed bodies of his family in Kibya.

He had only opened the cupboard because they had taken Mahmoud. The memories of Tadmur had been the very last to be taken out and examined. He had approached the memories with trepidation, only to find that they had lost their teeth. It all seemed far away, another lifetime. It was if it had happened to somebody else. It seemed strange that he was about to explain exactly that to the man in the office who kept him waiting. It wasn't Khalil Bishawa who had been in Tadmur Military Prison. It was Ahmad Mansour. They must have shared years together under the same roof without ever meeting. He wondered how Mansour had dealt with it.

At least he had survived. At least he now had the chance to resume some kind of life.

He had become so wrapped in his thoughts that he hadn't noticed that the office door had finally opened. The man must have already summoned him once because now his voice was tinged with annoyance.

"Mr Mansour. Please. You can come in now."

He was only young. Probably not even 30. He spoke the words slowly as if he was addressing an infant or a pet. "Please. Sit. Here."

He gestured to a metal chair. Khalil sat. The man sat at his side of the desk and spent a few moments examining papers. When he looked up he attempted a smile which came out looking like a grimace.

"So. Mr Mansour. English?" He finished the word "English" with verbal question mark and an exaggerated shrug of the shoulders.

"Yes. I do speak English. I am an English teacher in fact. I am surprised it isn't in the file."

This brought on a frown of concentration and a further leafing of paperwork. "Ah yes. Of course. Sorry about that. Must have missed it somehow. Anyway. Not to worry. The main thing is that you speak it, which makes things a lot easier I can assure you. Not always the case you know. Not at all. Sometimes they don't speak a word. Makes it bloody hard."

"Yes. I'm sure it does. I'm sorry, but I didn't get your name."

A blush this time. "No. Sorry. Of course. Jacobs. Ronald Jacobs."

Khalil held out a hand, which for a moment seemed to confuse the younger man. Then he twigged and took the proffered hand and shook. "Yes. Of course. Now. Mr Mansour. I gather that you are a Syrian."

"No. I am a Palestinian. I lived and worked in Syria. I was imprisoned in Syria. But I am a Palestinian."

"Yes. Yes of course. The thing is that I can't actually put down Palestinian. I mean in the paperwork. I mean, I understand what you mean of course. Obviously. The thing is, well according to the paperwork, well there is no Palestine you see. Where were you born Mr Mansour?"

"I was born in a small village near Jenin. In Palestine. You will know it as the West Bank."

"So maybe I could put down Israeli. I mean just for the paperwork. You understand?"

"I understand. I will bow to your better judgement Ronald. After all, you are the expert in these matters."

Jacobs looked at him quizzically. This one was a strange one. Very strange. Almost a cocky bastard and yet so polite. He had an uneasy sensation that he was getting the piss taken but he couldn't be sure. He spent a few minutes filling in essential details and ticking boxes. At least this time he could do it in English. Sometimes it took the best part of a day to fill in half a page. After a mere twenty minutes it was time for the nitty-gritty.

"Now Mr Mansour. It says here that you were persecuted in Syria and that you feel that you would be in real danger if you were to return. This is where things get a bit tricky. I mean, we know that things can be pretty bleak over there. Syria is on the list. Always has been. But that isn't enough on its own. We are going to need proof. You see, we can't just take your word for it. Now what proof will you be able to supply us with sir?"

"Are you familiar with Tadmur Military Prison Ronald?"

"No. I'm afraid I'm not."

"You will be able to find out about it. Take a look at the Amnesty International website. You will find something about my case there also. I was subjected to torture in Tadmur Prison. Everybody was. The cases are well documented. Amnesty have full details about the duration of my sentence."

Jacobs was scribbling away frantically. This one was a piece of cake. He would be off early tonight for once. Might even stop off for a pint or two on the way home. Bloody brilliant this one. Full details on the Amnesty International website. He spoke as he wrote.

"This is excellent Mr Mansour. Exactly what we need. Not often as clear as this."

"You say that you require proof Ronald?"

Jacobs looked up. "Absolutely, but I am sure that you have given us plenty of areas where we can verify."

Khalil stood and took off his jacket and hung it over the back of the metal chair. He then carefully undid the buttons of the cheap nylon shirt that he had bought for his journey to the West. Jacobs was struck dumb. He was wondering just what the hell was going on. He was about to say something. Then he understood. Khalil laid the shirt over the back of the chair and raised his arms. Slowly he turned around. Jacobs had never seen anything quite like it. The whole of his chest and stomach and back was a mass of scars and welts. He felt like some kind of voyeur. He felt as if he were being offered a glimpse into the abyss. He felt utterly out of his depth. He couldn't find a word, let alone a sentence. When he completed his slow rotation Khalil picked up the shirt, pulled it on and started to button.

"You said that you wanted proof Ronald. This is also my proof. This is what a man looks like who has been for many years in Tadmur prison. Maybe you can understand why it is that I do not want to return to Syria. I know that your paperwork does not recognise that there is such a thing as a Palestinian. That is not the case in Syria. They recognise Palestinians only too well. That is why they kept me in Tadmur. And tortured me. Because I am a Palestinian. That is my crime Ronald. It is a crime that carries a heavy sentence where I have come from."

"Mr Mansour. I'm . . . I don't know. I'm afraid I'm lost for words. Of course I will do all that I can. I can't make any promises but I feel confident that your case will be viewed favourably. Try not to worry. Now. The next thing is somewhere for you to stay. Sometimes this can be difficult but you are lucky. We have more vacant accommodation than is usual at the moment. I'm fairly sure that we will be able to find you a flat more or less straight away. You might have heard of a place called Sighthill?"

Declan had spent two days studying the first building on his list. It was rather a dismal-looking block of flats. At one time it must have been a part of a much larger scheme. Maybe there might have been ten similar blocks. Now they were all gone, flattened to rubble. The site where the demolition had taken place was half-heartedly fenced in. Even more half-hearted was a faded sign warning of danger within. He guessed that it could only be a matter of time before the last block standing met with a similar fate. More than half of the windows were boarded up. By bombing the place he was probably doing no more than saving the Council a few quids worth of demolition charges. There was no way that anyone would ever choose to live in the place other than sheer desperation. Maybe that was why the three-storey block had earned a stay of execution. Suddenly the Council had tenants to house who were desperate enough to say yes to anything. It was OK to house asylum seekers in such a dire place. There would have been uproar if they had suggested using it for stray dogs. He felt a disgusted anger at the treatment that was being handed out. The camp in Sidon had been twenty times poorer but at least there had been life there. There was no life here. Just frightened people hiding behind their doors waiting for the worst.

On the corner of the third floor there was a solid row of boarded windows. This was replicated on the floor below. No doubt there was damp or something. He broke into one of the flats on the top floor. The stink inside was diabolical. The floors were strewn with all the familiar garbage of a heroin squat. Needles. Burnt foil. Mouldy fast-food wrapping. Filthy mattresses. Empty bottles. A cloud of flies swarmed around him as he stepped in. The smell was seeping out of the bathroom where it was clear that the toilet hadn't worked for a very long time. A thick film of dust was enough to confirm that the place had become too hellish even for the desperados who had used it last. He worked quickly and placed a small charge in one of the cupboards. He then waited until after midnight to ease himself into another disused flat in the middle of the ground floor. This time he placed a much larger charge and made his way back to his small hotel.

He returned the next morning at eleven. He found a place to hide up in a long disused factory on the far side of the waste ground. He used a mobile phone to send the signal that sparked the charge in the top floor flat. He gave a small nod of satisfaction as he saw the main thrust of the explosion erupt upwards through the roof. The debris was thrown out across the waste ground. Perfect. Using a second phone he rang 999 and was connected to the police.

"OK listen. This is a message from the BNP. I'll only give it once. There has been a bomb at a block of flats full of asylum seekers." He gave the address. "Nobody is hurt. It was a warning. In exactly an hour there will be another bomb, which will take the whole place down like a pack of cards. Get your people there. Clear the building and get everyone back. Don't even think of trying to locate and diffuse the second bomb. This is a warning. We don't intend to kill the fuckers. We intend to make them leave. Any casualties will be down to you."

He cleared the line and tossed the phone to the floor. The reaction time of the Strathclyde police was impressive. Within ten minutes there were five squad cars at the scene. By this time there was a crowd of people who had fled the flats in the wake of the first bomb. The police moved them back and established a line 200 yards clear. He counted the police officers as they came in and out one by one. Six in. Six out. The last gave a vigorous all clear gesture to his superiors behind the line and then jogged to join them. Through binoculars he could see them all locked in earnest conversation. This was the time when they would considering whether to call in a bomb disposal team. He felt pretty confident that the building was completely clear. Why give them the worry? He used a third phone to detonate the second bomb. This was a big one. Once the dust had settled the dismal block had completely collapsed. He grinned. You've still got the touch Declan. Still got the touch.

All through the night Campbell had passed through new and different levels of tiredness. His shift had been due to finish at midnight. Now the sun was pulling itself over the horizon with the promise of another hot day and he was still on duty. Every copper in the city dreaded the Friday and Saturday night shifts when the good people of the city indulged in their traditional pastimes of getting blind drunk and stabbing each other. He had done a few pretty hairy shifts himself during his brief time in uniform. One in particular had ended in a near riot as a milling, fighting crowd of Celtic and Rangers fans had spilt out of a city centre night club with the avowed intent of killing each other. That night he had collapsed into his bed with a peach of a black eye and told himself that it couldn't get a lot worse. Dream-on Campbell. It just did. And the dire feeling in the pit of his stomach told him that this was only a start.

It had all started the previous afternoon when his radio had crackled out the news that there had been a bomb threat on the far side of the city. As the details emerged one by one, Campbell knew that the stakes were about to be raised. He gleaned more information from the local radio than the police. Already an explosion. Residents evacuated. Crowds held back behind a safety line. Then a massive explosion. Flats completely destroyed. No reports of casualties.

Police successful in emptying the building. Condemned flats used as temporary accommodation for refugees.

He got a call from the desk sergeant half an hour after Declan's big bang.

"It looks like trouble Campbell. We got a warning call. Claimed he was from the BNP. Thick Ulster accent. Shit storm's a coming. Watch your arse constable."

Whilst he was staring idiotically at his radio the first car had blown two streets away. As he hurled his car around the corner a second car went up. What in the name of hell was going on? As he radioed for back-up, two more cars burst into sheets of flame whilst the local kids leapt and danced and cheered. Suddenly it was like a chain reaction as the air was filled with the thumping sound of exploding petrol tanks. It lasted until eight o'clock by which time there were over 40 burning cars on the estate. He fed back the number plate information and in return found that an asylum seeker owned each and every one of the vehicles. There were plenty of policemen on the estate by now trying to clear the crowds of kids away from the pavements in case more cars blew. At thirteen minutes past eight the sergeant informed him that they had received another call. A Scottish accent this time, again claiming to be BNP. The caller promised that no more cars would blow that night. He assured the girl manning the line that the streets would be safe for the evening. The BNP had no interest in harming the rightful residents of Sighthill. It was a message he said. A message to the asylum seekers. Leave or things get worse.

At 10.45 things did get worse. Campbell was called to the fifth floor of block 15 to find a flat on fire. Outside on the pavement was a terrified family from Turkish Kurdistan. The oldest son had enough English to paint a picture for Campbell. There had been two men. They wore all black. Jump suits. Ski masks. They took the front door off with sledgehammers. They dragged the family out of the flat and used petrol to soak the furniture. They hammered on all the other doors on the floor and shouted that there was a fire. Then they lit the fire and took the lift. The mother was talking fast in a language that Campbell couldn't even begin to fathom. Her son did his best to translate her barrage of questions. Where could they go now? What would happen to them? She said they had nothing left. Everything they owned was in the flat. Campbell crammed them into his car and delivered them to the station. By the time he had left them sipping tea in one of the interview rooms the word had come in that there was another flat ablaze in Block 3.

Now in the bright light of the dawn he was attempting to console yet another family who had seen their home burn. They were from Iran. Like all the others they were terrified. They were the thirteenth and last family to be violently evicted that night. All he could do was to take them to the police station where the Social Services would do what they could.

The Recorder had received a call during the late evening, once again from a Scottish voice, claiming to represent the BNP. The message was clear and simple. The Government were to move all asylum seekers from the city of Glasgow. They were no longer welcome. Until the last asylum seeker was moved the BNP would maintain its campaign of forced evictions through fire and bombing. It was not their intention to cause casualties. The campaign would be put on hold as soon as the Government made a declaration of intent. The electronic version of the story was to dominate the first five pages of the paper that hit the Internet a little after midnight. All through the night journalists and TV vans poured onto the estate. By the time Campbell attended his fourth burnt flat incident a little after three he was besieged by reporters as he tried to console the family.

By this time he had collected enough officers to hold the baying mass of journalists back. He tried to talk to the family soothingly. They were Bosnians this time. Three young children wide-eyed with the horror of the night. A mother almost senseless with the memories of other horrors revisited. She was utterly immune to the frantic calls of the reporters as Campbell gently led her to a waiting police van with a blanket across her shoulders. Her mind was filled with images that had her taken years to drive away. She could see the moment that the big bearded Serbian soldier had split her husband's head with his sledgehammer. She could hear his delighted laugh as his men had cheered. She could smell the blood as it had flowed from the smashed skull into the wet soil of her vegetable patch. Again they had come with sledgehammers. She had been almost demented. Not her children. Please not the children. The man had dragged her out by the hair as she writhed and kicked and screamed. He had yanked out a whole tuft leaving a bald patch. He had shut her up with a fist to the face, and then he had lit the fire. She had been numb with relief. The sledgehammers were for the door, not the heads of her children.

Campbell got a look into her eyes as she climbed into the back of the van. He had never seen such eyes. They were filled with a horror that he could not imagine. All that he knew was that the family was from Bosnia. What kind of terror had driven them all the way to Sighthill? A young woman on her own with three children. No husband. And now this. He was too tired. It was more than he could take. He reached out to try to lay a consoling hand on her arm but she shrank back as if he were about to slash at her with a knife. She was beyond his reach. Maybe she was beyond anyone's reach. He carefully closed the back door and gave the roof a bang with the palm of his hand. As he stood and watched it drive through the cordon of reporters he felt a hand on his shoulder. Nicky.

He collapsed into her, his head bent down into her shoulder. She spoke softly into his ear. "Come on love. Let's get inside. Not in front of the cameras. Don't give them the pleasure. Try to stand up straight. Try and be strong."

He pulled himself back and followed her into the flats. She had a key for one of the meeting rooms that they used for their English classes. Once she had locked the door behind them she took him to her. All the strength seemed to have drained out of him. He was like a child. She held him for several minutes, quietly running her fingers through his hair. Finally he was able to sit up straight. His eyes were black with tiredness. She knew that he really should still have been signed off sick. His body was still laced with the bruises of his beating. It was her fault that he was here at all. Her fault that she was so pig-headed. Her fault that he had endured such a night. There was such despair in his eyes. When he spoke, his voice was little more than a whisper.

"What is happening Nicky?"

"Hate is happening. Hate is all around us. Worse than that. Organised hate. Thoughtful hate. Hitler hate. That is what is happening."

"It's going to get worse isn't it?"

"Oh yes. It will get worse. Much worse."

This seemed to switch him back on. He stood and shook his head to clear the fatigue. "No point moping then, is there. Have you been with Rosemary?"

"Yes. I got there as soon as I heard."

"How is she?"

Nicky smiled. "How do you think? On the warpath. Ready to take on the world. Crazy woman. Will you get off home now?"

He nodded. "Aye. I think so. There's been another call. Apparently that's it for the night. Hostilities are suspended whilst the government comes up with a statement. I should be able catch a bit of sleep. You?"

Again she smiled. "You won't believe this, but I have a new client to move in. Imagine it. Today is his first day of sanctuary in Scotland. God alone knows what he will make of it all. Hopefully he will speak a bit of English. I'm going to see him at eleven. I'll come back with you for a while."

"Poor sod. Where's he from?"

"Syria I think."

"Talk about out of the frying pan and into the fire."

At 10.30 that morning Declan flattened a line of four disused garages at the rear of a block of apartments in Cambuslang. This time the police were at the scene within minutes, hotly pursued by three TV vans. He counted the officers in and counted them back out and gave it ten minutes to be on the safe side. Then he dropped the main building like a pile of toy bricks. The weekend lunchtime news programmes all over the world carried the pictures.

Khalil was rather surprised by the knock at the door. His immediate reaction was to feel tense. Surely not. How utterly ironic if Brennan's men were to target him a mere couple of hours after he had taken up residence. A glance through the peephole alleviated his fears. Outside his door was a young woman would didn't look at all the type to cave in the door with a sledgehammer. He opened up.

"Hello."

"Oh hello. Is it Mr Mansour?"

"Hi. I'm Nicky. Nicky Jennings. Do you speak English?"

"Yes. I do."

She smiled. "Oh good. It makes things so much easier. I work for a charity. We try to help people to settle in. Try and explain how everything works."

He returned her smile. "How very kind. Please. Do come in."

My goodness. This one was different. He wore tired, shabby clothes but he was certainly a gentlemen. She walked into a room with the now familiar peeling wallpaper and threadbare carpet. He fell into the role of the host. "Please. Sit down. Here, let me put a jacket down for you to sit on. I don't think that the furniture is very clean. I was about to make some tea. Mint tea. A speciality from my part of the world. Have you had it?"

"Yes. Yes I have. One of my other clients." Nicky's voice trailed off as for a moment a sharp image of Mrs Khan in her kitchen came into her mind. She brushed the memory aside and gave a smile. "That would be lovely."

Khalil chatted as he boiled the kettle and arranged the small glasses that had been part of his meagre luggage. "This is a welcome surprise I must say. Have you been working in this field for long?"

His English was amazing. It was like listening to a 1950s film. Nobody spoke that way any more. "Oh, it isn't my job. I'm just a volunteer." She lifted her voice to make it carry into the kitchen. He appeared in the doorway.

"And what is your main job?"

"A teacher. English teacher."

This brought a broad smile to his face. "Really. What a coincidence. I am also an English teacher. Well, I was. I haven't taught for many years. I have a great fondness for your language. Evelyn Waugh is a great favourite of mine."

He disappeared back to attend to the boiled kettle. The situation was almost surreal. Here they were in this miserable flat with its tawdry old furniture with the world going crazy outside and here was a schoolteacher from Syria talking about Evelyn Waugh. It probably explained the way that he talked. He would have been quite at home in a Waugh novel. She could picture him in a dinner suit smoking a cigarette with a holder. "So, you are Syrian?"

He emerged with two glasses of tea. He passed her one and sat down on one of the lumpy armchairs. "No. I am Palestinian. Well, I always thought that I was. The man at the Immigration Department assures me that according to the paperwork it is quite impossible to be a Palestinian. Apparently we don't exist. So I am officially an Israeli now."

Was he joking? She really couldn't tell. Maybe he was just being ironic. He didn't appear overtly bitter. "I'm afraid I don't really understand everything about that situation. Did you originally come from Palestine?"

"Yes. I was born there. Near Jenin. You may have seen Jenin in the news?"

She conjured up images of Israeli tanks and bulldozers bearing down on crowds of young men with scarves wrapped around their faces who threw stones. "I think so. Yes. Of course I did."

"My family lived in a small village near the town for many, many years. They were forced to flee when the Israelis invaded in 1967. I was only a teenager then. We fled to Syria. I have lived there ever since. Well. Until now of course."

This was the part that she always found awkward. "And things were bad for you. In Syria?"

"Yes. I had rather a difficult time." His smile was in place but a shadow passed across his eyes. He was quick to change the subject. Not yet thought Nicky. Maybe not ever. He was the type of man to keep his secrets hidden far away from strangers. "Please Miss, or is it Mrs, Jennings. Could you explain what is happening here? There seems to have been rather a lot of trouble."

"It's Miss. But I would much rather you called me Nicky. As for the trouble, well, where do I start?"

She gave him a ten-minute run-down of the events that had over-taken Sighthill since the night of the killings. She did her best to gloss over the deadly seriousness of the threat. He would find out for himself soon enough. She didn't have the heart to hit him with every-thing on his first day. He heard her out with a thoughtful expression.

"It would seem that I have chosen a rather unfortunate time to arrive."

Understatement of the year Mr Mansour. "Yes. I'm afraid that you have. But there is no need to be too upset. I'm sure that the police will soon get on top of the situation. I have inside information. My boyfriend is a policeman. He works here in Sighthill. You will meet him no doubt."

Of course. The penny dropped. He had been bothered for a while by a feeling that he somehow knew this woman. Now he realised why. She was the lady from the riot. The one who had fought the mob off the policeman. She had looked like some kind of wild animal that night. It was why it had taken him so long to make the connection. It seemed almost impossible for this charming girl to be the one who had fought like a tigress. Remarkable. He masked his recognition well.

"I would like that. Now, you said that there are things that I should know."

"Yes. Yes there are. Why don't we start with the electric card."

For half an hour she took him through the basics he would need to settle into his new life. He sat patiently and took careful notes in a small notebook. What often took her hours, or even days, was easily completed in a few minutes. It was almost as if he already knew much of what she explained but wasn't letting on. She found it difficult to believe that this man had never been outside of Syria in his adult life. There was an urbanity, a sophistication about him. Maybe it really was just from reading. Well, it must have been. On impulse she continued.

"Campbell and I, that's my boyfriend by the way, are going for dinner tonight at the flat of one of the families that I work with. Rosemary and Moses. They are from Zimbabwe. I dare say Campbell won't be able to go now. Not with everything that is going on. It will be all hands to the pumps for a few days. But I will still go. Maybe you could come as well. I'm certain that Rosemary won't mind. She always cooks enough to feed a small village. I think you will like her. It will be a chance for you to start meeting people."

"I would like that very much indeed. Where do they live?"

"Block 14. But don't worry about finding it. I will pick you up. Shall we say seven o'clock?"

"Of course. I will be waiting."

He stared down from his window after she left. A feeling of guilt sat heavily with him. It had all seemed so different in the flat in Jeddah. Glasgow had seemed far away then. It hadn't been a real place. But it was all real enough now that he had arrived. Most of the fear and mayhem was down to him. Maybe it might have happened anyway. Probably it would. But he could still not escape the fact that the events of the last two weeks were more or less entirely of his doing. In Jeddah it had been easy. Only Mahmoud mattered. Nothing else. Now he had to come to terms with the damage that he was willing to cause to save his brother. He was putting so many people at risk. Thousands of them. People like the fine young woman who had come to offer her help. So many to save one. He became angry with himself. This was no time for weakness. For better or worse, he had made his decision. There was no going back now.

Outside everything was quiet. The view from his window took in the large courtyard that was framed by three huge blocks of flats. In the middle there was an area of grass that was in need of a cut. There was an 'all-weather' football pitch. And there was a playground. It had swings and a roundabout and a slide and a climbing frame. It was a beautiful sunny afternoon and surely the surrounding flats must have contained hundreds of children. And yet the playground was deserted. There was not a soul to be seen.

By the late afternoon the police had swamped the estate with just about every spare officer they could muster. Their problem was that they really didn't know what to do. It was out of the question for them to guard every car and flat. They had little expectation that anything would happen anyway. Already a picture was starting to emerge. Whoever was behind the upsurge in violence was clearly no fool. All had been quiet in the days that followed the riot. Only when the decision had been taken to pull back the extra police officer had trouble started up. Initial forensic examinations of the burnt-out flats and cars revealed nothing. It would have been a surprise if they had. All available witness statements agreed that the perpetrators had worn gloves as well as their black boiler suits and masks.

Door-to-door enquiries were half-hearted at best. It wasn't the sort of place where anyone would say what they had seen. Sighthill was bound by a set of rules that would not be broken. Police and journalists alike were met by the taciturn shaking of heads. Nobody knew a thing.

A few of the journalists hunted for Tac Brennan. They tried his flat and the pub but it was to no avail. He had anticipated that the predictable reaction of the authorities was that they would simply flood the area. He had arranged for his men to make their way to a holiday cottage he had hired 50 miles south of the city in Ayrshire. They all agreed to stay there for a few days whilst the coppers chased their tails. Tac was once again in the highest of spirits.

"Time to let the hair down lads. We're absolutely spot on so far. The bastards are absolutely shitting themselves. I have a contact in the local Social office. They're absolutely fucking overwhelmed. Totally. Hundreds are pouring in there. They all want out. We can leave things be for a while. Let them all stew. You guys are best staying here. I'll get back tomorrow and keep my ear to the ground. Now I suggest that it might be an idea for us all to get ourselves absolutely pissed, don't you?"

Khalil had spent the afternoon walking around the estate. There were clusters of police on every corner eyeing-up small groups of locals warily. He barely saw anyone who resembled an asylum seeker. They were keeping themselves behind locked doors. On a couple of occasions groups of kids shouted at him. It was nothing very serious. They scarpered as soon as the nearest policemen made toward them. There seemed to be the burnt-out shells of cars every few yards. He wondered what on earth would be done with them.

He took a bus into the city centre and when he got off he felt as if he had stepped into a different world. The pavements were teeming with shoppers in their colourful summer wear. It was ridiculous to think that just a couple of miles away there was a virtual war zone. On Sauchihall Street it was very much business as usual. Now that he was away form the estate he felt much more anonymous in the Saturday afternoon crowds. He bought a takeaway coffee and took a seat on a bench and watched the crowds go by. He wondered about Brennan's next move. He would no doubt hear from Sergei over the next day or two. The logical assumption was that nothing much would happen. It would be hard for him to manoeuvre whilst there were so many policemen on the ground. Much more likely was that he would lie low for a day or two then hit other targets across the city. Maybe he would even move out of town. That would force the police hand. They would have to pull officers back to cover more and more ground. Then he would be able to strike again. How long would he wait? He was under no particular time pressure. Waiting would be the most sensible approach. Every day that passed without incident would increase the pressure on the police. They could only maintain their numbers in Sighthill for relatively short time. He decided that it would probably be a week to ten days at least before Brennan resumed action. Time enough.

He checked the clock high on a grimy Victorian building. It was already past four. Time to get himself back. He bought two bottles of wine and a kilo of coffee to take along as an offering to Nicky's friend. The invitation had been completely unexpected. He had assumed that he would simply be left in his flat and left to his own devices. He wasn't sure whether this was a positive development or not. Maybe it could provide him with a short cut. Or maybe it would turn out to be a worthless distraction. Maybe he should have refused. But it was too late now.

Nicky arrived at seven as promised. It turned out that Rosemary's block lay across the courtyard with the playground. Had she really thought that he would have struggled to find it? Probably she had simply grown accustomed to the fact that so many of the families on the estate had grown terrified of even the shortest walk. He couldn't help but be touched by her consideration.

When he walked into Rosemary's flat he found it almost impossible to believe that it was more or less identical to his own. It was a vibrant blaze of colour. The walls and furniture were covered in the bold, blazing colours of her homeland. The windowsill was crammed with plants, and the smell of spicy food wafted through from the kitchen. Rosemary beamed at him and nearly swallowed his bony hand in hers.

"Welcome Mr Mansour. You come on in and sit. I am Rosemary. MOSES! COME IN HERE NOW! MR MANSOUR IS HERE! Sorry about that. My son he always has those headphones on his head."

A tall African boy appeared and shook hands rather formally. Khalil passed the carrier bag over to the hostess. "An offering. Nothing much I'm afraid."

Rosemary looked inside the bag and raised an eyebrow in surprise. "Wine Mr Mansour? I was thinking you were a Palestinian."

He laughed. "Oh, the wine is not for me. You are quite correct. I do not drink. But I was under the impression that the Scots and Zimbabweans enjoyed a glass. I will stick with the coffee. I think that you will approve of the brand."

She pulled the packet out of the bag and beamed when she saw that it was from her homeland. "Now where did you find this? It not coming from the Tesco shop down the road."

"It wasn't easy. I can tell you where to find the place. It is in the city."

"Well I think we are going to like you Mr Mansour. I think we might be inviting you again. What you say Moses?"

"Yes mother."

Nicky had remained quiet through it all. The man was extraordinary. He had been in Sighthill for less than a day and yet he had managed to arrive with coffee that must have come from a delicatessen somewhere in the city. She picked up one of the bottles of wine. She wasn't any kind of expert, but she felt pretty confident that it wasn't of the £3.99 variety that she tended to favour. Stranger and stranger.

The meal was a cheery affair. She noticed how adept her new charge was in the art of getting others to do all the speaking. Rosemary happily answered all his questions about life at home. He had the knack of steering her into the memories of happy times. Moses was drawn into speaking much more than he normally did. For once the quavering anger was absent from his voice as he told of days with his friends hunting with slingshots. She wasn't immune from his skills herself as he got her to talk at length about her school and the pupils and the problems. It occurred to her as Rosemary was preparing coffee that he had barely spoken about himself. It also occurred that they had barely spoken about the troubles that had engulfed Sighthill over the past week. How could he possibly be so disinterested? It was almost as if he already knew about everything that was happening. She wished that Campbell was with her to offer a second opinion on this fascinating man. There would be no point in asking Rosemary. By some utter miracle he had managed to completely charm her off her feet. Even Moses was taken with him. They were deep in a conversation about hunting. Khalil was telling him about an uncle of his who was a great hunter and how the people of the village would always call on him when a fox threatened their flocks.

They were easy together. Maybe the man could be good for Moses. The boy had been like an unexploded bomb for the last fortnight. Campbell had told her all about the incident with the politician. He had found the whole thing hysterically funny. The Deputy Minister for Justice being protected from the mob by the young boy from Africa. Nicky had laughed along but had felt anxious. There was a violence inside Moses that was barely contained. She had sensed it for a long time. On the surface he had taken the loss of his father and his family and friends well. Underneath she could feel his rage, and more and more the rage was being directed at what was happening in Sighthill. Possibly this strange man could be good for him. She hoped so.

A wave of tiredness hit her. She stifled a yawn and checked her watch. It was past eleven. Time for home. She got to her feet.

"Bedtime for me I'm afraid. I'm shattered. It has been a wonderful evening Rosemary. I do hope that you have enjoyed yourself Mr Mansour."

"I have. Very much. I will enjoy it even more if you will all please call me Ahmad. I will walk you to your vehicle."

"Oh there's no need. I'll be safe enough."

"It is not something that is for negotiation Miss Jennings."

"I too will come" said Moses rising from his chair.

As they watched the red tail-lights make their way to the T-junction at the end of the road between the great towering blocks man and boy stood in companionable silence until Khalil spoke.

"You know, I spent some time today looking down from my window. It was such a beautiful afternoon. And this seems to me to be a very fine playground. But there were no children. How can it be that there are no children playing outside on such a lovely day?"

"Scared. Everybody here is scared."

"Even children? These people would attack children?"

"It is common. It is usually other children. They are cowardly people here. They like to fight against small people. These people are not warriors."

Khalil shook his head sadly. "I have been in many bad places Moses. Many. Places of great danger. But I have never been in a place where the children are too frightened to play. It is a very bad thing Moses."

"This is true. It is very bad. Everything here is very bad."

"I think that the children should be allowed to play Moses."

The African looked at his new friend with interest. "What is it that you say?"

"Exactly that. The children should be allowed to play. It should be safe for them to play. It should be made safe. Maybe you might like to help me, Moses. Help me to make it safe?"

"I will help you."

"And will you tell your mother."

"No. My mother she is not need to know this thing."

272

"Maybe not. Perhaps we could talk about this tomorrow. Why don't you visit me at my flat? Let's say ten o'clock. You could bring some of your friends if you like. Friends who might want to help us make it safe for the children to play."

"I will come. I have these friends. They will help us in this thing."

Khalil caught a flash of the boy's huge white teeth before he jogged back to his block.

Daniel Morrissey pushed the cornflakes around his bowl half-heartedly. He couldn't seem to be able to find any appetite. He picked another paper off the heap before him. Same old, same old. Sighthill. Sighthill. More Sighthill. The whole bloody world had developed a bottomless appetite for Sighthill. Page after page of it. The news channels seemed to show nothing else. Blown-up buildings. Blown-up cars. Policemen patrolling what looked like a war zone. And somehow or another he had managed to place himself bang slap in the middle of the whole stinking mess. Or more to the point, Rosy had.

She was working her way through the pile of papers whilst nibbling away at a piece of brown toast. Wholemeal and organic of course. What else? She noticed his miserable expression.

"It's because it is so photogenic."

"What?"

"Sighthill. Makes for great photos. Great tele too. Perfect image of twenty-first-century urban hell. No wonder they're having a field day."

"It isn't some fucking backdrop to an arty film for Christ's sake Rosy. People live there you know. Sometimes I wonder if you actually give a shit."

His words washed over her. "Of course I don't dear. I'm just an over-privileged young middle-class girl who can't empathise with the trials and tribulations of the great unwashed. Not my job Daniel. That part is your job. I don't do bleeding heart I'm afraid."

Her hardness never ceased to stun him. But she was good. Unbelievably good. She would either get him a top slot or hung, drawn and quartered. There would be no middle way for Rosy. And if he was hung, drawn and quartered she would kiss him daintily on the cheek and move on to someone else. At least she was relatively honest about it.

"I'm worried about the meeting. He sounded pretty terse on the phone."

He had been summoned to a nine o'clock meeting with the First Minister and it was giving him a distinct trip-to-the-headmaster-for-a-caning feeling.

"Of course he sounded terse darling. What do you expect? He is in the spotlight. Racial mayhem on the streets of little old Scotland isn't part of the planned programme. There is no need for you to get in a tizz. He has the problem, not you. He needs you far more than you need him."

"Explain. Last time I looked he was my boss."

"For now. Maybe not for long. The buck stops with him. He is a dreary ex bus driver with about as much charisma as a jellied eel. The only reason he got the job was that he was seen as a safe pair of hands. There isn't a thing that he can say about all this that anyone will take a blind bit of notice of. He's grey. He's boring. And he's within an inch of being yesterday's man. You on the other hand are the young man of action. The public love you. They don't see that any of this business is your fault. They just see you sticking your lovely neck out to try and save the day. That's why he needs you darling. All you need to remember is who is wearing the trousers here."

"But what about policy? What on earth are we actually going to do about this?"

She spat out a short laugh. "Good lord, don't ask me. I just get you the TV with the right clothes and haircut. Don't ask me about policy. Is there one? It seems not. If there is then tell me. What are the options?"

"None really. There is no question of moving these people out of Sighthill. Where the hell would we put them? Nobody would have them anyway. There is no chance."

"Of course not. Money, money, money. Sighthill is the only cost - effective solution I dare say."

He was getting angry now. "It isn't just money Rosy. But money is important. The economy is as stagnant as a bloody pond and Westminster is getting fed up with writing cheques. We can't just ignore money."

"Obviously. Politics is all money. How much can you hoodwink the people into giving you? What can you spend it on to persuade them to give you their vote next time? Giving bed and board to asylum seekers is pretty far down the list of the voter's wish list. One up from all expenses paid Caribbean cruises for convicted paedophiles I should think. So. There is no choice really. They stay in Sighthill. The issue is how to stop the residents from killing them. Yes?"

"I suppose it is."

"So how do you do it? More police officers? Tough option. You can't just recruit and train extra coppers just like that. And if you take them from somewhere else the ordinary decent criminals will have a field day. Oh come on Daniel, you're not that thick. You know full well where this is all going."

"Oh do I really? Well please do enlighten me."

"At some stage somebody is going to have to bite the bullet and start talking about bringing the army in. Unless by some miracle the good people of Sighthill decide to get all warm and cuddly with their new guests. Can you see that happening? They're your people after all, or so you keep telling me."

"No." He felt sick. "That probably won't happen."

"Of course it won't. Look at what is going on Daniel. Bombs, evictions, this is organised. Thought out. Carefully planned. Whoever is behind all this isn't some skinhead outside a football ground on a Saturday afternoon waving a bike chain. Whoever it is isn't just going to stop. Maybe the police will keep a lid on things but it doesn't appear very likely. At some stage someone is going to have to put soldiers into Sighthill."

"I don't understand where you are coming from Rosy."

"It isn't your call Daniel. It isn't a call for the First Minister either. Soldiers on the street of a British city is a Westminster decision. As far as I can see it is bound to come at some stage. The sensible thing is to be the first person to realise it. Shake your head. Say how terribly concerned you are about the severity of the situation. Be the soothsayer. Be the one that sees it first. Then pass the buck and come out clean as a whistle. Because let's face it Daniel, at some stage you need to pass on this whole thing to someone else before it burns your fingers."

Now he was smiling. He had lain awake at night for hours wondering just how he could pass the buck. And Rosy had come through yet again. Soldiers. Perfect. Bloody perfect. "Of course I could still go across there. Just because Westminster was handling the problem wouldn't mean that I couldn't be seen on the front line."

"Obviously not dear. Maybe I'll even get the chance to dress you up in flak jacket."

Three hours later he marched into the Press conference behind his rather beleaguered leader. His earlier assessment had hit the man hard. He had vainly tried to find ways of avoiding Daniel's drastic assessment of the crisis. It would not be a call that he would relish. It would most probably be the end of him. The Party hadn't set him up in the job to dump a ton of crap on them. He had reluctantly agreed to the idea that it would be a good thing to gently float the issue to the press. To start the process of getting people used to the idea. He had been more than happy to pass the job over of giving the message to his younger colleague. Suddenly the First Minister's thoughts had turned to the prospect of three rounds of golf a week and more time at the villa in Spain.

"Gentlemen. Thank you for coming." The flash bulbs lit up Daniel's confident face. "We have had another bad weekend in Sighthill. Very bad. All the world is watching terrible images of race hate on the streets of Scotland's largest city. It must not continue. It cannot continue. Extreme right-wing elements are trying to blackmail this democratically elected government to change its policy of fairness and decency. I can answer their threat here and now. It isn't going to happen. Not now. Not next week. Not ever. This administration will never bow to terrorism, and let us all be very clear on this, the people who are orchestrating this vicious campaign of hate ARE terrorists. Terrorists of the very worst kind. Terrorists who are scaring people who are helpless and alone. People who have already suffered enough. Well I can confirm here and now that it will not work. Never. We will take whatever steps we have to ensure that those responsible for these outrages will never get what they want. If it means more police then so be it. If it means a request for troops then so be it. We refuse to be blackmailed."

It was as if a bolt of lightning had flickered its way around the room. The ranks of reporters had already been sitting up and paying attention. They had got used to seeing a bit of action when Daniel

Morrissey took to the podium. He was very much their kind of guy. You never knew what you were about to get. But he always offered a bit of value. Always gave good copy. But this was unbelievable. He had actually said the big "T" word. Said it in public for the world to hear. Not a quiet leak. Not unnamed sources. He had actually mentioned the prospect of putting troops onto the streets of a Scottish city. A forest of hands flew up as he wound up his briefing. He nodded to one at random.

"Jimmy Philips. The Sun. Tell me, what exactly would need for happen for you to order in the army?"

Daniel was marvellously unruffled, unlike the First Minister who looked like he had just discovered that he was sitting on a piece of chewing gum.

"Let me be quite clear about this. The Scottish Executive is not empowered to deploy the army to deal with a domestic disturbance. That decision remains the preserve of the government in Westminster. Therefore it will not be my decision to order the deployment. I will do all that I can to stay as close as possible to the situation on the ground and to brief my colleagues accordingly. If the First Minister feels as a result of these briefings that it is appropriate for him to contact Westminster then he will make that particular call. The final decision will be made in London. All that we can do is to make the best recommendations that we can."

He fielded a fusillade of questions with calm assurance before wrapping up the briefing. An hour later he was enjoying a rather fine lunch with admiring colleagues. His boss on the other hand was enjoying a less fulfilling afternoon. He received a call from the Prime Minister in London. He had really been quite shocked by the man's language. He would have never suspected it. Had he not realised that the army was already stretched to the limit in Iraq? Was he mad? By the time he put down the receiver the three rounds of golf a week and extra time to spend at the villa in Spain seemed a great deal closer. In fact they seemed like a bloody good idea.

Khalil checked his watch as he heard the knock at his door. Three minutes after one. Very punctual. The peephole revealed a young man in jeans and a leather jacket waiting.

"Mr Hendon?"

"Aye."

"Please come in."

Johnny walked in and cast a distasteful eye around the flat. "Nice place."

"I've been in worse. Please. Have a seat. Coffee? Tea?"

"Coffee will do. Can I smoke?"

Khalil nodded and brought over a metal litterbin for an ashtray. When he received his coffee Johnny took a sip and gave a nod. "Nice. I like a proper cup of coffee. So. You're the man then."

"I suppose I am."

"Happy so far?"

"Perfectly happy. You have been worth your fee."

"Good. I always strive to give proper value. So what's next?"

Khalil got to his feet and went to the window. "Come here a moment. Take a look. What do you see?"

Johnny joined him. "I don't know. Not a lot. Courtyard. Playground. Grass. What am I supposed to see?"

"Take a proper look at the playground."

Johnny did. "OK. Two swings. A slide. A see-saw. Government approved rubber matting. Climbing frame. Merry-go-round. It's a playground. Everything looks like it probably works. Lots of litter. A bit of graffiti. I don't know. What am I supposed to see?"

"What is missing Johnny?"

What was missing? How was he supposed to know? He had been intrigued to come and meet with the man who was at the centre of the whole thing. He hadn't quite known what to expect. Hadn't had a clue. He certainly hadn't expected a game of twenty questions.

"Christ, I don't know. What?"

"Children Johnny. Children. Imagine how many children there are up the flats around the courtyard. It is another sunny day. School is out. And yet there are no children. Why Johnny?"

"Because their parents as scared stiff. That's why. They are keeping them under lock-and-key. It's obvious."

"Obvious maybe. But it isn't good, is it Johnny? It can never be good when children are too afraid to come out and play in the sun, can it Johnny?"

This was absurd. "No it can't. But we live in a bitch of a world don't we. Where is all this leading?"

Khalil gestured him back to his seat where he lit up again. Khalil reached behind his chair and passed over a mirror. "I am aware of your needs Johnny. Please don't think that I will be offended. Go ahead if it helps you to concentrate."

Bloody hell. This was a turn-up. He was a cool one. The man. Johnny shrugged and proceeded to cut a line of cocaine and snorted it up through a crisp twenty-pound note fresh from the cash machine. Khalil watched him with a benign expression.

"OK. From tomorrow we will be making it safe for the children to play. Already there are some families who are willing to bring their children to the playground. We shall ensure that they are in no danger."

Johnny felt razor-sharp now. "Got you. I believe that it is called a red rag to a bull. Nice. Very nice. If you are looking for a way to yank Tac Brennan's chain then I think you have found it. What do you want me to do?"

Khalil told him.

Khalil took up his place on the broken bench at eleven the next morning. He turned his face upward to catch the warmth of the sun. He had brought bread and amused himself by tossing it to the floor for the pigeons to come and collect. Moses and his friends waited in the doorway to the flats. There were five others who waited in other parts of the courtyard. Ten of them in all. Ten who Moses had found and brought to Khalil. Ten who burned with anger for the things that had been done to their families. Ten young men who were tired of being pushed around and spat at. Ten young men who were ready to fight back. Ten young men from all four corners of the world – Bosnia, Turkey, Chechnya, Iraq, Sierra Leone, Zimbabwe. Ten young men united by the place that they had wound up. Ten young men whom Khalil knew were ready.

The first family came at ten past eleven. The father walked with his back held straight and his head high. Back home in Bosnia he had been a union leader in the shoe factory where he worked. When the Serbs had overrun his small town they had first raped and then executed his wife and parents. He had been lucky. He had been collecting his children from school. Without the children he would have fought. But they were most important. He had found them a sanctuary in Sighthill many miles from the killer squads. And now he would allow them to play. He helped them onto the see-saw and rocked them for a while. Then he joined Khalil on the bench.

"You have two beautiful young girls."

The man nodded, his face filled with pride. And they looked beautiful. One nine. The other one ten. Their blonde hair bouncing as they played. Their faces alive with the pleasure of being out of the flat.

More families arrived. Soon there were eleven children playing. The sound of their laughter echoed around the still air of the courtyard. Then the man gently nudged Khalil on the arm.

There were ten of them. He guessed that the oldest must have been eighteen. Maybe nineteen. He was the one he had spotted a few minutes before. He had come out of the main entrance of one of the blocks and watched the kids for a few moments before he had disappeared back inside. The youngest of the group was probably little more than fourteen. Khalil had seen most of them before over the last few days as he had quietly surveyed the ground that he had chosen.

Now they came towards the playground with a collective swagger. The older one was shouting and his comments received appreciative laughter from his followers.

"You best get off those fucking swings or I might just wrap that fucking chain round your Paki necks. What's that fucking smell lads? Fucking terrible isn't it. The smell of little fucking Pakis . . ."

He didn't seem to have noticed Khalil as he approached. He looked rather taken aback when he stood up. Khalil smiled politely.

"Is there some kind of a problem?"

The boy was stunned. Who did the old cunt think he was?

"You what?"

"I merely asked if there was some kind of problem. You seem rather upset."

Unbelievable. This was about to be one seriously dead Paki bastard.

"Aye. A've got a big problem you old cunt. A've got a problem with your stinking fucking breath. A've got a problem with these wee shites thinking they can come and play here."

He stood very close to Khalil to intimidate him. Khalil merely resumed in quiet reasonable tone.

"They are only children. Surely letting them play cannot present such a problem. I think it may well be best if you all leave now."

This brought a rather artificial guffaw of laughter. "Hear that lads. This old twat thinks we should leave. That right is it? And just what the fuck are you going to do about it?"

His face was so close that flecks of spit splashed onto Khalil's face. He took a handkerchief from his pocket and wiped it away. He sighed with an air of disappointment. "Maybe you should take a look around."

For a moment the boy sensed that he was about to be conned. Then he reasoned that it was unlikely. What was the old twat about to do when he turned his back? Run away? He wouldn't get far. He duly glanced over his shoulder to find Moses in the middle of a line of eleven. All of them cradled baseball bats. Within a couple of seconds the bravado drained out of first him and then the rest of his colleagues.

Khalil continued in the same gentle tone. "As I said. Maybe it would be best if you were to leave now. Why not let the children play? What harm can it do?"

To start with the boys backed away very carefully as if they were treading their way through a minefield. Once they were twenty yards clear they turned and ran. As they reached the corner the leader stopped and turned.

"You bastards are dead. All of you."

Khalil sat back down and pulled a book from his pocket. He had bought it on his trip into the city. It was Evelyn Waugh's *Decline and Fall*. He had not read it for years. It would pass the time. As it turned out there was not a great deal of time to pass. It was only twenty minutes after the boys had departed when four cars pulled up. The men who climbed out were clearly less than happy with the state of affairs. When Tac had been told of what had happened he had merely brought along a few of the men who had been with him in the pub. The ex-soldiers were all still in the cottage in Ayr.

He was seething. This wasn't part of the plan. This wasn't even nearly part of the plan. He had expected problems from the cops. He had even half-anticipated the threat of soldiers. What he hadn't even considered was that any of the asylum seekers would fight back. How could they? They came from different countries. They didn't even speak the same language. How the hell could they get themselves together enough to have a go? He had slapped the older boy hard across the face when he first heard his story. He had slapped him because he had been convinced that it was just bullshit. But the boy had stuck to it. Nothing changed in the second telling. And Tac had to accept that it was probably true. Baseball bats! The bastards had the cheek to threaten the lads with baseball bats. Unbelievable. And it had just been one man who had done the talking. An old bastard. Arrogant bastard. Maybe he was the one who had put it together.

By the time Brennan jumped out of the lead car he was fuming. He strode across the courtyard with the boy trotting to keep up.

"That's him Mr Brennan. The twat with the book on the bench. That's him."

Brennan marched over to where Khalil sat enjoying the sun as he read. For a moment Tac wondered whether or not he was simply going to ignore him. His temper was climbing. He was just about to start when the man carefully noted his page with a marker and pocketed the book. He looked up at Tac and smiled.

"Mr Brennan I presume. I thought you might come."

It was very hard for Tac to hold back from putting his lights out. There were people coming out of the flats now to watch. A mixture. Locals and wogs in separate groups. He concentrated on controlling his breathing. Not yet. Find out what the fuck is going on first. He managed to speak with reason.

"Exactly what is happening here?"

Khalil looked about him. "What you can see Mr Brennan. It is a fine afternoon. The children are playing. Nothing unusual in that, surely."

"I hear that you threatened some kids. I hear that there were baseball bats involved."

"Oh that." Khalil gave a light laugh. "It was nothing. I think it was just youthful high-spirits. Maybe they are unused to the heat. I think they saw our point of view in the end. After all, I'm sure you can see that it does nobody any harm if the children can have a play."

Brennan clenched his teeth together. He spoke very slowly. "I said that I heard that there were baseball bats. Were there baseball bats?"

"Oh yes. There were baseball bats. Rather unfortunate. I can assure you that I did ask politely first. Sometimes being polite isn't enough. Wouldn't you agree Mr Brennan?"

The audience was gripped now. Was the man stark staring mad? Didn't he know who he was talking to? Surely he did. He knew his name well enough. Tac was quite taken aback. "Tell me. Are you suicidal?"

"No. I don't think so."

"You've got bottle. I'll grant you that. You're a sad mad bastard, but you've got bottle. I'll give you five minutes. Five minutes and this playground is cleared. For some reason I'm feeling generous."

He reached into his pocket and lit up. Still Khalil was all reason.

"And the alternative?"

Tac blew out smoke and rolled his eyes. Crazy, crazy bastard. "The alternative is that I will beat you to within an inch of your life. The alternative is that you will live out the rest of your days in a fucking wheelchair. Is that clear enough for you or do I have to explain again?"

Khalil smiled. "Oh that is quite clear thank you. But I don't think you will do it."

"No? And why is that?"

Khalil drew aside the lapel of his jacket. For a moment Tac tensed, expecting to see a gun. No gun. A microphone. A microphone? What the hell was he doing with a microphone?

"JOHNNY!!" shouted Khalil.

Johnny Hendon stepped out from where he had been waiting inside the doorway to the flats. He waved cheerfully to Khalil.

"Yeah. Got it all. Nice and clear. Pictures too. Emailed it all off."

Khalil wasn't smiling any more. "You forgot your ski mask Mr Brennan. Rather complacent. Now beat me up if you wish. I think it would be a mistake. If not, then maybe you should leave now. Good day."

He pulled out his book and opened it up at the marked page.

Brennan was shaking with anger. His brain tried to take in his options. emailed. The fucker had emailed the whole thing somewhere. A full tape recording of his threats. Photos. He was stuffed. No options. He threw his half-smoked cigarette to the ground.

"This isn't over."

Khalil looked up from the page. "I never thought that it would be. Please be aware that this playground now will be available for children to play in. I will make sure that the children remain safe. I suggest that you remember your ski mask next time."

Brennan stared hard at him. To his own surprise he felt a tinge of unease. Some deep buried instinct was warning him. Who was this guy? He turned and marched back to the cars followed by his bewildered men.

Word spread around the estate that some old Paki guy had faced-down Tac Brennan. Nobody could quite believe it. Everybody wondered what would come next.

Tac Brennan almost took the front door of his flat clear off the hinges as he kicked it open. On the short journey back from the playground his temper had reached and surpassed boiling point. The men who followed him inside cowered into the corners of the room as he picked up a half-full bottle of scotch and hurled it against the wall. For a moment his eyes hunted out something else to throw. Then he realised that all eyes were on him. Time to find control.

"Right. Sit down. Stand up. I don't give a fuck. Just listen. That fucker is going down. And I mean all the way down. I want every one of you out there. Starting now. You get the word out. Tomorrow morning we close that old twat's playground venture down. I want bodies on the street. Hundreds. As many as you can get. It's a simple deal. They all get 50 quid each when they turn up and God help any of the bastards that I find sneaking off. Ten tomorrow morning outside his block. Let people know that I'm not fucking about here. People better turn up or watch their backs. Got that? Then fuck off. We'll meet up in the pub later."

Once the room was clear he dragged a mobile phone out of its case and dialled up his sergeants. "Jimmy. It's me. Get back here. Tomorrow we go big."

End. Another number.

"Nathan. I need a meet. The pub at noon. Never mind the last target. Things have changed."

When he had finished speaking he lit a cigarette and poured a big whisky. He was still shaking with rage. He knew that he had to calm down. He was behaving exactly how an amateur would behave. He was allowing temper to get the better of judgement. He had allowed the man to get right under his skin. He closed his eyes and forced himself to relax. Very gradually he managed to calm himself down. As his thoughts at last became a little more ordered he found that there really was only one question that was eating at him. Who the hell was this guy? He had known his name. Not that difficult. He didn't exactly keep a low profile in and around Sighthill. He had known that the men in the ski masks were down to him. Or did he know? Probably just guessing. Again, it wouldn't be too difficult. But how the hell had he been so damn calm. Christ, the old bastard must have been pushing 60. He had even opened his bloody book and started reading. Who did that? What kind of man could be so bloody cool?

He slumped back into his seat as it hit him that he knew exactly the type of guy who could show that kind of casual indifference to danger. After all, he had met with a few of them. There were the better officers that he had served under. The laid-back bastards who cracked jokes when the tracer bullets were filling the air. They were the strange ones from the SAS with their half-smiles and eyes that were somewhere else. Was the stranger really one of these men? If he was, it explained the bad feeling that Tac Brennan couldn't get rid off.

OK. Accept it then. So what does it mean? What do you do? There was no question of retreat. It wasn't in his make-up. No way. Time was beginning to press in. The bloody Minister had seemed pretty serious when he had talked about deploying troops. That would make things tough. Maybe even too tough. Even with most of the best boys away in Iraq they would still be able to find some pretty tasty lads to send in. Probably a couple of regiments form the north of England. Hard fuckers from Liverpool and Leeds with plenty of time in Ireland under their belts. They would just love to come up and have a go at the Jocks. The coppers were one thing but soldiers were another all together. His mates from the Paras would be OK. But the rest of them? No chance. All mouth. They would be hiding away in their flats once a few heads got broken. So they would be just eleven. Not enough. Not nearly enough.

So he needed to move things along. Go for broke whilst he still could. That was OK. It was what he was used to. It wasn't the way of the Paras to pick away at the edges of a problem with a careful plan. They would always go straight in with all guns blazing and fuck the consequences. So why change the habits of a lifetime. Maybe the old fucker thought that he had some kind of plan. Well that plan had better include an all-out fucking battle. Because that was what he was about to get.

Two thousand miles away Sergei listened to the tape with a beaming smile. Khalil had been right. The man was behaving completely predictably. It was almost as if he was sleepwalking his way to his nemesis. He had even fallen for the bait to make sure that the timing was right. It would be a Saturday morning that he would throw all caution to the wind and make his big move. Perfect. Time to make the few calls. Time for the dominoes to be lined up. The first call was to Khalil.

"It's me. I trained you rather well. It will happen tomorrow. Just as you predicted. Full on. No punches pulled. Are you ready?"

"I am ready. Thank you my friend."

The line was dead. All of a sudden the euphoria drained out of Sergei Mikhailovich. He realised that his part was played out. The brief conversation would probably be the last he would ever have with the man whom he had known for so many years. For a moment he had an image of the earnest young man who had come to his office at Patrice Lumumba all those years ago. It had been a time when they had all believed that they could make the world a better place. What difference had they ever made? None really. They had played their part. Nothing more. At least Khalil had one last chance to grasp a small victory in the face of their endless defeat.

Khalil met with Keeley and Declan in the coffee shop in Waterstones bookshop on Sauchiehall Street. He had stopped off in a public toilet to change into slacks and a jacket to make him less conspicuous. It was late in the afternoon and the girl behind the counter was counting down the minutes left before she could get the bus home to doll herself up for a Friday night on the town. Two students were idly flicking though books. Otherwise the three of them had the place to themselves.

Khalil spoke in a low voice as he stirred his coffee. "Sergei called. It will be tomorrow. Brennan will be coming with everything he has. As expected."

Keeley nodded. "Perfect. I will make some calls. Farouk spoke to Zaheer Khan last night. They can all leave as soon as you need them. Shall I arrange for them to come tonight?"

"Yes. As soon as they can. Meet them on the motorway. Bring them to Sighthill via the lock-up. It will be as well to move all the stuff from Sergei in whilst we can. We will need some of it tomorrow anyway. Bring them straight to my block. I will have space ready."

Keeley nodded. "Has Hendon done the article?"

"Yes. He called me half an hour ago. *The Recorder* will run it tomorrow."

"He got the photo?" asked Declan.

"He did. I think it is rather flattering."

Keeley chuckled. "Sergeant Brennan is going to flip his lid when he reads it. He must be bloody fuming already."

"He is" chipped in Declan. "I met him at lunchtime. Not a happy punter. Actually he's come up with quite a clever plan."

Declan ran over the tasks that he had been given a few hours earlier. They all kicked around Brennan's plans and concluded that they could only help their own cause.

Keeley brought over three more coffees.

"So. We are nearly there gentlemen. Is there anything else?"

Keeley nodded. "I've just got a couple of things to sort. I will contact Bland. I think that it would be good to put his lads into the mixer. I'll probably get them to follow up on your work Declan. I've also had another idea of how I can use Rufus." He ran through it and they nodded their approval. He then continued. "One last thing. It could be pretty hard getting in and out of Sighthill once everything goes off. We cannot rely on the TV people getting in. I know a man. He's a freelancer. He's been around the block a time or two. Balkans. Middle East. Africa. He won't get fazed when the shit starts to fly. I helped him get a start when I was with MI5. We helped him in Ireland. He helped us now and then. Good guy. Very discreet. I reckon I could get him up to work with Hendon."

Khalil considered the suggestion. It wasn't difficult to see the merit in it. They hadn't anticipated that Brennan could take things quite so far so quickly. The TV side of things would be critical. It would be foolish to rely on the ingenuity of the film crews to carve their way into Sighthill. He nodded. "You're right. It makes sense. See if you can arrange it. Is there anything else?"

There wasn't. They finished their coffees over more idle chat. Just as they were ready to leave Declan asked. "The article tomorrow. Do you think they will see it? Or will it be the TV?"

"They'll see it" said Khalil with complete certainty.

"Rufus?"

"Yeah man. Who's that?"

"It's Mr Burton, Rufus. I was wondering if you would be able to do a bit more work for me?"

"Hey Mr Burton. You know me. I'm here for you, man. Always here. 24/7 man. What's the gig?"

"I want you to get yourself into the BNP website. Put an article on the home page. I have also notice that they have a 'mailing out' facility. I thought that you could maybe use it to send out a message. Would that be a problem?"

"Normal payment terms?"

"Of course. I will have £500 delivered by courier before midnight."

"Then it's all cool man. Piece of cake. What about the message?"

"Give me an address and I'll email it to you."

"Leave it with me. It will be done my man. Have no fear. Rufus will deliver. Rufus always delivers."

Keeley fired up his laptop and spent half an hour reading through the archive of articles on the BNP website. Then he started to type.

URGENT MESSAGE!!!

This morning Daniel Morrissey MSP threatened to deploy soldiers on the streets of Sighthill to protect six thousand asylum seekers from the rightful residents. Protect them! Only a few short weeks ago three young Scottish boys were slashed to death by a crazed asylum seeker. The BNP has been warning about the dangers of allowing these terrorists into our country for months and months. Our warnings have not been heeded. Now when the residents of Sighthill are fighting to make their streets safe for children to play in, the Government are threatening them with troops. These threats show the lengths to which our so-called leaders will go to allow the mass contamination of our great country. The people of Sighthill are fighting the first battle in a war that will decide the future of every white British person on these islands of ours. Now is the time for all of us to stand shoulder to shoulder. Now is the time for us all to say "ENOUGH. NO MORE". Now is the time to stand and fight. There will be a war up in Sighthill this weekend. We need soldiers to win this war. For the sake of the future generations of white British people we must stand with the people of Sighthill this weekend. This is a chance for all of you who go to fight this battle to be remembered by history. One day you will be able to tell your grandchildren. You will be able to proudly say that you were there when the true inhabitants of our great nation at last stood up and started to turn back the tide. Our message is quite clear. Go to Sighthill. Go and fight for our future. Our time has arrived!!

He read and reread it and tinkered around until he was happy. Rambling sentimental drivel. Just right. He copied the file across to an email and sent it. By nine that evening every person who had registered for the BNP mailing list had received their copy. By midnight it was posted on the front page of the website. The BNP leadership were mainly to be found in pubs and clubs when their mobile phones started to ring. Very few were remotely sober enough to think about the problem coherently. There was a mildly frantic hunt for the member called Derek who looked after the website. By two in the morning it was established that Derek had flown out of Luton airport that morning for a week in Gran Canaria with his partner and three kids. Nobody really had a clue what to do. Most of them agreed during the course of their late-night conversations that they were actually quite happy with the message and they looked forward to meeting whoever had written it. Well over half of the senior men filled their cars with mates and hit the road north for Glasgow. It was going to be a weekend to remember.

Keeley's BNP message winged its way through cyberspace into Frankie "The Pitbull" Bland's computer a little after ten. It was already too late. The Pitbull had received a call from Mr Burton early that evening. He already had his men fully mobilised. Wives had been told. Girlfriends had been put straight. The boys were all primed and ready to roll. Bags were packed. Vehicles were fuelled up. The convoy of seven cars rolled out of Rathcoole a little after seven. Four hours later the bar on the ferry to Stranraer was jumping to the sound of Loyalist songs. By the time Keeley met them at a layby south of Ayr at four that morning they were mainly snoring away happily. Bland himself seemed remarkably sober considering the prodigious amount of lager that he had put away. He was more than happy with the role that Mr Burton had chosen for his team. He couldn't wait. It seemed like it had been a long time since they had all seen some proper action.

Khalil had sent Moses and his friends out and about to knock doors in the other blocks that afternoon. Word of the stand-off at the playground had got around fast. Most of the asylum seekers had received the news with terror. The situation they faced was already desperate. The fact that there were some among them who were intent on fighting back could only make it worse. However there were more young men who shared a desire to fight back. By seven that evening a further 35 were assembled in the meeting room in Khalil's block along with the ten who had stood with him at the playground that morning.

As Khalil stood up to address it seemed just like old times. Just like the camp in Sidon. Ranks of young men who had reached the end of their tether. Young men who had decided to fight back. He saw the same grim determination in their faces. Just like in Sidon, the men in front of him had come from far and wide. They shared no common language or political creed or religion. All they shared was their fate. For whatever reason they had been forced to flee their homeland to this bleak place. And instead of finding peace and the chance of a new life they had found only hate and contempt. And now they had had their fill. Now they would fight.

"It is good to see so many of you. People here think that we are helpless. They think that they can burn us out of our homes and we will do nothing. They think that they can keep our children locked away from the sunshine and we will do nothing. They see us as people who are worthless. They see us as people who are weak. I have only been here a short time. Only a few days. But what I see is different. I see people who have escaped from fear despite terrible danger. I see people who have completed journeys that many would have considered impossible. I see people who have found the strength to survive against all the odds. All we lack here is unity. Nothing else. Today we found some unity. We found enough strength to allow our children to play in the sunshine. It is only a small thing. But it is a start. It can be our first step towards finding our dignity. There isn't

*a person in this room who does not understand the importance of
dignity. A man can be beaten and tortured and see everything that
belongs to him taken away. But if he retains his dignity he will emerge
from the darkness in triumph.*

*'What we did today will not be the end. It will only be the start. We
have made people angry and tomorrow they will come for their
revenge. There will be many of them and they will be very, very angry.
Shall we hide? Or shall we fight? Now I must tell you the truth about
myself. I am not all that I seem. I have been sent here to help make
things better. Your problems here have not gone unnoticed. There are
people who are willing to help. Tonight a group of 50 men will arrive
here in Sighthill. They have volunteered to come and fight for the
dignity of every asylum seeker. Along with those of us in the room that
makes nearly a hundred."*

He paused to take a long, careful look around the room. He was not
disappointed with what he saw. His gaze was met with determined
eyes. So Khalil. You still have the old touch.

*"There is more. We will not only be a hundred. We will be a hundred
with a plan. A strategy. We will be a mob. A hundred can do much if
they are organised. Tomorrow we have the chance to win a great
victory. A famous victory. A victory for the oppressed people all over
the world. It is a rare opportunity, believe me. We all know what it is
to try to fight against tanks and planes and automatic weapons. It is
hopeless. But tomorrow there will be no tanks and planes. Only
people. People who are arrogant because they think that we are
weak. I ask you all to grasp this opportunity. I ask you all to stand
with me tomorrow. If there is anyone in the room who does not feel
that they are ready to carry out this task then please feel free to leave
now. You can do so with no shame. The path of violence is not for all
men. Our world would be an even more terrible place if it was."*

A silence hung in the room. There was only stillness. Nobody
moved. He would have been surprised if they had. Very slowly
Moses stood from his chair on the front row. He lifted a clenched fist
and shouted loud.

RED ZONE

"Bayete!!"

To all the others the word had no meaning. None of then knew that it was the battle cry of generations of young men of the Matebele. None of them knew that it was the battle cry for a king. None of them knew that it meant a pledge of allegiance from which a warrior could only be released by death. None of them knew of the times when warriors had shouted their salute before his nation's many bloody wars. They didn't know the detail but they could sense the tone. One by one they held their clenched fists up high and shouted out defiance in their many languages.

Khalil had his army. Tomorrow he would start the last battle.

Deep into the warmth of an Israeli night, Rachel Shultz was horribly tired. At university she had learned to study hard. Before each set of exams she had worked remorselessly with minimal levels of sleep. But it had been different then. An examination always had a fixed time and date. She would gear everything towards that time and date. No matter how hard she pushed herself there was always a finishing line. Beyond that line was the chance to relax and be with friends. It made the sacrifice worthwhile.

Now she was with Shin Bet everything had changed. Night after night she ploughed through papers and Internet pages feeling for a trace of her quarry. Now there was no finish line. There wasn't even the remotest guarantee that her search would ever bear any fruit. All the evidence suggested that she was wasting her time. The man she sought would be nearly 60 now. She shuddered at the thought of what he must have endured in the ten years he spent in Tadmur. The most likely truth was that he was dead. She had discovered that he had been taken from the prison early one morning in a Mercedes car. She knew nothing of what physical state he was in. She could only assume that it must have been terrible. The mere fact that money had been found was no reason to believe that he was still alive and in any state to present any kind of threat to Israel.

For days now she had sat for eighteen hours a day at her small desk seeking the needle in the haystack. Four nights earlier she had returned home after midnight to an enormous row with her boyfriend. He was home on leave from his posting along the fences of Gaza. He told her that he deserved more of her time. He told her that he only had three days. He demanded that she take time from her work. Her superiors would understand. Surely they would know what it was to be a soldier on the fence at Gaza. Rachel had refused. She had told him that the work that held her was vital. She told him that it wasn't only soldiers who had their duty. She had insisted that she would return to her desk at six the next morning. And he had left her with words of contempt. Since then there had been no call. Since then there had only been the eternal search. Why? What conceivable reason was there for her to drive herself on when everything suggested that her efforts were futile? The gut instinct of a tired old man. Nothing more.

She glanced over her computer screen to the door of his office at the far end of the large open-plan room on the third floor. As ever the window in the door gleamed a dull yellow from his desk lamp. Everybody else had left hours ago. Some had started making mocking comments about the new girl. She was trying to brown-nose to the great man. What was the point? He was the past. It wouldn't be long before they would pension him off. Breslow the dinosaur. Breslow the man from times that were past. She merely kept her head down and ignored them. They could think what they liked. She couldn't be bothered to rise to them. They wouldn't understand the way she felt. They would never know what she felt when he had shown her the tattoo from Treblinka. If he believed, then she would believe. It was a simple thing. She rubbed her eyes and resumed.

It was a little past three in the morning. Midnight in most of Western Europe. The newspapers would have posted their online editions onto the Internet. They had a program to trawl all the electronic media for keywords. Her fingers floated over the keys and set the program running. It took several minutes until the screen revealed the results. There were not many. One caught her attention. It was *The Scottish Recorder*. The headline of the article was:

'THE FIRST SHOTS IN THE PLAYGROUND WAR'.

The keyword that had guided her computer was *TADMUR*. She clicked onto the link with mild interest. As the screen filled with the article she almost fell off her chair. She dragged the drawer of her filing cabinet open and pulled out the image of the older Khalil Bishawa that the experts had produced. For a few moments her eyes flicked from the image to the screen and back again. It was remarkable. The image could almost have been a photograph of the man on the screen who sat on a bench in front of a set of swings. There were two smiling young children on the swings. Behind was a view of towering grey blocks of flats. The man looked relaxed. He wore an old suit and a shirt that suggested frayed cuffs. He looked remarkably well. A small smile played on his lips. Almost in a trance she read the story by a journalist called John Hendon.

"Ahmad Mansour arrived in Sighthill only a few days ago. He came from a place that few of us here in Scotland have ever heard about. The place was Tadmur Military Prison. Hidden away deep in the Syrian Desert, Tadmur Military Prison was for many years a place of nightmares. It remained in the shadows for a long time. Unspeakable acts of torture and depravity were part of the everyday routine in Tadmur. Thousands upon thousands of men like Ahmad Mansour were forced to endure the terrors of the regime. Thousands were murdered. Ahmad shakes his head politely when I ask him to speak about his time in Tadmur. I only found out what he must have endured from the Amnesty International Website. There is a full page dedicated to his case.

"He insists that he is one of the lucky ones. Many thousands of his fellow Palestinians were dragged off to Tadmur in the 1980s and 1990s having committed no other crime than having born with the wrong nationality. He was lucky because a relative died recently and left him sufficient funds to escape Syria. In a cruel twist of fate he has landed up in Sighthill.

"In the midst of the racial hatred that is sweeping the beleaguered Glasgow estate, he noticed one single sight that touched his heart. A playground. A playground that he watched from the window of his flat. A playground that was empty for all the hours of a sunny afternoon. He could not understand how could it be. He said that no matter how bad things were for his people in Syria there had never been a time when the children were too afraid to play. It was only here in this place of supposed sanctuary where children were locked away to keep them safe.

RED ZONE

"Yesterday Ahmad Mansour made his statement. Along with ten others he made the playground a safe place in which to play. The residents of Sighthill came to try and use physical force to drive the children back indoors. The hatred that was shown to the asylum seekers and their children was extreme. Ahmad Mansour is a man who is used to hate. Along with ten other men from the estate he forced the local residents to back down. This only happened because I was present with a camera that was emailing shots of the scene. They wore no disguise and had they attacked the asylum seekers I would have had clear evidence to pass on to the police. Mansour has no doubt that the men will come again. He fully expects that they will come again today in even greater numbers. He is determined that he and his men will not bow to intimidation.

"Once again there was little evidence of the police in the Sighthill Estate yesterday. Mansour and his fellow asylum seekers can expect little or no protection in their efforts to make the playground a safe place for the children. Yesterday there was still no clear word on the deteriorating situation from the Government. Today's events may well force their hand."

The tiredness had fallen away from Rachel the second that the image of the man by the playground had appeared on the screen. Her blood seemed to be pumping at about five times the normal rate. She wanted to leap to her feet and scream with joy. She wanted to hug everyone in the room. But there was nobody else there to witness her moment of triumph. Just the old man behind the door. She printed off the story and spent a moment straightening her clothes and running a comb through her hair.

At first there was no response to her tap on the door. She tried a second time, a little louder. This time there was a muffled response. She took it to be an affirmative and went inside. Breslow must have been asleep at his desk. He was in the process of dragging himself awake as she entered the room. For a moment he seemed disorientated, almost afraid. He pushed his steel glasses onto his nose and squinted at her. She thought that he looked terribly old; a frail old man lost in the loneliness of the hours before the dawn. Recognition came to his face.

"Oh. Rachel. It's you."

His pale hand automatically reached for his Marlboros. He lit up and pushed the mess of his hair into a semblance of order.

"Sit down Rachel. You work too late you know. Only old men like me should work so late. This is no place for you at this time. You should go home Rachel. This place will contaminate you."

She cut him short. Her eyes gleamed when she spoke.

"I've found him."

The words stopped him dead. A light switched on in his eyes.

"What?"

"I've found him. Here. Look."

She passed over the printout of Johnny Hendon's story and the likeness that the experts had come up with. He didn't move a muscle as he read. He took so long that she realised that he must have read the piece at least three times. He then swung his desk lamp round so that it poured light onto the two pictures. His eyes flicked from one picture to another. There was hunger in his eyes now. Only minutes before the eyes had been old and tired. Now they were alive with the gleam of the hunter.

"It's him." He made his pronouncement like a hanging judge. He drummed his fingers for a few seconds. "OK. I want everyone in here in two hours. No complaining. No excuses. Everyone. Make it happen Rachel. Go. Go now."

She jumped to her feet and turned for the door. He stopped her.

"Good Rachel. Very, very good."

She nodded in response. She had grown in the last hour. This was more than a result in an exam. This was the big game. The biggest game of them all. She had found her man. Now they would decide what to do with him. And she was part of it.

Israel's Interior Minister wasn't at all happy to be roused from his bed at 4.30 in the morning. He was even less happy that it was Mordechai Breslow doing the rousing. He hated the man. He always felt slightly soiled by even being in the same room as him. There was something of the reptile about Breslow. He had never met a man so cold. One of his great ambitions for his time in office was to be the one to cast the bastard onto the waste heap. He knew only too well that his country needed men like Breslow. It always had and it always would. He wasn't such a fool as to believe for a second that it didn't.

But he was also convinced that so long as men like Breslow were calling the shots, the war between his people and the Palestinians would be a war without end. He had never managed to feel sufficiently secure in his own position to make a real move to oust the evil old bastard. Maybe one day. And now he was here at his house before the sun was in the sky.

He could smell the bloody man's cigarette even before he opened the door to the living room where he waited. His wife would give him hell for it when she awoke. Breslow looked appalling. He looked as if he had slept in the same set of clothes for a fortnight. His ugly face was as pale as a sheet and his white hair stuck out in all directions in wild tufts. Somehow he managed to force civility into his voice.

"Mordechai. This is a surprise. Can I get you coffee?"

"Yes. Coffee. Coffee would be good. Just black. Black and strong."

The man was almost rambling. Maybe he had finally lost it and gone senile. Now that would be bonus. He nodded to his security man who made for the kitchen. He sat down carefully on an armchair facing Breslow. He was about to take a lead in the conversation when he was cut short.

"We've found Khalil Bishawa."

"Excuse me?"

"We've found Khalil Bishawa. You know him. The brother of Mahmoud Bishawa. We thought he was dead. He isn't. He is in Scotland. A place called Sighthill. He seems to be leading some kind of Peasants' Revolt."

The minister held out his hands in an expansive gesture.

"Hey Mordechai. Slow down! It is too early in the morning for me to go this fast. Take me through it slowly. Allow me to wake up."

The coffee arrived and Breslow brought his boss up to speed. He told him of the cryptic words spoken by Mahmoud on his first day of captivity. He gave him a résumé of the career of Khalil Bishawa before he had vanished off the face of the earth in 1983. He told him of what they had found out about his escape from Tadmur Prison in 1992. He told him of how they had found him in Glasgow. He gave a brief background into the events in Sighthill, as he understood them. At last the Minister held up a hand to stem the flow.

"This is excellent work Mordechai. As ever. Your department never ceases to astound me. However, I fail to understand the relevance of all this. Why do you feel it is so necessary to get me out of bed at this hour to hear all this? As I understand it Bishawa must now be an old man. He has been inactive for over a decade. So now he has taken up a strange crusade in Scotland. It is all thoroughly interesting, but I cannot see any reason for us to be overly concerned. I would suggest that he has probably lost the plot. It would hardly be surprising. Who wouldn't after ten years in Tadmur?"

Breslow answered in short, hard sentences. His voice rattled out like a machine gun at an execution. "One. Someone must have had money to get him out of Tadmur. They must have had money to have kept him off the map for ten years. Not little money. Big money. Real money. Why should he stop hiding now? Why is he arriving penniless in Scotland to seek asylum under a false name? No logical reason. Two. Don't tell me after ten years off the map that it is pure coincidence that Khalil Bishawa reappears just weeks after we take in his brother. No way. I don't believe in these kinds of coincidence. Three. Bishawa has only been in Scotland for a few days and yet look at him. He is all over their national papers. If he fled under a false name he must have wanted to hide. OK. Why not? But is this hiding? Hardly."

"So what are you saying?" The Minister was becoming intrigued despite himself.

"I'm saying that none of this is down to chance. There is a reason that Khalil Bishawa is in Glasgow. That reason will be involved with what has happened to his brother. These are not random events. They are part of a plan. It is what Khalil Bishawa does. He is a planner. One of their best. Trained by the Russians in the 1970s. Whatever the plan is, it represents danger to us."

"So why are you here Mordechai?"

"Because he is on the list."

The words hit the Minister in the face like iced water. The list. The list of the names of the leaders of the organisations they fought against. The list of those who were eligible for execution. The list that had been getting shorter every week since the Americans had given them their window of opportunity by invading Iraq. The list that had sent the helicopters into the skies over Gaza to fire their rockets. The list that had justified Operation Fox. The list that could only be automatically triggered if the target was in Israel or the Occupied Territories. Overseas was different. The UK was very different.

"No Mordechai. It is out of the question. The British would never forgive us. We gave up all that cowboy stuff years ago. Not a chance. No way."

Breslow wasn't fazed. He calmly lit up another cigarette.

"But there is a way. You need to read up on what is happening in this place Sighthill. There is more or less complete anarchy. A Minister in the Scottish Parliament even called for troops last week. For the next few days there will be chaos. The British will get control eventually. But until they do there will be an opportunity."

"What opportunity?"

"We take Bishawa out. We do it in the midst of all the chaos. He has set himself up as a leader of the people in this place. He is a natural target for the Far Right elements that are the cause of all the trouble. Were he to be killed then the blame would inevitably fall on them."

"But why is this so necessary?"

"Because we have no idea of what he plans. All we know is that it will be dangerous. This man is like a dog with rabies. There is only one way to ensure that he can do us no harm. We need to kill him to be sure. It is very simple."

The Minister couldn't argue with the logic. He would have to be completely convinced that the situation in this place called Sighthill was indeed as bad as Breslow suggested. That wouldn't be difficult. It would no doubt all be on the TV. If so, then yes, there was an opportunity. And yet these things so often went wrong and led to a propaganda disaster. That would be unthinkable.

"How can this be done Mordechai? There is so little time. How can you stage such an operation at this notice? How do we get a team in place?"

"No team sir. Just one man. That is all I would use."

"Cohen?"

"Yes. Of course."

The Minister realised that he should have guessed. Of course it would be Cohen. The quiet little man that Breslow used as his attack dog. The man who had once been introduced to the Cabinet after he had executed a Hamas leader in Amman. That had been an assassination on foreign soil of course. Cohen had killed in Lebanon and Egypt also. And he had never left a mess. There could be no argument about that. And now Breslow wanted to send his attack dog to Scotland. The risks were huge. But he could not fail to agree with Breslow's assessment. There was also risk in leaving Khalil Bishawa to forward his plan. Which was the safest path? He shook his head. It wasn't something to be decided now. It would only be decided by a full meeting of the Cabinet. Whether or not he decided to take it to his colleagues with his own recommendation was a decision for later. Not now.

"Proceed with a plan Mordechai. I will need a full briefing on the exact situation in Glasgow by lunchtime. I will need the bones of the plan. If you can convince me, I will take it to the Cabinet. That is all I can say for now."

Breslow was already on his feet, a smug smile on his face. "It is all that I had hoped for sir."

"If we do this Mordechai, there can be no mistakes. You understand that don't you?"

"I understand sir. There will be no mistakes. I will make sure of it."

Rachel was not the only Security Service night-owl in action. In London, Colin Freeman was spending his night in much the same way as his Israeli counterpart. However there was a difference in attitude. Rachel had been on the very cusp of despair in the moments leading up to her finding her electronic Holy Grail. Freeman was untroubled by any such uncertainties. All his life he had loved puzzles. Back home in Rotherham his mother had bought him puzzle books from Woolworth's almost on a daily basis. Her friends from the street would come into the house to drink tea and marvel at the youngster who tore through crosswords, which would have yielded them barely a clue. Excellence at puzzles had naturally followed into excellence in maths. His Grammar School had never seen anything like him. They put him through his A Levels at sixteen and he had won a Scholarship to Balliol College Oxford.

It was here that maths had evolved into computers. By the time that he embarked on his PhD a little after his twentieth birthday he had the whole wide corporate world at his feet. Instead he was seduced by the man from MI5 who lunched him at his club and offered him less than a tenth of the money that the big corporations were dangling in front of him. Money wasn't particularly important to Colin. What really mattered were the puzzles, and none of the big multinationals could offer him puzzles that could begin to compare with those at MI5.

This one was a good one. He had been enjoying it for many hours deep into the night. A colleague had brought it to him in the afternoon. He had said that it was a strange one. Nobody else could seem to get anywhere with it. A huge payment had entered a sleeping BNP account in the wee small hours and had bounced straight back out and into the ether. Who and what? Nobody could fathom it. Maybe Colin could help.

It had been a beauty. He had given up trying to track where the money had come in from. There was a time with any puzzle where you had to accept impossibility. With proper precautions it was possible to cover tracks completely. There were comparatively few who knew how to do it, but whoever had sent the money into the account in Croydon had been very careful. The route out of the account was more interesting. It was without doubt tidy enough, but nowhere near as sophisticated. For hour after hour his fingers had thumped away at his keyboard as he had untied the knots one by one. Colin found it half an hour after Rachel made her big breakthrough. Mr George Brennan of Sighthill, Glasgow was the man at the end of the chain. OK. So where next? There was something familiar about Sighthill.

He typed the keyword into a search engine and soon skip-read enough articles to come up to speed with the situation. He entered "Brennan Sighthill" and found out all about the ex-sergeant whose son had been murdered. This Brennan was known as Tac Brennan. Was it the same man? He checked the man's MI5 file. Yes. Same guy. George Brennan AKA Tac Brennan. Was there a BNP connection? A small one. Just the one meeting attended. Well, one meeting must have been enough. He opened up the internal files covering the upsurge in violence in Sighthill. Words jumped off the page at him. Co-ordinated. Carefully organised. Evidence of planning. Well executed. So. His colleagues suspected some organised force behind the trouble on the estate. He returned to the search engine and steered his way to the BNP website to be confronted by the call to arms that Rufus had posted on the Home Page just a few hours before.

He sat back and chewed at his pencil for a moment. The puzzle was all but complete. He started to scribble down the key facts.

Tac Brennan. Ex-Sergeant, Parachute Regiment. Twenty years service. Has an account in Nassau. Well-concealed.

Means what?

Very good accountant. Nothing declared on Tax Return. Collecting Income Support. Typical low-level gangster.

Son killed by asylum seeker.

Has attended a BNP meeting.

£250,000 transferred through BNP account into his Nassau account.

Levels of organised violence in Sighthill escalate.

BNP website calls on volunteers to travel to Sighthill.

He checked his notes and nodded. The puzzle was as complete as it was going to get. The only piece missing was where the cash had come from and that piece was not available to find. There was enough. More than enough. He picked up the phone and dialled the duty officer. "It's Colin Freeman here sir. I think you should come. I have something you should see."

The duty officer didn't dither. He got his boss out of bed and he in turn did the same to his. A meeting was held at six-thirty accompanied by copious amounts of coffee. After an hour, a senior operative was dispatched by helicopter to Glasgow to brief the Chief Constable of the Strathclyde Police Force in person.

Mordechai Breslow breezed back into the office at five-thirty that morning. Everyone was in and there was electricity in the air. Nobody knew yet what was up, but it had to be something. The only reason that meetings were called at six in the morning of the Sabbath was either war or something big.

"Ten minutes" said Breslow as he marched through his office door. He was running on all cylinders now. He hadn't been absolutely sure of the support of the Minister. The stupid man had been quietly trying to find a way of undermining him for months. Idiot. Breslow had tracked his efforts with little concern. There was no need. There was a file that contained some remarkably clear photos of the Minister looking as if a heart attack was imminent as he energetically took one of his younger secretaries from behind. The set of photos had travelled with him to the meeting in the inside pocket of his jacket. He would have taken them out if he had to. There had been no need. Now he returned the pictures to the file in the bottom drawer of his filing cabinet. It was one of what he called his rainy day files.

Once the drawer was locked he grabbed the phone and dialled up his opposite number in the Mossad.

"Avi. It's Mordechai."

The voice on the other end of the line was less than amused. "Fuck off Mordechai. It's too early. Ring later."

"Not a chance. Time to rise and shine Avi. We've found Khalil Bishawa."

Now the voice was wide-awake. "Go on."

Breslow took him quickly through the facts. After ten minutes he concluded. "My girl has done a quick assessment. It isn't perfect. All she has used is the Press. It feels like this man Brennan is the main player. Too much of a coincidence for him not to be. Decorated ex-Para loses son and organised violence breaks out. I don't buy the grieving father bit. I need more Avi. Much more. I need it yesterday."

"Sure. How long do you think the window will be open?"

"Two days. Maybe three."

The Mossad man whistled. "Fuck it Mordechai, it's tight. OK. Give me a few hours. I'll come back at lunchtime. How much help will you need?"

"Minimal. Information mainly. My man will need equipment and basic advice. Other than that he will be solo."

"Will you send Cohen?"

"Yes."

"Will the Cabinet sign it off?"

"I don't know. I think so."

There was a pause. "Don't fuck it up Mordechai. You know what will happen if you fuck it up?"

"I know what will happen."

"OK. I'll call. Bye."

"Goodbye Avi."

Thomas Rogerson was looking forward to his morning. As soon as his alarm had got him out of bed a little after seven he had opened the curtains a crack to see wall to wall blue skies and not a breath of breeze. It was a perfect summer morning for Captain's Day and the previous evening he had spent an hour and a half at the driving range hitting them like Tiger Woods. A low score was beckoning, maybe even low enough to win. He was about to start getting his clubs into the boot when his mobile phone rang. "Tom. Hi. Any chance of squash on Wednesday?"

"No. 'Fraid not. All tied up. Maybe next time?"

"OK. See you then."

"Yes. Ciao."

With a slight air of resignation he put his golf clubs back into the cupboard under the stairs and left the house. Thomas's grandfather had changed the family name from Rosenthal to Rogerson a year after he had moved to Britain in 1935. He had been one of the lucky ones. He had managed to bring most of the assets of the family jewellers in Frankfurt with him. By 1939 he had used the money to good effect. He had purchased a family home in Golders Green and a jewellery store off the Strand. He had succeeded as the rest of his family had been exterminated. The old man had died in 1956. His son had taken up the reins. It had been Thomas's older brother who had been earmarked to become the next generation of Rosenthal/Rogerson jewellers. This had meant that Thomas had been allowed a choice of careers. Like many in the mid-1970s he had chosen to take a year out from study before going to university. He had spent the time working on a kibbutz in Tiberius. Towards the end of his stay he had been taken to one side to meet a visitor from Tel Aviv who had asked whether or not he would like to work for Israel. He had agreed to do so without hesitation. He owed it to the memory of the old man who had saved the family only to die of a broken heart from the guilt of being the only one to live.

It had been the Mossad who had guided Thomas towards MI5 and in 1980 he had duly made it into his targeted profession. They had all hoped that he might be a high flier. Sadly he had been something of a disappointment in this respect. He never really knew why. Maybe he wasn't as bright as his colleagues. Possibly. However he always harboured a suspicion that the main reason that his career had only progressed at a snail's pace was that his grandfather had originally been called Rosenthal.

He didn't allow his lack of fast-track promotion to completely limit his effectiveness. Thomas excelled at sport. He played Rugby for the second fifteen at Harlequins. He had a three handicap on the golf course. He was an excellent squash player and he sailed at weekends. Sport soon made him friends within MI5 well above his lowly station. He became a favourite partner. A good man. Decent chap. Bloody good sportsman. The sort of chap who it was fine to talk about things with on the way up the eleventh. As a result it was comparatively rare that Thomas could not collect the bits and pieces of information that were requested by Tel Aviv.

The squash appointment meant a meeting at two hours from the phone call on a bench on Wimbledon Common. The junior man from the Embassy was happily throwing bread to the pigeons when Thomas walked past him tapping a copy of the *Guardian* against his leg. When he turned and walked back to the bench it was unoccupied. The man had left his paper. Thomas picked it up and turned to the sports page. He glanced at his watch and a look of mild shock passed over his face for the benefit of anyone who may have been watching. He got to his feet and moved away quickly like a man who had just realised that he was running later than he had realised. Later he read the note that had been hidden in the middle of the paper.

"Find out everything about situation in Sighthill.
Is Brennan behind recent events?
Send all known about Brennan. Urgent."

He went into work and had a number of casual conversations in the corridors. It wasn't difficult to get the answers. The place was buzzing after the morning meeting. There was something big in the air. The BNP were about to make a major move. It had come from nowhere. There would be questions. How on earth had they missed it? They had no idea that anything like this was in the offing. It all seemed to be down to an ex-Para sergeant called Brennan. He'd only been to one meeting but they were funding him. Dangerous bastard. The lid was about to be blown off. Everyone was jumping about like scalded cats. A top man had shot up to Glasgow in a chopper to brief the Chief Constable. Thomas's report was back in Tel Aviv by early afternoon, well in time for Mordechai's brainstorming session.

It was approaching nine o'clock in the morning when Campbell Swann turned his car into Sighthill. Yet another glorious day was in prospect and already the temperature was rising. Once upon a time such a day would have heralded a trip to the countryside, maybe even an evening away in a small hotel in the Highlands if he had the whole weekend free. He could barely remember the last time he had enjoyed a weekend off work apart from his stay in hospital. Once again he had not finished his shift until after 2.00 a.m. only to be informed by the sergeant that he would have to be back on duty by eleven the next morning.

It had been a bizarre night on the estate. Numerous cars had started to arrive after midnight. The wide avenue that ran through the heart of Sighthill had become something of a street party. Most of the cars seemed to bring heavily tattooed men with a variety of English accents. A check on the names of garages on the number plates told him that the visitors had travelled from a variety of small English towns, Halifax, Burnley, Sunderland. By the time he had knocked off there were cars arriving from Luton and Barking and Swindon. The atmosphere was that of a summer carnival as packs of lager were pulled from boots and the growing crowd mingled with each other. Technically he could have intervened on the pretext of too much drinking in public, but the look of the visitors suggested that such a course of action would be the prelude to riot. He had spent his hours cruising around reporting back number plates to the station. A little after one a senior officer had arrived to take a look at the situation for himself. He had looked a worried man as he described the article on the BNP website. He had clearly been utterly disgusted by the decision of the top brass to keep their forces back to avoid inflaming the already volatile situation.

The situation in the courtyard of Rosemary's block was no less confusing. There were a number of white vans with registration marks from east Lancashire. Young Asian men that he had never seen before were unloading boxes and carrying them into the flats. At one o'clock, two large articulated lorries rumbled onto the estate and made their way into the courtyard. Once again Campbell requested a strong back-up force to investigate. Once again he was denied. Eventually he returned to his flat, fuming at the decision of his bosses to bury their heads even further in the sand.

When he had got home Nicky had been waiting for him.

"Where the hell have you been?"

She was clearly well primed. "Where the bloody hell do you think I've been? Sighthill. Just like always. Bloody Sighthill. I might as well get myself a flat up there. I've about had it up to here with the damn place."

"Well that is tough because we are going back. I've had Rosemary on the phone all night. She doesn't know what is happening. Moses seems to have disappeared. There are all kinds of strangers arriving. There . . ."

He held out his hands to stop her. "Hey. Easy for Christ's sake. I've just come back from there, remember. There are vans and wagons and hundreds of cars. I know Nicky. What do you think I've been doing all night? Sitting in a lay-by reading the paper?"

She blew out her cheeks. "Sorry. I've just got myself all wound up. I've been worrying myself nearly sick. Please. Come on. We have to go. Rosemary thinks that maybe you can talk to Moses. She thinks that he might listen to you. She is frightened that he is about to do something stupid. I am Campbell. Please we have to go."

She was like a human hurricane he thought. "OK. OK. We'll go. llBut not now Nicky. I've had it. Seriously, I'm out on my feet. I need some sleep. Give me until eight. Then we'll go. I don't start until eleven. That will give me time to find him. But don't hold your breath. I'm not sure that Moses is about to listen to anything."

She nodded and her shoulders slumped. "Of course. I'm sorry. I should have thought. You must be shattered. Go on. Get yourself to bed. I'll bring you a cup of tea. Have you eaten?"

"No. But I'm not hungry. Tea will be fine."

He was almost out for the count when she brought in his tea.

"Campbell?"

"Ummm"

"What is going on? I mean the vans and lorries and everything."

"They are getting ready for war. All of them. The BNP have sent out a rallying call on their website. Come to Sighthill and fight for the future of White Britain. They're rolling in from all over, Lancashire, Yorkshire, London, everywhere. As for the guys at Rosemary's block? Don't know. East Lancashire number plates. Asians. Who knows? All I know is that it will all go off tomorrow and the brass have decided that the best thing to do is to keep a low profile. I don't think there is a thing we can do Nicky. But I will try to talk to Moses. Of course I will, but . . ."

He had never finished the sentence. Sleep had taken him. Nicky on the other hand had found sleep impossible to find.

As they made their way through the estate it was clear that many more cars had arrived through the night. The pavements were strewn with empty cans. Some had even brought their barbeques and the air was thick with the smell of cooking bacon. The crowds got thicker as they got closer to Rosemary's block. There was singing now. Flags of St George. Nazi salutes. Skinheads. Nicky felt as if she was stuck in some kind of a nightmare. Hostile glances registered Campbell's uniform.

The crowd stopped 300 yards short of the entrance to the block. There were queues here. Lines of up to twenty men and boys led two tables where men who Campbell recognised as Brennan's cronies sat. As he passed one of the tables he caught a glimpse of bank notes being handed across the table. What the bloody hell was this? Then for a few yards everything was calm until they entered the courtyard. Here there was every bit as much activity as outside. There seemed to be many strange faces to Campbell. They stood with each other in small groups and smoked. There was no sign of the vans but the two lorries were parked on the grass either side of the entrance to the close. Amazingly enough the playground in the middle was filled with children. Their laughter as they played seemed completely at odds with the seething tension that filled the air. Rosemary saw them as they got out of the car and came over. Her face held none of its usual good humour.

"It is good that you have come. There are crazy things here. Many strangers. They have come to fight. All of them. Moses will not speak to me. He will not listen. He wants to fight. You must stop all this Campbell. It will be bad. Very bad. It is the man Ahmad who brings this. He is make them all fight. All the boys. He make them crazy for a fight."

She pointed to the bench by the playground where Khalil sat talking earnestly with Zaheer Khan and two other men. Moses was part of a small group behind them. Every inch of their body-language spoke of trouble. They walked across and Campbell shouted Moses over to him. Others in the group eyed his uniform suspiciously. The tall African came to him with reluctance.

"What is happening Moses? Your mother is worried."

"Nothing is happening Mr Swann. I am talking with my friends."
The boy couldn't look him in the eye.

"Bullshit Moses. You know it. I know it. Don't lie to me. At least
spare me that."

Moses nodded. "Yes. It is true. There will be fighting here Mr
Swann. You should go now. You go with Miss Nicky. You make her
safe now."

Campbell gave a short angry laugh. "Who do you think I am?
Bloody Superman? Even he wouldn't get Nicky out of here. You
know what she is like."

"She determined woman Miss Nicky."

Campbell struggled to think of what he could say. "Look Moses.
I know there will be fighting. I'm not daft. When it starts you
should be with your mother. She will need you to keep her safe. You
should do this."

The boy's eyes flashed in anger. "I am Matebele Mr Swann. When
the men fight the women stay with the children and the cattle. No
Matebele man stays with the women."

Campbell could see that it was pointless. He tapped the boy on the
shoulder. "OK. I promised Nicky I would try. I've tried. Try and take
care Moses."

"I will be OK Mr Swann. Today we win this fight."

"Have you any idea how many of them are out there?"

"I don't care how many. We will win this fight. You will see this
Mr Swann."

If all the men in the courtyard were in the same mood as Moses,
Campbell couldn't help but agree. There was a strange air of
calmness about the place. It was a total contrast to the growing mob
that waited outside. He called up the number of the station from the
memory of his phone.

"Hi Sarge. It's Campbell. I'm in Sighthill. This place is going to
blow sky high in about 40 minutes. I don't suppose that the brass are
about to change their minds. I don't suppose that they have time to.
But pass the message on anyway. Yeah. I'm at the playground. I'll
stay here. I'll keep you posted."

Khalil looked up from his conversation and saw the young woman
striding over to him. He stood and offered her a seat at the bench.
"Good morning Miss Jennings. Please join me."

She was tired and fuming mad. "No thank you. I would however like to know just what the hell is going on. Things were already bad enough here before you came. But now . . ." She looked about the courtyard. "Now . . . now they are just going to get worse. Why are you doing this? Why are you pushing these people? Can't you see that they have been through enough."

Khalil allowed the smile to leave his face. Why indeed? What if you knew the real truth young lady? How mad would you be then? He pointed to the children on the playground. "This is why Miss Jennings? Things cannot get worse than when children are too afraid to come out and play. Well, as you can see, now they are playing. Sometimes we have to make the decision to make a stand. We must decide when it is worth it. I feel that it is worth it so that these children have the chance to play. Maybe you disagree, but take a look around. Many here do not disagree. They are willing to fight for these children. I see it as something noble. I am only sorry that you disagree."

She struggled to maintain her indignation but couldn't. How could she argue with his words? She wanted to. All of her instincts hated the idea of violence. But what did she know? All she had known was a safe quiet life. These people had been through the darkness. If they wanted to take a stand then what right had she to be angry? There was nothing she could think of to say. She sank down onto the bench beside him and watched the smiling faces in the playground. Maybe he was right. Maybe they were worth fighting for. It seemed such a small thing. The chance to sit on a see-saw in the sunshine. And yet in that moment it seemed as if it was worth almost anything. Yet again she felt quite mesmerised by this strange man.

Campbell came over looking forlorn. "Sorry Nicky. I tried. No go I'm afraid."

She had known the answer already and nodded. "Well at least we tried Campbell. We had to try. This is Mr Mansour by the way. I told you about him. He is the reason for all of this."

Khalil laughed. "Oh I wouldn't go as far as that Miss Jennings." He held out a hand. "I am delighted to meet you Mr Swann. I have already heard much about you during my brief time here. All of it good I must say."

Campbell shook the proffered hand. So this was the man. There was nothing outwardly impressive about him. Not tall. Well under six foot. Very thin. A face that looked as if it had lived too much life. And yet he could sense the man's aura. He was frighteningly calm. Very certain somehow. Oh yes. He could see that here was a man that other men would follow. No doubt he was also behind the vans from Lancashire and the lorries on the grass and the strangers who talked in small groups. In time he would understand more of what had brought this man to Sighthill. But not now. Now the clock was ticking down. Everyone knew it. Khalil continued to speak.

"I feel that you should take Miss Jennings away now. Things will become dangerous very soon. You too should go I think."

Campbell shook his head. "Nicky won't go. Not a chance. She will stay with Rosemary. I'm not going either. I think that I might just make it my business to stay very close to you Mr Mansour. I wonder if that will put me in danger? What do you think Mr Mansour?"

Khalil shrugged. "From the men outside, maybe. Not from me. I hear that you are a fine man Mr Swann. Why should I wish to hurt you?"

Campbell grinned with little mirth. "Good. Then I shall stay close and observe and at some stage I will no doubt be forced to arrest you."

Khalil returned his smile. "If that should be the case, then so be it."

At that moment their attention was drawn by a sudden surge in sound from the avenue outside the courtyard. The mob was starting to roar.

"I think that they are coming, yes?"

Campbell nodded. "Yes. I think they are."

Tac Brennan checked his watch for the umpteenth time. 9.47 The numbers were unbelievable. He had been told about the BNP website at midnight the night before. When he had left the pub he had been astounded to find cars already arriving. He had spent most of the night mingling with the men who had driven into Sighthill from all over Britain. Lots of them were just thugs. Pumped-up morons swilling down lager and showing off their tattoos to giggling girls. Others were much better. They were older ones. They were the ones who were going steady on the beer. Several of them had done time in the services. He swapped stories with them about Crossmaglen and Bosnia. He even found one who had been at Goose Green with him. By the time he had left the street to catch a couple of hours of kip there were over 200 of them. Not bad. Bloody good in fact. He gave a silent nod to the mysterious Mr Burton who would have undoubtedly been behind the whole thing.

The only problem with having such a surprisingly large number of guys at his disposal would be the issue of command and control. There would be none. By the time the moment came, over half of them would be pissed out of their minds. The lads from the estate wouldn't be much better. There would be no question of any tactics. All that could be done was to keep them under wraps until the right moment. Once they went in there would be nothing he could do to control the situation. His biggest worry was that the coppers might try to flood the area. He had been gambling on the fact that they wouldn't. He had done a good job in convincing that idiot Morrissey that the best way forward was for the cops to take a softly softly approach. The pratt had bought into it. Campbell had been up and down the street all night. He must have let his bosses know what was about to go down. Would they listen? Brennan had hoped not. By nine-thirty he was happy that he had guessed right. The only evidence of the Strathclyde police was the helicopter that had hummed overhead for most of the morning.

He had checked with his most reliable men how many locals had come forward to collect their cash. By 9.35 there had been 237. That gave him a force of nearly 450. He could see that most of the crowd were well and truly fired-up. If he had been watching them from the other side of a barricade in West Belfast he would have know, that he was about to be in for a tough old day. They weren't perfect, but they would do. They would be far too much for the small gang of wogs who were waiting in the courtyard. They were about to learn their lesson. In particular, the old arrogant twat from the day before was going to pay a very heavy price. Brennan had decided that it was a price that he would make him pay personally.

9.51. OK. Time to go. He moved among his chosen lieutenants.

"Four minutes. We go at 9.55. Got that? Kick them to shite."

9.54. A minute to go. He pulled on a ski mask on and waited for the calls.

9.55. The mob started to roar in unison. It started to walk forward. Somewhere near the back the familiar terrace chant of "Here we go! Here we go . . !" Started up. It spread through the ranks quickly. By the time they were a hundred yards short of the entrance to the courtyard it had grown in volume. As Brennan looked around he saw a sea of faces belting out the song. They were mainly ugly faces. Red from too much beer and sun. Veins sticking out as they strained to hammer up the volume.

Only twenty yards now. 9.57. At the entrance. There he was. That bastard. Standing by the playground like some kind of statue. Ten of them with him. All of them with their baseball bats. All very still. He had to give it them. They had some guts the silly bastards. No kids today. No chance. So much for the safe playground. The adrenalin was pouring through him now. So they thought that they could threaten him. On his turf. No way. No fucking way.

The mob was gathering at the entrance. Their chant had hit a peak of volume. They were jumping up and down shaking their fists. They were ready for it. They were inflamed by the sight of the eleven men who stood so very still with nothing separating them from the mob other than a hundred yards and a low wall. 9.59. Time.

Brennan let out a scream and ran forward. For a moment he was way back in time. For a moment he was wet through and howling like a madman as he charged behind Colonel H. Jones towards the flashing Argentinean guns. The mob took up his lead instantly and followed with 450 similar screams.

Declan had been able to watch the scene below take shape from the spot he had chosen on the roof of the block across the avenue from the one where the mob was closing in. He checked his watch. 9.57. Just three minutes. Brennan was obviously going to take them in seconds before he did his stuff. Sensible. Professional. He felt an unavoidable gnawing sensation as he watched the advance and the sound of their chanting came up to him. There must have been 500 of the bastards. He had watched them as they had arrived through the night. Lots of them were just regulation idiots. But among them were plenty of genuine hard men. In particular the twenty lads from Rathcoole who had come across with Bland made him shudder. They had now divided into two groups, which were stationed at either end of the estate covering the main approaches. Both of these entrances were now blocked by a collection of vehicles. They had been stolen through the night and brought to the estate. There were cars and vans and even a school bus. They were parked tightly together right the way across the road.

Declan had placed explosives in the drain that ran under the road underneath where the vehicles were parked. He had used more explosive than he had ever used before. It was about to be one hell of a bang. He checked his watch.

10.00

Boom. Boom. The two bombs went off simultaneously. Some of the cars were lifted clean off the road as the force of the blasts split apart the tarmac and thrust upwards. For a moment there were two orange flashes and then further crump sounds as the petrol tanks of the vehicles ignited. For several minutes the view was obscured by billowing clouds of black smoke. Then slowly it cleared enough to reveal the extent of his handiwork. The vehicles had been thrown together in a crazy twisted pile of metal. They looked as if a child with a tantrum had attacked his collection of metal toys with a claw hammer. Both ends of the avenue were completely chocked up with 25 tons of twisted metal. Declan gave himself a small nod of approval and made for the door to the emergency stairs.

Campbell could not control the shiver of fear that ran through him as he heard the chanting mob draw closer. Then they came into view. 50. 100. More. 200. Still coming. 300. 400. More. Christ, how many more were there? He had been concentrating so hard on the sound of the crowd that he hadn't noticed Khalil's signal. Fifty men had trotted out from either side of the courtyard and crouched behind the low wall. Now Campbell looked at them more closely. What the hell? Each carried a perspex riot shield. Where the hell had they come from? They had batons. Some kind of police issue. What were they doing now? Surely not. No way. They were pulling on gas masks. It was crazy. It couldn't be happening. Impossible. And some of them had something else. Not batons. Something vaguely familiar. Of course. He remembered the demonstration they had been given by the policeman from Baltimore. Electric prods capable of immobilising even the most demented rioter. How the hell . . .

The mob screamed. The mob charged. Somewhere not far away he felt the roar of a huge explosion. Maybe two explosions. There was a gentle tap on his arm. It was Mansour. Cool as ice. The bastard looked as if he were on a coach trip on the banks of Loch Lomond.

He passed a gas mask to Campbell. That same faint smile on his face. Who the hell was this guy?

"Here. You will need this."

Brennan closed the distance. Fifty yards. forty. He could feel the shake of the ground pounded by 900 pairs of feet. Thirty. Boom! The bombs . . . Nice, Bang on time. Clockwork. Fucking clockwork. And still the old bastard hadn't moved. Still he just stood there like stone. All of them. Mad crazy bastards. And Swann was there with him. What the fuck did he think he was playing at? Well maybe it was time for him to go down as well. Why not?

Just the small wall now. Twenty yards and he would be there. Twenty yards and he would kill the bastard. Why not? They had killed Kevin. They had it coming. No evidence here. He was just one of 400 in a black mask. Safer than safe. He would slash the bastard's throat, just like they had slashed his Kevin's throat . . .

What? Out of nowhere there was a line of men behind plastic shields. How? They must have been waiting behind the wall. The weight of the charge took those in the front crashing into the wall as the shock of the men with the shields made them lose their step. Brennan managed to keep his feet. Suddenly the man beside him screamed in agony. What? His soldier's brain automatically slowed. Something behind the shield. A bar. A long bar. The man hadn't swung it. He had merely prodded. Such pain from a prod. No way. Then he got it. Electricity. Holy Christ. The prod was coming at him now as if in slow motion. He managed to twist his body clear of it by mere inches. It touched the man behind him who howled. Something else about the men behind the shields. What? Think Tac. Work it out. Fuck. No. Gas masks. And the men at the back were lobbing something into the crowd. Shit. Gas. Shit.

The charge had been stopped dead at the low wall. There was utter panic at the front as men were thrown to the floor by the electricity. The momentum of the charge was forced out to the sides as those at the back strained to get into the action, utterly unaware of the plight of those at the front. More men with shields emerged from either side of the courtyard and stopped the sideways thrust of the mob. The 400 attackers were now contained by three lines of tightly packed men who applied pain with their electric prods and batons. The CS gas was spreading now, causing even greater panic in the crowd. Those at the back were beginning to realise what was happening. Soon the first of them broke off and ran for the main avenue. The few became many within seconds. Soon the whole mob was streaming out of the courtyard.

Brennan had realised within seconds that his attack was doomed. He fell back carefully with a handkerchief clamped over his mouth and nose. The men with the shields were moving forward now, dragging those who had fallen and been trampled. A mere five minutes after he had initiated the charge Tac Brennan was back on the avenue outside the courtyard. One by one those of his men who had fallen were tossed out into the road. The crowd were running away in all directions. Soon he stood alone amidst a mess of moaning injured men. His gaze never wavered. The man had never once moved. Still he stood there in the same place beyond the wall. It was too far to be sure but Brennan could sense the mocking smile on his lips.

Then all of a sudden he could see him no more. The two lorries were both reversed into the opening until the backs of their trailers touched. With a hissing release of air the tyres were slashed. The entrance was completely blocked. The sheer speed and magnitude of his defeat took Tac Brennan a moment to deal with. Then he found calm. He spoke to himself quietly.

"You're a dead man. Whoever you are. You're a dead man."

The pilot of the helicopter had been relaying a running commentary back to headquarters. He had found it hard to keep the disbelief out of his voice as the scene below unfolded. He reported that the crowd that was advancing down the avenue was in excess of 300. He described the moment of the charge and the two explosions at the entrances either end of the estate. Back in the incident room Chief Superintendent David Finlay had heard enough. He was an old-fashioned Glasgow copper. For hours he had been fuming at the pathetic way that his superiors had been tip-toeing around the problem. At 2.00 a.m. he had demanded that they should place roadblocks at all entrances to Sighthill to stop and search arriving vehicles. His request had been rejected. At 5.00 a.m. he had requested permission to send in a strong force to get in among the men who were gathering and to get in position to break-up any developing problem. Once again his request had been rejected.

Now he decided that he wasn't even going to ask – and bugger the consequences. There were bombs going off and some kind of open war seemed to be breaking out in the heart of his city. No way was he ready to sit on his hands any more. If they decided to fire him, then so be it. Luckily he had taken it on himself to move every available man in the region into position ready to move at short notice. Now he ordered them in. All of them.

Two minutes after he sent his units forward the pilot reported confusing developments. The mob seemed to have broken. Men were running in all directions from the courtyard. Two lorries were being used to block the way in. There was a lot of smoke down there. It was hard to see. Something must have happened.

Finlay frowned and tried to puzzle out what could be the reason for this unexpected turn of events. A mob of over 300 had attacked. He knew who they were. They had been running number plate checks all night on the arriving cars and had come up with a choice selection of far right wing nutcases. They would have been joined by Sighthill's finest who hardly had a reputation for being shy and retiring. As a group of over 300 men they were a pretty bloody intimidating lot. And yet their attack seemed to have been thrown back in a matter of minutes. What the hell had happened up there? He knew one thing for certain. He needed to get a lot closer to the situation.

The lead units of Finlay's intervention force sped towards Sighthill with sirens blazing. They made an impressive sight. Eight heavily armoured vans designed for riot situations were accompanied by five patrol cars. Inside each van twelve policemen in full riot gear stared at each other from bench seats. They had been building themselves up for hours for the moment. Now it was about to be show time. This was going to be a big one.

As he threw his van around the last corner the driver's eyes widened in surprise. The road into the estate was entirely blocked by a huge pile of smoking, mangled vehicles. He slammed on the brakes and skidded to a halt twenty yards short of the barrier. Above him the helicopter pilot reported that the intervention force had been blocked at the edge of the estate.

One by one the vehicles pulled up and bodies spilled out. The officer in charge radioed for instructions. They came back instantly. "Go in on foot. Control the situation." He was in the process of turning to bark out his instructions and to arrange his force into squads when the first petrol bomb exploded into a sheet of flames ten feet away from him. Within seconds they were under concerted attack. The road seemed to be on fire. Already some of his men were screaming.

The drivers had by and large reacted well. The vehicles were reversing backwards fast. One squad car was engulfed in flames. Another had a gaping hole in the window as a result of a thrown brick. Officers were helping the wounded to their feet and hauling them away from the barricade. They made their retreat in total disorder, only stopping when they were 400 yards clear. Ambulances were called up and the officer reported in. He was told to hold position and await instructions.

Frankie Bland and his men were jubilant. They watched the retreat of the police with their fists held high. How many of the bastards had there been? Must have been over a hundred of the fuckers. And they had broken them and sent them legging it like a bunch of schoolgirls. Just the ten of them. Ten men from Rathcoole. Fucking amazing. One for the annals.

Tac Brennan jogged up and took in the situation. There was a car in flames and obvious mayhem amongst the group of police a few hundred yards up the road. He nodded. At least there was some good news. He needed time now. Time to regroup. Time to get some kind of handle on the situation. What he certainly didn't need was hundreds of coppers throwing their weight around. The men from Belfast had certainly given them a bloody nose. If it had been the Paras who had come at the barricade they would have attacked again straight away. No messing. Regroup and back at them. Not the cops. They would spend ages with their fingers up their backsides trying to work out what the hell had happened. How long would it take them to try again? Hours. Had to be.

He went over to Bland. "Nice one. Fucking magic. I'll organise you more men. More petrol bombs. Hold for as long as you can. They won't be coming for some time yet."

Bland beamed. "We'll hold your fucking barricade for just as long as you like. No surrender. That's us. No fucking surrender. What happened down there?"

Brennan shook his head. "Christ knows. The bastards were waiting for us. Riot shields. CS gas. Everything. I haven't worked it out yet. I'll need some time."

"You're fucking joking me. CS gas? Where the fuck did they get that from?"

"I haven't got a clue."

Declan's explosions had been the signal for the two-man Para teams to go into action. They each worked one of the blocks. The flat burnings of a few days before had been carefully considered warnings. Now Brennan had decided that it was time to start to clear the area. The chaos of the riot would provide perfect cover for the operation. They had discussed the idea of the mass-torching of flats at length. Eventually it was decided that it wasn't an option. So many flats on fire would set whole blocks alight and there wasn't a chance that the Fire Brigade would be on hand to sort it out. The last thing Brennan wanted to do was to burn out as many of his own people as asylum seekers. The solution had been a simple one. One masked man would smash in the door with a sledgehammer. They would both charge in and drag the inhabitants out into the corridor. They would give them a bit of a belting and push them into the stairwell and move on to the next address on the list. Behind them gangs of five or six kids would go in and smash the place up. They were under strict instructions to keep moving and not piss about rooting for keepsakes. They were told that any of them who were pissing about would get a kicking themselves. The going rate for flat wrecking on the day was £100. Tac Brennan had found no shortage of takers.

They had done their best to estimate the time required to clear each flat. Ten minutes seemed a sensible, conservative guess. Six flats an hour. Five teams. Four hours. 120 flats each containing an average of three of the bastards. Nearly 400.

As it turned out the two-man squads managed to average a fraction over five minutes per flat. Like with anything, they found that they speeded-up with practice. After two hours they were working with the practised efficiency of SS men clearing a Polish Ghetto. After four hours they had managed to clear and wreck over 200 flats.

Finlay arrived at the scene twenty minutes after his attack team had been thrown back. Three ambulances had beaten him to it. He watched with growing anger as three policemen were gently lifted inside with bad burns. There were others with heads streaming with blood from being hit by bricks and rocks. Most of the others either looked on or huddled together in small groups. Fiasco. A bloody fiasco.

He started to inject some order into the situation. Within five minutes he had them checking vehicles and equipment and reforming themselves into squads. They were sullen in their work. None of them fancied having another go at the men behind the cars.

The command vehicle had arrived and Finlay directed it to the playground of a primary school. Once inside he demanded to be patched through to the pilot of the helicopter.

"OK. The barricade first. What do you see?"

He checked through the window as the chopper turned and hovered over the wrecked cars.

"There are about ten of them. All wearing ski masks. More arriving I think. There seem to be a lot of petrol bombs. They're all lined up ready. Piles of stones and bricks too. They seem organised."

"Damn. What about the block at the far end?"

"Same story."

"What else?"

"There is a lot of activity. It seems like people are being beaten. All over the place. It looks like a mass brawl down there."

Finlay took off his glasses and rubbed at his eyes. It was a nightmare. Beyond a nightmare. They had ordered him to hold back and now the situation was completely out of control. He shuddered to think what the hell was happening on the streets a few hundred yards away from where he stood. Somehow he would have to get his men in there but he would need numbers, and numbers would take time. What was about to happen in the meantime didn't bear thinking about.

He started making his calls. He said that he wanted every man who could walk. He said that he needed them yesterday.

Tac Brennan took a moment to take in the situation. It was extraordinary, but things had somehow worked out much better than he could have hoped. The attack on the courtyard had been a disaster but it had worked in his favour. It had meant that there were hundreds of angry men out on the street looking for someone to take out their rage on. There was no shortage of targets as clusters of terrified asylum seekers were emerging from the blocks. Everywhere he looked there were groups of men laying into prone figures on the floor. OK. Time to think out the next step. He called his men around him.

"Right. We need to organise this. We can't just kill the fuckers. We need them out. Start to make it happen. Herd them to the barricades. I'll make sure the lads know to let them through. It will give the cops something else to think about for a while. Move it."

He checked his watch. Time was racing by. Already it was past eleven-thirty. How long should he leave the lads in the flats? A while yet. He decided to give them until two. He called each team and arranged for them all to meet up in his flat at three. Next step Sergeant. Come on. Work it out. It was what you wanted. So now you've got it. His instincts yearned to find a way to have a go at the men in the courtyard. It didn't matter that things had worked out in his favour. He was boiling mad at the nonchalant ease with which they had thrown him back. They had read him like a book. That was what really hurt. They had played him for a mug. But of course it wasn't they. He knew that. It was him. The arrogant bastard from the playground.

He cursed himself because he was letting his temper run away with him. Stupid. Think it out properly Sergeant. Work out the situation. There was no possibility of another attack on the courtyard in the near term. They would be ready again. They were better organised. Better equipped. Better everything. Whatever action he took next would need a heap of thought and planning. No point shooting from the hip. He would only wind up looking like a twat again.

Recommended action sergeant? Leave them be. They had locked themselves in. Fine. Leave them for later. The good news was that his operation was well on the way to achieving the prime objective. Already his lads were beginning to spread the word and groups of asylum seekers were being pushed and poked towards the barricades. He had sufficient forces to completely clear them out. So what was the best way to ensure that it continued? Time. He needed to buy enough time to finish the job. As long as he was able to keep the cops on the far side of the barricades the operation could only become more successful. Once he had identified the prime objective he moved on to working out how to achieve it. His forces were at present safely contained within the estate. They were well-motivated and morale was high. There was no ammunition required for the work so logistics was not a problem. How long would they need? At the rate things were moving another 24 hours would just about do it. What was the main threat? The army could well be called in now, but that would take time. Certainly more than 24 hours. In the meantime the police presented the main threat to the success of the operation.

He grinned now that his brain was working properly. What was the threat? That they would muster sufficient forces to break through into the estate at which point the morale of at least three-quarters of his force would collapse. He needed to keep them outside for 24 hours. His instincts were always those of a Paratrooper. Only ever defend if you have to. Attack was always the better option. As the boots and fists flew he conjured up his counter offensive.

Finlay looked over to the barricade with a sinking feeling. For ten minutes a growing number of figures had started to emerge. There were heads pouring blood. There were those who could only walk with support. There were women crying and screaming. There were kids with their small faces etched in shock. It looked like footage from Bosnia. But it wasn't Bosnia. It was Glasgow. His city. And all he could do was to stand and watch as it happened in front of his eyes. He felt a burning shame. More ambulances were arriving at the scene all the time. As the refugees from the estate reached the police lines they were led aside to receive medical attention. Soon the road was filled with figures wrapped in blankets looking harrowed. His town. Five minutes earlier he had cursed bitterly under his breath as a second helicopter had appeared in the sky over the estate. The bloody press. At this very minute they would be beaming pictures around the world. He had bawled out an assistant. Get them away. He didn't care how. Tell them they were endangering the police helicopter. Tell them anything. Just get them out.

Now another officer came up to him in trepidation.

"Sir."

"What?"

"The press have arrived sir. A TV van. Just back there."

Finlay spun round to see a young woman being wired-up whilst a cameraman found his range. Bastards.

"Get them back. Now. And I mean right back."

"How far sir?"

"Why not try fucking Carlisle!"

"Sir?"

"Oh for Christ's sake, just use your bloody initiative."

A few moments later the sound of a commotion behind him drew his attention. The young woman was not going quietly. She had been on the verge of starting her dramatic report live from the Sighthill riot. For three years she had been standing out in the rain interviewing the winners of dog shows or councillors campaigning against car parks until her big moment had arrived. The whole thing was awesome. Everywhere she looked there were wounded people crying and moaning. It was massive. And she was first. She was about to be networked half-way across the planet. The very minute that she assumed her very best grave expression a bloody constable had pushed away the camera.

"Sorry miss. You will have to move back. The area isn't safe."

The serious concerned expression was replaced by pouting temper.

"Not a chance. Not a fucking chance. This is a free country. How dare you."

The cameraman made to steer her back to the van with a gentle hand on the arm. She swept it away.

"Get off!! Get your fucking hands off me"

"Kirsty."

"I'm not having this. Get that camera back out." Her eyes were filling with the bitter tears of frustration. How could this happen? It was her moment. Nobody else's. It could lead her anywhere. How dare they.

"KIRSTY! Just get in the bloody van will you."

This time he pushed her and the floodgates burst and the tears of injustice flowed. Finlay grinned to himself in satisfaction. Serves the silly bitch right. He waved over one of his sergeants. "Get a cordon up. Way back. Keep them out. We've got enough problems without having that lot with us."

"Sir."

"He went back inside the command vehicle and started making calls. Already every force within 100 miles had been committed to sending every spare officer they could muster. He could do no more than shout down the phone and make sure that they arrived as quickly as possible. He called three other officers around him and they did their best to estimate how long it would take for the reinforcements to arrive. Maybe there would be enough by eight o'clock. Certainly by nine.

"OK. We will look to go in at ten. I want bulldozers. I don't care where you find them. I want three of them. Big ones. We drive them at the barricade in a line. Straight through. The lads will go in behind in vans. Once inside we fan out and take charge. OK? Sort it out."

"Sir?"

"Not now for Christ's sake!"

"But sir . . ."

"WHAT!!"

The young constable looked ready to wet himself.

"Chief Constable sir. And the Deputy Justice Minister. Outside sir. Want to see you sir. What should I say sir?"

For a moment he felt an irrational urge to hit the young man in the face. Come on Finlay. Get a bloody grip. He took a long deep breath. "OK. Send them in. Gentlemen, you best step outside please."

The command vehicle cleared and Sir David Haston climbed up the steps followed by Daniel Morrissey and a man he didn't know. Haston's face was a dangerous shade of red. He was either hopping mad or about to have a massive heart attack or both. Whichever outcome could only spell even more bad news.

"Finlay." The Chief Constable spat out the greeting like a mouthful of sour milk.

"Good morning sir."

"I think not Finlay. I think not. A fucking fiasco more like. You know Morrissey, yes?"

Finlay nodded. The politician's face was a sickly grey that was a long way from the vibrant confident image that he portrayed on the TV.

"And this is Davies. Davies is MI5. Flew up from London this morning. It's not good Finlay. Fucking awful in fact. In a nutshell, the BNP is bankrolling this man Brennan to the tune of £250,000. Christ alone knows what he has spent it on. He has certainly bought his fair share of explosives. Maybe weapons too. We have no idea. I think we can also assume that he will have hired in some pretty savoury individuals. That about the shape of it Davies?"

Davies had the laconic voice of a public school education. Finlay sensed mockery in his tone. He felt like hitting him as well.

"'Fraid so. We have been running checks as fast as we can. It appears that there are several NCOs who served in the Parachute Regiment with Brennan who don't seem to be at home. Could be innocent of course, but we don't think so. Our assessment is that Brennan has used some of the money to hire them as some kind of mercenaries. I'm afraid that we have also had word from Stranraer that cameras have picked up Frankie Bland and twenty of his men. We haven't tracked them all the way yet. We're working on the CCTV images now. But I think that it is fair to assume that they are here. It seems that we have some rather unpleasant individuals in Sighthill at the moment."

Haston sat down and started fiddling with his pipe. "So Finlay. Bring us up to speed. Where do we stand?"

Finlay explained the state of play regarding extra officers. He ran them through the timetable that he had drawn up. He presented his bulldozer plan. All three men went over to the window to take a look at the barricade a few hundred yards away. Haston puffed out sweet-smelling tobacco thoughtfully.

"Bulldozers hey. Not bad Finlay. Not bad at all. That should give them something to think about. When?"

"22-hundred sir."

The Chief Constable made a humffing sound and sat back down. "And all we can do until then is to sit and wait whist Brennan gets on with it. This is a bloody pogrom you know. Ethnic bloody cleansing. Know that Finlay?"

"I do sir."

Haston turned to Daniel. "Well Morrissey. I suppose this comes down to you. In my book bulldozers are a political decision. Are you going to make it?"

Daniel felt like a rabbit in the headlights. This wasn't how any of this was supposed to have panned out. He was only just coming to terms with the fact that only days before he had shared a beaming photo opportunity with Tac Brennan. He had driven the bastard over to Edinburgh to ask his advice. It had played beautifully at the time. Of course it had. Tac Brennan had been a media darling. War hero loses son to psycho killer. They had lapped him up. Not any more.

War hero takes a quarter of a million from BNP to stage Sighthill pogrom wasn't going to make him anybody's darling. And Daniel Morrissey like a stupid, stupid twat had driven him all the way to Edinburgh to publicly seek his advice on how to handle the situation in Sighthill.

On the way over in the car he had made the mistake of thinking that it couldn't get any worse. That was before he was hit with the sight of the line of human misery emerging from the barricade. That was before he had been told that it was his call whether or not to send police officers into Sighthill behind three bulldozers to face a bunch of maniacs from the UDA as well as ex-paratroopers all of whom were probably armed to the teeth. His call? No way. Not a chance in hell.

"I feel that in this matter I will have to follow the advice of the experts on the ground. I will be happy to follow the course that you gentlemen recommend."

Haston cast him a malevolent look through the clouds of tobacco smoke. Typical spineless chinless gutless bastard politician. First sign of trouble and he was running for the hills. He didn't feel like speaking to him. The best he could come up with was another humffing sound. Daniel felt withered by the gaze. He knew that he was way out of his depth. Worse still, he knew and they knew that as soon as the truth about Tac Brennan got out he would be finished. Time to make himself scarce.

"Well gentlemen. I think that I have seen enough. I need to get back to the city. Keep me informed."

Haston stared out at him as he did his best to look assured and confident as he strode over to his car.

"Jumped-up little pratt."

"Si." said Finlay.

Davies just smiled.

Campbell was finding it hard to get a grip on what was happening. The overwhelming success of Khalil's tactics had stunned him. He had thought that the man was crazy. He had proved himself to be anything but. As the two wagons had blocked out the entrance he had turned and asked.

"How? Where did it all come from? All this equipment?"

Khalil had merely smiled. "We have friends Constable. Good

friends. Friends who decided that it was time that we were given help to stand up. Now if you excuse me, I have things to attend to. I presume that you are not about to arrest me just yet?"

Campbell had simply shaken his head. He felt like a spare part. All around him the men who had thrown back the attack were smiling and clapping each other on the backs. Not surprising. He had watched Brennan as he had charged at them at the head of the mob. He had felt the killing rage in the man's eyes. For a moment Campbell had been transformed himself. He was more or less resolved that he would possibly be killed by the mob. Before it happened he would have had Brennan. He would have beaten the bastard to within an inch of his life. Brennan had only been 25 yards short when he had hit the wall of plastic shields. Campbell had seen the look of utter consternation on his face as he was thrown back. It had been worth the price of the ticket.

All he could think to do was to go and find Nicky and Rosemary. By the time he got to the flat they were both at the window. He joined them. Nobody spoke. The view outside was enough to make them all speechless. All along the road asylum seekers were being knocked to the floor and beaten. Men, women and children. None were being spared. He watched for a few moments and felt sick to his stomach. Nicky leant into him and he put an arm around her. Tears splashed down onto his shoulder. Finally he gently eased her away.

"That's enough."

She tried to pull him back but he was too strong.

"Campbell . . ."

He was already gone. Once he was back in the courtyard he found Khalil and spun the smaller man around with tug on the shoulder of his jacket.

"Have you any idea what is happening out there?"

"I'm sorry?"

"They are dragging them out of the flats and beating them. Women. Children. They are beating them on the ground. Someone will die. Do you have any idea what you have done here? You are nice and safe behind your wagons. What about the people out there?"

Khalil kept his face calm but the words hit him hard. It hadn't supposed to have been this way. He had assumed that Brennan would concentrate all his forces on the courtyard. He hadn't seen it coming.

Brennan had used the attack as cover for clearing the blocks. He cursed himself. It was so obvious. He had been too sure. Too arrogant. He had committed the cardinal sin of underestimating his man. He knew that the development had no relevance whatsoever to his plan. He knew what Sergei would have said. Of course there are always civilian casualties. They can't be helped. We need to focus on the big picture. We cannot afford to be weak. There had been a time when Khalil had been able to harden his heart and follow the way of Sergei. He had been younger then. More certain. Not any more. He had opened Pandora's Box and now the poison was pouring out. All for his mission.

"What do you expect me to say Constable? It is a bad situation. It is not I who am beating these people." Weak words. Lying words.

"Give me 50 men. We make a charge. Straight up the middle of the street. They won't be expecting it. Use surprise. We go fast and hard. The others will follow up behind and get as many as we can back in here to safety."

"You will do this?" Khalil was impressed by the tall young man.

"Of course I will. I'm a policeman. Remember? I'm the one who is supposed to keep people safe."

Khalil nodded. "All I can do is ask. I cannot demand. Everyone here is a volunteer."

"Good enough. Get on with it."

Finding enough volunteers was not difficult. Just about every one of the young men in the courtyard had been on the wrong end of beatings. They had been the ones who had been chased outside the school gates. They were the ones who were jostled into corners in the playground. They were the ones who had walked with their heads bowed to ignore the abuse and the taunting. For once it had been them who had been doing the chasing. They were all still high on it. They felt indestructible. Immune from failure. They all wanted more.

Campbell waved them into a semicircle. White faces. Brown faces. Black faces. United now. All a part of Mr Mansour's unlikely army.

"OK. Here's how we do it. When they open up the gap between the trucks we go out in single file until the first man reaches the far side of the road. Then we form a line. When I am happy with the line we go. When we go, we scream. We scream so loud that we will break winsdows with the noise. We go and we don't stop. Any of

Brennan's men get belted. Any refugees get passed back. Nobody hangs back. If we scream loud enough they will run. At the moment they are all scared of the electricity. When I say stop, we stop. We close ranks and we return backwards. We keep the line. We will need to protect the men behind who are collecting the wounded. All clear."

He had four translators who ensured that every man was fully up to speed with the plan. Heads were nodded. Moses had joined him.

"You will allow me to run at your side Campbell. You Scottish men forgot how to use a shield and a fighting club many, many years ago. I will watch out for you."

"We'll see who can't use a club you cheeky sod." There was no point not admitting it. He felt on top of the world. For months he had held himself in check and he had followed the rulebook to the letter. He had watched his partner being murdered. He had picked Nicky off the floor after a beating. He had spent a miserable time in a hospital bed himself. All the time he had bitten his tongue and done the right thing whilst Tac Brennan and his men laughed and sneered and made a mockery of the law that they knew could never touch them. Well all bets were off now. He weighed the riot stick in his hand. It felt good. Really good. No more rule books now. Now the rule book was out of the window.

"OK. Let's go."

An Asian voice shouted, "Moses. You giving us your war cry. You shout it!"

Once again Moses bellowed out the ancient battle cry of his tribe. Once again they answered with their own.

Tac Brennan was pacing his flat waiting for two of his men to report in when a change in the sound of the street outside drew him to his window. Once there he froze. A long line of men with shields and batons were charging down the width of the avenue. In front of them other men were turning and running in all directions. Some were too slow and they were felled by heavy blows. The asylum seekers merely stood still and allowed the charge to sweep by them. The charge faced no opposition whatsoever. All of his best men were elsewhere. The soldiers were still clearing the flats whilst Bland's team manned the barricades. All that was left was the rabble. None had the stomach to stand and fight. Not after the humiliation in the courtyard. As the line drew nearer he could see that there were men behind who were picking up the asylum seekers who had been left on the ground. They were guiding them back towards the courtyard. Others had soon caught on and they were running towards the sanctuary of the advancing line.

He clenched his teeth together. Once again he had been out-flanked. He fumed at himself. Once again he had completely underestimated his opponent. He had assumed that he would hide behind his wagons. He had been complacent and now he was paying the price. He tried to guess the number of refugees who were streaming back towards the safety of the courtyard. 200 probably. It wasn't the end of the world. Their flats and possessions were still all smashed up. It was unlikely that any would want to stay. He was still managing to meet his goals. But he had been beaten again. He had been caught napping and the basic weakness of his force had been exposed. Their morale would be shattered now. One beating was bad enough. Two was not far short of disaster. Grudgingly he had to admit that for a moment he had lost the initiative.

The line was almost level with his window when it halted. They kept perfect order. The shields were drawn together. Then carefully they moved back, presenting a solid line of plastic. He squinted to get a better view. Surely it couldn't be. No way. But as he watched he realised that the tall figure in the heart of the line was Campbell Swann. What the hell was he doing? It was becoming a little rather more than annoying. Tac Brennan was getting tired of giving Swann the benefit of the doubt because he had bottle. Tac Brennan had had enough of him. He added him to his list.

Finlay was listening to the excited voice from the helicopter. The man was almost gabbling. He cut in on the running commentary.

"Slow down man. I can barely understand a word that you are saying."

The tinny voice was apologetic. "Sorry sir. There is some kind of a charge. About 50 men from the courtyard. They are the ones with the shields. The asylum seekers. They came out and formed a line and charged. They are gathering up the wounded and getting them back. Lots of wounded. Must be 200."

"Is there much opposition?"

"No sir. They are all running. All of them. Wait a minute. The line has stopped. Repeat. The line has stopped. They are moving back now. Slowly. They are facing forward with the shields and walking backwards. Covering the ones at the back helping the wounded. Very organised sir. Bloody hell . . ."

"What?"

"I just took her down low sir. Swann is in the middle of the line."

"Swann. Who the hell is Swann?"

"Constable Swann sir. Campbell Swann. It's his beat sir."

Of course it was. He was the one who got the beating on the night of the riot. Teague had been his partner.

"Just what the hell does he think he is doing?"

"Can't answer that sir."

"Is he in uniform?" What an absurd question. What the hell did it matter.

"Yes sir."

The pilot kept up his commentary as the line slowly moved back all the way to the courtyard and the wagons were once again closed together. Finlay asked of the room in general.

"Could somebody find out if Swann has a mobile phone please. If so, get the number for me."

Five minutes later he dialled up the number.

"Yes."

"Is that Constable Swann?"

"It is."

"This is Finlay. Chief Superintendent Finlay."

"Oh. Morning sir."

"Could you brief me on just what you are doing please Swann."

The line was silent for a moment.

"I am trying to offer assistance where appropriate."

"Assistance like leading a 50-man baton charge with riot gear. If you look up you might notice that we have a chopper overhead."

Another silence.

"It seemed the best way to help the wounded sir."

"Did it now? Well never mind that. I need a full report. Who is behind all this?"

Campbell looked across to Khalil who was listening to half of the conversation. He gave a small shrug. "You must do your job Campbell."

Swann nodded. "Mansour sir. Ahmad Mansour. He is one of the asylum seekers. That is on the inside sir. I would suggest that Tac Brennan is in charge of things on the rest of the estate."

"Yes. We already know that. Who is this Mansour?"

"Just a moment sir."

Campbell turned to Khalil again. "He wants to know who you are."

"I am just a man from Palestine who wants to make it safe for children to play in the playground here. Tell him that."

Campbell duly relayed the message. Finlay shook his head. "Are you telling me that this is what it is all about? A bloody playground?"

"It would appear so sir."

"How many are in there Swann?"

"Fighters, about a hundred. Civilians. I don't know. Probably 200 from the street. Maybe another 300 in the flats."

"And equipment? What about that?"

"Quite substantial sir. So far I have seen shields, gas masks, CS gas, riot sticks, electric stunners . . ."

"Electric stunners!! Where in Christ's name did they get those from?"

"There is Russian writing on them sir."

Finlay rolled his eyes. Electric man-stoppers from Russia. It was lunacy. He was becoming more and more convinced that he would wake up any moment. "OK Swann. Keep the phone on. Report any developments to me on this number."

"Yes sir. One more thing sir. We have four or five badly wounded people here. From outside. They need attention pretty urgently."

"Nothing I can do Swann. The Estate is blocked at both ends. No way I could get an ambulance in."

"Use a chopper. Get the Mountain Rescue boys here. We can use a winch. Sir."

"OK. Good-thought Swann. I'll arrange it."

Finlay gave the order for the chopper to be called up. A phone was held out to him. What now. "It's the station sir."

He grabbed the receiver "Finlay here."

"We thought that you should know that there is a live commentary running on Radio Clyde sir. It is Johnny Hendon. He's been on for the last hour."

"Hendon. Where the bloody hell is he?"

"In the courtyard sir."

"In the bloody courtyard. How the hell did he get in there?"

"Don't know sir. He hasn't said."

"Oh for Christ's sake. OK. Thanks. I'll get someone to tune-in."

He slammed down the phone. One thing after another. He sent a man to go and sit in his car and listen and to report anything worthwhile. Another officer reported that the diggers had arrived and where would he like them.

"Is there not one single man here willing to use their bloody initiative? Just put them out of the way somewhere. Try the football field at the back of the school."

He took a mug of coffee and closed his eyes for a moment. When had it become part of his job description to be in charge of parking-up diggers?

Johnny Hendon was having a ball. He had always quite fancied himself as a cutting edge live reporter. In his early days with the media he had attended a couple of interviews with the BBC but it had never come to anything. Well Johnny boy, they always say that it comes to he who waits.

"Pretty quiet now Sally. They are trying their best to take care of the wounded. Some of the injuries seem pretty bad. I have heard that there is a Mountain Rescue helicopter on the way to get them out. We have also got our first clue about the demands of the people here. Ahmad Mansour is demanding full-time security measures to be pledged for the playground. I can tell you that there are some children there now. They have just come out. Six of them. I suppose they must be about five or six years old. Their mums are with them. This is what the situation all boils down to. It is down to kids being allowed to play out on the swings, something that 99.9 percent of us take for granted. But not the residents of Sighthill. The residents of Sighthill have had to go to war to make a playground safe. Well Sally, they seem to have won the first battle of their war. The evidence is there to see. Four little girls. Two little boys. One roundabout. One set of swings. This is Johnny Hendon talking to you large and in charge from Sighthill, Glasgow."

He cut the line and laughed. Crazy days Johnny. Crazy days. He pulled a mirror from his pocket and cut two fat lines of cocaine and snorted them back. He closed his eyes and wallowed in the undiluted luxury of the hit. Once the rush had settled he dialled another number and waited.

"Yes." It was Roseanne's voice. The dreamy long-legged Roseanne. Rosy. Rosy. What do you make of all this Rosy? In a spin Rosy?

"Hi. I need to speak to Danny."

"Who is this?"

"Johnny Hendon."

Her voice was cold as an east coast wind. "The Minister isn't taking calls from the media at present. He is rather busy."

"Don't get so uptight. Just tell him I'm on the line. He'll talk to me Rosy. Guaranteed."

She looked over to where the Deputy Justice Minister was busy with sitting on his hotel bed with his head in his hands and muttering to himself. She had tried her best to get him to pull himself together from the minute they had walked into the room after he had claimed to have an important call to make. For a few minutes he had lost it completely. He had gone almost purple as he had screamed and raved that it was all her fucking fault and that he should have never listened to her because she was a fucking stuck-up bitch and a tart and that his career was fucked out of sight because of her. She had patiently waited for the tempest to blow over and then had ordered him to sit down and spend a minute or to sorting himself out. She had presented him with a half-full tumbler of Scotch, which he had gulped down and ever since he had sat with his head in his hands mumbling about how nothing was fair and that they would all say that it was his fault.

In many ways Roseanne couldn't help but agree with him. There wasn't a lot that a man could not spin his way out of as a politician. But inviting a BNP mercenary over to ask for his advice a week before the very same man revealed himself as a grade-A Nazi was probably one of them. It seemed that the "boy made good" from the South Side had gone as far as he was about to go. The rise had been a fine thing to behold. She didn't plan to be around to watch the fall.

What the hell. Maybe Hendon might talk some sense into him. She pushed the phone at him. "Take it. It's Hendon."

He grabbed at the phone. "Why don't you just fuck off Johnny? You've screwed me. All of you. Hope that you're happy now."

Johnny laughed. "Don't be a twat Danny. Remember. I'm your get-out-of-jail-free card. I'm your salvation. I'm your man Danny Boy."

Part of Daniel seethed at the happy-go-lucky tone. But another part sensed the merest trace of hope. "How?"

"I told you Danny. Remember. I told you that when the shite begins to fly I can get you to the man. The man the whole wide world wants to hear about. The main man in charge in war zone Sighthill. I can put you next to Ahmad Mansour, Danny. Think about it. Morrissey in eleventh-hour peace deal. Morrissey saves the day. Fearless Minister brokers dramatic deal in Sighthill. Bloody hell Danny, I can turn you into John Wayne."

"Oh yeah. Just like that. And how do you suggest I manage that? I don't know if you have been to Sighthill lately but there are about million skinheads and UDA men behind barricades with petrol bombs. Something tells me that they won't be about to stand back and doff their caps when a ministerial car wants to drive in. The place is a war zone in case you missed it."

"I didn't miss it Danny. I'm here. I'm doing live broadcasts for the radio. It's a bloody rip. You need to expand your thinking Danny. In a while they are going to be sending in a chopper to winch out the badly wounded. Well what goes up can come down Danny. Wounded people can be winched up and deputy Justice Ministers can be winched down. Think about it Danny. I have a cameraman here. Ladies and gentlemen, we are proud to present live footage of Deputy Justice Minister Daniel Morrissey being dropped into the courtyard in Sighthill to negotiate with Ahmad Mansour. I know you'll do it Danny, so don't pretend you won't. Mansour will be calling this afternoon. He will say that he will talk to you and only you. We'll take it from there. OK Danny? Ciao."

Daniel stared at the phone in disbelief for a moment. Then he jumped up and waved a clenched fist at the imagined ranks of his enemies. He turned to Roseanne with triumph in his eyes. "Rosy, we're back in business."

When he explained why, she had to agree that he was almost certainly right. Maybe against all odds the skyrocketing career of Daniel Morrissey still had a mile or two to run. By the way he stuck his tongue halfway down to her intestines she decided that she was no longer a fucking stuck-up bitch and a tart.

Almost the whole of the Operation Fox team were assembled by 3.00 p.m. Tel Aviv time – 1 p.m. Sighthill time. All of them were buzzing with the implications of Rachel's late-night find. Breslow had kept his suspicions about the second Bishawa brother firmly under his hat. As far as the majority of the team around the table were concerned, Khalil Bishawa had disappeared permanently off the map in the early 1990s. Now Mordechai stood and revealed his findings with the flourish of a master magician. The years had fallen from him. He seemed to be a man in his prime as he rattled through his briefing. He took them through the whole story. An early morning exit from Tadmur prison. A reappearance as a known political prisoner called Ahmad Mansour. A new role as the leader of the resistance of a small group of asylum seekers in an area of Glasgow called Sighthill. He played them footage from the *BBC News 24* Channel. He played tapes of Johnny Hendon's dramatic live reports for Radio Clyde.

They bounced ideas around the table for over an hour as they tried to dig down into the motivation for Bishawa's extraordinary activities. Collars were loosened. Ashtrays were filled. Voices were raised. Hands were waved. Only Noah Cohen sat back from it all. Only Noah Cohen and the quiet girl with the dark eyes who was once again covering for the first choice secretary. Noah sat still as stone wearing a look of mild disinterest. She filled page after page of paper with shorthand, pausing only to brush away an errant lock of hair as it fell across her eyes.

Consensus was reached after an hour and ten minutes. The consensus was that Breslow's evaluation was as good as was possible. There was no realistic way that they could anticipate exactly what Bishawa's plan was. However, they agreed that the coincidence was far too great. Whatever he was doing had to be directly related to capture and internment of his brother. Logic therefore dictated that the plan would inevitably present some kind of genuine threat to the people of Israel. Once that point was established the only sensible course of action was that Khalil Bishawa should be eliminated as quickly as possible before his plan was allowed to run its course.

Breslow was delighted. He had been worried that the argument may have raged for the whole afternoon. Consensus in an hour and ten minutes exceeded even his wildest hopes. At 4.30 p.m. the report from London was brought to the table. It was backed up by a live telephone update. After further heated debate they agreed that they could not rely on the present chaotic situation in Sighthill lasting for more than 24 hours. This started up the key debate on how the operation could be carried out. Mordechai lit Marlboro number thirteen of the afternoon and prepared to battle it out.

To everyone's surprise the discussion was brought to order by the insistent banging of a hand on the table. The hand was as thin as a claw and covered with a lattice of blue veins. It belonged to Eyal Weissman who at 93 was the oldest and the wisest of the grand-masters who had been brought in to mastermind Operation Fox. He was a legendary figure to all who sat around the table. For over 60 years he had provided counsel to all the leaders of his country from David Ben Gurian to Shimon Peres. His was a voice that was always listened to even though it was now reedy and frail.

"If I may, I would like to point some things out. I hesitate to go against the spirit of open debate and I only do so because I feel that time is of prime importance here. Mordechai, you have called in the old men because you want us to give your plan a certain elegance. You are seduced by Operation Fox. But my boy you are deluded. There is no room for elegance here. There is no time for elegance. We are agreed that Bishawa must be eliminated. We are agreed that the ideal conditions to carry this out may only last for a further 24 hours. We have no time to reconnoitre the ground. We have no time to insert a team. Noah sits here with us in this room a minimum of ten hours travelling time from this place called Sighthill. I see only one way here Mordechai. I feel sure of this. Noah must leave now. He will be met by one of our people as soon as he gets off the plane. I assume that he has the required identity papers prepared and ready?"

"He has."

"Good. Our man will drive him straight to Sighthill. There is an El Al flight that arrives at Heathrow at 6.00 p.m. London time. This means that Noah should be in Sighthill before midnight. Our man will supply Noah with a weapon. We must gamble that Noah will indeed find a way into the estate. He has got into many worse places. At this point we must assume that he has a maximum of twelve hours to complete his mission. People, we have all watched the pictures. Bishawa has enclosed himself in a tightly defended area. How can

Noah find a weak point in such a short period of time in a place that is totally strange to him? He can't of course. He will need someone who knows the place intimately, someone who is familiar with every nook and cranny. Do we have such a man in place? No. Of course we don't. Do we know of such a man? Yes. Yes we do. This man Brennan is the one who can help Noah to get into the castle that Bishawa has built for himself. This would put Noah within striking range of the target before dawn tomorrow. Gentlemen I am convinced that it is the only way. We must decide now. If this is to be done, then Noah must be on the next plane."

Nobody was inclined to question the words of Eyal Weissman. It was Mordechai who took it on himself to ask the one question that they all wanted to ask.

"But Eyal. The man Brennan. How can we know that he will help Noah? How can we know this man? He is a stranger to us."

Weissman tapped at the table with his pencil. "But of course we cannot know this Mordechai. How could we? We must gamble, and like any gambler we must assess the odds. Will he help? Sure, why not? The man was a Paratrooper, he will not be squeamish about killing. Bishawa has humiliated him twice. He will be tired and wondering how long it will be before soldiers attack him. His heart will be filled with hate for what Bishawa has dared to do. He is the SS Commander who bears the shame of a successful uprising in the Ghetto. He will take Noah as a sign that all is not lost. By dawn tomorrow this man will be ready for a last throw of the dice. Do I know this? No. Do I feel this? Yes. It is a gamble my friends. But there is a certainty that must guide you all in this gamble. Without the help of Brennan this thing cannot be done. That, my friends, is the certainty."

The nods around the table were enough to tell Mordechai that the old man had won his case. "OK. It is adopted. Noah. You must go. We will get you to the airport. I will get the green light from the Cabinet whilst you are in the air." Noah Cohen stood from the chair where he had heard them all out quietly. One by one they rose and went to him to shake his hand. He didn't acknowledge their words of encouragement verbally. He merely nodded his head. Mordechai was the last in the line.

"As always Noah. As always, it comes down to you. Go well my friend."

This time there was a trace of a smile and then Noah Cohen left the room. Papers were picked up and packed into cases. There was the start of the murmur of small talk. The replacement secretary halted the packing up.

"Excuse me sir. Mr Breslow. A name. Can you give me a name? For the operation sir."

Breslow creased his forehead in thought and then smiled as an answer came to him. "Yes. Of course Deborah. Swansong. Operation Swansong. A swansong for Khalil Bishawa. Maybe a swansong for me also. Operation Swansong."

He snapped his folder closed and headed for his office to begin the process of persuading his Cabinet to sanction an execution.

Deborah put her notes on her desk and left the building. She joked with the girls around her that she needed some air after a few hours of breathing Breslow's filthy tobacco smoke. Outside, the evening was starting to cool after a baking hot day. At lunchtime on a weekday the grass would have been filled with workers from the offices catching some sunshine and eating their packed lunches. Saturdays were quiet in the Shin Bet Headquarters. Now the grounds were deserted. She made a play of strolling around aimlessly and rolling her shoulders to rid herself of stiffness. She reached a small copse of trees filled with the sound of crickets. Everywhere was very quiet. She pulled out her phone.

"They are sending him tonight. He is to arrive by midnight. He will make contact with the man Brennan. He makes the kill tomorrow morning."

There was only silence at the end of the line. She was shaking as she put the phone back into the pocket of her cardigan. Later she would throw it out of the window of the bus that would take her home to her flat.

Tac Brennan opened the door of his flat to two thirteen-year-old boys who he had picked off the street an hour and a half before.

"Come in lads. Grab a pew. Want a coke or something?"

"Aye. Please Mr Brennan."

He passed then a couple of cans and sat opposite them on the arm of his chair.

"So. Come on. Did you manage to get out?"

"Aye. Nae bother Mr Brennan."

He hadn't for a moment imagined that they would have had any bother finding a way off the estate. He knew for a fact that the pair of them had been two of Sighthill's more enterprising burglars from the age of ten. Getting in and out of places was their speciality. Brennan had sent them out to check out was happening at the police lines.

"Come on then. What's going on?"

"There's loads of them Mr Brennan. Hard to say how many. We were watching for about twenty minutes and there was more arriving all the time. I reckon there must have been about 300."

Brennan divided by two-thirds and felt that 200 would be nearer the mark. He allowed the boy to carry on.

"We found the van you was talking about. Big thing. Like one of those massive mobile homes you see bands travelling about in on MTV. All white it was."

"Where?"

"On the playground at the primary school."

Brennan nodded. It was what he had half expected. The gates were big enough and it was the best stretch of tarmac around. "What about the playing field at the back of the school? What are they using them for?"

"Nothing much. Just some diggers. They were parking one up when we were there."

"Who was?"

"The coppers. Well, they weren't actually parking it. It was the blokes who had brought it who were parking it. They had to back it off one of them wagons used for carrying big diggers and dump trucks and that."

"A low loader?"

"Don't know. Maybe. Anyway. Three coppers were showing them where to put it. There were two others there all ready. Same type. From Motherwell."

"What kind of diggers? Did they have the big buckets on the front?"

"No. They had them flat plate things. You know. For shoving stuff and that."

"Bulldozers?"

"Aye. That's them. Bulldozers. Three of them."

Brennan grinned. "Good work lads. Bloody good. Here you go. Fifty quid each."

Their eyes lit up. Christmas had come well and truly early.

"Thanks Mr Brennan. Thanks a lot."

"Aye. Nae bother. Now bugger off the pair of you."

He closed the door on them and sat down. Three bulldozers. Of course. It was perfect. It couldn't have been better. A few minutes later the Irishman arrived. Tac talked him through his next task as he scribbled a map and passed it to him.

"So. Can you do it?"

"Sure. Why not. What time do you want it?"

"21.30 hours."

The Irishman nodded and left. Brennan was in the process of offering a silent vote of thanks to Burton for giving him Nathan and Bland when the man himself called him.

"It's Mr Burton here. You OK?"

"Aye. Nae bad. A few hitches but we're getting there."

"More than a few hitches from what I gather." The tone was neutral but mildly threatening. Brennan bridled. "Look sunshine. This is a combat situation we have here. Fancy plans are all well and good until the thing gets started. Things happen. Things change. It's just how things are. You know that."

"On what basis do you say that you are making progress?"

"Because we are clearing the flats. Hundreds of them. We're cleaning them out and trashing them. They won't be staying in Sighthill. Not after this. There will be nowhere for them to stay. They won't want to stay. I'm telling you Mr Burton they are on their way out."

There was a pause. "Very well. I understand. Please be aware that we have invested a considerable sum of money in you Mr Brennan. We expect results. I presume that you understand that."

This was too much. "Don't you dare threaten me Burton. You threaten me and I'll . . ."

A new sharpness in the voice cut him short. "You'll what Mr Brennan? Think about it. You have no idea who I am. You have no idea where I live. You have no idea who I represent. I, on the other hand, know all there is to know about you. I can stop you breathing whenever I want Mr Brennan and don't forget it."

The words sent a chill through Tac Brennan. It had happened without him noticing. He had walked into the shite right up to his neck and he hadn't even noticed. Time to chew back the temper.

"Fair enough. Don't you worry. Your clients will see value for their money."

"I do hope so Mr Brennan. For your sake. Now. Tell me what contingency plans you have for Mansour?"

No point bullshitting. "None as yet. I'm focusing on the main goal. Clearing the flats. Next I need to keep the cops out of here. I have something in place for this evening. Then I will deal with Mansour."

"Tell me about the police."

Brennan skimmed through his plan. Burton sounded a little happier. "Good. Very good. Excellent in fact. Now I can help you with the Mansour situation."

"Go on. I'm all ears."

"My people have access to excellent intelligence. Better than you would believe. For some reason the Israelis have a problem with the man Mansour. They recognised him from the newspaper articles. I don't know what the problem is. It doesn't matter. They are sending one of their men over. Their best. His orders are to assassinate Mansour. He is under orders to ask for your assistance. You will give him anything that he wants."

"Gladly." Brennan's head was spinning. The whole thing just kept escalating. "What do you think he will need?"

"Access to the courtyard. He will go in quietly, find a position, make the hit and he will be gone. I gather that he is a man who doesn't miss. All he will need is a way in. Find it for him Mr Brennan."

"Will he be going in on his own?"

"That is the plan. But I want you to send Nathan in with him. It isn't up for negotiation. Make sure he realises that. He doesn't have much of a choice. We want one of our people in there with him. Just in case. You can plan what to do about the rest of them on the assumption that Mansour will be dead. I doubt that you will find much opposition once he is gone."

"OK. You've got it. As long as he gets into Sighthill I'll sort him out."

"He'll get in. Goodbye Mr Brennan. We will speak tomorrow. Good luck."

The line was dead before Tac Brennan could reply.

David Finlay forced down another mouthful of the foul coffee that came with the command vehicle. It seemed typical somehow. The money had been found for thousands and thousands of pounds of state of the art command and control equipment and then some lackey had been sent out to buy the cheapest filthy coffee they could find. He had a howling, blinding headache by now. Six Anadins in the last hour hadn't even touched it. Twelve minutes past ten. The deadline for his bulldozer move had been moved back hours before. The required numbers were still drifting in. Now the time was set for one in the morning. They had assessed that the men they were about to face would be tired and dulled by a full day of drinking and inflicting grievous bodily harm. Maybe it had been a good thing that the reinforcements had been slow to arrive. Now they would have the cover of darkness to launch the attack.

The door opened and a tall army colonel entered.

"Which one is Finlay?"

David waved a weary hand. "Over here."

The officer marched over to extend a hand.

"Leatherdale. Colonel James Leatherdale. Queen's Lancashire Regiment."

The argument about bringing in the army had raged for most of the afternoon. The Strathclyde Police had been adamant that they could handle the situation given enough time. Daniel Morrissey had been convinced that they couldn't. The First Minister in Edinburgh and his emergency team had agonised endlessly. In the end it was the TV pictures that came from Johnny Hendon that swung the day. They showed the view of the avenue from within the courtyard. They showed the road filled with what looked like hundreds of men bearing makeshift weapons still beating and herding desperate asylum seekers towards the exits of the estate. The whole world had become witness to the brutal ethnic cleansing that was being carried out. In the end it had been the Government in London who had forced the issue.

The reputation of Great Britain Plc was being shredded by the minute. The land of Shakespeare and rolling green fields and red double-decker buses was beginning to look like some two-bit hole in the Balkans. It wouldn't do. Frantic calculations were being made about where the share prices would open on Monday morning. It looked like everyone was about to sell. London had decided to hedge its bets. The police would be given the opportunity to take control of the situation through the night. At the same time soldiers would be deployed in readiness to take over the following day if the police failed in their assault. Finding troops had been difficult. The British Army was stretched to the limit with commitments all over the world. In the end the best option was the Queen's Lancashire Regiment which could deploy 612 men within 24 hours.

Finlay cleared away papers so that the soldier could sit. "Is that your lads arriving now?"

"No. Just me and my Adjutant. We came up by car. The lads should be here by about eight in the morning. I'm just on a reccy. What is the situation?"

"No change really. We are still building up numbers. We should be on target to go in at 0100. We're pretty confident. Want coffee? It comes with a government health warning."

The Colonel shook his head. "We're going to need somewhere to establish ourselves. About the size of a football field. Any ideas . . ."

The sentence was lost in the midst of the sound of three huge explosions. A few yards away from the command post three bulldozers which had been leased by a plant hire company from Motherwell were blown into worthless mangled lumps of twisted metal. The argument over the 200,000-pound liability would rage on for the next eight months

Frankie Bland had his eyes glued to the luminous dial of his wristwatch. The very moment that the digital display clicked to 22:15 the air shook with the roar of Declan's bombs. He clambered over the barricade and waved his men forward. The 200-yard gap between the roadblock and the police lines was bathed in the white light from the mobile floodlights which had been erected. Most of the police were instinctively making their way towards the source of the explosion when they heard the roar of the men from Rathcoole. The sight of the twenty howling men in ski masks froze most of the officers where they stood. They had been in the midst of making preparations for their attack. Instead they were being charged themselves by a group of raging maniacs. By the time that Bland's group were twenty yards short, the beginnings of a makeshift line were being formed. At this point the Irishmen stopped and lit their petrol bombs and started to hurl them. The sheets of flame spread panic among the police ranks, which broke and retreated fast. Frankie Bland stood for a moment and gloried in the result of his charge. This was one that would be talked about in the club for years and years. With a sense of reluctance he waved his men back. By the time they climbed back behind their defences their attack had lasted less than five minutes. The twenty men of Rathcoole had sent over 200 policemen into a frantic retreat. It was to become the stuff of legends.

All of the personnel in the command truck were crammed against the windows trying to see what had been blown up when the door flew open. They turned to see masked men piling in. Finlay managed to get out the words "What the . . ."

Then he was flattened by a fist to the face. He instinctively tried to make himself as small as he could as he was kicked repeatedly. He sensed that the same was happening to all the others. His eyes were clamped shut. He could hear the thump of landing blows. Then he could hear the sound of thousands of pounds worth of hi-tech equipment being smashed to pieces by baseball bats. Then all he could hear was the sound of those around him on the floor groaning.

He dragged himself to a sitting position and gingerly pulled out a handkerchief to hold to his bleeding nose. His head was spinning and he felt utterly disorientated. Next to him the Colonel was heaving himself to his feet. He spat out two broken teeth into his hands and examined them with extreme distaste.

"What the hell was that?" Finlay asked nobody in particular.

The Colonel wiped the blood off his chin with the back of his sleeve and chuckled. "In the old days, I mean when the Russians were lined up against us in Germany, we used to practise. In the event of a Soviet attack the role of the Parachute Regiment was to penetrate their lines and hit their command and control centres." He gave the wretched-looking Chief Superintendent a bloody, gap-toothed grin. "You've just got what Ivan would have got if he had ever tried it on. The only difference is that we would have all been dead as dodos if Brennan and his lads had been playing big boys rules."

Finlay shook his head, quite unable to come to terms with what had happened. Leatherdale smoothed down his tunic. "Looks like it is over to us then."

"Aye. I would say so. Best of British and all that. Have you any clue what one of those bulldozers will cost to replace?"

"None at all whatsoever" said the Colonel cheerfully. "But it will be a bloody fortune."

Daniel Morrissey was pleasantly surprised by the tone of the First Minister. He had been expecting fireworks when he had called to report the news of Brennan's commando raid on the Strathclyde Police Mobile Command Centre. Instead the voice of the older man in Edinburgh was subdued.

"It's OK Daniel. I have heard all about it already. I have just put down the phone. The Home Secretary has already been briefed by the Colonel of the Queen's Lancashire Regiment who has apparently lost two of his two front teeth. The Home Office has now taken full charge of the situation in Sighthill. Operational control has been passed over to Colonel Leatherdale and some bloody spook called Davies. It seems that they think that this sort of thing is all a bit too much for us new boys in Edinburgh."

The First Minister was about to go on to say what a jumped-up, pompous prick the Home Secretary was and that he sounded smug as a fucking bug but he decided that it would not be statesmanlike. Instead it was Daniel who spoke.

"I have just spoken with the man Mansour. He wants to negotiate. Face to face."

"Well you better pass it on to Leatherdale then."

"He insists that he will only speak to me. It has to be face to face. Tomorrow morning at eleven in the courtyard."

"Oh well that is just marvellous then. You can jolly on in there in your Ministerial Rover and blow Tac Brennan a big fat kiss on the way past." The sarcasm leaked out of the earpiece of the phone. Daniel smiled.

"Actually, no sir. I can use a helicopter. The same one that evacuated the wounded this morning. I've sorted it. They can drop me in there tomorrow morning."

The First Minister pondered the idea for a few moments. The more he thought, the more he liked it. Let London be seen to play the heavy hand with the soldiers. Why not? He could wash his hands of all the nasty stuff. Whilst London smashed their way into Sighthill with soldiers in riot gear, Edinburgh would drop their man in from a helicopter in a last-ditch attempt to avoid bloodshed. It was almost beautiful. There was a bounce back in his voice when he spoke again.

"Splendid Morrissey. Absolutely first bloody rate. I'll arrange things."

"Will they agree? I mean London?"

"I am not intending to ask them. I shall be telling them. Maybe there is something buried about twenty feet deep in the Constitution that says that we do not have the right to do this, but even with 200 lawyers on the case they wouldn't find it by eleven tomorrow morning. Oh no Daniel. We won't be pussyfooting around asking for permission on this one. Not a bloody chance."

The reality of what he was about to do suddenly hit Daniel now that the last obstacle had been removed. "Oh. Right. Excellent. Thank you sir."

The leader sensed the sudden uncertainty. "You are quite happy to go through with this Daniel? Bloody brave and all that. I wouldn't order you in there. Has to be your choice."

"Oh no. I'm fine sir. Anything I can do to help."

"Good man. It won't go unnoticed. I should think that the divine Roseanne will find a way of leaking it to the Press."

"Yes. I dare say she will."

"Splendid. Well keep me informed won't you?"

"I will sir."

He poured himself a big scotch and wondered what on earth he was playing at. Then he rang Ahmad Mansour and told him to expect him to drop in at eleven the next morning.

Keeley was pacing the floor of his hotel suite like a caged lion when the door was knocked. It was Farouk. He had flown in to be there for the finale. Just as they were sitting down to coffee the phone rang.

"Burton."

"It's me." As ever Khalil's voice was steady. "M has just confirmed. Tomorrow at eleven."

Keeley grinned. It was just fantastic. Every aspect of what had seemed such a crazy plan was coming right. "It's agreed. Morrissey will be dropped in there tomorrow at eleven. I can't believe it."

"Any more word on Cohen?"

"No. Nothing. Brennan is expecting him. He will get him inside. He's agreed to send Declan in with him."

Farouk nodded. Then he grinned as well. It was impossible not to. Keeley punched out another call.

"Brennan."

"It's Burton. More information. Daniel Morrissey will be negotiating with Mansour tomorrow morning. Eleven hundred hours. He will be dropped in by helicopter. We can assume that Mansour will be out in the open waiting for him. Make sure that you brief the man from Israel fully. It will be his opportunity. If you can, get him in there before dawn."

"If he arrives in time, I will."

"Your attack was outstanding by the way."

"Value for money?"

"Oh yes Mr Brennan. Excellent value for money."

He tossed the phone down onto the settee. "We are nearly there my old friend. Now all we need is for Cohen to get in."

"He'll get in."

Brennan had taken the call in the kitchen. The men from the raid were happily toasting each other with cans of cold lager. It could have turned into a major session but all of them were only too aware that the operation was very much ongoing. The Irishman sat apart, as ever will a distant half-smile. Brennan waved him over.

"A word. We'll go in the kitchen."

He closed the door. "There is a development. Burton called. Apparently the Israelis want Mansour dead. No idea why. I don't care to be honest. They are sending a man. He is due to arrive sometime through the night. His orders are to take out Mansour."

The Irishman's eyes widened for a moment.

"He has also told me that they are going to drop Daniel Morrissey in by helicopter at eleven hundred in the morning. The assessment is that Mansour will be out in the open to welcome him. Burton wants all assistance to be offered to the Israeli. That means we need to get him into the courtyard. He also wants you to go in with him. He didn't say why. That's between him and you. I hope he's paying you enough."

"He's paying me plenty."

"Good. One of my lads, Gerry, lives on the ground floor of one of the blocks round the yard. His wife and kids are in there now. He'll take you round. Show you which window. I've found some rope. When you go back with the Israeli you can call from a mobile and they'll throw the rope down. Simple. That gets you in. Then it's down to you."

Declan nodded. The man was right. It was simple. The simpler the better. "What about afterwards? When it's done?"

"Up to you. Get out the way you go in I suppose."

"No. Not that. The whole operation."

Brennan lit up. "I think I'll be knocking it on the head. There was a soldier in the Command van. Full Colonel. I reckon that the army will here by the morning. Then we'll just be pissing in the wind. I'll tell the lads to break out. If everyone goes at once most of them should be able to scarper. No point everyone getting their heads stoved in for nothing. We've done OK. There won't be any wogs in Sighthill for a long time. You can bugger off too. We're more or less all done. Hold the Israeli's hand and fuck off."

"OK. Fair enough."

"If you are ever looking for any work just call me, yeah?"

Declan gave a trace of a smile. Hell would freeze over first. "Aye. You never know."

Noah Cohen was dropped off a mile from the estate at one in the morning. The confirmation of the Israeli Cabinet had been phoned through when they had been driving past Penrith on the M6. Breslow had got his green light.

The streets were filled with people. Hundreds had turned out to be close to the action. The clubs of Glasgow were to have an unusually quiet Saturday night. It was easy for him to blend in. He wore a light waterproof jacket and jeans. His pistol and Uzi were wrapped up in clothes in the small rucksack on his back. There was no point in trying anything fancy. No time for it. If he was stopped and searched it would just be bad luck. For an hour he drifted around the streets carefully, getting a feel for the ground. On the drive up he had been able to study the maps that they had got hold of in the embassy.

The police were clearly in a state of chaos. They hadn't even begun to start the process of sealing off the estate. When he made his move it was ridiculously easy.

Once he was inside the estate he found the streets to be even busier. Just about everyone seemed to be drunk. Burgers fizzed on barbeques. Groups competed with each other as to which could sing the louder. There were empty beer cans everywhere. He found a man who seemed rather less drunk than the rest and tapped his arm for attention.

"I need to find Brennan."

The big man looked him up and down. The dismissive expression slowly faded. Later he tried to describe the moments to his mates. He wasn't big or anything. Small really. Nothing to him. But he was a right evil fucker. "Up there." He pointed up the avenue. "His flat's in that block up there. Last on the right. Ask anyone."

Noah nodded his thanks. Ten minutes later he was shown into Brennan's flat. He recognised the ex-sergeant from the newspaper pictures that they had shown him. When their eyes met across the room they both knew each other for what they were. They were two men who had been in the same places. Tac Brennan stood and cleared the room. Cohen waited patiently. It was strange, almost as if he were expected. Maybe he was. Maybe their people in London had managed to make contact with this man. When they were alone Brennan waved him to a chair.

"I'm Brennan. What can I do for you?" He had wondered whether he should let on that he already knew about the mission. He decided against it. He had no idea how Burton had come upon the information. Letting on might scare the man off. Better to act dumb.

"I think our interests may be the same." The accent was quite strong. The voice was very soft. A voice that probably wasn't used very much. It was always the quiet ones who did the killing.

"Go on."

"I come from Israel. My people want Ahmad Mansour dead. I am to kill him. I think he gives you too many problems, this man. I think it is good for you if he is dead. You can help me. Get me close to him."

"You don't beat about the bush do you? What's your name?"

"I do not have a name."

Brennan laughed. "I don't suppose you do." He wondered whether he should make a show of thinking it over. He got up and pulled a can of coke from the fridge. "Want one?"

"Yes. I will take one." Brennan tossed it over. Cohen opened the can and took a careful sip. His strangely dead eyes never left Brennan as he sat back down. Tac decided to play the game for a while.

"It's all a bit far-fetched. I mean an Israeli hit-man turning up out of the blue. How do I know you're not just some nutter who's been watching too much TV?"

"You don't. What does it matter who I am? If I am what I say I am, then Mansour will die. If I am merely pretending, then maybe Mansour will still die. If I am just some crazy man, then Mansour will live. If this was to happen it does not harm you. I think you people call it a 'no lose' situation. Yes?"

Brennan nodded. Christ, they had given the bastard a tough mission. There certainly couldn't have been much time for planning. Get in there and brazen it out. That must have been the extent of it. And the little bastard must have said OK and got on the plane.

"Sure. That's what we say right enough. You look the part to me. Soldier. Yes?"

Noah nodded.

"Aye. Me too. Well I was. Twenty years in the Paras. You been in long?"

Another nod.

"Pretty good your lot. You don't fuck about, I'll give you that. OK Mr No Name. I'll get you in there. I'm happy enough for you to kill the fucker. You should get a decent chance in the morning. We have a politician who wants to be an action hero. The silly bastard is getting himself dropped in by helicopter tomorrow morning to negotiate with Mansour. Your man will probably be out in the open. It will happen at eleven o'clock."

Noah nodded again. It was good information.

"I'm going to tie one set of strings on you. I can't think what harm you can do but I'm a careful man. Always have been. I'll send one of my boys in with you. He can be a guide if you like. He's a good man. Steady as a rock. He'll help you if you need it. He'll just make sure that you do what you say you're going to do. Fair enough?"

"It is fair." Noah kept his expression vacant. It was a rather irksome development. But only a minor one. If necessary he would be able to dispose of the man. It wasn't a major issue. "When will you get me inside?"

Brennan checked his watch. "Let's say four shall we? My man will be back by then. Good enough for you?"

"It is good. Please. Do you have somewhere where I can sleep? I should rest."

"Yeah. Through there. Just lie on the bed. Nobody will disturb you."

"Thank you." Brennan watched him close the door of Kevin's room. A cool one he was. Cool as bloody ice.

Mary Tanner, Gerry's wife, duly opened the living room window when he called her on his mobile phone from where he waited outside.

"What the fuck is going on Gerry? Me and the kids have been trapped in here all fucking day whilst you are out fucking about . . ."

He shushed her loudly. "For fuck's sake Mary. Keep it down will you. Now listen. See this lad with me. He'll be coming back in a bit. He's called Nathan. There will be two of them. When he calls, you open the window and chuck this rope down. Here. I'll throw it up." He threw up a coil of rope, which she caught and tossed into the room behind her grumpily. "When he calls, throw down the rope and they will climb up and get out of the front door into the block. Simple. Got it?"

"Never mind if I've got it Gerry. Why the fuck should I piss about with your silly games whilst you're swanning around with the lads on the piss?"

"Try a grand out for size."

"You what?"

"Like I said. Do this, and we get paid a grand. Cash. You can get that new suite you've been whinging on about."

Now that did make a difference. Mary had been whinging on about a new suite for well over three years whilst every penny they had disappeared into the bookies. She decided that she would happily shag this Nathan for a new suite, let alone just throw him a rope.

"Aye. All right. I'll do it. Just mind your shoes are fucking clean when you come it. I don't want my carpets all shat up."

Whilst husband and wife were negotiating, Declan discreetly placed a small magnetic box on the wall side of a drainpipe and flicked a switch. The box would send out a location signal that could be picked up within a radius of half a mile.

"Closer and closer" he murmured to himself.

"You what?" asked Gerry.

"Ah nothing. Just saying it's a nice place you have here."

Khalil jumped slightly as the receiver in his pocket let out a peeping sound. He pulled out the monitor and confirmed that the signal was active. Seconds later his phone rang. Declan's voice was hushed, urgent.

"Can't talk long. He's in. We're coming at 0400. Block 4. Follow the tracker."

Khalil checked his watch. Nearly three. He realised that he should be tired. When had he last slept properly? It seemed like days. But now yet another surge of adrenalin kicked into him. He felt it was a wonder that his system had any adrenalin left. The stars were bright overhead. The great black shapes of the blocks reached up for the night sky. It had only been a few days since he had been shown into the flat that was supposed to be his home. The few days felt like months. He had come to like Sighthill. The people were fighters. More to the point, the fight was almost a fair one. For two days the two sets of residents had fought each other to a standstill. However they had fought with fists and sticks and stones. To the best of his knowledge nobody had died. There had been something almost old-fashioned about their little war. No jets had suddenly appeared to drop napalm or cluster bombs or phosphorous. No huge tanks had crashed through the walls to blow the arms and legs off fleeing children.

His train of thought made him smile. What kind of a desperate life must he have led for him to be feeling nostalgic towards a place just because people only beat each other with sticks? No matter how he tried to dress it up in his own mind, his own contribution had been a questionable one. He had mobilised the anger of young men and turned it into courage and defiance. His line of young men with their shields were very much like the young men of Gaza and Jenin who threw their bricks and stones at the tanks. For a while it had made everyone feel better about themselves. All around him he had seen people who were proud because they had at last managed to fight back. Heads were held a little higher. Backs were a little straighter. For once they had not simply allowed themselves to be bullied and pushed and mocked.

What he was aware of which everyone was not looking at was that the sun would rise the following morning. And when the sun rose these people would find that their flats were wrecked and burned. They would find that the meagre homes in which they had sought sanctuary were no longer there. It was a heavy price to pay for a little bit of pride, a little bit of self-respect. It was a price that his own people had been paying for 50 endless years. They had fought and fought and where had it got them? A few lousy miles of land. Towns that were hemmed in with high walls and razor wire. An economy that was non-existent. 50 years and his people were still caged in like animals. Still surrounded by watchtowers and guns. It had been a huge price to pay for pride and defiance. Tomorrow would bring the same for these people. Right now he saw eyes that were shining with achievement. He saw groups who were laughing. It was a happiness that would be no more than a fleeting moment.

Moses was chatting with three of the Asians from Burnley. Khalil shouted him over.

"Sorry to interrupt. I need a bit of help."

"Of course. What can I do?"

"I need you carry something for me."

"It is not a problem."

The man from Israel never spoke as he and Declan made their way to the back of Block 4. He just walked quietly along with his small backpack hanging casually over his shoulder. Occasionally he gave a nod to groups of men around campfires and barbeques. He was nondescript. A small nothing man who would never merit a second glance. If any of you only knew, Declan thought as they passed the drunken elements of Brennan's makeshift army. If you had the first clue your jaws would hit the pavement. The small bloke with the rucksack and balding bloke with his hands in his pocket. The Israeli assassin and the Irish terrorist out for a pleasant stroll.

When they arrived at Gerry's window he casually leant against the drainpipe as he dug in his pocket for his phone. He flicked the switch on the tiny box. Mary answered the call and opened the window. The rope dropped down.

"I'll go first" said Declan.

Cohen shrugged.

Declan climbed the rope and jumped into the living room where the irritable-looking woman waited. He gave her a smile and turned back.

"OK. Toss me your bag."

The Israeli obliged and started up the rope with more agility than Declan had managed. He reached the tope and started to swing himself in. For a moment he was off balance as he had both hands on the rope as he threw his legs over the sill. Declan took his chance. He thrust a hypodermic needle hard into Noah's exposed flank. He caught the momentum of his swing and yanked him into the room hard. He hit the floor with a look of surprise. Declan already had a revolver in his hand and the muzzle pointed straight at his forehead. Cohen's expression was almost relaxed. His thoughts were already drifting as the huge dose of sedative started moving around his system. Declan reached into his pocket and hit the "send" button on his phone. There was a ringing sound outside the door of the flat. The door flew in. Mary was about to scream when the very calmness of Khalil's voice halted her.

"No. No need. You are in no danger. None at all. Just sit down please. Good. Thank you. OK. Me and my friends will leave now. Nothing more. I am going pull the phone out of the socket and take away the rope. You would need to jump from the window to tell anyone about this and I don't think that you will do. Much better to stay here and look after the children and forget that any of this ever happened for a few hours. He pressed a bundle of twenty-pound notes into her hand and gave her a warm smile.

"I hope that will cover any damage to the door. Sorry for the trouble. Really."

He nodded to Moses who tossed the unconscious figure of Noah Cohen over his shoulder. Then the three men left. Mary counted the notes with a kind of numbed sense of wonder. £1500. £1500 that would never get within half a mile of a bookies. £1500 that would mean a new suite and a wide screen TV. And the bastard Council could pick up the bill for the door.

Tac Brennan's youthful spies visited his flat as the first light of dawn was tinting the sky. He waved them inside. They both accepted cans of Coke. Tac was feeling the pace. The constant tension of the last two days had drained him. In the days when he had been in the field with his company there had always been times when he could find a corner and get his head down. Any lull in the action was kip time. Strategy had never been his problem. There were no toffee-nosed officers to decide what everyone was going to do next this time. This time it had been down to him call the shots, and the pressure was beginning to tell.

He had spent the hours before the dawn walking the streets, chatting with those who were still awake. He had returned to his flat feeling discouraged and despondent. Everyone was tired. The novelty had worn off. The blocks were all but cleared. Huge hangovers were starting to kick in. The wild army that had charged the courtyard the day before was little more than a pitiful rabble with sore heads. He was down to a reliable force of 30. He was happy to hang his hat on the lads from the Regiment and Bland's lads seemed to still be up for anything. He knew that his options were almost zero. They had caught the cops with their pants down with their raid. It wouldn't happen again. They were firmly on the back foot. Now he would find out what was happening outside.

The two boys told him about the soldiers. Lots of them. They had helmets and camouflage uniforms and everything. They had English accents. From the North. Like Oasis. They were all fired-up for the morning. It had been no more than he had expected to hear. He gave them another 50 quid and sent them packing. As he heard their exited voices recede down the corridor he was suddenly hit hard by a wave of grief for his son. He remembered all the times when the voice in the corridor had been Kevin's. He wouldn't hear it again. In the end it had been what all of this had been about. Kevin. It hadn't been so much revenge as something to fill the time. Something to steer his mind clear of the black agony of his loss. Had he found his revenge? Were the hundreds of smashed flats and broken heads any kind of compensation? Not really. Not at all.

And now the slow light of the dawn was signalling the end. The only thing left to him was to try to rally some kind of defiant last stand. What was the point? There would only be himself and a few lads who were all completely knackered, up against a Regiment of northern bastards who were itching to kick a few heads in. He could easily imagine the talk that the sergeants would give the lads. They would tell them that there were Paras who had gone rotten. They would jog their memories that the Paras thought they were God's fucking gift. They would suggest that it was time that the cocky bastards had a kicking. A proper kicking. What would it gain? Not a thing. It was time to wrap the thing up.

Then he would have to decide what he was going to do with himself. Surprisingly enough he was suddenly a wealthy man. The lad from Sighthill had come good against all the odds. It seemed daft to feel down when he had a quarter of a million in the bank care of Burton.

He started making calls and summoned the lads to the flat. They filed in one by one, all of them tired, all of them ready to call it a day. There were no complaints when he explained that they would wind things up at eleven hundred hours. He explained the exit strategy. Everyone was on board. It had been a crack. A real crack. Maybe they would all do it again sometime. Hands were shaken and backs were slapped. They left each other with promises to stay in touch. By six-thirty Tac Brennan sat alone with the walls closing in on him. He was confident enough that his plan would work. It was important to him that the lads should all get away clean. Now there was only one last skirmish left in his little war, and that was beyond his control. All that was left was the man with the quiet expression and the deadly eyes. The man who had been sent to make the kill.

Roseanne was surprised by the way she felt. She had never been a sentimental girl. The complete opposite in fact. It had come from her mother who must have had every ounce of sentiment drained out of her the day she was born. Ever since she could remember she had used boys and men as meal tickets. It had been a game that her mum had taught her well. A quick brain can only get a girl so far. Her tits and arse would always take her further. Put the two together and a girl can go far. Men were all sad pathetic creatures who never quite stopped missing their mothers. Just like her stupid father who had flitted with his secretary years before. Use them up and throw them out darling. She had always followed her mum's advice to the letter just like any nice girl from Stirling should have done. There had been a long list of meal tickets. At school and university they had been her ticket to the right parties and nights out where everything was always paid for. In the workplace it had been much the same with promotion and salary thrown in.

Daniel Morrissey had always been a perfect mark. He would never shake the feeling of social inadequacy that his upbringing in the Glasgow's housing schemes had left as a legacy. He needed someone to show him what to wear and which order to use the cutlery at the posh dinners. He needed someone to teach him how to show a bit of class. She had found her rough diamond and polished it until it gleamed. Already she had received offers from other politicians in Edinburgh and Westminster who had noted her remarkable success in creating the Daniel Morrissey brand. The next steps up the ladder would take her close to the top floor, and her not even 25. Mummy was delighted. The fact that Daniel's rise had been so meteoric had been a concern. Those who rose too fast always crashed and burned. It was as inevitable as night following day. She had to be sure to jump off before the runaway train fell off the edge.

On several occasions over the last week she had been convinced that the time had come. The pressure was chipping away at the Deputy Minister and the cracks were opening up. It was only a matter of time before he made an absolute arse of himself and sent his career into freefall.

She had been about to walk the day before at the hotel when he had sat on the bed with his head in his hands. She had been on the very brink of picking up her handbag and making the exit. Only the call from Johnny Hendon had held her back. There was to be one last throw of the dice after all. And what a throw of the dice it was. A drop from a helicopter into a war zone. Epic. Magnificent. Selling it to the media had been the easiest task she had ever undertaken. Her charge was just about to become the most popular politician in Britain and her career options would be enhanced accordingly. It was surely her moment of triumph. So why on earth was she not elated?

Daniel was pale and drawn, his forehead creased into a frown as the RAF man explained how the harness would work. It suddenly hit her what he was about to do. It wasn't a tough speech or a photo opportunity. He was actually about to drop down into the middle of God alone knew what. It wasn't spin. It was real life. And he was actually about to do it.

Everything seemed ready. He seemed somehow lost in the bulky jump suit that they had dressed him in. He turned to her with a sheepish attempt at a confident grin but there was pure terror in his yes. To her own astonishment she threw herself at him and hung on tight. To her even greater astonishment there were tears pouring down her cheeks. She pushed her face into the rough canvas that covered his shoulder. "Just come back safe Danny."

She could feel mother's disapproval from 30 miles away. So what? If she wanted to be pathetic she would be pathetic. He eased her off him and climbed on board the Sea King helicopter.

Colonel Leatherdale was among his men. It was where he was always the happiest. Word had got round through the night that the old man had had a right kicking. It had not been cause for any sniggering. The old man was all right. One of the coppers had said how he had just spat two teeth out and had a laugh. Now he was out and about and right as rain. His mouth must have been hurting like a bastard but he didn't show it. There would be some payback. They all knew it. The word had been passed down. Some minister was going to drop in from a helicopter where the Pakis were holed up at eleven. Every man and his dog would be watching. They were going to give it five minutes. Then they would go in and break a few heads. No problem.

The Colonel was quite content with what he found on his rounds. The lads were sound as a pound. Raring to go. Fired up. Bloody good lot, his lads.

Daniel looked out of the open side of the helicopter with fascination. It was his first time. Below him was the familiar landscape of his home city. He leaned forward as far as the harness would allow him and spotted the familiar blocks of Sighthill approaching fast. He had been feeling queasy and scared but now as his destination drew near he actually felt better.

There were already two other helicopters on station above the estate. Phone calls had been made. The media were permitted to be there this time. It was important that everyone could see that the Government was going the extra mile. Seeing the Minister going in would help to calm the situation. The Chief Constable had met the news with his familiar snort. Typical politicians. Anything for a couple of lousy votes.

The broad avenues of Sighthill were now just a hundred feet below them. The place was heaving with people. There must have been hundreds and hundreds out there, many of them with their faces turned up to the sky. The crowd was at its thickest at the two barriers at either end of the avenue. Daniel couldn't fathom what they were up to. It was hard to tell from where he watched. There seemed to be little threat about the crowd. He could pick out lots of women and children and elderly. It was more of a queue than a mob. Then he saw that they were funnelling out through gaps in the road blocks and making their way across the empty ground towards where the men of the Queen's Lancashire Regiment were waiting to stage their attack. They were leaving. All of them.

Leatherdale watched the slowly advancing crowd with amazement. They had started to approach at five minutes to eleven. In front were women with pushchairs and prams and old-age pensioners. Kids skipped along and laughed. He climbed up on top of a Warrior armoured car and could see that behind the barricades there were many more. Hundreds and hundreds. And he couldn't help but chuckle. Tac Brennan had done them again. He was getting his lads out. He was using the book. Use any means possible to exfiltrate when the situation becomes untenable. His lads would be in the middle of the crowd that slowly made its way toward him. There would be no broken heads after all. Brennan had assessed the situation and called it a day. Sighthill was emptying out.

Khalil watched the big yellow helicopter as it slowly dropped toward him. He had heard the news of Brennan's exodus several hours earlier. Sergei's listening device had been good to the last. The news had been welcome. His playground war had run its course. Now there were only the last rites to finish off. He could see movement in the hatch. A figure emerged and slowly came down toward him.

When Morrissey's feet were firmly off the ground Khalil stepped forward to help him out of the harness. He then stood back and waited as the politician rather self-consciously peeled off his jump suit. Once it was off, he didn't quite seem to know what to do with it. In the end he folded it roughly and placed it on the ground. Khalil smiled and held out a hand.

"Good morning Mr Morrissey. Thank you for coming." The smile and the civility and the excellent English came as a surprise to Daniel.

He hadn't had a clue what to expect but this was a complete surprise. He duly shook the offered hand and nodded. Khalil continued.

"I think it is best that we go somewhere private to talk. Don't you? It would not be easy with so many eyes on us."

Daniel blinked and felt very unsure of himself. He really was at a loss. Somewhere private? Was it safe? He was annoyed at himself for the stutter in his voice.

"Yes. Well of course. But there are considerations. I mean. Well security I suppose."

"Of course. I can understand your concerns. It is quite natural. I am sure that Constable Swann here will be more than happy to act as chaperone." He waved to Campbell who duly joined them. "I am suggesting that you might accompany us for our meeting constable. The Minister is rightly concerned about his safety. Is that acceptable?"

"Aye. I'll come along. You'll be fine sir. Don't worry." Campbell was more than happy to go along. He was unashamedly intrigued to see what Mansour was about to ask for. Khalil held out a hand, every inch the perfect host.

"Good. Maybe you will both step this way. I have a room prepared."

The meeting room in the Shin Bet headquarters was thick with tension. Every pair of eyes was glued to the screen, which relayed the live pictures from *BBC News 24*. They watched the figure emerge from the helicopter. They watched it slowly descend toward the figure who waited on the ground. The figure that was in a space all of his own. The figure that was completely exposed and vulnerable. It was like waiting for an over inflated balloon to burst. It was like waiting for a scary bit in a film. They all knew what was about to happen, but they would jump higher than anyone else when the bullets hit.

Nothing happened. The figure reached the ground. The figure took off the overalls. The men shook hands and talked. A tall policeman joined them. They started to walk. No shots. No sign of Cohen. Maybe he hadn't considered the situation to be right. Maybe he had some alternative plan. Everyone slumped back in their chairs and allowed the tension to drain away.

Mordechai Breslow stared at the screen with a fixed expression. The moment had come. The moment had passed. Something had gone wrong.

Tac Brennan was watching the same pictures. Like the Shin Bet team he felt himself wound up to the limit as Morrissey reached the floor. Nothing happened. The three men went inside the block and disappeared. For Christ's sake, he had laid it out on a plate for the bloody man. The Paki had stood out there all alone. Why the hell had he not taken him down?

Something must have gone wrong.

They took the lift. True to the tradition of millions who rode lifts every day, they rode in silence. The floor numbers illuminated one by one. At nineteen the number stayed lit. Beyond nineteen was only the roof. Khalil stepped out and gestured down the corridor with chipped paint and greasy floor tiles and a faint smell of urine. The door to the flat at the far end was waiting open.

Campbell went inside and stopped so abruptly that Daniel bumped into him. Then Daniel saw the scene that had halted the constable. A man with a ski mask was waiting in the middle of the room with a machine gun levelled at belly height. Daniel took an instinctive step back only to feel the shape of a gun barrel in his back. Behind him the still calm voice of Khalil spoke. "Please. Do not panic. There is no immediate danger. Go inside please. Sit down. That's right. Campbell if you could sit here please. Mr Morrissey, you sit here. By the table. That's it. Fine."

There was another man. He was on the chair next to Campbell. His ankles were taped to the legs of the chair. His arms were secured behind him. He watched them with a bored, disinterested expression. Khalil kept his gun on them whilst Declan secured them in the same manner as Noah. When the task was completed, Khalil laid down the gun and sat on the table to face them. Behind him was a very new-looking computer. Beside him was a telephone.

"Now. Firstly I must apologise. As you will have gathered, things are not what you expected. This is a hostage situation I'm afraid. I will explain how things stand. My name is not Ahmad Mansour. I am in fact Khalil Bishawa. Maybe you have heard about my brother Mahmoud Bishawa. He was captured by the Israeli Security Forces and he is now detained and awaiting a trial that will mean a death sentence. The gentleman here is called Noah Cohen. He is a soldier with the Israeli Defence Force. A better description is that he is an assassin. He was the one who led the raid to capture my brother.

"So. Why are we all here? I will explain. The purpose of what has happened here over the last week was to put my picture in the media. The Israelis believed that I died many years ago in Tadmur Military Prison in Syria. As you can see, I did not. Our plan was simple. Once they knew that I was alive they would feel threatened. Like my brother, I have fought for the freedom of my people for many years. Fifty years in fact."

The sheer number of years seemed to make him pause momentarily. "We felt that the Israeli reaction would be predictable. Once they were assured that a state of near anarchy prevailed here in Sighthill they would send Cohen to assassinate me. It is his speciality. He has been doing this kind of thing successfully for many years. As you can see, Mr Cohen is indeed here. This time we were waiting."

He gave Noah a sympathetic smile.

"So. Where do we go from here? Well, what we actually have is a hostage situation that nobody is even aware of. In the next room there is a huge amount of Semtex that I can trigger by pressing this button. I am assured that the explosion would take the top five floors of the block and throw them all over Sighthill. To avoid this happening and all of us losing our lives I will now need to persuade the Israelis to release my brother. If they do, we can all continue our lives. I will make the call now."

Nobody spoke. Declan had taken up a station by the window and looked almost bored as he casually cradled his weapon. Campbell's brain furiously tried to work out if there was anything he could do, only to reach the conclusion that there wasn't. Daniel was so consumed by terror that it took all his concentration to stop himself from crying. Noah looked as if he were about to nod off.

The receptionist at the front desk of the Shin Bet Headquarters answered the call in Hebrew. Khalil asked to be connected to Mordechai Breslow in the same tongue, giving his own name in the process. Two minutes later he heard the single word. "Breslow."

"Good morning Mordechai. It is Khalil Bishawa. I will speak in English for the benefit of my guests. I am sure you know who they are. No doubt you have your television on. To confirm, I have Deputy Justice Minister Daniel Morrissey and Constable Campbell Swann here with me. They are quite unhurt. I also have Noah Cohen of your army with me. Oh yes Mordechai. He is right here I'm afraid. I will give you a website address. When you log-on and find it you will see that I have a webcam, which will show you live pictures of my three guests. Let me know when you see the pictures Mordechai."

Breslow nodded to his nearest colleague who tapped into the site. Immediately the picture of the three men on their chairs filled the screen of every computer in the room. There was a sharp intake of breath and muttered swearing. Breslow thrust a Marlboro between his lips and lit.

"OK Bishawa. We have the pictures."

"Good. I must give you credit for this small detail. It has been a great comfort to see that Mahmoud is alive and well every day. Now. Right now these pictures are only being watched by a very few people. You know how the Internet works Mordechai. It is a secret policeman's nightmare. I can have these pictures made available to everyone on the planet at a moment's notice. You understand this Mordechai?"

"I understand."

"Good. So. This is the situation. I have three hostages and a very large bomb. If I detonate the bomb I will destroy the top half of the building and kill everyone in the room. I will ensure that everyone is well aware of the reason why. The consequences Mordechai? Not good. A dead policemen. A dead politician. Allegations of an Israeli assassin. Not good. But very containable. You would have no great qualms about stone walling the allegations and of course Noah here is very expendable. So there is no need for you to play your 'we never negotiate with terrorists' card' Mordechai. We already know the script. Therefore the question is, can we make the consequences sufficiently bad for you to play ball? I think we can."

He reached into his pocket and took out three syringes.

"Remember the name Sergei Mikhailovich, Mordechai. Of course you do. Both of you crossed swords often enough. You will also know that he and I worked together for many years. We were close. We still are. He has offered me assistance. No doubt you have been wondering where on earth all the equipment came from. Well, there is your little mystery solved. So what is in the needles Mordechai? This is the result of many years of research that was undertaken by the old KGB.

They found traditional interrogation techniques to be less than satisfactory. Suspects who were tortured had a bad habit of dying before they could tell all that was required of them. Instead they came up with chemical solutions. You know about them of course. Think about it Mordechai. Think about how it would be if I administered these chemicals to Noah here and questioned him. Think about what would come out. All the killings. All the places that you ordered him to carry out your work. Names. Dates. Places. Times. Places where you should never have been. And it will all be on film Mordechai. On the Internet where you cannot stop it. There for the newspapers to watch. There for the Americans to watch. There for anyone in the world to watch. Consequences Mordechai. Could you stonewall this kind of detail? I think not. Consequences."

Again he paused for a moment. "Time to talk about the deal Mordechai. You need to deliver my brother to the centre of Ramallah within two hours. I will tell you where. You will take him in an armoured column and leave him. I will receive a call when he is safe. Then I will surrender to Constable Swann here. This offer is completely non-negotiable. Your leaders are faced with the question of how much face they want to lose. They either lose a lot of face by releasing my brother. Or they lose an incalculable amount of face by having the deeds of Noah Cohen made public to the world. A straight choice. Two hours is plenty of time. Two hours or Noah gets his medicine and the broadcast will begin. I will call in 90 minutes Mordechai. Goodbye."

Khalil ended the call. Daniel and Campbell looked as if they had witnessed a landing of the Martians. Noah's head was down. It was worse than he had dared to imagine. Far worse.

Mordechai Breslow replaced the receiver gently onto its cradle. All around the table eyes were cast down. Nobody wanted to look at him. The extent of the crisis was breathtaking. What was about to be the culmination of his career had in moments become the nemesis. He picked up the phone and spoke to the Minister.

"We have a disaster sir. A complete disaster. I suggest you get over here right away. My people will fill you in when you arrive. I am leaving now. I resign. I make one suggestion. Accept the terms that Khalil Bishawa is offering. There is no choice. This time we are beaten. We must accept the defeat. I will pass the phone to Rachel now. She will explain. Goodbye sir."

He duly passed the handset to an astonished Rachel. The voice of the Minister was screaming out of the earpiece. Breslow seemed not to notice. He rose from his chair very slowly and pulled on his rumpled jacket. Still none of them could bear to look. As he made his way to the door he was waylaid by a small, bony hand. Eyal Rosenberg had risen from his chair with difficulty.

"This man Bishawa has learnt to play chess Mordechai. He has learnt the game that we believed was our own. He has become a master. A grand master. There is no shame when you lose to a grand master. You must go with pride my friend. What man could have foretold this?"

Mordechai took the pale little hand in his and smiled his appreciation at the words. "One man did, Eyal. One man did and I was too arrogant to believe him. Mahmoud Bishawa told me on the day that we took him. He said that Khalil would set him free."

The old man nodded and Breslow released his gentle grip. He left the building where he had spent such a great part of his blighted life.

It was Campbell who managed to speak first.

"It's all true isn't it?"

"Yes. All of it."

"And you'll do it won't you. Blow us all up. If they say no."

"I will."

The policeman closed his eyes for a moment. "How? How can you?"

"Do you have a brother Campbell?"

"Yes. I have two brothers."

"Once I had a mother and a father and two sisters and a wife that I loved and a beautiful baby girl. All of them are gone, Campbell. All of them are murdered and gone. Murdered by the Israelis. Murdered by the same people who stole our home. All I have left is my brother. That is how Campbell. That is how."

To everyone's surprise Noah spoke for the first time since he had come round from the sedatives. "It is our war. Only we can understand. Only when you lose someone can you understand how it is. It is why we become monsters."

"You too?" asked Khalil.

"Yes. My mother. It was a bomb in a café in Tel Aviv. I was only a boy. I was in the toilet when it happened. When I came out she was cut in half. Everything below her waist was gone. My father never recovered. He died a few months later. It is why I have killed. It is why all of us kill. We know no other way."

Khalil looked to the window where Declan still hadn't moved. He gave him a short shake of the head to warn him not to speak. His Irish accent would have been too much of a clue. The Irishman stood up straighter as Khalil went to him.

"It is time for you to go now my friend. There is no need for you to stay here. You cannot affect the outcome. It is out of our hands now. Please, this is no time for us to argue. Go for my sake. Maybe there will be a day when we shall meet again. If not, then it has been my privilege to call you my friend."

For a moment Declan hesitated then he accepted Khalil's brief embrace. He leaned his gun up against the wall and left without looking back. Khalil stared at the closed door. "OK. Well we have some time on our hands. I think we should do what we intended to do. Let us discuss the situation here in Sighthill. I have some suggestions. Not terms. It would not be fair for me to dictate terms.

'Mr Morrissey, everything that has happened here is down to two men. Myself and Brennan. All of his people have escaped in the crowd outside. My people on the other hand remain in the courtyard." He looked down from the high window. "The soldiers are arriving. I presume that they will do nothing until you give some kind of word. I hope so. I feel that these people have been punished enough. There isn't a man who fought who hasn't suffered. It is the reason why they were willing to fight. What good would prosecuting them do? How on earth could you gather evidence that would stand up in court? You will no doubt have guessed that we have considerable financial backing. I can promise that any man who is taken to court will have the very best legal representation that money can buy. Surely this will only lead to embarrassment for your Government. Do you agree?"

Daniel was just beginning to get a grip on himself. "I suppose I can see your point. What do you suggest?"

"A full amnesty for all involved, with two exceptions. Myself and Brennan. We were the architects of all that has happened. Although your Government must share in the responsibility for allowing the situation here to get so bad in the first place. You can make a call to your First Minister. Get him to agree and there will be no more trouble here. Let's have a safe, clean end to all this. I would also ask for full-time security to be provided at all the playgrounds where asylum seekers as housed. A modest enough cost, surely."

Daniel nodded. It wasn't just the fear. He could see the logic. He had a politician's instinct for a clean way out of an awkward hole. He dictated the number for Khalil to dial. The phone was set to speaker mode.

"It's Morrissey sir. I have made some progress. I need your thoughts."

He outlined the offer on the table. His boss's instincts were entirely in tune with his own. He agreed to make a televised statement in half an hour. He said that he would arrange for the army to hold position outside for an hour. Khalil phoned Zaheer Kahn and explained the agreement. The playground war was officially over.

After brief and bitter recriminations the Israeli Cabinet accepted Breslow's recommendation. There was no way that the world could hear of the things that Noah Cohen had done. The damage would take years to repair. The only option was to swallow their pride. They would get Mahmoud Bishawa again. They could get the toothpaste back into the tube. They would simply have to be patient.

The Minister came into the room 50 minutes after Breslow had departed and took his seat at the end of the table to await the call. He grabbed the phone when it rang exactly on time.

"Is that you Mordechai?"

"No. It's Stein. Breslow has gone. Breslow is finished. You deal with me."

"OK."

"We accept. Mahmoud Bishawa will be in Ramallah within the next twenty minutes. We will not accept the terms for the exchange."

"Go on."

"There are soldiers outside. We demand that the officer comes to you. We must see Cohen handed over to the officer in charge. Only then will your brother be released. You can keep hold of your detonator. If we try a trick you can still use it."

Khalil thought quickly. It seemed OK. He had wondered if they would leave the exchange to trust. It was always going to be the moment of maximum risk. "OK. I will arrange it. I will receive a call the moment that your column reaches its destination. Tell them no shooting. It is arranged. There will be no stones thrown today. They go in. They leave my brother. When I have this confirmed and I hand over the detonator and the gun. Are we agreed?"

"We are agreed." Stein slammed down the phone and felt physically sick with rage.

Leatherdale was confused by the instruction. The Minister's voice had sounded somewhat strange. Tense certainly. He supposed that it was only to be expected. He rode up to the nineteenth floor with one of his sergeants. The scene in the flat took him completely by surprise. Morrissey, a policeman and a man he did not know were tied to chairs. The man he recognised as Mansour was standing by a table covering him with a sub-machine gun. He sensed his sergeant lifting his weapon. He put out a hand and gently eased it back down.

"No sergeant Watson. I think not. It seems we have a tricky situation here."

Khalil spoke. "Would you two go and stand behind the chairs please. We are nearing the end of a hostage situation gentlemen. My brother is about to be released from custody by the Israeli army. The moment this happens it will be confirmed to me by telephone. I will then surrender myself and allow you to free these gentlemen. The web cam is sending live footage to the Shin Bet Headquarters in Tel Aviv. Do you understand?"

Leatherdale nodded and took up the requested position. "May I ask your name please?" enquired Khalil.

"Colonel Leatherdale. Queen's Lancashire Regiment."

Khalil passed the details to Stein who in turn confirmed that he could see the Colonel on the screen.

Salim heard the approaching engines at the same moment as the rest of the crowd. The word had been let out twenty minutes earlier and it seemed as if the whole town had taken to the street. He could see them now. Three armoured vehicles approaching through the small gap left by the throngs of people on the pavement. There was no shouting. No talking even. Just silence as the small convoy approached the designated address. He stepped out into the road and raised a hand to halt the lead vehicle. A young captain jumped down and his eyes flitted across the faces in the crowd nervously. "Are you the one?"

Salim nodded. "It is me."

The officer nodded for two of his men to open the doors at the back. Mahmoud blinked at the unaccustomed brightness of the sun. One of the soldiers passed him his crutches and he hobbled toward his uncle. Salim already had the phone to his ear.

"Khalil. It is Salim. He is here. He is with me . . ." The sound of hundreds of cheering voices drowned out the rest. Khalil put down the gun and the detonator.

"Gentlemen. It is over. My brother has been freed. Will you allow me a word with him?"

Leatherdale nodded, having checked that his sergeant had now raised his weapon.

"Mahmoud? Mahmoud is that you?"

"It is my brother. It is me. I am safe."

There were tears pouring down Khalil's face. "Stay safe Mahmoud. We will meet again before our time comes to die. Now I must go."

He put the phone down and looked up with moist eyes. "It is over. He is safe."

He held out his hands. Campbell who had been untied cuffed him. "I'm going to read you your rights now. What should I call him Mr Morrissey?"

For a moment Daniel did not catch his meaning. Then the penny dropped.

"Ah yes. I see. I suggest that we keep it simple. I think that it would be best for all concerned if he were to remain as Ahmad Mansour. Best for all of us."

"Ahmad Mansour, I am placing you under arrest. You have the right to remain silent . . ."

Tac Brennan had lost interest in the television. He had watched the First Minister's statement with disgust. An amnesty. So typical. They were just going to let them go. All of them. All except the bastard Mansour. He had considered getting out himself but he couldn't find the energy. Let them arrest him. They would never make any of it stick. He would beat any charges they dreamt up. Running away would only make it easier for them. He went to the fridge and took out a beer. When would they come? Soon probably. Well let them. It didn't seem important.

He was halfway through his can when there was a knock at the door. Very good boys. Quick off the mark. He didn't bother to check the peephole. He knew exactly who to expect.

He was wrong. Instead of the anticipated squaddies there was a man in civilian clothes with a silenced gun.

"Mr Brennan. Step inside please. Sit down. Very good. I'm Davies by the way. I work for the Government. Everyone has decided that you are a bit of a pain in the arse. People are worried that you might just become a bit of a hero-martyr figure for the Far Right. Now that wouldn't do at all. Better that you are the ex-Para gone bad who took 250,000 pounds from the BNP and did away with himself. Goodbye Mr Brennan."

Davies shot him through the side of the head before he had time to register the threat. Davies worked quickly. He wrapped Brennan's fingers around the butt of the gun then allowed his limp arm to fall. The gun bounced on the carpet. He quickly checked about the flat and left.

The Coroner was more than happy with the evidence presented to him that Tac Brennan had ended his life by his own hand.

His was the sole fatality of the Sighthill Playground War.

EPILOGUE

Khalil's time in Barlinnie Prison had passed easily. His trial had been something of a tame affair. He had pleaded guilty to the offence of inciting a riot. The judge had taken into consideration the extreme conditions that had prevailed at Sighthill and he accepted that there had been considerable provocation. However he had also noted that Ahmad Mansour had refused to divulge where he had sourced the sophisticated equipment which had been used in the insurrection. Bearing this in mind, he had sentenced Ahmad Mansour to seven years.

The Government had done an outstanding job of burying the hostage situation. The weapons and Semtex had been spirited away and Leatherdale and his sergeant were sworn to secrecy. Cohen was returned to Israel on an El Al jet and the British Government had let their Israeli counterparts know what they thought of having assassins on their soil in the most vigorous of terms.

Khalil had been more than happy to settle into the steady rhythm of life of the prison. After his experience with many of the residents of Sighthill he had wondered how the other prisoners would be with him. To his surprise they were fine. The legend of the Sighthill battles had become firmly entrenched in Glaswegian folklore. The fact that he had faced down Tac Brennan and 400 skinheads, Paras and general hard men counted heavily in his favour. To his astonishment he became something of a favourite.

He was sure that he was the only inmate of Barlinnie who viewed the old jail with such fondness. He was the only one who had endured ten years of living hell in Tadmur. There was no comparison. The fact that he knew that the war was over for both himself and Mahmoud gave him a surreal feeling of contentment that he had never known before. He was never short of visitors. Rosemary and Moses came every month. Campbell and Nicky weren't quite so regular. Zaheer Khan had driven up from Lancashire on three occasions. Farouk and Declan were both as regular as clockwork. Even Daniel Morrissey found time for a private chat during a ministerial visit. But today was special.

The visiting suite was crowded with the usual sample of young mothers and wives and mothers and fathers. Hosts of children seemed to get told off by the second. Arguments broke out every other minute. Bags of heroin were discreetly passed during frantic bouts of snogging. He sat alone at a table at the back of the room and stared through the fog of cigarette smoke to the entrance door.

And he saw them. They were Sunday-best smart. Salim looked around at the near mayhem of the visiting area with a look of fierce disapproval. Mahmoud had already spotted him. He grinned and pointed ironically at the false leg under his trousers. He approached with barely a limp. Khalil smiled back. His brother looked so much younger. It was as if the cares of the of the world had been lifted from his shoulders. For the first time in more years than he could remember there was a hint of the old Mahmoud in his eyes. He could almost feel the same zest for life as the five-year-old boy who had headed out into the night to help to trap the fox.

A child howled at a dropped Barbie Doll. Mahmoud stooped slightly awkwardly to pick it up and pass it back. The little girl gazed at him with saucer-like blue eyes and then returned his smile.

They didn't speak when Mahmoud came to the table. They embraced and held onto each other for a long moment. Then Salim joined in. A few of those at the tables nearby looked over and sensed a special moment.

It had been 50 years. 50 years since the three of them had stood and looked back at the smoke that hung over the small town of Kibya. They were old now. Their war was over.

They had kept to their pledge.

THE END

Other titles available from Glenmill Publishing

NOVELS

The Cull
by Mark Frankland
£5.99 plus £1.00 P&P

Terrible Beauty
by Mark Frankland
£6.99 plus £1.00 P&P

Red Sky in the Morning
by David Cherrington
£5.99 plus £1.00 P&P

Hot Property
by John Peel
A £1 donation to the North West Cancer
Research Fund is included in the cover price
£6.99 plus £1.00 P&P

CHILDRENS STORIES

The Drums of Anfield
by Mark Frankland
£4.99 plus £1.00 P&P

The Drums of Hampden
by Mark Frankland
£4.99 plus £1.00 P&P

**To order a copy please complete
the order form at the back of the book
or tel. 0776 149 3542**

Order Form

Name   --

Address   --

Telephone   --

Email   --

Please send me ----------------- Copies of

Please send me----------------- Copies of

I enclose a cheque for -----------------------

Please make cheques payable to:
'Glenmill Publishing'

Return this form to:

        Glenmill Publishing
        Glenmill
        Dumfries
        DG2 8PX

Or Telephone   0776 149 3542